EVEN

Andrew Grant was born in Birmingham in May 1968. He went to school in St Albans and later attended the University of Sheffield where he studied English Literature and Drama. After graduation, Andrew set up and ran a small independent theatre company which showcased a range of original material to local, regional and national audiences. Following a critically successful but financially challenging appearance at the Edinburgh Fringe Festival, Andrew moved into the telecommunications industry as a 'temporary' solution to a short-term cash crisis. Fifteen years later, after carrying out a variety of roles – including a number which were covered by the UK Official Secrets Act – Andrew escaped from corporate life, and established himself as a critically acclaimed author. He is married to novelist Tasha Alexander, and lives on a wildlife reserve in Wyoming, USA.

ANDREW
GRANT

EVEN

PAN BOOKS

First published 2009 as a Thomas Dunne Book for Minotaur Books
an imprint of St Martin's Publishing Group, New York

First published in the UK 2009 by Macmillan

This edition first published 2021 by Pan Books
an imprint of Pan Macmillan
The Smithson, 6 Briset Street, London EC1M 5NR
EU representative: Macmillan Publishers Ireland Ltd, 1st Floor,
The Liffey Trust Centre, 117-126 Sheriff Street, Upper
Dublin 1,D01 YC43
Associated companies throughout the world
www.panmacmillan.com

ISBN 978-1-5290-5451-4

7 9 8 6

A CIP catalogue record for this book is available from the British Library.

Printed and bound by CPI Group (UK) Ltd, Croydon, CR0 4YY

Visit **www.panmacmillan.com** to read more about all our books
and to buy them. You will also find features, author interviews and
news of any author events, and you can sign up for e-newsletters
so that you're always first to hear about our new releases.

For Janet Reid and Pete Wolverton;
my agent, my editor, and now my friends

EVEN

ONE

When I saw the body, my first thought was to just keep on walking.

This one had nothing to do with me.

There was no logical reason to get involved.

I managed two more steps. If the alleyway had been a little cleaner, there's a chance I might have kept on going. Or if the guy had been left with a little more dignity, the scene might not have bothered me so much. But the way he'd been discarded—dumped like a piece of garbage—I couldn't let it pass.

Maybe it was because I've had a few close calls in filthy alleyways myself, over the years. Or maybe because I have nowhere to really call "home," either. But whatever the reason, I could feel a strange connection with the washed-up tramp. It was too late to give him any practical help—he was clearly dead—but I thought I could at least get someone to come and take care of his remains. I felt I owed it to him. Or even to myself. If I was a Good Samaritan for this helpless guy now, perhaps someone would do the same for me when my time came. I didn't relish the idea of my bones returning to dust in a heap of cheeseburger wrappers and used condoms.

I stepped into the alley. The body was four yards away. It was lying on its back with its feet toward the sidewalk. Its arms were stretched out the opposite way, pointing back into the narrow passageway. The wrists were close together —not tied—and the hands were partly obscured by the debris that covered the ground.

I moved closer and saw there were bullet holes in the tramp's clothing. I counted six. But it wasn't the number that caught my eye. It was the pattern. A neat T shape. Four across the chest, level with the shoulders, and two below, straight down the sternum. Very precise shooting. The work of a professional. A police marksman, maybe, or a soldier. Not something you'd associate with a dead tramp. And not something you can easily ignore.

Thoughts of calling the authorities suddenly took a backseat.

I examined the body from all sides. It was crumpled and slack, like a puppet with its strings cut. The best I could do with age would be ten years either side of fifty-five. There was no way to be more precise. His hair was graying and unwashed, and there was three or four days' stubble on the tramp's face. His nails were ragged and dirty but his hands were smooth, and he had the clothes of an office worker. He was wearing a navy blue cashmere overcoat, a gray single-breasted suit, a fine-weave oxford shirt—originally white or cream?—and a pair of scuffed, black, wing tip shoes. I had a picture in my mind of a ruined lawyer or stockbroker. He had quality garments, but all of them were stretched out of shape and each one had a variety of tears and holes and stains. The coat and jacket had lost all their buttons. The pants were held up with string. The leather soles were hanging off his shoes in several places. He'd lost his tie. Wall Street was only a few blocks away. If he had been some kind of professional, what a fall from grace the guy had suffered. He stank. I could smell piss and puke and booze. He was seriously unpleasant to be near.

I went through his pockets. I had to work slowly, because he was covered in blood and I didn't have any gloves. I started with his coat. At first it seemed to be empty, but as I pulled it open I found that a hard rectangular object had slipped through a hole into the lining. I worked it clear and saw it was a flat glass bottle, half full of a clear, colorless liquid. The label said it was vodka. I didn't recognize the brand. There was nothing else hidden away with it, so I moved on to his jacket. The first inside pocket was completely torn away, but I found something in the other side. The tramp's wallet. It was still there. Whoever had killed him hadn't bothered to take it.

The wallet was slim. It was made of shiny black leather, and it looked old. The corners had worn away, it was in holes where it folded, and the silk lining was torn inside. It was slightly curved, as if he normally carried it in the back pocket of his trousers. The credit card spaces were all empty, but where the cash would normally be I found a dog-eared Social Security card. It gave his name—Alan James McNeil—and a number, 900–14–0471.

I put the wallet back and stood up. My next step would be to work back along the trail where the body had been dragged through the garbage. I wanted to find the exact spot where McNeil had been killed, and see if anything there would explain why the body had been moved or how the guy had ended up as a victim. But before I could start, I latched on to a sound from behind me. A vehicle. Moving fast. Coming in my direction. It could have been a coincidence, but I was doubtful. There had been no other traffic all the time I'd been in the alley. And the way the body had been left, it was possible someone was coming back for it. Someone with questions to answer.

I moved into the shadows at the mouth of the alley and looked out, down the street. I was right. A car was approaching. A large, pale blue Ford sedan with white lettering on the side and a lighting bar on the roof. An NYPD radio car. I couldn't risk being found lurking at a crime scene so I stepped forward to beckon it over, but before I could raise my hand the driver gave a short burst with his lights and siren. Then the car surged toward me. I watched it come closer and swing into the alley, wallowing on its suspension as it bounced over the curb. I had to step back or it would have hit me.

The car doors opened and two policemen climbed out. The driver drew his pistol. He held it two-handed, above the door frame, pointing steadily at my chest. The passenger was holding a short-barreled shotgun. Given the width of the alley, it didn't much matter where he was pointing it.

"Stand still," the driver said. "Don't move."

The officers were both around five feet ten. They were powerfully built and looked in good shape. Neither seemed fazed by the situation. They'd moved calmly and swiftly when they got out of the car, reacting in perfect unison without needing to glance across or speak to each other. Now they were standing stock still, concentrating, alert without being anxious. Their neat blue uniforms summed them up perfectly. They were nowhere near brand-new, but still a long way from worn out. Trying anything with these guys would clearly be a mistake.

"Hands where I can see them," the driver said. "Slowly. Do it now."

You could see where this was going. They had the wrong end of the stick, but I knew there was no point trying to change their minds. Uniformed police are the same the world over. Once they set out to do something, they do it. Argue with them, and you just make it worse. So I raised my hands to shoulder height, fingers extended, palms toward them.

The passenger slotted his shotgun back in its cradle and came round toward me. As he moved closer I could see the name KLEIN engraved on a shiny plate beneath the shield on his chest.

"Hands on the hood," he said, reaching around to push me between the shoulder blades with his right hand.

I leaned on the front of the car and he jabbed at my

ankles with his right foot. I shuffled my legs a couple of inches farther apart, and looked over at the driver. His badge gave the name KAUFMANN. I focused on it while Klein patted me down. He worked fast. He started with my left arm, running both his hands all the way down from my shoulder to my wrist. He did the same with my right arm, then checked my body, my waist, both legs, both ankles, and the pockets of my coat and jeans. He found nothing.

"Clear," he said from behind me. "No gun."

Kaufmann nodded, but he didn't relax in the slightest. His weapon was motionless. My eyes were drawn to the muzzle. It was still pointing at my chest. The tramp had been shot in the chest. Minutes ago, a few feet from where I was standing. I felt the skin covering my ribs begin to tingle.

"I'll tell CSU," Kaufmann said. "Don't worry. They'll find it."

Klein pulled my left arm around behind my back. I heard the snap of a heavy press stud being unfastened, then a ratchet closed rapidly. Cold metal bit into the skin of my wrist. He grabbed my right arm, pulling me upright at the same time, and secured the second handcuff.

"What's your name?" he said.

I didn't answer.

"Where's your ID?"

The cuffs were digging into both my wrists. He'd tightened them far more than he needed to.

"What happened here?"

I looked at the front of their car. There were a few minor chips and scratches in the paintwork, and a small crack in one of the headlight lenses.

"Did you kill that guy?"

Lower down, on the fender, there was a sticker offering a reward if you phoned a special number after a cop had been shot.

"OK, I've had enough. You're coming back to the station house. Let the detectives sort this out."

Klein took my left arm just above the elbow and led me to his side of the car. He opened the back door, reached up to put his hand flat on my head, and guided me inside. He made sure I was clear, then slammed the door behind me. The seat was square and hard. The car was wide, but there wasn't much room for my legs because of a thick glass screen that rose up from the floor, isolating the rear of the cabin. The surface was scratched and cloudy, obscuring my view through the windshield. I sprawled out sideways and tried to keep my weight off my hands.

The air in the back of the car was warm and stale. I could smell industrial disinfectant. It had a strong sweet scent, but it wasn't quite enough to cover the lingering odor of dirty, sticky humans. I looked around and saw there were greasy marks on the window next to me. From people's foreheads. Previous occupants must have rested against the glass. I started to breathe through my mouth. I wished there was some way I could keep my hands off the upholstery.

After five minutes another car arrived. It parked carelessly, sticking out from the curb at a lazy angle next to the entrance to the alley. It was another Ford. The same model as the radio car but with plain, dark blue paintwork. It needed a wash. There was a red, flashing beacon on the dashboard. Two men got out without switching it off. They appeared to be in their fifties, and were wearing suits and raincoats with gold shields hanging from their breast pockets. The men moved slowly and deliberately. Both looked a little overweight.

An unmarked, white box van pulled up on the other side of the car. Two men in navy blue overalls jumped down and walked over to join Kaufmann and Klein. As they came closer I could see woven cloth NYPD badges on their sleeves. One of them turned back toward their vehicle for a moment, and I read CRIME SCENE UNIT in tall white letters on his back.

The technicians started looking into the alley. The guys in suits looked into the car, at me. The taller one came over to my side and peered at me through the glass, like a kid drawn to a repugnant reptile at the zoo. His shield identified him as a detective, but it didn't give a name. Only a number set into the metal at the top. After twenty seconds of staring he called the others together. Kaufmann and Klein closed their doors so I couldn't hear what was being said. I watched them talk for a couple of minutes. They were very animated. Then the group moved to the front of the car. I could make out lots of hand movement from the uniformed officers. They kept gesturing and pointing at the body, at me, at things in the alley, and at something out on the street. I couldn't make out what it was.

The taller detective brought the conference to a close, and the officers came and got back into the car. Neither of them looked at me. Kaufmann started the engine and backed out into the street. Then the car pitched forward and we sped away from the alley.

And, I thought, away from any more trouble.

TWO

Ask me where I live these days, and I'd struggle to find an answer.

I do have an address, obviously, but that doesn't help much. It would just point you to a half-empty apartment in the Barbican, in London. One bedroom, Cromwell Tower, nearer the top than the bottom. I've owned it for years. Bank statements still get sent there, and copies of bills, but that's about all. I haven't set foot through the door in seven months. The time before it was fifteen months. Home for me has become a succession of hotel rooms. Different cities, different countries, one after the other, rarely a break in between. Memories of one place blur into the next. That's been the way for fifteen years now, so I'm comfortable with it. But I still recall the first hotel I ever stayed in. It was in Edinburgh, not long after I left college. I was broke. A soft drinks company was looking for recruits. For sales and marketing. I didn't know much about either, but the money was good so I gave it a shot. I filled in the forms. Then they invited twenty of us up to their local Holiday Inn so they could pick out the five best candidates. We were there for one night. When I went to check out the next morning, the receptionist asked if I'd enjoyed my stay. I said apart from the work, yes. And I was about to go when I heard someone else being asked the same question. A guy called Gordon, from Cambridge. Only his reply was very different. He wasn't satisfied at all. His pillows had been too soft. His towels had been too rough. And worst of all, they'd sent up the wrong kind of honey with his breakfast.

They may have sounded petty, but Gordon's complaints really unsettled me. I could hardly move my feet to walk away. Each word felt like a sharp finger poking through my skin and gouging at my innards. How had such a shallow little weasel spotted all those flaws when they'd completely passed me by? What was wrong with me?

I mulled over the whole episode on the journey home and eventually the answer came to me. It was actually dead simple. I'd really been aware of it my whole life, in a vague kind of way. Gordon's bleating had just brought it into focus. It came down to this. What you see depends on what you look for. You can enjoy the positives, or seek out the negatives. It's your choice.

I'd gone one way, he'd gone the other.

I still take that path, as far as I can. I don't know about him. Because they didn't offer me the job.

I love the city at night. I prefer it to the day. The darkness draws out a wider spectrum of people, not just shoppers and office workers. Sounds carry farther. Everything you see feels closer and more personal. And the shadows are never far away, whenever you need them.

Kaufmann drove fast. Neither officer spoke. Away from the alley the streets were still busy. They were full of cars and taxis and limos and vans. A few people were still out walking. There were tall buildings all around, made of brick and stone and glass and concrete. They were squashed in on top of each other, bearing down, connecting you to the darkness up above.

The journey didn't last long. Less than six minutes. The station house was only a dozen blocks away and Kaufmann took a direct route, basically northwest, toward the Hudson. He stopped outside an eight-story, stone-fronted building midway down a side street. Police cruisers and unmarked sedans were parked at forty-five degrees from the curb, jutting out evenly like fish bones. We joined the end of the row. Klein came round and opened my door. I shuffled out and he led me to the end of a metal railing that separated the sidewalk from the street. Kaufmann caught up with us and we followed him along to a pair of solid, studded wooden doors at the center of the façade. Big keystones were set all around the doorway and on either side a bright green lantern was hanging on a metal bracket.

Inside, the reception area was small and cramped. It smelled of dust and floor polish, like a school. The walls were painted apple green, which is supposed to be a calming color, and there were notices plastered everywhere. About a quarter showed monochrome photofit images of people the police wanted to question, and the rest gave pedantic warnings about every conceivable petty misdemeanor from smoking in the building to dropping litter in the interview rooms.

Kaufmann approached the reception desk and rested his elbows on the wooden counter. Another uniformed officer emerged from a back room and leaned over to talk to him. The pair of them spoke for a minute. They seemed to know each other. This was probably a familiar ritual. I wouldn't be the first person Kaufmann had dragged in at the dead of night. Finally the officer behind the desk laughed and slapped Kaufmann on the shoulder. He pressed a button, and a gate in a waist-high glass barrier to our right swung open. Klein ushered me through, then led the way down a flight of stairs that followed around three sides of a square elevator shaft.

The next corridor opened up into a broad square lobby area. The far wall was divided into two sections. The right-hand part was wider. It was made of metal. The surface was painted gray, with large rivets set into it at regular intervals. The remainder was blocked off by dull, dirty white metal bars. The other walls were made of whitewashed stone, and the floor had been covered with some kind of speckled, shiny material. It felt like being in a cellar. The atmosphere was cold and vaguely damp. There were only three windows. They were long and narrow, set high up in the left-hand wall. All were closed. It didn't look as if they could be opened. There were no handles, and they were covered by thick metal bars.

A uniformed officer sat behind a battered wooden desk to our right. He was hunched over, concentrating on a computer screen. His badge gave the name JACKMAN. When he saw us he pushed the mouse away and stood up.

"Evening, fellas," he said. "What have you got for me?"

"Just this one guy," Kaufmann said. "Collar off a homicide on Mulberry Street."

"You're in luck, then. Got one vacancy left. Who caught the case?"

"Don't know. Norman and Johns were at the scene. Said they'd be leaving it for the day tour."

"No problem. I'll find out later. What's the guy's name?"

"Don't know. He wouldn't say."

"OK then—let's have a look at him."

Jackman took a shiny metal dish from a filing cabinet behind him and came around to our side of the desk. He worked his way methodically through my pockets and put each piece of my property in turn into the dish. He ended up with eighty cents in change, eighteen dollars in bills, and the card key from my hotel. He added my watch to the pile. It still didn't look like much. Jackman stood and studied the dish, gently stirring the contents with his stubby index finger as if weighing up whether there was enough for a bona fide citizen to be carrying. After a moment he frowned, put the dish back down on the desk, and searched me all over again. He pinched his fingers along the seams of my clothes, squeezed the edges of my collar, and inspected the inside of my boots. It was a much more thorough job than Klein had done in the alley, but it turned up nothing more.

Jackman took the dish over to the other side of the desk and tipped the contents into a clear plastic bag. It was twelve inches tall by eight wide. Large enough for a gun or a knife. No wonder he seemed so disappointed with my sorry collection. He sealed the top, and held it up to the light as if to emphasize how little my possessions amounted to. Then he stuck a label on the bag and dropped it into the top drawer of the cabinet. Without looking he nudged the drawer with his elbow, and while it was still grinding slowly back into place on its worn runners he made his way around to the bars.

Klein took his gun out of its holster and laid it on the corner of the desk. Then he grabbed my elbow and pushed me forward. Jackman took a bunch of keys from his belt. They were large and heavy, something you might imagine a medieval jailer would use. He unlocked the center section of bars and swung them open. They hinged outward, toward us. Klein shoved me through the gap. Jackman followed him, then pulled the gate back into place and made sure it was secure.

The wall to the left was blank. So was the one at the far end. To the right was a row of cells. There were five. They were identical. The front walls were made of bars. There was a gate in the center of each, all with a heavy lock. The sides were gray metal, three inches thick, filled with broad rivet heads. I realized the panel you could see from the lobby was the outside of the first cell. The rear walls were whitewashed stone. They were all covered in graffiti. It was scratched, rather than written or painted. A pair of benches ran parallel with the side walls. They were made of metal and had been bolted to the floor. The only other item in each cell was a toilet. The bowls stuck out from the rear wall. They were also made of metal—stainless steel—and none of them had a seat.

Klein led me past the first four cells. They were all occupied. There was a single person in the one nearest the lobby. A young guy. He had stained, shapeless clothes, lank greasy hair, and sunken features. He was standing hunched over near the toilet, looking wide-eyed and confused. There were five people in the second cell and four in each of the next two, but I could see the door to the last one in the row was standing open. It was folded back on itself, flush with the bars. When we reached it Klein let go of my arm. Jackman took over. He pushed me into the cell, and kept going until my shins were touching the toilet bowl. My nose told me it was a while since anyone had cleaned it.

"Look straight at the wall," he said. "Now, keep looking at it. When I uncuff your left wrist, immediately put your hand on top of your head. Do the same when I uncuff your right wrist. Understand?"

I didn't reply, but he released my wrists anyway.

"Good," he said. "Now, stand still. Do not move until you hear me close the cell door. Understand?"

I listened to his footsteps retreat across the cell floor. It sounded as though he were walking backward. He stopped, and the door slammed shut, squealing on its hinges as it was dragged through 180 degrees. I heard the keys jangle as he worked the lock, and then two sets of footsteps receded down the corridor.

The graffiti in my cell was fascinating. It covered every inch of stone from floor to ceiling. People must have stood on the benches and even the toilet to find space. I saw people's names, gang names, sports teams, including one English soccer club, political slogans, insults about the police, opinions of rock bands and movie stars. But mainly obscenities. And for some reason those were mostly in clumsy attempts at rhyming couplets, so they really made no sense at all.

I gave it a couple more minutes, then picked a spot on one of the benches and tried to get some rest. It wasn't easy. The giant rivets kept digging into my spine and shoulder blades so I had to slide my back to and fro along the wall until I found a comfortable position. But even then, wherever I looked in that narrow space my eyes couldn't avoid settling on one cold, hard object or another. The toilet, the other bench, the bars, the floor, the walls. This was definitely not what I'd had in mind for my last night in New York. I'd worked hard. I'd done a good job. I deserved a night to myself. But on the other hand, if the last few days had worked out even a whisker differently, I might not have had any time left to spend anywhere. Maybe this was just fate balancing the scales a little.

Without consciously intending to, my hand moved up to touch the back of my head. It was still sore. Two nights ago someone I was working with made a mistake. It was their miscalculation, but I was the one to pay the price. A piece of flying glass had cut me. A big piece. It had sliced my skin, right through to the bone. So I had to admit, annoying as the situation was, things could have been a lot worse. It wasn't as if I'd never been locked up before. It comes with the territory. As cells go, this one wasn't too bad. It was a bit small maybe, and pretty spartan, but relatively clean. And I was in there on my own. There's nothing worse than being crammed in with a horde of unwashed lowlifes, spewing out their foul breath and trampling on your feet. Plus, I wouldn't be in there long. Not like the hopeless cases you normally find in these places. Sad, desperate people clinging to the fruitless fantasy they weren't going to spend the rest of their lives in jail. For me, clearly, it was only a temporary problem. A bump in the road. Nothing more.

Because in a few hours, I'd be on a plane back to London.

THREE

I first moved house when I was still in kindergarten.

It was because of my dad's job. He worked for the government and for some reason they found it essential to transplant us from Birmingham to London. One large English city to another. On the face of it, not too big a change. But for a six-year-old, different worlds.

Looking back, violence was inevitable. I had a different accent. A different vocabulary. I was used to different rituals and routines. And it was the 1970s, after all. With hindsight, what happened the first time I set foot in the playground wasn't a huge surprise. For a moment I stood on my own, looking around, getting my bearings. Then I noticed a group of kids coming toward me. I counted about twenty. All boys. At first I was pleased, thinking they wanted to play or to make friends. Two of them came right up close. The rest gathered around. They formed a tight circle. And started to chant.

Fight, fight, fight.

I'd never encountered a situation like that before. My old school had been happy and peaceful. I had no experience to base my response on. Only instinct. And it was telling me the danger had to be snuffed out fast, before things got out of control. I focused on the two boys in front of me. They were the biggest. Clearly a year or two older than the rest. One was a little taller than the other. And a little broader. That made him more of a threat, so I decided he had to go down first.

I was surprised, but one punch was all it took. It left him rolling on the ground, a mess of blood and snot and tears. Then I turned to his pal. Only I couldn't hit him. He'd already run away, along with the rest of their little gang. And after that, until the day I left, they never came near me again.

It wasn't a very good school. That was the only lesson I learned, the whole time I was there.

But I can't complain. It's served me well over the years.

I woke to the sound of footsteps on the far side of the gate. They were approaching the lobby. I could hear three sets. Two were confident and purposeful. The other was shuffling and reluctant. They drew closer, then stopped. I heard voices. One was Officer Jackman, starting the property-bagging ritual. The others were unfamiliar. I guessed it was around 2:30 A.M., Monday morning. I'd most likely been asleep on the bench for less than two hours.

Two of the cells only had a single occupant. Mine, and the one nearest the gate. If the guy in that one was as stoned as he looked, I knew they wouldn't risk putting anyone in with him. Which meant I was about to get a new cellmate. I sighed to myself and leaned across to get a better view down the corridor.

Jackman was the first to appear. Behind him, two more uniformed officers were struggling with a prisoner. He was quite tall—about six feet two, only a couple of inches shorter than me—but incredibly wide. Everything about him seemed distorted. His legs, his arms, his chest, his neck—they all looked stretched sideways, like a regular TV picture on a wide-screen set. He was wearing tight, dark blue jeans with white patches bleached into them, army-style boots with the leather stripped away to expose the steel toe caps, and a faded burgundy sleeveless sweat top. His head was completely shaved. He had a flat, square face apart from his nose, which was crooked from being broken too often. But the most eye-catching thing about him was the tattoo on his neck. It was a line of swastikas. They were scarlet, outlined in black, and drawn so that the hooks at the end of each arm were joined together in an unbroken ring.

Jackman opened the door and the two officers heaved the Nazi into my cell. They really put some effort into it, but he still came to a halt after one step. Jackman followed, but didn't try to push him any further. The officers stayed close and drew their nightsticks. They looked tense. Their eyes didn't leave the big guy's back. One of them had grazed knuckles on his right hand. The other had red patches on his forehead and a cut about an inch long to the side of his left eye. Maybe they were afraid the Nazi might kick off again. Or maybe they were hoping he would.

Jackman began to gingerly remove the Nazi's handcuffs. They were stretched to their widest setting to fit around his huge wrists. There was no "keep looking at the wall" speech this time, but the Nazi put his hands on his head anyway, without being told. I guess he was no stranger to the routine, and he wasn't stupid enough to give the officers behind him any excuse to go to work with their nightsticks.

The Nazi remained completely still until the officers had locked up and pulled back to the lobby. Then he glanced over his shoulder to make sure I was watching, and stretched his arms up high over his head. The stench of stale sweat grew stronger. With his arms still extended, he unlaced his fingers and showed me that the way he'd been holding them, it was as if he'd been giving a V sign to the officers behind him. He half turned toward me, and the solid slabs of his cheeks folded into a huge smile. He began to chuckle, and finally broke into a braying laugh.

I kept my expression as neutral as possible and looked away, keeping track of him out of the corner of my eye. His laughter slowly trailed off and an embarrassed, sulky frown spread across his face. Then, slowly and deliberately, he turned to fully face me.

"The hell are you?" he said, as if seeing me for the first time.

"No one for you to worry about," I said.

"The hell you doing in my cell?"

"But that could change. . . ."

"The hell you doing on my bench?"

"Oh—this is your bench?"

"Yeah. And I want to sit down, asshole."

"Sit on the other bench."

"No."

"Then stay standing up."

"I want to sit on my bench. Now."

"What makes it your bench?"

"I'm telling you it is."

"It's your property?"

"Yeah."

"You own it?"

"Right."

"So what happened? Did you buy it?"

"What?"

"The police department sell it to you?"

"Eh?"

"Your mummy write your name on it, so you wouldn't lose it in the playground?"

"The hell?"

"Or did the guards name it after you? 'The Imbecile Nazi Memorial Bench?' In memory of your brain? Assuming you once had one."

He took a moment before trying to answer this time, and I watched as his giant fists balled up by his sides.

"Last chance," he said, stressing each word individually. "Off the bench. Right now."

"What's your name?" I said.

"What?"

"Simple question. What's your name?"

"Derek. Why?"

"Well, Derek, let me ask you one last thing. 'No' is a short word. Which part are you struggling with?"

For ten seconds he loomed over me, pulling a pained expression as though I were a dim-witted acquaintance who was trying his patience. Then he shrugged, sighed, and made as if to turn and walk away. But instead of putting any distance between us he immediately spun back around toward me, using the momentum to throw a huge right-handed punch straight at my face. It was powerful. He had all his weight behind it. I would have had a serious problem if he'd hit his target. But subtlety wasn't his strong suit. I watched what he was doing, and at the last moment I whipped my head across six inches to the right. It was far enough. His fist flew past my ear and tried to bury itself in the metal surface of the wall. I could feel the vibration running right down my spine. I don't know how many bones he broke, but from the pitch of his screams as he clutched his hand and staggered back toward the toilet, I'd guess most of them.

I checked the corridor. There was no sign of anyone coming to investigate.

"On the gate," I called. "Officer Jackman. This guy has a problem. You need to move him out of here. He needs help."

There was no reply.

"Out of luck, asshole," the Nazi said, taking a step toward me. "They never move me. Takes three of them. So it's just you and me till morning. And I ain't the one gonna need help."

"Derek, it's only a bench," I said. "It's not worth getting hurt over."

"I'm not gonna get hurt," he said, taking another step. "You are."

"Derek, I've given you one chance. I'm not giving you another. Now sit down and be quiet."

He stayed where he was for another thirty seconds. Just long enough for me to hope he might have the sense to let it drop. But no. People like him never do. He started to move toward me again. I eased onto my feet and backed up against the bars, ready to go.

"Derek, don't do this," I said. "It's really not worth it."

He took a final step, close enough for me to nearly choke on his vile breath. Then he smiled and shaped up to hit me with his left hand. It was a good idea, but again he lacked sufficient finesse. He just couldn't disguise the movement in his right leg as he pulled it back, getting ready to kick me. So before he could complete his move I launched myself off the bars and swung my left elbow around, driving it into his temple.

He was already off balance preparing for the kick, so the force of the blow knocked him right off his feet. He fell backward, spinning around toward the side wall. The back of his head crashed into the metal. He slumped down, smashing his right temple into the bench. His momentum kept him going and he half bounced, half rolled face-first into the rim of the toilet and then down onto the floor. His left temple cracked against the ground and he finally came to rest between the bowl and the side wall. As his head connected with the concrete an arc of blood shook free from his shattered face, splattering the legs of "his" bench with little shiny droplets.

That was the closest he got to his prize.

After the medics had dragged the Nazi away Jackman came back and stood in the corridor, staring in at me through the bars.

"What was that all about?" he said.

I looked at him and shrugged.

"You do that to him?" he said.

"Me?" I said. "No."

"So what happened?"

"No idea. The guy just collapsed."

"And you were doing what? Sleeping?"

"No. Calling you to come and help him. I guess you didn't hear me."

"Let me see your hands."

"Why?"

"The guy just collapsed, all on his own, and somehow got his face all smashed in. That seem a little strange to you?"

"No."

"You didn't help him on his way?"

"No. I didn't touch him."

"Show me anyway."

I shrugged and pulled my hands out of my pockets. I held them up so he could see my palms.

"Other side," he said.

I turned them over. There wasn't a blemish to be seen. Jackman stared intently as if hoping something would magically appear if he looked hard enough. Then he glared at me, snorted, and stalked away to the lobby. I thought about calling him back. The morning suddenly seemed a long time away. I was tempted to ask him to call the consulate for me. I know the right people. They could pull me out in no time. The NYPD would be told to forget all about me. Then I thought about all the paperwork that would involve me in when I arrived in England. The endless, stupid questions I'd have to answer. Maybe a reprimand of some kind. So I decided against it. I was safe where I was. I'd done nothing wrong. There was no reason not to let things run their course.

As long as I got to JFK on time, no one ever need know what had happened.

FOUR

You never get a second chance to make a first impression.

That could have been my new school's motto. When the teachers finally showed their faces in the playground that first day all they saw was me on my feet and the other boy on the ground. I was new, and one of their guys was hurt. It was clearly my fault. I was marked down as a hooligan. A thug. Someone with a faulty attitude who needed close supervision. I was kept in at lunchtime for a month. Banned from the playground for the rest of the term. And barred from soccer indefinitely.

Things weren't much better in the classroom. If I asked a question the teachers wouldn't take it seriously. They just said I was being disruptive. Then they'd send me to sit at the back, on my own. Report me to the headmaster. Write moaning letters to my parents. Give me bad reports. It made no difference what I was questioning, or whether I was right or wrong. Whenever real life didn't match their comfortable theories, it wasn't the theories they doubted. It was real life.

That never made any sense to me.

And nothing's happened in the meantime to change my mind.

The day-tour detectives didn't arrive too early. Somewhere in the region of 9:30 A.M., I'd guess. There were two of them. A uniformed officer named Cauldwell let them into my cell. He must have relieved Jackman when the night shift went off duty.

Apart from wearing suits instead of uniforms, the detectives reminded me of the officers who had picked me up in the alley. They had the same weathered, capable appearance, though one of them was a little younger. Probably in his early forties. He was the first to speak.

"My name's Detective Gibson," he said. "This is my partner, Detective Harris."

I nodded.

"We've been assigned to your case," Gibson said. "We need to get a couple of formalities out of the way, then I thought we could go upstairs and get this whole thing worked out?"

"Got any coffee upstairs?" I said.

"As much as you can drink."

"Any food?"

"Maybe some doughnuts. Could be stale."

"They'll have to do," I said, standing up. "Let's get on with it."

We stopped on the first floor for photographs and fingerprints, then carried on up to the detectives' squad room on the fourth. It was basically an ordinary open-plan office, but there was a strangely austere, regimented feel to the place. The rows of storage cabinets behind the administrator's desk were inch-parallel, and they were all neatly closed. There were no keys in any of the locks, and no papers peeping out from between any of the doors. The desks were evenly distributed around the room. There were six pairs, all facing the same way, all with identical chairs tucked in underneath. The surface of each one was absolutely clear, apart from the matching computer keyboards and mice. There were no mugs or family photos or personal effects of any kind, and the sleek flat-panel monitors were all switched off. There was nothing on the windowsills, and all the trash cans I could see were completely empty. It felt more like a furniture showroom than a place where real people did important work.

Harris and Gibson led me around the side of a small booth that had been built in the center of the room. We passed the entrance and kept going toward the far wall. A line of doors was spaced out along it. There were six. We headed for the last one, which was almost in the corner. INTERVIEW ROOM THREE. Harris flipped a slider across to the OCCUPIED position and pushed the door open. Lights set into the ceiling flickered on automatically as Gibson and I followed him inside.

The room felt small and cramped after the expanse of the main office. The ceiling was lower, and the blinds were shut across the window, blocking out any natural light. Most of the space was taken up by a wooden table. It looked solid and sturdy, as if it were built to withstand some abuse. It had already taken some, judging by the dents and blemishes in its surface. There were three chairs around it. Harris took the one at the far side. Gibson guided me to the next one, which was on its own at the long side of the table.

"Make yourself comfortable," he said.

The remaining chair was to my left, so there was nothing to block my view of a mirror built into the opposite wall. It was rectangular, four feet high, six feet wide. I smiled into it politely in case anyone was on the other side, already watching.

I'd expected Gibson to sit down as well, but when I turned back to him I saw he'd moved across to the door.

"Back in a minute," he said, and left the room.

I looked at Harris. He didn't seem to be paying any attention to me at all. He was just leaning back in his chair, vaguely smiling, and staring into space. There was a tape strip alarm running along the wall, a few inches from his shoulder. I found myself wondering how quickly he could reach it. Then I saw him glance up to the corner of the room above the door. I turned to look, and saw a tiny CCTV camera mounted on a metal bracket where the walls met the ceiling. A red light next to the lens was blinking steadily.

Maybe that's why he was looking so smug.

Gibson returned to the interview room carrying a notebook, some papers, and three white polystyrene cups with lids.

"No doughnuts," he said as he sat down. "Sorry."

"Just don't tell me you put milk in my coffee," I said.

"No. For you, I guessed no milk, no sugar."

"That's a relief."

The detectives were silent as I took a sip of coffee. It was surprisingly good. A little cold, maybe, but I allowed myself a moment to enjoy the strong, bitter taste. Gibson left his cup on the table and watched me. Harris emptied his with a single gulp and wiped his mouth on his sleeve.

"Now, before we start, I need to tell you something," Gibson said. He spoke really slowly, as if he thought I might not understand. "It's important you should know, you can have an attorney present if you want one. But before you make a decision on that, I think you should hear what we've got, and let me tell you what you can do to help yourself. Then, you can decide which way to go when you know all the facts. What do you say?"

"Fine with me," I said. "I'm not looking to drag this out."

"OK then, let's not waste any more time. I just need you to sign something to say you've passed on the attorney for now, and we're in business."

Gibson took a ballpoint pen from his jacket pocket and handed it to me. Then he shuffled through the papers he'd brought back with him, selected a single sheet, and slid it across. I scanned my way down the page until I came to a box at the bottom. Someone had highlighted the outline in yellow. It was too small for my signature, so I just scrawled right across the bottom of the page. Gibson reached over and gathered up the pen and paper. He looked at the form for a moment and frowned.

"Nope," he said. "Can't read that. And the guys downstairs told me you don't have ID, so maybe you can start by telling us your name?"

"David Trevellyan," I said.

"And where are you from, David?"

"England. Originally."

"Thought I recognized the accent. So what are you doing in New York?"

"Working. I'm here on business."

"What kind of business?"

"Telecommunications."

"And is that why you were out on the street last night, David? You were doing telecommunications work?"

"Of course not. I'm a consultant, not an engineer."

"What does that mean?"

"It means I work with corporate clients. Give them advice. Help them with strategy, overcoming operational problems, that sort of thing."

"What kind of problems were you overcoming last night?"

"None. I wasn't working last night. I've just finished a contract and I don't have to be back in the U.K. until tomorrow, so I was taking a night off."

"What kind of contract was it, you just finished?"

"Government."

"No offense, but why would the government hire a British consultant? Don't we have plenty of our own?"

"Not your government. The British government."

"If it was the British government, why are you in the United States?"

"I was working for the Foreign Office. I started at the embassy in Washington and then moved on to the consulate here in New York."

"Where were you before Washington?"

"On another job. In Paris."

"Paris, France? You came directly from there?"

"That's right."

"When?"

"Six weeks ago."

"Then you came directly to New York?"

"Right."

"When?"

"Three weeks ago."

"Been here ever since?"

"Haven't set foot outside Manhattan."

"And your contract finished, when?"

"Yesterday."

"Yesterday was Sunday."

"So?"

"What time yesterday? Morning? Afternoon?"

"Late afternoon. The project owner's based in London, so I had to wait at the consulate until sign-off came through."

"What time was that?"

"Five-thirty."

"People can verify that?"

"Of course."

"Good. 'Cause we may need to talk to them. We'll come back to you for names if we do."

I shrugged. It would be a pain, but I could find some people to say the right thing if he really insisted.

"Now, let's see if I got this," he said. "Five-thirty, you're at the consulate getting a sign-off on your project. Midnight, you're in an alley with a corpse."

"That's right," I said. "Six and a half hours after finishing work, I was unfortunate enough to discover a dead body."

"Fill in the gaps."

"I left the consulate, obviously. Went back to my hotel. Had a shower. Got changed. Went out for a meal."

"Where?"

"At a small restaurant. Fong's, it was called."

"Who with?"

"No one. I went on my own."

"What about the receipt?"

"What about it?"

"It wasn't with your things."

"So?"

"So where is it?"

"I don't know."

"Why not? What did you do with it?"

"I paid cash. I didn't keep it."

"Convenient."

"How is it convenient?"

"Anyone see you there? Staff? Customers?"

"Sure. Try eating out alone and not getting stared at."

"Maybe we'll go ask. OK. What else?"

"I finished my meal. Started walking back. Saw the body. It was in an alley off Mulberry Street. I checked to see if I could help the guy, and was on my way to call 911 when your colleagues arrived."

"Why not call on your cell phone?"

"Don't carry one. I don't like cell phones. They fry your brain."

"So, you just found the body lying there?"

"That's right."

"It was already there when you went into the alley?"

"Right."

"Already dead?"

"Afraid so. I did check, but it was too late."

"And that's it?"

"That's it."

"Doesn't quite add up, does it, David?"

"Doesn't add up how? That's what happened."

"Think about it. You're a businessman. A consultant. A respectable citizen enjoying a well-earned night off. And with all the wonders of New York City to pick from, you choose to spend your time in a shit-filled alley where there just happens to be some bum's body, still warm, full of bullets? Sorry. Doesn't work for me."

"That's not what I said. I told you, I spent my evening in a restaurant. I found the body afterward, when I was walking back to my hotel."

"Why were you walking? Why not take a cab?"

"And I only went into the alley because I saw the body lying there. You could see it from the street. Other detectives were there. And uniformed officers. Check with them. They'll confirm where it was."

"We don't care where the body was, David. We only care about how come there was a body."

"And if you know anything about that, now would be the time to tell us," Harris said, looking at me for the first time since we entered the interview room.

"You need to work with us on this, David," Gibson said. "If you're straight with us now, maybe we can help you. But if you keep lying to us, we'll make sure this whole thing falls right on you."

I sat and looked from one to the other. I felt insulted, more than anything. If I had been lying, there was no way anyone would know about it, least of all either of these guys.

"You should be looking to get out in front of this, David," Harris said. "Be smart. This is your last chance to do yourself some good."

"We'll find out later, anyway," Gibson said. "But then it'll be too late to help. You need to tell us now."

"I've told you what I know," I said.

"Look, I don't believe you're a bad guy, David," Harris said. "But if you didn't mean what happened, you need to let us know now. Stop wasting our time."

I took another sip of coffee.

"Maybe the guy attacked you?" Gibson said. "Forced you into the alley?"

"Yeah—maybe it was his gun," Harris said. "He used it to get you into the alley, you struggled, the gun went off . . . ?"

"So it was an accident?" Gibson said. "You never meant to kill him. That would definitely help you."

"But if that was how it happened, you need to tell us," Harris said. "Then we can help you with your statement. Make sure it shows you in the best light."

"You think it might have been an accident?" I said. "I'm curious. Would that be a single accident, where the gun went off six separate times? Or six individual accidents, one after the other?"

"Hey, David, we're just trying to help," Harris said.

"I appreciate that," I said. "So listen to what I'm telling you. I found the body. Nothing else."

"If that's how you want to play it—fine," Harris said. "But there's something else you should know. Someone saw you."

"Saw me find it?"

"No. Saw you kill the guy."

"Nonsense."

"No, David, it's true. They called 911."

"How do you think the radio car got there so quick?" Gibson said. "It was there before you even left the alley, right?"

"Maybe someone did call 911," I said. "Maybe they did see who killed the guy. But it wasn't me."

Harris reached into his jacket and took out a tape recorder. It was a tiny, handheld one such as people use for dictation. He held it up so I could see clearly what it was, then stood it upright on the table in front of him. Both detectives were looking at me intently. Harris's lips were glistening.

"Anything to add, now's the time," he said.

I picked up my cup and sloshed the dregs around for a moment.

"I could do with another coffee, actually," I said. "This last bit's gone a little cold."

Harris scowled.

"This is taken from the 911 voice recorder," he said, reaching out to the tape machine.

A synthesized female voice gave out a date. March 15. That was yesterday.

"New York Police Department Central Emergency Reception," it said. "The time is 23:57 hours. Agent 8304."

"Nine-one-one Emergency," a real operator's voice said, taking over. Her voice sounded harsh and metallic through the tiny speaker. "Your name, telephone number, and address, please."

"Please, just help me," a man's voice said. It was high-pitched and trembling. "I've just seen a guy get mur-dered." He was breathing hard, and I could hear some light traffic noise in the background.

"I understand that, sir, but I need to start with your name, telephone number, and address."

"OK, it's Andy Newm—"

Harris leaned forward and pressed a button. The voice on the tape squealed and jabbered for a moment, so I couldn't make out any more details. Then Harris let go of the machine and I heard the operator speaking again.

". . . me what you saw?"

"OK, well, there was, like, this guy. A big guy. He went into the alley. Up to a bum. The bum saw him. Stood up. Real slow. Shaky on his feet. Like he was drunk or something. The guy pulled a gun. The bum just stood there, looking at it. Then he backed up. Kept going back. Right back. All the way to the wall. He tried to climb on the Dumpster, but the guy . . . the guy just . . . shot him. In the chest. A bunch of times. Like, bang, bang, bang, bang, bang, bang. And that was it. The bum was dead."

"What happened next?"

"The bum fell down. On the ground. The big guy just left him there. Then I ran. Didn't want him to see me."

"Where is this alley?"

"Near Canal Street. Mulberry. Off there."

"And where were you when this was happening?"

"Right there, on the street."

"Are you sure the man with the gun didn't get a look at you?"

"No. I was hiding. Down from the kids' playground."

"Did you get a good look at him?"

"Yeah. I got a real good look."

"Can you describe him?"

"Sure. He was white. Tall. Bout six four. Black leather coat. Round collar. Sort of medium length. Didn't reach down to his knees. Black jeans. Black boots. But the weird thing about this guy was, he had a big chunk of hair missing. Back of his head."

"What, like he was going bald?"

"No. Like it had been shaved off. Like for an operation or something. I thought maybe he was mental, or had a lobotomy or something."

"But you said the bald patch was at the back of his head?"

"Yeah, I said the back. Had stitches in it."

"How many stitches?"

"A lot. Maybe ten or fifteen."

"OK, and can—"

Harris switched the machine off.

"David, I notice you're a white male," he said. "You're about six four tall, wearing black boots, black jeans, and a black three-quarter-length leather coat. And the collar is . . . round."

"Your point being what?" I said.

Harris got up and walked around behind me. I felt him lean his weight on the back of my chair. His breath was warm on my neck. I watched him in the mirror, making a show of examining the back of my head. I guessed he was focusing on the shaved patch. That, and the line of twelve neat stitches running across the center of it. I was beginning to resent that scar. It wasn't the only one I had. It wasn't even the largest. But it was causing more than its share of trouble.

"Anything you'd like to share with us, David?" he said.

"Yes," I said. "I think I will have a word with my lawyer, after all."

Harris looked irritated. He shot a sour glance at Gibson, and dropped back into his chair.

"You can do that, David, if you want," Gibson said slowly, as though he were talking to an imbecile. "But if you do, we can't help you. We can't even talk to you. You'll stay in jail while we check into all the unsolved homicides from while you were in New York. And in D.C. It'll take months, if you go that way."

"But it's not too late to talk to us," Harris said. "Help us now, and we'll try to keep you out of the system. Get this thing cleared up real quick. That's what you said you wanted."

"Not anymore," I said. "Now I want to speak to my lawyer."

"David, calm down," Gibson said. "All we're saying is, we've heard the caller's side of the story. Why not tell us yours?"

"I've told you already," I said. "You didn't listen. Now I want my lawyer."

"Let's not be hasty, here, David," Gibson said. "Look at it from our side. Think how this thing looks."

"It looks like a frame," I said. "It looks like you can't be bothered to do your jobs. Now—my lawyer. Fourth time. I won't ask again."

"At least tell us why you moved the body," Gibson said.

I folded my arms and kept quiet.

"When that guy called 911, the body was at the back of the alley," Gibson said. "That was at 23:57."

"Four minutes later, when the uniforms arrived, it had moved to the front," Harris said.

"You were the only one at the scene," Gibson said.

"So it had to be you who moved it," Harris said.

"Only question is, why?" Gibson said.

I didn't answer.

"Like we said before, David, we don't think you're a bad guy," Harris said. "We think you felt bad about what happened. We think you dragged that body nearer the street 'cause you wanted it to be found. You wanted to put things right."

"That shows remorse, David," Gibson said. "Remorse is good. Remorse could really help you. But you have to tell us."

"Your lawyer will tell you to keep quiet," Harris said. "But he doesn't have to live with this thing. You do."

"So, if you were sorry, if you were trying to put things right—tell us about it," Gibson said. "You'll feel a whole lot better."

"And save yourself a whole lot of jail time," Harris said.

"Because if you don't talk to us, we'll have to pull in that witness," Gibson said. "And with a description of you like he gave on the phone, he'll pull you out of a lineup in a second."

"And that would change the game, David," Harris said. "Big-time."

"Make what you did look premeditated," Gibson said.

"Self-defense would be out of the window," Harris said.

"Manslaughter would be out," Gibson said.

"We'd be talking about murder," Harris said. "Think about that."

Gibson slid his pen and a pad of paper toward me.

"Write what happened, the way we told you," he said. "Or write your lawyer's number. Your choice."

I wrote down a number.

FIVE

The first thing I do in the morning, if I'm not in jail, is read the papers.

I enjoy them well enough from Monday to Saturday. Sundays aren't so good, though. There's too little news. Too much opinion. And a huge sheaf of magazines to deal with. Like the ones I picked up at Charles-de-Gaulle on my way over to start this last job. There was a whole supplement about people's attitudes to work. Why had they taken their jobs? What did they like about them? What did they not like? What would make them leave? The answers had been spun out into four pages of bar graphs and diagrams and pie charts. All the usual reasons were there—money, status, promotion, hours, travel. But according to the journalists, the biggest factor was "interaction with colleagues."

Not something you'd expect to see in my profession.

Although, just once, I met someone who made me wish it was.

Tanya Wilson looked pretty much the same as the day I

first met her in Madrid, three years ago. She was five feet eight, slim, with an elegant blue suit that combined perfectly with her plain white blouse and low-heeled navy shoes. Her dark shoulder-length hair was pulled back from her face, as usual. She'd always preferred that style, despite the way it emphasized the sharpness of her features. I remember thinking at our original meeting that she looked like a lawyer, and today, with a battered leather briefcase and narrow metal-framed glasses, the impression was stronger still.

For a moment neither of us spoke.

In our profession, when it comes to relationships, there's a line you don't cross. Or at least, you don't if you have any sense. Tanya and I both understood, but we'd come close to crossing it anyway that spring. Perilously close. Maybe a couple of toes had actually crept over to the other side. I'm pretty sure mine had. I think hers had, too. But before we could abandon reason altogether and leap right across with both feet, fate intervened. I was sent to Morocco, to collect someone.

It should have been a routine trip. Four days, maximum, there and back. Tanya was handling the arrangements so I had no reason to worry. And as you'd expect, the job started flawlessly. Travel documents, flights, currency, accommodation, vehicles. Everything went exactly according to plan. There wasn't even the slightest hint of a hitch until the end of day two. Then, when we were thirty minutes away from our rendezvous, that all changed. There was an incident with our Jeep. It was caught in an explosion. Some sort of improvised roadside device, I assume, but there was no proper investigation into what kind. I never found out who planted it. How it was triggered. What happened to our contact. Who cleaned up the mess. Or how the remains of the driver—someone I'd known for ten years—ended up back in Scotland for a memorial service I couldn't attend. All I can remember is waking up in a hospital in Rabat, two days later. It was a dismal place. The lights were down low and I thought I'd been left there alone, but as I drifted back into consciousness I realized that someone else was with me. It was Tanya. She was standing at the end of my bed, silently watching me, with a single tear glistening in the corner of her right eye.

Tanya visited me every day after that. First in Morocco, then in Spain when I was sent back to recuperate. Some days she could only grab a few minutes. Others she was with me for hours on end. But however long we were together, all we could think about was getting some real time to ourselves. Alone. Away from doctors and nurses and squeaky hospital furniture. It was becoming an obsession. Rules and conventions and protocols wouldn't have stood a chance. Nothing would, if fate hadn't showed its hand a second time.

The same day I was discharged from the hospital, Tanya was transferred. I never heard where to. She was just there one day, gone the next. That's the way it goes in our world. There was nothing either of us could do. But she's been on my mind a lot since then. I often wondered, if our paths crossed again, would I feel the same? And that old question was just raising its head when Tanya broke eye contact and turned to close the interview room door. She checked it had latched and then came over toward the chair Gibson had been using. A subtle hint of sandalwood and bergamot drifted over to me as she moved and I felt a tiny shiver ripple the skin between my shoulder blades.

I guess I had my answer.

"Sorry, David," she said as she sat down. "I got here as quickly as I could. Have you been waiting long?"

"One thousand and forty-nine days," I said.

Tanya looked blank for a moment, then broke into a shy smile.

"I am sorry," she said. "I only flew in yesterday. Started here this morning. Didn't know you were even in town till I heard the call come in from the detectives. Then I had to check a couple of things. It's been a while since I crossed swords in the American courts."

"You're fresh in and they gave you the case?" I said.

"I took it. I didn't give them a choice. My stock's risen a little, these last couple of years. And I couldn't leave it to anyone else. Not once I realized they were talking about you. I'm the only one here who knows what you're really like."

"What am I really like?"

"Oh, no. I'm not answering that one. So. I haven't seen you for a while. How've you been?"

"Can't complain. Still in one piece. You?"

"Fine. Or I will be, once I get you out of here."

"Heard the latest?"

"Think so. I spoke to the detectives before I came in. They have one dead body and a pretty strong impression you're responsible for it. Plus lots of circumstantial evidence. And a recording from an eyewitness. It sounds like a mess, David, quite frankly."

"It's bogus, is what it is."

"I know that. But the point is, we'll have to work a lot harder. Knowing they have that kind of testimony will make you more of a flight risk. And with you being a foreign national, it could be a problem."

"Flight risk? What do you mean?"

"When we ask for bail. The judge won't agree if it looks like you could run."

"Sorry, Tanya—what bail?"

"To get you out of here. Oh, hold on. Wait a minute. You weren't going to ask London for . . . ?"

"Tanya," I said, nodding toward the observation mirror.

"Don't worry," she said. "They can watch us, but not listen. Not while I'm present. They wouldn't risk it. So, tell me you weren't about to mention the d-word?"

I didn't answer.

"You were, weren't you?" she said. "You were going to ask to be hooked out. From the U.S.A. Are you mad?"

"Is that a problem?" I said.

"Don't you get operational bulletins anymore, David?"

"Of course."

"And do you read them?"

"Absolutely. Whenever I'm in an office, with nothing better to do."

"You don't, do you? Our people make the effort to put out useful updates so you know what's what, but do you take any notice? No. You're still ignoring our advice. Until you're in trouble. Then you expect us to wave a magic wand."

"What's magic about getting me pulled out? Embarrassing—yes. Heavy on paperwork—yes. But hardly out of the ordinary. I worked with a fellow in Nairobi who got dip-exed from three jobs in a row. Admittedly, he did get canned after the last one, but this is my first time. What's the problem?"

"Diplomatic exfiltration may have been common practice in the past. It isn't now."

"Why not?"

"Does the name David Robinson mean anything to you?"

"Should it?"

"Surely you've been briefed on this. Didn't you read . . . Oh, all right, I'll spell it out. Robinson was a U.S. Marine. He was posted to Grosvenor Square. Last year, just before Christmas, he was picked up by the Met. Charged with indecently assaulting a female student in the toilets of a nightclub in Soho, somewhere. Washington came through. Wanted him pulled out. London refused. Said it was a civilian offense, in civilian premises, while he was off duty. Insisted he stay in the U.K. to stand trial like anyone else."

"Seems fair. Did they nail him for it?"

"It never went to court. Robinson killed himself in jail the night before the hearing."

"Good result."

"Maybe. But that's not the point."

"What is?"

"The liaison protocols. Washington tore them up."

"But that's not workable. How can you—"

"Officially sanctioned operations are still covered. But that's all."

"Problem solved, then. Tell them I was sanctioned."

"I can't do that, David. These guys aren't fools."

"So what do we do?"

"Go for bail, like I said."

"Don't know. How long will it take?"

"Depends when your arraignment is. The DA will argue you should stay in custody. We'll argue you should get bail. Then it's up to the judge."

"What's the earliest it could be? I'm due back in London tomorrow. I'm on a flight out this afternoon."

"David, it's time for you to face facts. You're not going to be on that plane. And being late home is the least of your worries. First we have to get you out of here. Then we go to work on your defense. As for the arraignment, I'll push for an early hearing. Otherwise they'll move you."

"Where to?"

"A regular jail. They only have holding facilities here."

I looked at Tanya, and it was obvious she could tell

what I was thinking. We both knew what kind of place she was talking about. Outdated. Overcrowded. Unsanitary. Crawling with degenerate criminals.

"David, think about this," she said, reaching across and placing her hand over mine. "Don't do anything stupid. Ever since this Robinson thing, Washington has been looking for payback. They want their pound of flesh. Give them the chance, and they'll take it from you."

The droplets of blood from the Nazi's face had congealed on the bench legs and turned a dirty brown, like specks of rust. Harris spotted them when the detectives returned me to my cell. He went straight over for a closer look. Maybe word of the incident had spread around the building while we'd been upstairs.

"Know anything about this?" he said.

"Absolutely nothing," I said.

"Nothing, huh? Just like you know nothing about the guy in the alley? Well, we do know something, David. We know you killed that guy. So what you need to do is stop lying and tell us what happened, while we can still help you."

"What I need to do is sit here and wait for my lawyer to get me released."

"You can try," Harris said. "But trust me. You'll have a long wait."

Harris was wrong. I only had to wait forty minutes. At dead-on one o'clock he was back with Gibson, standing outside my cell, waiting for Cauldwell to work the lock. Only this time, he had his handcuffs ready.

"On your feet," he said. "Turn around. Show me your hands."

He fastened the cuffs and gave each one an extra squeeze, making sure they were clamped really tight around my wrists.

"Ms. Wilson works fast, doesn't she?" I said.

"What?" Harris said.

"Ms. Wilson. My lawyer. Works fast, to get me released already."

"You're not being released, jackass. And this has nothing to do with your lawyer."

"No? So where are we going?"

"We're not going anywhere. You are. The FBI is here."

"Why? What do they want?"

"Like you don't know."

"I don't know. Why is the FBI involved?"

"Enough. Shut your mouth. Not one more word, or you're going to take a beating right here."

Three men were waiting for us near the reception desk. I'd never seen any of them before. The little glass gate swung open as we approached and the oldest of the group stepped forward. He had short, graying hair and a bulging stomach that hung down over his belt.

"My name is Lieutenant Hendersen, NYPD," he said. "I'm here to inform you that at 12:05 P.M. today, jurisdiction in your case was assumed by the Federal Bureau of Investigation. These gentlemen are agents. We've completed the paperwork. They'll take it from here."

"I'm Special Agent Lavine," the taller of the other two men said, stepping up alongside Hendersen. He was a shade over six feet tall, slim, with broad shoulders and short blond hair. His gray single-breasted suit was well cut, and his white shirt looked crisp and new next to his dark, striped tie. Cuff links peeped out from under the sleeves of his jacket, and I caught sight of initials embroidered onto his shirt pocket when he moved. He wouldn't have looked out of place in a tailor's window, other than for his face. It looked tired and drawn, with deep lines etched into the skin around both eyes. The third guy looked much more awake, almost bouncing on the balls of his feet. His clothes were similar, but he was an inch taller, six inches wider, and a good ten years younger. He stepped into line a moment later, moving slowly as if working hard to resist the urge to reach out and grab me.

"This is Special Agent Weston," Lavine said. "You're with us, now. Come on. Time to go."

"The FBI are taking over?" I said to Hendersen. "Why?"

He ignored me.

"What about my arraignment?" I said. "Does my attorney know about this?"

Hendersen sneered at me.

"Good-bye, Mr. Trevellyan," he said, and turned to walk away.

Gibson handed my bag of possessions to Agent Weston, and Harris removed his cuffs from behind my back. I went to rub my wrists, but before I could get the circulation going again Lavine had grabbed them and snapped on his own cuffs. They were of a slightly different design, but every bit as uncomfortable.

Weston took my arm and guided me out through the main door. He led me along the sidewalk to a plain white van parked at the end of the line of vehicles. Lavine opened the rear doors and Weston bundled me inside. The load space was empty apart from an old gray blanket like the kind moving companies use to protect furniture. It was crumpled and stained, and smelled of mildew. I pushed it away with my foot. I didn't like to think what it might have been used for.

I don't know which agent took the wheel, but whoever it was had a heavy right foot. The rear tires screeched as we lurched forward, and the van crunched into every pothole and swerved around every corner after that. The interior was pitch-dark, and as I bounced helplessly around, banging and bruising myself on the hard metal surfaces, it reminded me of a story I'd once heard. Something an old-time U.S. Army intelligence guy had told me. About the CIA in Vietnam. He said they used to load Vietcong suspects onto helicopters, put sacks over their heads, and fly them around for a while before taking them in for questioning. They got the most drugged-up, whacked-out pilots they could lay their hands on and just let them go crazy for a couple of hours. Then the prisoners would come staggering out, sick to their stomachs, totally disoriented. Much more likely to talk. Apparently a couple of times the poor guys were so out of it they actually believed they'd landed in the United States, and gave it all up straightaway.

"So where are we, then?" I said to Weston when he finally opened the rear doors, twenty minutes later. "Saigon?"

He didn't answer.

"Quantico, maybe?" I said.

He gestured for me to get out.

"Federal Plaza, at least?" I said, looking over his shoulder at the parallel rows of square pillars and grimy, oil-stained floor. "Because I've got to tell you, I'm not impressed with the decor."

Weston reached into the van and leaned forward to grab my arm. His jacket gaped open and the rough black polymer grip of his service weapon stood out against his clean white shirt. I let him tug impatiently at my sleeve for a moment, then shuffled toward him until I could swing my legs around and get my feet on the ground.

I stepped away and saw we were in the corner of a large, rectangular basement garage. There were only four other vehicles. Identical Ford sedans, standing in line to the side of the van. They looked new and shiny. They were much larger than European cars, but even with all the empty spaces each one was parked neatly within the yellow lines.

There were no other people. Apart from the two agents and me, the place was deserted. No one to witness anything that could happen there. A notice on the wall said the owners—some bank—denied responsibility for any damage that may be caused. I couldn't see which bank because someone had taped a piece of cardboard over the name with JUDAS handwritten in large red capitals. Next to the sign were the remains of a metal bracket. It was like the one above the door in the police interview room. A short length of wire was dangling from it, neatly cut at its end. I looked around the rest of the garage. Similar brackets had been mounted on the pillars at regular intervals.

Now, they were all empty.

Maybe the cameras had been recovered by the bank when it abandoned the building. Maybe they'd been stolen while it was lying derelict. Or maybe they'd been removed for another reason.

I backed up against the side of the van, just in case.

Lavine broke the silence.

"Hey," he said, standing in front of a pair of turquoise wooden doors set into the wall. "Will you hurry it up?"

Weston turned to look at his partner, and that gave me a decision to make. My eyes were drawn to his neck. Cervical vertebrae are notoriously delicate. Even wearing handcuffs, I could sever his spinal cord with one sharp snap. Then I could reach down under his arm and take his gun. A Glock 23 holds thirteen rounds, but I wouldn't need that many. One would be enough. Two, if I went by the book. Lavine would be finished before he could take his own weapon out of its holster.

I passed.

If all I was supposed to have done was kill a tramp, why was the bureau so interested in me? What made it worth trampling all over the NYPD and dragging me away to this building? There was too much I didn't understand.

So you can call it curiosity. Or professional courtesy. But either way, I decided to play along.

SIX

There were always plenty of books in the house when I was a kid.

A lot were borrowed from the library. Others had been inherited from relatives. But a few had been bought for me. I remember the first one my parents ever gave me, after I'd learned to read for myself. It was a collection of proverbs and fables. Some of them seemed pretty old-fashioned, even in those days. Some didn't make much sense. Some I've forgotten the detail of.

And others, I should have paid more attention to.

Ones like *Curiosity killed the cat. . . .*

The turquoise doors were the only way I could see to get out of the garage, other than the vehicle ramp at the opposite side. They had obviously been heavily used. The paint was worn and peeling, and the corner of the right-hand door scraped on the ground when Lavine pushed it open. Weston and I followed him through into a small concrete-walled lobby. There was an elevator to our right, but Lavine ignored it. He kept going and disappeared up a set of stairs at the far side. They only went up one level. We trudged along behind him and caught up just before he reached a heavy gray door at the top. He held it open for us and we emerged into a large, bright, open space.

I paused to check my new surroundings, but Weston grabbed my arm and hauled me past a deserted reception counter that ran along the left-hand wall. It would have been wide enough for three people to work behind, but now I could only see one chair. All the usual receptionists' paraphernalia was missing—sign-in books, visitors' badges, telephone switchboards, computer screens—and there was no other furniture in the whole area. It must have been some time since the place was occupied. A layer of dust covered the floor, making the marble tiles feel a little greasy under-foot, and a few small spiderwebs clung to the angles of the tall window frames.

The bottom six feet of glass had been covered up with sheets of coarse blockboard. One section was boarded up on the inside, as well. It was next to the far end of the counter, in line with a semicircle of black textured rubber set into the floor. It looked like the remains of a revolving door. It would have led to the street, but now the thick wooden panel blocking the opening was braced with two stout planks. Each was held in place by six heavy steel bolts. You'd need some decent tools to get through there, now. Or a little C4.

Weston didn't release my arm until we reached a line of shiny silver posts. There were five, dividing the recep-tion area on one side from a twin bank of elevators on the other. I guess they would have originally held hinged panels—probably glass, judging by the brackets—to control access into the building. Now their fittings were broken and there was nothing to fill the spaces between them. We walked through, past a double door leading to some offices, and headed toward the elevators. A door in the far corner was labeled STAIRS. For a moment I thought Lavine was going to make us climb again, but he reached out and pressed the call button instead. The indicators above three of the elevators were blank, but the fourth one was already showing GROUND. Its doors parted, and the three of us filed inside.

The elevator had buttons for twenty-four floors. Lavine hit the one labeled "23." The doors closed gently, and almost imperceptibly we began to ascend. The elevator's walls were covered by some sort of rough sacklike material hanging from small metal hooks near the ceiling. I pulled back the edge of one of the sheets and found it was protecting a mirror. I presume it was the same on the other walls. If so, I was glad they were hidden. I didn't need an endless sea of those agents' miserable faces reflecting all around me.

The display gradually wound its way up to 23. We stopped moving and the doors silently slid apart. Weston pushed me out first. He guided me around to the right, away from the elevators, and then steered me along the corridor until we reached an enormous open-plan office. Two lines of storage cabinets were laid out along the center of the room, forming a kind of pathway to a glass supervisor's booth that jutted out from the end wall. The cabinets were low—less than waist height—and a gap after each third one gave access to groups of desks on either side. They were pushed together in fours to form parallel rows of identical crosses. These were arranged alternately one against the cabinets, one against the windows all the way down the room. The nearer ones were completely bare, except for a tangle of wires spilling out from the exposed cable trays at the back. Farther away several computer keyboards were scattered around, all with their leads neatly coiled up, and I could see a handful of old telephone headsets mixed in among them.

The last couple of desks on the right looked as if they hadn't been cleared yet, and the ones at the far end on the left had been moved out of position. They'd been pushed aside, and the space between them was filled with chairs. At least a hundred. They were piled high on each other at impossible, drunken angles. Some had their arms hooked together to hold them in place. Others had fallen off and were lying on the floor, blocking the entrance to the booth.

Lavine flipped a couple of the fallen chairs onto their wheels and rolled them through the glass doorway. I had to stand aside as he came back out for another one, and I ended up squashed against the last desk on the right. I could hardly see any of its surface. It was covered with pizza boxes, Coke cans, coffee mugs, newspapers—all kinds of junk. The next desk was clinical in comparison. It held neat piles of papers and folders, several pens, a cell phone charger, and a pair of laptop computers. The screensavers had kicked in on both of them. One had a floating FBI shield that rippled as it moved. Homer Simpson was showing his backside on the other.

Two maps were pinned to the wall behind the desks, completely filling the space between a pair of windows. At the top was a large-scale street map of Manhattan. Clusters of red dots and blue triangles had been marked on it, along with a series of times and dates from the previous week. Below that a color-coded linear diagram was superimposed on an outline of the United States. The key said it was a schematic of the national railroad network. A set of black-and-white photographs had been stuck around the top right-hand border. They showed men's faces. I counted five. All of them would be in their mid to late thirties. They looked scruffy and unkempt, but basically cared for. Certainly not a pack of tramps. Arrows had been drawn connecting them to points on different railroad lines. All the points were on routes that fanned out from New York.

And all the men in the photos looked as if they were dead.

I sat right at the rear of the booth. Lavine had pushed my chair all the way in, so my back was literally against the wall. The agents sat facing me. They were shoulder to shoulder, pressing forward, blocking me in, trying to make me uncomfortable.

No one spoke for eleven, maybe twelve minutes. Then the fingers on Lavine's left hand started to drum against his thigh. He fought it for another minute, and then his mouth got the better of him.

"How're your veins?" he said. "Good?"

"Hope they're not," Weston said. "Hope they have to really dig around in there, trying to find one big enough."

"You know you're looking at the needle," Lavine said. "New York's a death penalty state. Being English won't save you."

"But hey," Weston said. "That's what you get when you start snapping people's necks."

I allowed myself a little smile.

"Snapping necks?" I said. "Didn't the NYPD tell you? The guy I found in the alley had been shot."

"The guy in the alley had been," Lavine said. "But the other five guys all had their necks broken."

"What five guys?" I said. "The NYPD were only trying to frame me for one. What is this? Rollover week at the bureau?"

"The guys who were found by the railroad tracks," Lavine said. "I saw you looking at their pictures, outside."

"I've never been near one of your railroads."

"Don't waste my time. We're not here for a confession. Forensics will take care of that. We're here for something else."

"Truth is, we don't know when things started going wrong for you," Weston said. "We don't even know for sure if they did. Maybe you just killed those guys 'cause you liked it."

"But either way, we don't care," Lavine said.

"So why are we talking?" I said.

"Because you have something we want," Weston said.

"A name," Lavine said. "Help us with that, and we can take the death penalty off the table."

"We can save your skin," Weston said. "And we're the only ones who can."

"The only ones," Lavine said. "You need to understand that. You need to be real clear. Take a moment. Think about it."

He leaned back, his fingers moving faster now.

"You want help with a name?" I said. "Why? Is one of you expecting a baby?"

"Michael Raab," Lavine said. "Who gave him up to you?"

"Who told you how to contact him?" Weston said. "Who he was? How to recognize him?"

"No idea what you're talking about," I said.

"You're not thinking straight," Weston said. "We have you. We can bring the hammer down any time we like."

"And believe me, we would like to," Lavine said. "The only thing we want more than you is the name. Who gave Michael Raab away?"

"Are we on to weddings, now?" I said.

"He went to that alley specifically to meet someone," Weston said.

"The alley where you were found," Lavine said.

"Someone with an English accent," Weston said.

I shrugged.

"You called him," Lavine said. "You set the meeting up."

"Wasn't me," I said.

"We heard the 911 tape," Lavine said. "You didn't pick him at random. You targeted him. Why? How did you know who he was?"

"Someone gave him away," Weston said. "Who?"

"You're barking up the wrong tree," I said. "The only people in that alley were me, and the tramp. And he was already—"

"Not 'the tramp,'" Lavine said. "Mike Raab."

"No," I said. "The tramp's name was Alan McNeil. I saw his Social Security card. His number was—"

"No idea where that came from," Lavine said. "Something he must have picked up. We'll look into it. But get this straight. His name wasn't McNeil. It was Michael Raab."

"And he was no tramp," Weston said.

"He looked like a tramp," I said. "Smelled like one, too."

"Because he was undercover," Weston said.

"Michael Raab was a Special Agent," Lavine said. "I knew him for twelve years. He was my partner. And my friend."

SEVEN

One year my father organized a fete at the local community center.

That would have been OK, except that he made me help. It meant he wouldn't let me buy anything until the customers had finished picking over the stalls, leaving behind only mangled piles of worthless rubbish. He didn't believe in gambling, so the raffles and lotteries were out of the question. The only thing I could do, apart from wander around spotting thieves and pickpockets, was the single game in the place that involved skill rather than chance. And even that was stretching the point. All you had to do was throw Ping-Pong balls into empty toilet bowls. You got three shots for five pence. I remember wondering why they bothered. It would have been easier just to hand over the prizes at the start.

I had a go anyway, and went home with three goldfish. They spent the next few months cooped up in a bowl in the kitchen, between the sink and the toaster. None of them did anything. They just floated aimlessly around while people stared in at them through the glass.

I never really gave them much thought, once they were home.

But after the next hour, I knew how their lives must have felt.

The agents withdrew from the booth without saying another word and for fully sixty minutes they hung around outside, observing me. Some of the time they were sitting, tinkering with their PCs or muttering to each other. Some of the time they were on their feet, standing still or wandering about aimlessly. But all the time, at least one of them had his eyes glued to me, watching me waste even more of my time.

Eventually Lavine's cell phone rang. He answered quickly, as if he'd been expecting the call. He talked for a minute, gesturing with his free hand even though it was obvious the other person couldn't see him, and then spun abruptly around to look at me. His face seemed to turn a shade paler, and as he listened I could see his expression change from surprise to bewilderment and finally something close to disgust.

Weston just looked angry when Lavine spoke to him after the call ended. They talked for another minute, then drew their handguns and Lavine stepped cautiously toward the booth. He pushed the door open with his free hand, keeping to the side so that his body was never between Weston and me.

"Stand up," he said. "Get out."

This time they did everything by the book. It was as

though their actions were being scrutinized by a hidden assessor and they were determined not to get a bad score. We went back through the main office, around to the elevator lobby, and across to a door in the far corner. It led to a staircase. There was no corporate decor, here. Just a gray floor, gray walls, gray handrails, and a gray ceiling. Different sizes of gray pipes were attached to the walls by plain, functional brackets. The place was cold and it echoed, a little like the inside of a battleship.

We went up one level, to the top floor. Two men were waiting for us. They were wearing neat gray suits like Weston and Lavine, and both were holding guns. As we approached they backed off through a door at the top of the stairs and took up defensive positions on the far side.

This floor had the same basic layout as the one below, but instead of passing through an open plan area, the corridor led us between two groups of more modest-sized rooms. There were individual offices on the right, and meeting rooms on the left. Several of the office doors still had name plates. I saw PETER MOULDS, NIGEL GOWER, DEREK WOODS. That one was open. I looked inside. The furniture was gone, but the carpet was a different class and there were outlines on the wall where pictures would have hung.

We continued along the corridor until we reached a pair of wide doors at the far end. The pale veneer was richly polished, and a plaque on the right-hand side read PRINCIPAL BOARDROOM. Lavine knocked lightly, twice, just below it.

"Come," a male voice said.

Lavine pushed the door halfway open and Weston bundled me through the gap into a large, square room. It was the full width of the building, and all three external walls were floor-to-ceiling glass. There were no blinds, and my eyes were immediately drawn to the tiny people milling around, far below. We were so high there was no sense that the building could be rooted in the same streets. It felt more as if we were floating above them, completely disconnected from everyday life.

Inside, the room was dominated by an enormous table. It was easily thirty feet long by ten feet wide. The surface was made from black granite, so highly polished it looked as if it were wet. I ran my eye all the way along, but I couldn't see any joins. It seemed to be a single slab. That would explain why it was still there. The partition walls must have been built around it. There would be no way to get it out now—it was too big.

Three men were sitting at the far side of the table, facing me. They appeared to be in their mid-fifties, and had the pallid complexion of people who don't see enough sunshine. Their suits were plain and nondescript. They had crisp white shirts and sober ties, and each wore his graying hair in a neat, conservative style.

The man in the center of the trio wore narrow, wire-rimmed glasses. He was looking down at a folder on the table in front of him. It held a half-inch stack of papers, but I could only see part of the top sheet. It was a computer-generated form. A photograph was clipped to the top, obscuring a quarter of the page. It showed a man's face. It was clean shaven, and the hair was tidier and shorter, but there was no doubt I'd seen the person before. Less than twenty-four hours ago.

Dressed as a tramp.

Weston put his hand on my shoulder and guided me toward a broken-down typist's chair. It was on its own on our side of the table, lined up opposite the three older men. Its blue cloth covers were badly torn. Clumps of stuffing were poking out of the holes, and various levers and handles were dangling from its base. I looked at Lavine as I lowered myself gingerly onto the seat, but he wouldn't make eye contact. He just turned his head away and shuffled farther along the table to my left. Weston removed his hand and slunk away to my right, leaving me isolated. On the other side of the table the man with the glasses closed his folder and pressed his fingertips against his temples for a moment. Then he dropped his hands and began to speak.

"Forgive me," he said. "Closing a personnel file for the last time is never easy. Allow me to introduce myself. I am Bruce Rosser, deputy director of Special Operations with the FBI."

"I'm David Trevellyan," I said. "But you knew that already."

"I did," he said, solemnly nodding his head. "Now—my colleagues. On my left, Louis Breuer. On my right, Mitchell Varley, also with Special Operations. Agents Lavine and Weston, you've already met."

I looked at each of them, but didn't say anything.

"Mike Raab was a good agent," Rosser said. "He'll be missed."

"Yeah, well, everyone's a saint, once they're dead," I said.

"No. Mike really was one of the good guys. I knew him pretty well. Mentored him, his first couple of cases, back when I was in the field. We used to play cards. Any chance we could find. All night, sometimes."

"Beats working, I suppose."

"How about you, Mr. Trevellyan? Do you play?"

"No."

"Shame. You should. You really get to know someone, that way. How they think. How they plan. How they adapt. How they bluff. How they lie. You know, if I had to get the measure of someone right now, given a regular interview or one hand of cards, I'd go with the cards."

"Is that right?"

"Yes, sir, it is. And you know what else I use them for?"

"I could suggest something."

"Problem solving. Ever gathered all the facts, but just can't see how they fit together? Cards can give you the answer. Help you put the pieces in place, one at a time."

"I'll bear that in mind."

"You know what? Let's do more than that. Let's play right now," he said, reaching into his pocket and pulling out a pack. They were white with a gold band around the edge and a large, ornate eagle design embossed in the center. They looked well used. "One hand of blackjack. For

Mike. And for you. Help you straighten out your situation. I'll deal. You tell me when to stop."

"Stop," I said.

He carried on shuffling, then laid the pack facedown on the table.

"Ready?" he said.

I didn't answer.

"OK, here we go," he said, turning over the top card. It was the two of clubs. "Lavine and Weston told you about the bodies. We've found five, male, near railroad tracks, their necks broken."

The second card was the four of diamonds.

"I assigned Mike after the second one was found," he said. "It was slow, but he was getting somewhere. He followed the trail to New York City. Set up in here, to stay under the radar while he was undercover."

Next was the two of hearts.

"Yesterday morning, he missed a regular contact."

Two of spades.

"We followed protocol. Spoke to the local police, emergency rooms, everyone else. At midday we heard the NYPD had found Mike's body."

Three of clubs.

"And they also had his killer in custody."

Three of diamonds.

"With eyewitness testimony on tape."

Four of spades.

"Which indicated a leak inside the bureau."

Rosser leaned back and gestured to the line of cards.

"So, how are we doing?" he said.

"How should I know?" I said. "I told you. I don't play."

"Just look at the cards. Add them up."

"Seven."

"Don't count them," he said, after a moment. "Add up the values."

"Twenty," I said.

"Twenty, that's right. A good hand. Almost unbeatable. The guy who killed an FBI agent, served up on a silver platter. A lot of people would stick with a hand like that."

"But you're not going to."

"Maybe. Maybe not. Let's think about it. Break the puzzle down a little more," he said, splitting the cards into three piles. "See, I think we actually have three problems here. You follow?"

"You have a dead agent," I said. "You have someone killing railway passengers. And you think you have a leak in the bureau."

"Good. We're on the same page. And these problems— separate, or connected?"

"Can't say. I don't know enough about the case to connect them, but if they're not connected, that would be a pretty big coincidence."

"And I guess we both feel the same way about coincidences, right? So let's start at the beginning. The railroad guys. They weren't passengers, the victims."

"So who were they? Employees? People living near railroad lines?"

"No. Free riders."

"Who?"

"People who hitch rides on freight trains."

"They still do that? I thought leaping onto moving trains went out with the Depression."

"Most people think that. It suits us. And we don't go out of our way to correct them. The fewer know about it, the fewer start doing it."

"Maybe. I just wouldn't have thought it was such a big deal."

"It's not al-Qaeda, granted. But it's big, and it's getting bigger. Try this. Right now, this moment, guess how many free riders are out there?"

"I don't know. Twelve?"

"No. Any given time, around two thousand. And a group that size, it needs to be managed."

"Really? Sure you're not exaggerating? There's not a bit of budget padding going on here?"

"We're certain."

"How do you know? About the numbers. Do you have people standing on bridges with clipboards, counting?"

"Not exactly. But we do keep a close eye."

"How?"

"Not your business."

"OK. So why do people do it? To save the price of a ticket?"

"It started that way, years ago. But now it's a way of life. Bums, with nowhere else to live. Illegal immigrants, sneaking into the country. Vets, from Nam. And lately Iraq, obviously. And Afghanistan. It's the closest to peace some of those guys are ever going to get, now."

"It doesn't sound very peaceful to me."

"I don't know. Riding around, alone, in an empty boxcar. That rhythm you get, with the wheels on the rails. It lulls crazy people into a kind of trance. Or lying under the stars, on an open trailer, winding slowly through the mountains. It's like being on vacation, for them."

"So what do you think happened? Did some vet start taking out his post-traumatic stress on these bums?"

"No. We don't get much trouble with the vets. They're mostly pacifists, now. They just want to be left alone."

"Who then?"

"Another kind of person altogether. Someone who doesn't need to ride the rails. Someone who wants to."

"Why?"

"Because it's against the law. Because it's fun. The greater the danger, the greater the thrill. People get all romantic about it. They think they're modern-day cowboys, riding the last freedom trail around America."

"Oh, please."

"They do. It's true. Or how about this? Because it's a great place to kill people no one will miss, and then disappear before the bodies are found. It's like a recurring stain."

"It's happened before?"

"Many times. Four years ago, a guy killed eleven. The last guy, thirteen."

"You caught them?"

"Raab's team did. Eventually. But there's over a hundred and seventy thousand miles of track in the major routes alone. That's a lot of places to hide. Or you can run. One side of the country to the other in three days flat. Or cross into Mexico. Or Canada."

"And wherever you go, you don't leave any records."

"You got it. No tickets. No credit cards. No hotels. Nothing."

"So if the guy's still in the wind after five murders, what changed? Why would he suddenly think the net was closing? Late-onset paranoia?"

"Someone told him. Warned him. That's the only answer."

"Now you're being paranoid. It's more likely Raab just showed his hand somehow. He probably screwed things up himself."

"No. For two reasons. One, we've traced every step he took. He didn't give himself away. We know that. And two, this guy didn't just spot some anonymous cop breathing down his neck. He had specifics. Who was running the investigation. Where they'd be. When."

"But that's high-level information. How would a bum or a vet get access to it?"

"You've got to understand the kind of guys we're talking about. They're not garden-variety lawbreakers. There's a whole subculture building up around this. There's a lot of juice involved."

"You said they were bums and vets."

"I did. And they're still there, sure. But now we've got

movie stars doing it. Rock stars. Tycoons. Guys who are used to getting what they want, when they want it, regardless."

"So?"

"I'm talking about powerful guys. People with contacts. Especially the business guys. They all have politicians and public officials in their pockets. One of them must have a hook in the bureau, as well. It's not good, but it happens."

"So the guy who killed these riders was tipped by his buddy in the bureau?"

"Yes."

"And then he took Raab out to save his own skin?"

"Yes."

"It was the same guy?"

"That's how we saw it."

"What do you need to complete your hand?"

"An ace."

"Then go ahead. Deal your last card."

"If it is an ace, we're going to start the paperwork on you," Rosser said, his hand hovering just above the pack. "You still want me to do it?"

I nodded.

Rosser flipped the top card over and covered it with his hand. He moved so fast all I saw was a blur of red, blue, and yellow against the white background. There was no sign of any numbers. Then he looked straight at me and raised his hand.

It was a grotesque character in a harlequin suit, standing on the north pole and showering the globe with dozens of tiny cards.

"Oh, my," Rosser said. "Would you look at that."

"The joker," I said. "How appropriate. Nice meeting you."

"Wow, slow down. Maybe we need to look at this thing again. If the train killer and Raab's killer are different people after all," he said, separating the three piles of cards, "maybe they're still connected some other way. What do you think?"

I didn't answer.

"Let's talk about this guy on the trains," Rosser said. "He's some kind of maverick entrepreneur. He's rich. More than rich. Loaded. Would he be the kind of guy to, say, wash his own shirts?"

"I doubt it," I said.

"Do his own ironing?"

"No."

"Drive his own limousine?"

"Unlikely."

"So, would he be the type of guy to go up against a federal agent on his own?"

"You think he killed five other people."

"They were spaced-out vets. That's a whole different ballgame. Plus, they were a hobby. This is business."

"So?"

"He'd approach it the same way he approaches everything else. He has the money, the contacts, the established pattern of behavior. He'd hire someone to do it for him."

"Maybe."

"No. Definitely. Now the question is, if you were hiring someone for a job like this, what kind of person would you choose?"

"No idea. Never had a problem I couldn't solve on my own."

"But if you did, what would you think of this as a résumé?"

Rosser pulled a sheaf of papers from under Raab's file and tossed it across the table toward me. I scrabbled it up from the shiny surface and looked at the top sheet. It was the printout of an e-mail.

The following information is for research and analysis purposes only. It should not be used as the basis for overt or covert action against Lieutenant Commander Trevellyan or any other Legation Resource Unit personnel.

So Headquarters wouldn't help me, but they were quick enough to roll over for the FBI—weasel words or not.

"Legation Resource Unit," Rosser said. "Used to be plain old Royal Navy Intelligence. Am I right?"

I didn't answer.

"Which section?" he said. "C?"

I shrugged.

"Corporate rebranding meets diplomatic security," he said. "Wow. Do the men in bow ties feel any safer?"

I stayed silent.

"You're really a sailor, then?" he said.

"Of course I am," I said. "A world record holder, me."

"What for?"

"Solo global circumnavigation. In the dark. Backward."

"Really?"

"No."

"No, thought not. Bet you can't even swim."

"Amazing. No one's ever said that to me before. Royal Navy. Water jokes. You made that jump pretty fast. But if you're going to ask me where I left my battleship, you know what? Don't bother."

"OK. I won't. Smart move, by the way, giving the NYPD an unlisted consulate phone number. First thing we checked, when they gave us your file. Your bosses in London were real impressed. Shows a lot of strategic awareness, for a guy who's supposed to be covertly guarding the place."

"That's not relevant," I said, turning back to the wad of papers. "The contact was unscheduled. I followed standard procedure. They know that."

The first part of the report was a summary of my service record. It started with my initial assignment to Hong Kong and carried on with an entry for most of the places I'd been sent to since then. I scanned the next seven pages and saw Washington, Canberra, Moscow, Paris, Lagos, St. Petersburg, Berlin, Tel Aviv, La Paz, Vienna, and half a dozen others. It covered the last fourteen years of my life, going all the way up to the mission I'd just completed here in New York. Nine weeks' work, four people's lives, and twelve stitches in the back of my head, all boiled down to fifty sterile words.

"Here we are," I said, pointing to the paragraph as well

as the handcuffs would allow. "This proves it. I couldn't have been involved with this train thing."

"We know that now," Rosser said. "But keep going. It gets more interesting."

The next section listed some of the training the navy had put me through. I skipped that part. Too many memories of freezing, wet nights on the Welsh mountains. And also because I was hoping the final few pages would contain one thing in particular.

I wasn't disappointed.

It was the psychological evaluation the navy had carried out during my recruitment. I'd never seen it before. Normally, they're guarded like the crown jewels. I started at the beginning.

> *David is an adaptable realist, relying on what he sees, hears, and knows for himself. He is hardworking, righteous, fiercely independent, and convinced that his cause must win above all else. David is optimistic and positive, living mainly in the here and now. He pushes others as hard as he pushes himself, and would prove a challenging adversary.*

"Turn over," Rosser said. "Check the parts I've marked out."

Three sections on the next page were outlined in yellow.

> *David appears not to be overly concerned with the needs of others, and may resort to extreme practices if anything threatens to get in his way.*

David's rather impersonal approach to life may leave little time, tolerance, or compassion for other people. He may adopt an "if you've got a headache, take an aspirin" attitude, which indicates a lack of empathy.

David dislikes being told what to do, or how to do it. He may frequently rebel against the rules, and in so doing will strongly resist attempts by others to regulate his behavior.

"What do you think?" Rosser said. "Makes you an ideal candidate for the hired help, doesn't it?"

"Because a shrink thinks I may lack empathy?" I said.

"No. We know why you got involved. And it clearly had nothing to do with empathy. Mitchell?"

Mitchell Varley, the guy on Rosser's right, lifted up a slim black briefcase and balanced it on his lap. He popped the catches and took out a small, clear Ziploc pouch. It contained a fragment of charred paper about an inch wide. He held the tiny bag at arm's length for a moment, gripping it between his finger and thumb, then gently placed it on the table.

"You have some ash in a bag," I said. "Should I be impressed?"

"We searched your hotel room," Varley said. "Guess those bill wrappers didn't burn quite as good as you figured. This was from a ten-thousand-dollar block. Enough in the room for five of them. What was that—the down payment? Half before, half after? That's the normal deal?"

"So a hundred thousand dollars was the price of Michael Raab's life," Rosser said. "Question is, have you got what it'll cost to save your own?"

EIGHT

It was early in December when we moved away from Birmingham.

I remember the date because I'd just been given a part in the school nativity play. It was my first one. I was going to be Joseph. The plot wasn't too convincing, but acting it out sounded fun. I was disappointed to miss the chance, at first. But at my new school we heard all sorts of other Bible stories. Some were much better. David and Goliath, for example. That was the best of all.

The hero shared my name, for a start.

And when the chips were down, I liked how he stepped up and faced his enemy alone.

The reflection of Rosser's pale, humorless face floated in the polished granite like a ghoul hovering over a giant over-turned gravestone.

"Downstairs, was the death penalty mentioned?" he said.

"It might have been," I said. "I can't remember. People are threatening to kill me all the time. And yet, here I am."

"Good. Because I've changed my mind. I've got something else lined up for you."

"An apology? A first-class ticket back to London?"

"An eight-by-ten cell," he said, reaching to his left and slowly drawing the edge of his hand across the shiny surface. "Think about it. That's about a quarter of the size of this table."

"I don't see a judge in here."

"Eight feet by ten. Your whole world. Twenty-three hours a day. How long would you last?"

I didn't answer.

"Not long, a guy like you," he said. "So this is what you're going to do. Go back downstairs with Lavine and Weston. Tell them about the guy who hired you. Every last detail. Help us take him down. Him, and his rat buddy in the bureau. Then, maybe we'll think about sending you back to London."

"I can't do that," I said. "There's no one to tell them about. No one hired me. I'm not involved."

"We can prove you are. Don't kid yourself. Force us into court with this and the whole thing will land right at your door. It'll destroy you."

"You can prove nothing. And London will never stand by and watch me walk into a courtroom."

"They've already agreed. You've been disavowed, Mr. Trevellyan. You're not a lieutenant commander anymore. You'll walk into that courtroom a private citizen. It'll be you and a public defender against the bureau's attorneys. How do you think the cards will be stacked then?"

I didn't answer.

"Don't believe me?" he said. "OK. Louis—get London on the phone."

Thirty-five minutes later the door swung open and Tanya Wilson strode into the room. She was wearing the same smart suit as before, but had replaced the briefcase with a small, blue leather handbag. There was no sign of the prop glasses and her expression was aloof and impatient, like an executive who had been called into a meeting with people she thought were going to waste her time. She scowled at me as though that were my fault, then took a quick look across the table.

"Afternoon, gentlemen," she said, and introduced herself.

I glanced at Tanya's watch. It had just turned five to four.

"Ms. Wilson," Rosser said. "Sorry to drag you across town, but you have some information for Mr. Trevellyan?"

"I do," Tanya said. "Though I'd appreciate a moment's privacy with him. This episode has been embarrassing enough. London wouldn't thank me for airing any more of their dirty laundry."

"Understood. Agent Lavine—find Ms. Wilson a suitable room down the hallway. Will five minutes be enough?"

Tanya nodded. I got to my feet and we followed Lavine back out into the corridor. He led the way to the first door on the right. Tanya pushed it open and stood aside for me to go through before her. She followed me in and seemed surprised to find Lavine hard on her heels. He walked to the center of the room and turned slowly around, surveying the blank walls and empty floor space. The only object to be seen was a set of emergency evacuation instructions. They were in a plain clip frame on the wall to the side of the door. It had a glass front. Lavine removed it on his way out.

"Four minutes thirty," he said. "I'll be right outside."

"What are you doing here, Tanya?" I said. "It seems you're not my attorney anymore."

"No, I'm just a messenger now," she said, stepping closer and taking hold of my lapels. For a moment I thought she was going to reach up and kiss me. At least I hoped she was. "I've been sent to tell you something."

"What is it?"

"London has been on the phone," she said, letting go of my coat and taking a step back. You can always rely on Headquarters people to dampen the moment.

"And?"

"I'm sorry, David. There's no easy way to say this. They dressed it up in a load of bullshit, but the bottom line is, London is washing their hands. As far as this current situation is concerned, you're on your own."

"They're cutting me loose?"

"I'm sorry, David. I wouldn't personally go this way, but it's London's call."

"That's ridiculous. Why?"

"This dead agent. The eyewitness. Something about some physical evidence the FBI found at your hotel."

"That's nothing."

"It's something to Washington. Whatever they found, it somehow convinced them you've been freelancing. They say they're coming after you personally unless you give up your client."

"And London? They believe that?"

"They don't know either way."

"So they just gave me up, anyhow?"

"It wouldn't be the first time someone crossed the line. And Washington thinks they've got a traitor in the bureau, which is making them extra crazy."

"That's their problem. London should have stood up."

"I'm sorry, David. I agree with you. I think they're making a mistake. I tried to argue with them, but who am I?"

"Don't worry about it, Tanya. It's not your fault. You didn't go over there and remove their backbones."

"I still feel bad, though."

"That's life. Shit happens. It's what you do about it that counts."

"But what can you do? You didn't kill their agent, and you don't have a name to give them. It's a lose-lose situation."

"Something will come to mind."

"Like what? If you don't cooperate they'll think you're

holding out on them. They'll come after you extra hard, out of spite."

"It won't come to that."

"How can you avoid it? The moment they get you in a courtroom, you're finished. The odds are totally stacked in their favor."

"So maybe I won't go into a courtroom."

"David, there's no way to avoid it. Without London's help you don't have a choice. Face the facts. You're stuck with it, so we'll just have to think of a different approach. Something to balance the scales a little."

"Such as?"

"This legal aid person Washington is offering? Their public defender? Forget him. Hire a better lawyer. It would be expensive, but if you worked with them to build a really strong case you could beat the FBI at their own game. And make London eat humble pie at the same time. How sweet would that be?"

"Work with a lawyer?" I said, moving over to the window. There were fewer people on the street now, and the ones that were left seemed somehow smaller and farther away. "That's one option."

There was a bang on the door.

"Sixty seconds," Lavine said, from the corridor.

"His watch must be fast," Tanya said. "Arsehole. So anyway, decision time. What are we going to tell Rosser when we go back in?"

"Tell him whatever you like," I said, crossing to the opposite corner of the room. "But for now, do me a favor. Stay where you are."

"David? What are you doing?"

I found a spot where I'd be concealed by the door when it opened and got into position, lying on my back with my right knee slightly bent and my arms stretched out above my head, as straight as the handcuffs would allow. Then I slowed my breathing right down and relaxed my whole body until it was perfectly still.

Lavine didn't knock a second time, and he came into the room well before the final minute was up. He took a step toward Tanya and then stopped abruptly with one hand still holding the door. After a moment the closing mechanism pulled the handle clear of his fingertips and it swung back into place with a bang.

"Where is he?" Lavine said.

Tanya nodded in my direction. She looked nervous.

If Lavine had been sensible and headed back to the corridor for help I'd have had a problem. But he didn't. He came over to gawp at me. People can never resist the sight of a body. I should know.

I stopped breathing altogether as Lavine approached. He stepped into the gap I'd left next to the wall, bent over me, then knelt down for a closer look. I could feel his breath on my cheek. It was damp. I guess he was worried, wondering how to explain this fiasco to Rosser.

Before he could move away I whipped my right leg up, hooked it around the back of his head and dragged him down toward me, trapping his neck between my thighs and jacking myself up into a sitting position at the same time. My arms were still above my head, and in one continuous movement I swung them over and brought them down in front of me, slamming the edges of my fists into his left temple like a pair of sledgehammers.

Tanya rushed over and stood for a moment, staring down at the pair of us entwined on the floor. She looked completely aghast. Then, without me asking, she began to haul Lavine's slack body off my leg.

"David, what on earth do you think you're doing?" she said. "How are we going to fix this?"

"Give me a hand," I said. "I need his keys."

"What's going on inside your head? Why did you attack him? Talk about making yourself look guilty. Who's going to believe you now?"

"Tanya—keys."

"Things were bad enough already. Now you've made them a thousand times worse. Just be quiet for a minute. I need time to think."

"We don't have any time. I need to be out of here before they come looking for Lavine. They'll wonder where we are."

"You're running away? Things are getting a bit tough, and this is how you react?"

"I'm not running away, Tanya. Never have, never will."

"Then what are you doing? You might as well sign a confession. Do you want to die in jail?"

"Stop thinking inside the system, Tanya. I gave it a

chance. It came up short. Now it's time to take care of business for myself."

"How?"

"Find out who's framing me."

"Then what? Have you thought about this at all? Have you got any idea what you're going to do?"

"Bring them back here. Accept Rosser's apology. Go back to work."

"You're taking the law into your own hands? You really think that's the best way to go? You'll be a fugitive. A cop killer. The FBI, NYPD, everyone you can think of will be out there, hunting you down."

"They can try, Tanya. It's nothing new. And who else is going to sort this crock out? Lawyers? I don't think so. Washington? Too busy throwing me to the lions. London? Sitting back, watching. You? Running around, delivering messages?"

Tanya turned away. Her breathing sounded sharp and fast but she made no attempt to speak.

"I'm sorry," I said. "That wasn't fair."

"No, it wasn't," she said, without moving. "I've been trying to help ever since I got your call."

"I know. But if you really want to do something helpful, please, get me the damn keys."

Tanya found them in Lavine's pants pocket, which was the first place she looked. She pulled them out, stalled for a moment while she pretended to examine his Bart Simpson key ring, and then very hesitantly released my wrists.

"OK," she said. "So I'm an accessory now. What else can I do?"

"Nothing," I said, taking Lavine's gun and $130 in bills from his wallet. "London has washed its hands. You can't get involved."

"Hello? News flash—I am involved. I want to be. What London's doing is wrong. I'm not going to just stand by and see you stabbed in the back."

"Sure?"

"Absolutely. Why not? In for a penny, in for a pound."

"You'll end up in hot water."

"Not necessarily."

"OK then. Maybe there are a couple of things you could do."

"Tell me."

"Keep your phone on. Hook me up with the right people when I'm ready to come back in. No one too trig-ger-happy."

"You've got my number. What else?"

"I'll tell you in a minute," I said.

Something on the wall had caught my eye. About waist height, fifteen inches in from the corner. From a distance I thought it was just a dent, but looking up from the floor I wasn't so sure. I moved closer and saw it was actually the mouth of a metal socket. It was square, about half an inch across. The plaster had been chipped away all around it, disguising the shape. I ran my hand across the surface and into the narrow alcove that formed where the two walls met. I reached up inside the dusty channel but didn't find anything. Then I moved my hand down again and my fingers brushed against something cold and metallic. I took hold, pulled, and it came away from its moorings quite easily. It was a steel bar, shaped like the starting handle from a vintage car. One end was squared off. I tried it in the socket. It fitted perfectly.

I turned the handle gently, but nothing happened. I tried a little harder, and very gradually the entire side wall began to move. It was sliding away toward the far side of the room and gathering up like a concertina between two banks of windows. I could have wound it all the way back to join our room up with the next one, but there was no need. I stopped after a dozen turns, leaving a space just wide enough to squeeze through.

I poked my head through the gap and quickly scanned the room. It was a similar size, also empty, with nothing on the walls. I didn't go through. There wasn't time for a thorough inspection, but that didn't matter. I could see enough from where I stood. A socket for winding the folding wall back into place—this time with a metal plate around it—and a door leading to the corridor. Everything I was going to need.

Tanya had her back to me, still gazing down at Lavine.

"That other favor," I said. "Tell them I overpowered their guy on my own. Don't mention that you found the keys. Then say I knocked you down, and you don't know what happened after that. OK?"

"Do you think they'll swallow it?" she said.

"Just keep it simple, don't elaborate, and stick to your story."

"I'll try."

"Oh, Tanya?" I said, pulling the handle free from its socket. "One last thing. I need you to scream."

She didn't disappoint. I kissed her—just for luck—then hooked her legs out from under her. She went down, hard, already yelling before she even landed on Lavine. I dived through into the next room. The handle slotted into place and I quickly started turning. A door opened in the distance. It sounded like the boardroom. Rosser and the others coming to investigate. More footsteps thundered down the corridor. Two people, running. Coming from the opposite direction. The agents who had been stationed by the elevators.

The wall inched across as if it were being pulled by a snail. I turned the handle even faster and the edge finally slotted home just as I heard the door fly open on the far side. People rushed in. I heard them milling around. Their voices were raised. They sounded angry and confused. I moved over to my door, eased it open a crack and peeped out into the corridor. It was clear. I opened the door wider and slipped through. Then I had to wait there for a moment, easing the door closed against the mechanism so it didn't bang into the frame.

But thanks to Tanya, there was no one around to see me.

NINE

Stairs are your enemy, my Escape and Evasion instructor used to say.

He repeated it constantly, never missing a chance to drum it into our heads. At first I thought he must be mad, but pretty quickly I came to see his point. Run up or down enough of them and your legs turn to jelly, however fit you are. Bad if you're carrying a tray of coffee back to your office. Worse if there are people with guns waiting for you at the other end.

I figured that with their top brass in an insecure building the bureau guys would be doing everything by the book. The agents who had been stationed by the elevators would be the inner perimeter. I didn't have to worry about them. I'd got through, and I'd hear if they tried to follow me. But there'd also be an outer perimeter, either on the ground floor or in the garage. And probably a backup vehicle outside on the street. That put a lot of stairs between me and anyone with a hostile disposition.

I decided to take things nice and slow.

*

I stopped on the twentieth floor to see if anything was happening with the elevators. There was only one in service—the same one that Lavine and Weston had taken me up in—and the display showed it was on the ground floor.

I stopped again on the first floor. This time I went straight through the lobby area and down the corridor, looking into all the various rooms. The first few on both sides were empty. Then I found one with a desk in it. That wouldn't work. Too big to carry. A large cardboard box had been left in the next room, but it was damaged. Too flimsy to stand on. But in the next room—the last but one—I found a small set of wooden shelves tucked away in a closet in the corner, next to the window. They were three feet wide, two feet high, and nine inches deep. Sturdy enough, and a perfect size. I picked them up and headed back to the elevators.

I went directly to the active one and hit the call button. The doors parted after a few seconds and I moved inside. I placed the shelves in the center of the floor, climbed up on them, and shoved the escape hatch in the ceiling just hard enough to partially dislodge it. Then I laid the shelves on their side, hit the buttons for the tenth and the ground floors, and stepped back out into the lobby.

Without making a sound, I ran down the one remaining flight of stairs. I slowed down as I approached the door to the reception area and peered through the coating of dust on the little window. I saw four men on the other side. They were wearing black utility suits with FBI in large yellow letters on their backs. Three were standing, looking at the active elevator. The other was facing the other way. He was talking on a handheld radio, his empty hand pressed against his free ear.

His conversation ended and he turned to join the others. He gestured with his arms and they moved to form a shallow horseshoe facing the metal doors, an arm's length apart. They all drew their weapons. I checked the floor indicator. The elevator was on the tenth. The display blinked. The elevator had started moving. It was coming back down. None of the agents reacted until it reached the second floor. Then, in unison, they raised their Glocks and took aim at the join in the center of the doors. I took hold of the handle in front of me and gently started to twist.

The elevator reached the ground floor. The agents were like statues. Their legs and backs were taut, their necks strained forward, all their senses focused in front of them. The elevator doors slid apart. At the same moment, I slipped into the lobby through the gap I'd made and carefully eased the door back into place. That put me six feet away from the nearest agent, directly behind him.

For a moment, all four stayed perfectly still. The agent who'd been on the radio was the first to move. He crept forward toward the elevator, his pistol snapping up and down between the abandoned shelves on the floor and the crooked escape hatch above them. As he moved, I moved. He went forward. I went sideways. He reached the entrance to the elevator, only looking up now, satisfied the car was empty. I reached the line of silver posts and kept moving, slowly and smoothly, until I was level with the entrance to the garage stairs.

Without warning, the elevator doors timed out and began to close. Another agent stepped up and hit the call button. The doors paused at the halfway point, then slid apart again. The two agents moved forward, together now, into the elevator itself. I edged backward, nudged the door, and disappeared silently down the steps.

I was at the bottom of the final flight before I realized I'd forgotten one detail. There were no windows in the turquoise doors leading to the garage. It would be impossible to tell if there were any more agents lurking on the other side. And no time to set up another diversion.

I gave the bottom of the left-hand door a sharp jab with my foot. It moved about twelve inches, its trailing edge grating harshly against the concrete. I slid across so that I was covered by the wall and waited for a reaction. There wasn't one. No shots. No voices. No one coming to investigate. I waited another minute. Still no response. So I drew Lavine's pistol, took a deep breath, and stepped through the gap.

There were more vehicles in the garage than when I arrived, but no people. Another three identical white vans had appeared next to Weston and Lavine's, and two more black Fords were parked alongside the four I'd seen earlier. A couple of spaces farther down there was a pair of even larger black sedans—Lincolns—and opposite them, a shiny Cadillac with dark privacy glass.

Taking one of the vehicles was out of the question. I

didn't have the time or the tools to deal with the trackers. Not that I minded—staying one step ahead in a city is always easier on foot.

The exit ramp was on the other side of the garage. I made my way across, climbed up, and slipped into the empty security booth at the top of the slope. It gave a clear view of the street. There were vehicles parked along both sides. They were mostly sedans and SUVs—older models, dirty, with a few dents and scratches—but diagonally opposite the entrance there was a clean, white van. It was the same make and model as the four in the garage. A sign saying BAXTER ELECTRICAL was attached to the rear panel, but it wasn't fooling anyone.

A steel-blue Jeep Cherokee turned into the street and cruised slowly between the lines of parked cars. It stopped, and reversed into a space a couple of slots behind the van. Two men got out. Both were wearing suits. The driver slung a black nylon computer bag over his shoulder. He locked the Jeep from his remote and they crossed the street, heading toward the garage. I waited for them to draw almost level and then drifted out of the booth, a couple of paces in front. It wouldn't have fooled anyone keeping a proper watch, but I didn't have time to wait.

As we walked I could hear a couple of vehicle engines on the move. They sounded like cars. Nothing more powerful. I risked taking a look over my shoulder and saw the white van was still in place at the curb. The guys from the Jeep were behind me, looking down, trudging along in silence. They stayed with me until the next corner when I peeled off to the left.

Two cars followed me. Black Lincolns. The first one drew level then braked to match my pace. It was far too slow to be regular traffic. The bureau guys in the van must have been on the ball, after all. I looked for some cover— an entrance to a building, a ramp down to another garage, an alley, a fire escape, anything to get off the street—but there was nothing I could use. Just a long, blank wall.

I turned to run back the other way. The cars responded, surging up onto the sidewalk. One cut across in front of me, blocking me off. The other came from behind, penning me in. The one in front was way too keen and its huge bulbous fender slammed right into the brickwork.

On a normal day that would give me my way out. I'd shoot the guys in the car behind me and slide over its hood while the other two were still wrestling with their airbags. And when they'd disentangled themselves and tried to follow, I'd shoot them, too.

But today wasn't normal. I was dealing with FBI agents. Killing them wasn't an option. Nor was fighting my way out. These were trained, motivated guys who thought I'd killed one of their own. The situation was too volatile. Things would escalate too quickly. I was on the wrong side of the line already, and if one of them got seriously hurt, there'd be no way back for me. In the circumstances, I had no choice. Annoying as it was, I'd have to let them take me back in.

And next time, be more careful.

The guys from the rear car got out and walked toward me. There were two of them. They would be in their mid-twenties, with black, slightly shiny suits and dark, glossy hair. Both were holding weapons. The driver had a Colt .38 Super in polished stainless steel. The passenger had a Smith & Wesson 1911 Performance Center in glassbead black. Expensive pieces of hardware. Flashy. Not the kind of thing you'd expect Quantico to approve.

The passenger tucked his gun into his waistband and came over to search me. It was my third time in seventeen hours. I'd be surprised if it was his third time, ever. He didn't even turn me around. Just put his left hand on my chest to hold me against the wall and checked me over with his right. The urge to gooseneck his left wrist and force him onto his knees in front of me was almost too strong to resist. Instead I held my arms out, kept quiet, and let him have a good rummage around in my clothes. Lavine's gun went into his waistband, next to his own, the money went into his back pocket, and the handle I'd taken from the meeting room seemed to confuse him, so he just dumped it on the ground.

"Give me your hands," he said, reaching forward and grabbing both my wrists.

He'd left himself completely open. I was amazed the FBI could have sent such amateurs to arrest me, knowing what they knew. Quite insulted, actually. Then something struck me about how they'd driven into the wall. How their vehicles had functioning airbags. How they were using shiny handguns in the field. How comically inept their search technique was. Put it all together, and there was only one explanation.

They weren't FBI agents at all. I looked down at the guy's face and smiled. He wasn't off limits any longer. My head started to roll back. The muscles in my neck began to tighten, all on their own. It was as if some kind of magnetic attraction had developed between my forehead and the bridge of his nose. But before I could split his skull, another thought hit me. It stopped me in my tracks. This was no random mugging. These cowboys were out in too much force for that. And how had they known to target me in particular? What I looked like? Or where I'd be?

Someone had been helping them. And that was good.

Because now they were going to help me.

TEN

When I was four years old my grandparents bought me Snakes & Ladders for my birthday. Chutes & Ladders, they call it in the States. But whatever the name, it was my favorite toy for quite a while. And all because of the first time we played with it. I remember the anticipation, waiting for the old folks to get ready. Then lining up the counters next to the board. Picking up the dice. Rolling. And getting a . . . one.

I was disappointed. It was a terrible score. The worst you could get. I was obviously doomed. I took my counter and gloomily reached toward the first square. Then I noticed the ladder. It sprouted from the bottom corner and ran all the way up to square 38. It would carry me nearly halfway home with my first move.

From despair to hope in a single moment. It was an amazing feeling.

And when the fool from the Lincoln pulled a long white cable tie out of his pocket and wrapped it around my wrists, I felt something like it again.

*

I knew the guy from the car wouldn't have been able to tell me anything useful, himself. He was too low down the food chain. But the person who sent him would be a different story. And this idiot was going to save me the trouble of tracking him down. I nearly laughed out loud, even when the driver popped the trunk and gestured for me to climb inside.

We were on the move for fifty minutes. It was absolutely dark in the trunk, but apart from being cramped and a bit airless, I didn't really mind. The carpet was thick and soft, and there was a raised ledge that made a kind of pillow. The big sedan's suspension was much more civilized than the FBI van, it didn't stink like the NYPD car, and the driver was taking it nice and steady. I'd been in hotel rooms that were less comfortable.

The first part of the journey was all stops and starts, so I guessed we were still in the city. Then there was a really rough section with tight twists and turns and lots of tire noise. After that a long, smooth, fast road with a couple of sweeping right-hand bends. The last five minutes were slower, then we turned left into some sort of rough yard or driveway. We snaked right and left, then crunched to a halt. The car paused for a moment. Then it rolled forward for the final few yards before coming to rest. The engine note died away. A car door slammed. Footsteps passed me. A mechanical clanking sound started up somewhere close. It lasted twenty seconds. Then there was silence.

The trunk lid opened, and all I could see was the inside of a roll-up garage door looming above me. The panels were made of wood. They ran horizontally. Each one was ten inches high, with some kind of dull brown coating applied to them. Rails ran up the sides to a winding mechanism that was fixed to the rough plasterboard ceiling.

The door was less than an inch from the car's rear fender. I stood up in the trunk and looked around. The front of the car was touching a wooden pole, sticking straight upright, with a red circular reflector attached to it at windshield height. There was a blank unplastered wall to our left, and room for two other cars to our right. The driver was in the center of the empty space. He was leaning against a round metal pillar, his hands in his pockets, looking pleased with himself. The passenger climbed out and went to stand next to him, also with a smug grin on his face. Then a plain wooden door in the opposite wall scraped open and another man stepped into the garage. He would be in his fifties, and was heavyset with dark, wiry hair and an open, friendly face. He was wearing a black polo shirt with some kind of golf club logo, beige trousers, and boat shoes. He could easily have been a lawyer or stockbroker, home for a long weekend and killing time before the Tuesday-morning rush.

"You two," he said. "Where are your manners? Help our guest."

My feet were on the ground long before the passenger ambled across to the car, so he just took my elbow and steered me toward the internal door. The older man stepped through first, leading us into a basement area. It was basically a long rectangle, but with a block taken out

at our end for a set of stairs. Another area was paneled in
at the far end for something—I couldn't see what—which
made the remaining space into a shape like a capital H.

The floor was gray concrete throughout. There were
wooden shelves all around the walls with piles of suit-
cases, bags, plastic containers, and cardboard boxes neatly
lined up on them. There was a lot of stuff in there, but you
could have emptied the place inside ten minutes. The ceiling was the only part that wasn't tidy and organized. It
was mostly boxed in, but in several places the boards were
missing and wads of pink fiberglass insulation were hanging down. Either the place had recently been searched, or
they had a major mouse problem.

The corner between the door and the stairwell was
taken up with a washing machine, a dryer, some ironing
equipment, and various baskets of clothes. The older man
ignored them and hurried straight through, heading for the
alcove on the opposite side. That was about the same size
as the laundry area, and was also fitted out for a particular
purpose. But not with white goods. Two giant cages had
been crammed in there. They must have been ten feet deep
by six wide and seven high. The floors as well as the sides
and roofs were made of heavy-gauge wire mesh. Each one
had a mesh door at the front. Both were padlocked.

The cage on the right, next to the stairs, was empty.
There was a person in the other one. It was a woman. She
was lying curled up on her side in the far corner, facing
away from us. Her clothes looked smart. She had gray-
green trousers, a matching suit jacket, and black low-

heeled boots. I watched her carefully. Her shoulders flexed slightly as she breathed, but otherwise she didn't respond to our arrival in any way.

"Need the john?" the older guy said.

"No," I said.

"Hungry? Thirsty?"

I didn't answer.

He took a bunch of keys from his pocket and unlocked the empty cage. I stepped inside.

"Hang in there," he said. "I'll be right back with some food. Then you can eat. Or not. It's up to you."

The guys from the car trailed meekly away after the older man. Their footsteps were hard and hollow on the bare wooden stairs, and the ceiling creaked loudly as they walked about above my head. I was glad they'd gone with him. With them all out of the way I could start to look around. I'd never been in a cage like that before. I wanted to know how it was made. Where its weaknesses were.

"Don't you know what these things are?" a female voice said. It sounded harsh and irritated. I looked around and saw my neighbor had stood up. She was tall. Five eleven, allowing for the heels. It hadn't been so obvious when she was curled up.

"They're dog cages," she said. "Made to hold big, angry dogs. Dobermans and Alsatians, for God's sake. And you think you're just going to claw your way out? Some finger-nails you must have."

"Have you seen any dogs around here?" I said.

"I didn't say I'd seen dogs. I said these were dog cages.

Which they are. Look." She pointed with her right foot to a metal tag attached to the mesh low down at the side of her cage. It said HOUND COMPOUND INC.

If these were dog cages, where were the dogs? I'd had more than my fill of trouble with them in the past, and there was no room in my plans for them now. Especially not big, angry ones. I scanned the rest of the basement. There were no leads or bowls or baskets. No packets or cans of dog food. No dog paraphernalia of any kind. No dog hairs on the floor. No smell of dogs. And no sound of barking.

Maybe the dogs were dead.

Maybe a previous owner had left the cages behind.

Or maybe these cages hadn't been bought with dogs in mind.

A door banged above us, then I heard footsteps on the stairs again. The three guys reappeared. The older one was carrying a rectangular tray. It was brown plastic with fake wood grain like they use in cheap cafeterias. Two items were on it. Something tall and square wrapped in shiny white paper, and a small bottle of Coke. It was plastic. There was no cutlery.

The driver took the tray and the older man fished in his pocket for the keys. He motioned for me to move back then opened the door. The driver put the tray down just inside the cage. He moved slowly and kept his eyes on me until he'd stepped back out and fixed the padlock into place.

"There you go," the older man said. "Enjoy."

"Thanks," I said. "Maybe I will. Then what?"

He studied me for a moment, as if deciding whether to answer.

"Someone wants to speak to you," he said, finally.

"Who?" I said. "When?"

"Someone important. They're on their way now. Be here soon. Better eat. Might not get the chance, later."

He stayed and looked at me levelly for another few seconds. It didn't seem threatening. More like he was curious about me. Then he turned and led the others back upstairs.

I picked up the tray, took it to the back of the cage and sat down. I took a mouthful of Coke—nice and cold—and then unwrapped the white paper package. A sandwich was inside. The largest sandwich I'd ever seen in my life. It was fully three inches thick. There were two large chunks of white bread crammed with dozens of slices of pastrami and big wedges of Swiss cheese. Mustard was dripping out between the layers. Fitting it into my mouth would be quite a challenge.

"This is huge," I said to the woman. "Like some? There's plenty for both of us."

She came across to the boundary of the cages and had a look.

"Don't like pastrami," she said.

I shrugged and picked up the sandwich.

"Suit yourself."

The woman waited until I'd finished eating and then moved down inside her cage so she was level with me. She leaned forward and took hold of the wire. Her hands were close together, about shoulder height, and I could see her wrists were bound with the same kind of cable tie as mine.

"Same jeweler?" I said, raising my arms. She smiled.

"Sorry about before," she said. "If I was rude."

"Don't mention it."

" 'Cause I could really use a friend right now. Think we could be friends?"

"No. I shouldn't think so."

"Oh. Why not?"

"Different taste in sandwiches. I might want more pastrami, you'd insist on something wholesome—it would be a disaster. We'd probably kill each other inside a week."

"Oh, yeah. I see what you mean. Could be a problem, the food thing. Think we could work around it?"

"Maybe. In the circumstances."

"That's good. 'Cause I really need to talk. You mind? You're not one of these silent, solitary-type guys are you?"

"Me? No. I'm like the village gossip."

"Good. But, you know, I'm not normally chatty like this. If we were in a bar right now, I'd be trying to decide whether to take my hat off to you or punch you in the face."

"Well, given you're not wearing a hat, I'm glad we're where we are."

"Nothing personal. Just I've got a funny feeling you're in the same line of work as me."

"I doubt that very much."

"How so?"

"Bit of a coincidence, both of us ending up here, if we were."

"I don't agree. You follow the same story, you end up in the same place. You're bound to."

"You're following a story? You're a reporter?"

"Like you're not. And forget about following. You're not following. You're stealing. My exclusive. And somehow getting further with it than me. You asshole. You must be very good."

"Listen, don't worry. A reporter is the last thing I am. Journalists and me—we're like oil and water."

"Really? I'm offended now. What's wrong with reporters? Everyone should mix with us."

"Nothing's wrong. But let's just say we don't really seek publicity, where I work."

"Where do you work?"

"My office is in London. I do a lot of telecoms consultancy. For the government. Tend to be a bit secretive, some of those guys."

"Sounds interesting. That why you're in New York?"

"See? That's why we don't mix. Can't help yourself, can you?"

"Sorry. But my problem is, if you were lying, that's exactly the sort of thing you'd say."

"Good point. Maybe next time we meet I'll be picking up the Pulitzer and you'll be on table Z, crying into your Chardonnay."

"You know about the Chardonnay? Now I'm really suspicious."

"Yeah—I was there last year, at the ceremony. Hiding behind the curtains, deciding which big scoop to steal."

"Then you would never have got mine. I never talk about a story until it's published. Except to my editor. It brings bad luck."

"It brought bad luck anyway. I'm guessing it was your story that got you in trouble?"

"So it would seem."

"What happened?"

"Two guys—the same two that got you—set up a meeting. In a parking lot. Said they had information for me. Then they pulled guns. Put me in the trunk of their car. Drove me out here. It was horrible. I nearly puked."

"Any idea where we are?"

"Not really. But it's quiet. And from the length of the drive I'd guess maybe Connecticut? Upstate New York?"

"When did they grab you?"

"Three days ago."

"Been here all that time?"

"Apart from trips upstairs, to the bathroom."

"Will anyone have missed you? Raised the alarm?"

"No."

"What about your editor?"

"Haven't got one yet. I pitched it to everyone. No one bit."

"So you're working it on your own, anyway?"

"Yeah. Pretty stupid, huh?"

"No. I like that. It shows commitment. But what were you stirring up that's worth all this trouble?"

"You really don't know?"

"Wouldn't waste my time asking if I did."

"Could take a while."

"Doesn't look like we're going anywhere."

"OK then. It basically started as a social justice piece. I got details of all the homicides in Manhattan over the last twelve months. It was a long list, so I broke it down by clear-up rate. Then I looked at the NYPD's results. I wanted to see how much is based on the victim's background."

"What did you find? Anything conclusive?"

"Oh, yeah. No doubt about it. Institutionalized discrimination, from one end of the city to the other."

"Based on what?"

"It's like this. If a Wall Street guy gets hit, the police go hell-for-leather. The killer's as good as caught before the knot gets tied on the toe tag. But if it's a bum, the detectives go straight to the paperwork. Kick it down to Open Unsolved."

"Are you sure?"

"Absolutely. They even have their own code for it. 'NHI'—No Human Involved."

"It wasn't like that last night. I found a bum's body and the NYPD were all over me like a rash."

"That was different. The way I heard it, there was something a bit special about the victim."

"How did you hear that? I thought you were locked up in here?"

"I overheard the guys talking, before they went to pick you up."

"How did they know?"

"I just heard them talking," she said, shrugging her shoulders. "So is it true? The victim was an FBI agent?"

"Yes, he was," I said. "But they only found that out later. The NYPD didn't know at the time."

"See, this federal thing is confusing me. I looked into all the organized groups that could possibly enjoy killing bums. Or benefit from it. Gangs, property developers, white supremacists, psychos, other bums, you name it. And the bureau didn't factor in once."

"So?"

"So what am I missing? I've got a lot riding on this story. If there's a huge hole in it, I need to know."

"There's no hole. The feds aren't involved in your story."

"But their guy was disguised as a bum. He was killed in Manhattan. That's a coincidence?"

"Why not? It's a big city. Must be dozens of investigations going on, all the time."

"What were they looking at, then, the guys you spoke to?"

"Don't know," I said. After all, she was still a reporter. "They kept their cards pretty close. But it was clear they were only looking at things that happened outside the city."

"You're sure?"

"Absolutely."

"Then thank goodness," she said, turning her back to the dividing wall and sinking to the floor. "I thought I'd missed something. If all this was for nothing . . ."

I shifted around the corner so I was sitting nearer to her. We ended up almost back to back, our right shoulders separated by the mesh. Her thick black hair was spilling through into my cage. Some of it was touching my arm. She twisted her head to look at me and a strand tickled my cheek. It smelled of coconut.

"What's your name?" I said. "I want to look out for your byline."

She smiled.

"Julianne," she said. "Julianne Morgan. You?"

"David Trevellyan."

"David, can I ask you something? I'm curious."

"Sure."

"About the FBI. Did they give you a hard time?"

"Not especially."

"Why did they pull you in, then?"

"The NYPD had a tip from a bogus eyewitness. It threw them off the scent for a while."

"But the feds believed you in the end?"

"We came to an understanding."

"They didn't want to throw you in jail while they checked out your alibi, or whatever?"

"They may have preferred me to hang around a little longer."

"So why let you go? Did you pull some lawyer trick?"

"Dialogue had stalled. It was time to explore other avenues."

"What does that mean?"

"I felt I could contribute more to solving the case if I was free to operate in a less restricted environment."

"In other words, you escaped?"

"If you like."

"Oh yes, I do like. How? What did you do?"

"Not much. Just walked out the door when they weren't looking."

"Yeah, I'm sure. Any chance of fixing it so these guys aren't looking? So you could walk out of here, too? And take me with you?"

"Absolutely. When the time is right."

"When the time is right? When will that be?"

"Someone's coming to talk to me. It would be rude to leave without having a chat."

"Screw 'rude.' I've been here three days."

"Another couple of hours won't hurt."

"David, ever thought what they'll do when they don't need us anymore? Like maybe after they've talked to us?"

There was another bang above our heads, then two people's footsteps clattered down the stairs. Julianne slumped forward like she'd been shot.

"Too late," she said.

The two younger guys appeared from the bottom of the staircase.

"Your boss here?" I said.

They ignored me and crossed to the front of Julianne's cage. The guy who'd driven me here had the keys. He opened her door. Julianne stood up and backed away.

"Where are you going?" he said. "Come on. Out."

Julianne didn't move. The driver stepped into her cage. She retreated. He followed her into the corner, grabbed her upper arm and hauled her out. The passenger pulled the door shut after him.

The padlock was one of the old-fashioned English kind. You can't just click them shut with one hand—you have to hold the hasp in place while you turn the key. They're more awkward to use, but I prefer them. No effort has been wasted on decoration or convenience. It's all gone into making them solid and functional. They look uncompromising, like they belong in an ancient jail or dungeon. My door had the same kind.

The driver finished with the key and the two guys moved back toward the stairs, dragging Julianne between them.

"Don't worry," the driver said as they passed me. "You're next."

That would be fine for me.

Maybe not for Julianne.

Certainly not for them.

ELEVEN

So far, all my assignments have been in cities.

All except one, that is. It started out OK. I had a roof over my head, running water, cooked food. But things soon went downhill. It spread into the jungle. In Colombia. And I hated it. The entire place was full of creatures that spent every waking moment trying to kill you. Everything that walked or crawled or slithered or swam or flew was absolutely lethal. Even the frogs were poisonous. Apart from one type. Some exotic species that was all covered in bright red and yellow blotches. They'd evolved that way to fool people into thinking they were dangerous, apparently. Like the guys who'd taken Julianne, in many ways. Only there was a problem with that approach. Some predators fell for it and walked away, unwilling to take the risk. The rest just steamed in harder.

That may have worked for the frogs, half the time.

But neither result was going to suit me.

Julianne was brought back after only twenty minutes. I took a good look at her as the driver shoved her through the cage doorway. She seemed pretty composed. Not in any obvious pain, anyway. I tried to catch her eye but she didn't lift her head. She wouldn't stop staring at the floor.

The driver opened my door and glared across at me, alert and anxious. He was standing bolt upright, chest out, chin up.

"Your turn," the driver said. "The hell you waiting for?"

"Nothing," I said quietly, making sure not to look him in the face.

I hesitated for a moment, then wearily hauled myself to my feet. I made a real meal of it, slumping my shoulders and bowing my head. Another few seconds slipped away. The driver was beginning to relax, not perceiving a threat. Another long pause dragged by and, finally satisfied, I crept timidly out of the cage.

The passenger took my right arm and held it while the driver swung the cage door shut. When he had both hands on the padlock, concentrating, I stamped my right heel down sideways into the passenger's left kneecap. He yelled, dropped my arm, and doubled over in pain. Struggling for balance, he hopped drunkenly back, hunched up, hugging his injured leg to his chest.

The padlock hit the floor. The driver was starting to react. His right hand was moving to his waistband, toward the shiny .38. But before he could grab it, my left elbow reached the side of his face. It was hard to get the power with my wrists bound so close, but I caught him well enough. His head flopped sideways, full into the frame of the cage door, and he went down.

I turned back to the passenger. He'd straightened up and was taking some weight on his left leg again. His face was twisted with fury. His left hand was clenched into a fist, and as I watched his right hand appeared from behind his back, holding his .45. I sprang forward, slamming into him, hands out in front of me, pushing his arm back down. The gun jammed into his groin. I went to twist his arm up and around, ready to break his elbow, but I couldn't get the leverage with my wrists tied. I was short of options, so I just drove my forehead straight into his face. It was rushed, but still enough to break his nose—I heard the crack—and knock him backward onto the floor.

He dropped the gun as he went down. I kicked it sideways under the nearest set of shelves. He lay still for a moment, then rolled onto his front, struggled onto all fours, and clawed himself upright using the wooden frame like a ladder. He turned to face me. Blood was gushing from his nose, covering his chin, and already soaking into the front of his shirt. He took a limping, unsteady step toward me. I let him take one more, then swung my right knee up hard, high into his rib cage. He folded over in front of me, too winded to yell any more, so I smashed my fists down into the base of his skull, stepped aside, and left him to fall.

The driver's Colt had fallen out of his waistband when he went down, so I leaned over and retrieved it. It was a nice weapon. The wooden grip felt good in my hand. My thumb hovered over the safety. Two each in the head would seem like a fair return. But that would be too noisy. It would attract the wrong kind of attention.

The driver had landed facedown, so I put his gun in my pocket and knelt down beside him. I put my right knee between his shoulder blades and took hold of his head, hands by his ears, ready to twist.

"David," Julianne said, in a kind of hissing whisper. "What are you doing?"

She was at the front of her cage, only a couple of feet away. Her fingers were through the mesh and her eyes were wide and staring.

"Oh, my God," she said slowly, her voice shaking. "You're going to kill him."

It was a long time since I'd worked with civilians. I'd forgotten how they can react in this kind of situation. Failing to neutralize those guys would be ridiculously naïve. Let them live, and you know what would happen. They'd pop up later, guaranteed, trying to put a bullet in your back. But on the other hand, I couldn't tell how she would respond to seeing me do it. If she panicked I wouldn't be able to take her with me. She'd been upstairs. She might be useful. And if I had to leave her behind, I couldn't see her getting out on her own.

That wasn't really a problem. I'd only just met her. It was too soon to say I really liked her. But this whole thing had started because I'd tried to help someone. The old tramp in the alley. Or the agent, as he'd turned out to be. I was too late then, but there was still a chance with Julianne. I didn't want to walk away without at least telling myself I'd given it a decent shot.

I took a careful look at her. She was trembling. Her

breathing was fast and shallow. I decided I couldn't take the risk. She was too close to hysteria already.

"Kill him?" I said, sliding my hands smoothly around to find his carotid artery. "Are you joking? I'm doing first aid. I've got to check his pulse. And breathing. Make sure he's not hurt."

I got off the driver's back, picked his keys up off the floor, and opened Julianne's door. She took two quick steps back. Her arms were out as if to fend me off and her hands and fingers were rigid. I went back to the bodies. She stayed in the cage.

"We need to search them," I said. "Come and give me a hand."

I rolled the driver onto his back.

She didn't move.

"We need a knife," I said. "Or scissors. Something sharp. To get these ties off our wrists."

She came to the cage door.

"We haven't got long," I said. "Someone will come looking, soon."

"What do you want me to do?" she said.

"Start with him," I said, nodding toward the driver. If she was hesitant already, seeing the passenger's blood wasn't going to encourage her any. "Turn out his pockets. Put the stuff in a pile on the floor. I'll do the same with the other guy."

She came out and moved cautiously away from the cage. She knelt down next to the driver, stretched out her hands, and touched him delicately on the hip. Her hands hovered there for a moment and then slid slowly toward his pants pocket, but as her fingertips reached the opening she snatched them back as if she'd been stung.

"Can't do it," she said. "I'm sorry. It doesn't feel right."

"You can," I said. "One pocket at a time. Pants and jacket. Just stick your hand in, grab whatever's there, and pull it out."

She didn't look convinced, but she had another try.

The passenger's pockets were disappointing. Apart from three cable ties and $400 in notes there was nothing I could use. Julianne had similar luck with the driver, except that he only had $260 in his wallet.

Neither had anything with a blade.

"Not very impressive," I said. "Put the average ten-year-old to shame, where I grew up. But never mind. We'll find something upstairs. We'll start with the kitchen. There are bound to be knives in there."

"Good thinking," she said. "Let's go. I know the way."

"Hold on. I need to put these guys where they won't cause trouble. We'll use the cages."

The driver's legs were blocking the door to the cage I'd been in so I grabbed his pants at the ankles and heaved them to the side, out of the way. His body bowed awkwardly from the waist, but his jacket didn't follow the curve. It didn't fold properly. There was still something inside it. I looked at Julianne. She looked away.

"Well?" I said.

"Well, what?" she said.

"I told you to look in his jacket."

"I did. I thought I'd got everything."

"Doesn't look like it."

"Don't start. I never wanted to search him, anyway. That was your genius idea. So if I missed something, big deal."

"Unless it's a knife . . ."

I checked his pockets again, myself. All were empty except the one inside his jacket. It held a brown envelope. It was folded over in both directions to form a little package, about two inches by three and a half. I unwrapped it. It was A5 size, unsealed, with no name or address. There was no marking of any kind.

"What's inside?" Julianne said, curious now.

I opened the envelope and shook the contents into my hand. It was a Social Security card. About a hundred years old, judging by the creases and stains. It was hard to read. I could just about make out a name—Charles Paul Bromley—and a number, 812–67–7478.

"What do you make of it?" I said. "Does it look normal?"

"Well, yeah, pretty much," Julianne said. "But I wonder why he kept it in an envelope, not his wallet? Seems a bit unusual."

I wrapped the card up and put it back in the driver's pocket.

"Maybe it wasn't his," I said, thinking of the one in Agent Raab's jacket. "We'll figure it out later. No time now."

Julianne halfheartedly guided the driver's feet while I

dragged him into the cage, attached his wrist to the back wall with a cable tie, and went back for the passenger. I put him in Julianne's cage and secured him to the side wall, well out of the driver's reach.

"Happy now?" Julianne said. "Can we go?"

I took the padlock from Julianne's cage and fixed it onto my door.

"What are you fiddling around with now?" she said.

I picked up the other padlock and hooked it onto Julianne's door.

"You've already beaten the crap out of them and tied them to the walls," she said. "Who do you think they are? A pair of Houdinis? Let's just get out of here before someone comes."

I locked the padlocks and tossed the keys into an open box on one of the shelves. It wasn't a perfect solution—those guys were still breathing—but at least it would slow them down. And sometimes, you just have to go with what you've got.

Julianne went up the stairs like a greyhound out of a trap. She didn't waste any time in the hallway, either. It was a spacious, rectangular area with tall white walls, quarry tiles on the floor, and a dramatic angled ceiling above a galleried landing. There were two internal doors to our left, an external door on the far side—I could see bushes and a brick path through a window—and a wide arch in front of us leading to a formal living room with two low white sofas, several abstract paintings on the walls, and a variety of tall bookcases overflowing with hardbacks.

Julianne ignored all these and headed through another, narrower archway to our right. It led to a combined kitchen/family room. The center of the space was taken up with a large blue L-shaped sofa and a glass coffee table on wheels. It sat on a rug with a Picasso-style design woven into it, and was piled high with all kinds of magazines and catalogues. Fashion, design, music, cars, art, you name it. A long bookcase ran all along one wall—hardbacks at the bottom, paperbacks at the top, except for one section that held five small trophies. Next to that was an elaborate wood-burning stove, and in the far corner there was another doorway. I couldn't see where it led.

The kitchen was separated by a peninsular unit that housed some cupboards and a dishwasher. The worktop was black granite, immaculate, uncluttered by kettles or toasters or other utensils. The sink was under a small window that looked onto a screened porch. It was empty. There was another archway in the wall to the left leading to a dining room, as well as some more units and a gas cook top. Next to the cook top was a wooden block holding five steel-handled chef's knives.

"Grab one of those," I said. "The center one."

"A knife?" Julianne said, disappearing through the archway. "Scissors would be better. There must be more cutlery somewhere. I'll check through here."

I had no idea what she was thinking, turning her nose up at a chance like that, but there wasn't time to argue. I put the driver's gun down and took out the knife. It was solid and heavy with a gleaming five-inch Sheffield steel blade. There were five drawers under the cook top. I opened the top one a couple of inches and wedged the knife inside, sharp side up. But before I could get enough pressure on the blade to cut the tie, I heard footsteps from the dining room.

Two sets.

Julianne came into the kitchen first, followed by the older guy who'd brought my food. His right arm was around her neck, and he was holding an old Army Colt to her left temple. She was standing stiffly, back arched, grimacing. He was smiling. His throat was unguarded. I closed my fingers around the knife blade. It was a good weight for throwing. How much did I want to save this woman? It was unlikely I could stop the guy getting one shot off. But certain I could stop him getting two.

I heard the clatter of heavy feet on wooden stairs. Someone was coming down. They paused in the hallway and then appeared through the arch. It was someone new. He was huge. At least six feet seven. His head was shaved and he had to duck as he came in. He was wearing a smart blue suit with a white shirt and striped tie. It was hard to tell without the hair, but I put him in his late thirties. Apart from his freak size he looked like a businessman stepping out of a meeting to grab a coffee.

"What's going on, George?" he said. "Where's Jason and Spencer?"

"Don't know," the older guy said. "Found this bitch

sneaking around, and him in here playing with the utensils. Haven't seen the pretty boys."

"Where are Jason and Spencer?" the tall guy said, looking at me.

"Who?" I said.

"The two guys I sent to fetch you."

"Oh, them. Downstairs."

"Dead?" he said, looking at the knife.

"No. Just . . . resting."

"George, take the woman back down there. Lock her up, and see what's going on with those fools."

The tall guy stepped aside to let George get past with Julianne. Her eyes stayed on me, wide and frightened, as if begging for help.

"Let's you and me go upstairs," the tall guy said. "We need to talk."

I didn't move. The knife was still in my hand.

"Going to use that?" he said. "Go ahead. I'm not carrying."

He held his arms out to the sides, as if inviting a search.

I stayed where I was.

"Come on," he said. "Let's go. My boss is upstairs."

I didn't reply.

"Come on," he said. "My boss is waiting. That's not good."

"Your boss?" I said.

"Right. Wants to talk to you."

"You think I'm one day old?"

"What?"

"You think I was born yesterday? You snatch me off the street and lock me in a kennel like a dog because your boss wants to talk?"

"OK, look, I won't bullshit you. The thing with the kennel—that was wrong. But with everything jumping off at once—journalists sniffing around, FBI all over the place, you suddenly on the loose—we had to move fast. We made some mistakes."

"Just a few."

"We know that, now. We should have shown more respect, but we needed you off the street."

"Why?"

"To keep you out of anyone else's pocket. We heard some rumors. Needed time to check them out."

"Rumors? About me?"

"Look, put the knife down. Come upstairs. Hear what we've got to say. It'll make sense. And what's to worry about, anyway? If we wanted you dead, you'd be on the slab already."

"I'm not meeting anyone like this," I said, holding up my hands.

The tall guy came over and very gently took hold of the knife handle. He waited for me to clear my fingers, then severed the tie. It fell to the floor, leaving a narrow red welt around both my wrists.

"Happy now?" he said. "So let's go."

He slid the knife back into the block, picked the driver's Colt up from the countertop, and turned to lead the way.

As he walked toward the hallway he slipped the gun into his jacket pocket. It rattled against something metal.

And as sincere as the guy had seemed, I doubt it was his keys.

TWELVE

Several of my previous assignments had been missing from Rosser's file.

A number of them had taken place in the United States. One was in California. I'd been sent there to infiltrate a cell phone company where we suspected some employees were selling transcripts of sensitive short message service messages. The scheme had been well hidden. It took three months to flush out. I'd felt strange working in the same office for so long, but in the end a little part of me was sorry to leave. Not because of the people, though. Most of them were crooks. It was more about the way you were looked after. There was gym membership. Concert tickets. Discounts at local stores. You don't even get free parking in the navy.

Another strange thing was the company newsletter. Different departments telling each other what they were doing. That's a weird concept. The magazine was nicely produced—glossy paper, plenty of photos—but the lack of real news meant they had a lot of ads and bogus articles. One was written by a psychologist. Every month someone gave him pictures of a manager's office and he revealed all kinds of insights based on how they kept their work-space. Once we learned that the papers strewn all over the desk of the president of Human Resources showed she was a really caring person. The next month we found out that the way the VP of engineering arranged his stationery demonstrated a sound grasp of complex technology. I was certainly convinced.

That psychologist would have loved the large rectan-gular room the tall guy took me to next, at the end of the landing corridor. It had a white-stained wooden floor, plain white walls, and a white ceiling that sloped sharply to one side. There was a wide window at the far end and double closet doors built into the wall on the left. An L-shaped desk ran along the other wall and stuck out halfway across the room. Behind it was a single chrome and black leather chair. There were no piles of papers or letter trays or pen holders. The only thing anywhere on the desk was a small, white laptop. Its screen was folded down and there was no sign of it being connected to anything. And there was no printer, router, fax, or phone.

The space between the desk and the door was filled with a boardroom-style table. It was made from light wood with rounded corners and beveled edges. The table-top was polished like glass and I couldn't see a single mark or scratch or blemish. There was a flap, eight inches by twelve, set into the surface at both ends. They were prob-ably to conceal power outlets. Three chrome and leather chairs were arranged along each side—precisely parallel—and two more were lined up at each end.

A projector sat in the middle of the table with its cable in a neat coil at its side. It was pointing at a screen on the wall next to the door. The other walls were bare, except for a print of Magritte's *Ceci n'est pas une pipe*, which hung over the desk. The original is in the L.A. County Museum. I noticed it when I was tailing a couple of suspects on that mobile phone job. I remember liking it. Finding a copy of it here seemed strange.

"Take a seat," the tall guy said. "Won't be long."

I chose the chair in the center on the far side. He took the one nearest the exit. Farther down the corridor a door slammed. Footsteps approached. One set, light but confident, moving fast without rushing. They paused, and then a woman entered the room. The way she strode in made it clear that we were the ones invading her domain, not the other way around.

The woman had ginger hair. Fiery red, not orange. It was cut long at the back and sides to emphasize her long, slender neck and delicate jaw. Her skin was pale and flawless, and her wine-red lipstick brought out a wild green glint in her eyes. Her clothes—jacket, vest-style top, slacks, and pumps—were all black. They looked expensive. From a distance I put her at around thirty-five, but when she came over and took the seat opposite me I guessed she was at least a decade older.

She sat and looked straight at me for a full fifteen seconds. Her eyes seemed to glow from behind her bangs like a cat's and she had the calm, unrushed air of someone in complete control of herself and everything around her.

"You're from out of town, so you probably don't know who we are," she said.

I didn't answer.

"So we'll start with some ground rules," she said. "We're not like the police. Or the FBI. We don't care about guilt or alibis. We have no rules or procedures. All we're here to do is talk about a proposition. Something we can both benefit from. Any bullshit from you, and the conversation ends."

"OK then," I said. "No bullshit. What can we do for each other?"

"We can help with your current problem. You can do us a small favor in return."

"What current problem?"

"Your FBI problem. They don't like you very much. Not anymore. Not now they think you killed their agent."

"They're mistaken."

"We know."

"How do you know?"

"Because we killed him."

"You did? Why?"

"No reason. We have lots of balls in the air, any given moment. Every now and again one gets dropped. It's no big deal."

"It is from where I'm sitting."

"OK," she said, after a moment. "Truth is, it was a mistake. Our guy didn't watch him long enough. We didn't know he was an undercover agent."

"An agent disguised as a tramp," I said. "But why kill a tramp?"

"That's not relevant."

Then I made the connection. The Social Security cards. Raab was carrying one. It was old and filthy and used. The guy downstairs had another. They were stealing identities. From tramps. And probably selling them. Rosser had mentioned illegal immigrants using the railroads. They were exactly the kind of people who'd need new papers. Maybe that was how Raab had got caught up with these guys.

"So Agent Raab was killed by mistake," I said. "That's nice to know. His family will be delighted. But how does it help me?"

"It doesn't," she said. "In itself. But if we give you the guy who pulled the trigger, that would work. Might even throw in the gun. They run ballistics, you're free and clear."

"Why would you do that?"

"When the FBI pulled you in, you met three main guys?"

"Right. Rosser, Varley, and Breuer."

"Good. That's what we heard. So this is what you do. Contact the FBI. Tell them you have the real shooter, and you want to bring him in. But you'll only hand him over to the same three guys you already met. Say you don't trust anyone else. Can you do that?"

"I know someone. They could set it up. But why those three guys?"

"We have a problem with one of them."

"Which one?"

"Mitchell Varley."

"What sort of problem?"

"His continued existence."

"Intriguing. Why?"

"Ancient history."

"Not that you're one to bear a grudge . . ."

"Let's just say our paths have crossed before. More than once."

"They have? Excellent. I always enjoy a good bit of vengeance. What did he do?"

"Doesn't matter," she said, and I saw her left hand slip down from the table into her lap. "But my guy's going to correct the situation."

"How?" I said.

"With a .22. One shot, close range. Straight through the temple. But don't worry. You'll be in no danger. The bullet won't even come out the other side. It'll just rattle around, turning his worthless brain to mush."

"And that's your small favor?"

"Put our guy and Varley together. That's all we want."

"Then I'm sorry. I can't help."

Air hissed from between the woman's clenched teeth.

"You were with Varley for what, an hour?" she said.

"Less," I said.

"And now you're ready to die for him? Must have been some conversation you guys had."

"That sounds vaguely like a threat."

"No, not a threat. Just Plan B. Because aside from the chance to rid the world of Mitchell Varley, there's still this thing with the dead agent. I've got to deal with it somehow. If I'm not giving you the shooter, I'll have to do something else."

"Not my problem."

"Absolutely your problem. The feds already thought you did it. Escaping confirmed that. Now they've got a hard-on for you like you wouldn't believe."

"So?"

"So we leave your body where it's easy to find. They'll close the case on the spot. Never even look in our direction. So, time to lose this sentimental crap with Varley. Otherwise . . ."

"There is no sentimental crap with Mitchell Varley. He barely said two dozen words to me. And frankly, I wasn't impressed with what he did say. I couldn't care less what happens to him."

"Then what's the problem?"

"Well, let's just think about it for a moment. I bring your guy in. He immediately kills Varley, who's only there because I specifically asked for him to be. How's that going to look? I'll be lucky if the others don't shoot me on the spot."

"They won't shoot you. They'll thank you."

"For what? Getting their friend killed?"

"No. For saving them."

"How am I going to do that?"

"Seen *In the Line of Fire*? At the end. Like that."

"You want me to take a bullet?"

"No. Just make it look like you were willing to. Appearance is everything. The second Varley gets hit, you yell at the others. *Get down, he's got a gun,* like that. Then jump in front of them. It'll look like you saved Rosser and Breuer, not set up Varley."

"What happens to your guy?"

"He goes for the door, under cover of your heroics."

"And after that?"

"His problem."

"What if he doesn't make it?"

"Then it's my pawn for their queen. Varley's worth it."

"Does your guy see it the same way?"

"He knows it's a risk, obviously. But I've made it worth taking."

"What if he goes after one of the others first? Or me?"

"He won't."

"Why not?"

"He has his instructions," she said, standing up and moving toward the desk. "He'll follow them. That's what my people do."

"What's your name?" I said.

"Lesley. Why?"

"I was thinking Agripinilla, for some reason."

"Know anywhere in the city where you could do this?" she said, opening one of the desk drawers and taking out a cell phone. "Or do you want me to find you a place? Needs to be away from their building. Nowhere with witnesses. Easy access."

"How about the building they took me to this afternoon?" I said. "It is theirs, but it's not fitted out yet. No one else uses it."

"Metal detectors? Cameras?"

"No."

"Good. And the location's OK," she said, switching the phone on and bringing it over to me. "You already know the layout. Ties in with wanting to see the same three guys. All right. Go ahead."

I left the phone on the table.

"Two more things," I said. "One—I spent last night in jail. Today I've had a coffee, a sandwich, and a Coke. No way am I meeting these guys tonight. Tomorrow at the earliest. And I'm not staying here. I want a night in a decent hotel, with a decent meal, which you're paying for."

"Be safer here," she said. "People are looking for you."

"People are always looking for me. It comes with the territory."

"Well, OK, I guess. I'll send a couple of guys with you. What else?"

"Julianne Morgan. The woman you've got locked up in the basement. I'm taking her with me."

"You want the woman?" she said, glancing at the tall guy. "Why?"

"She got mixed up in this by mistake. She's got no idea what's going on. She's no threat to you. If Varley and this other guy of yours don't make it through—too bad. They knew the risks. They made their choices. She didn't."

"What will you do with her?"

"Take her to the city. Let her stay in the hotel tonight, and cut her loose in the morning. I'm hardly going to want a journalist hanging around me tomorrow."

"Well, why not? OK. You can have her. Saves us having to get rid of her. But she rides to the city in the trunk. We'll have cars watching you. Let her out anywhere this side of the river, she'll be dead before her feet touch the sidewalk."

"I can live with that," I said, wondering if Julianne could.

"Now make the damn call before I change my mind."

Tanya answered on the first ring.

"This is David," I said.

"David?" she said. "Are you all right? Where are you?"

"Those contacts you had at Federal Plaza. Are they still in place?"

"What's up? Is someone listening?"

"Yes. Could you call them? Set something up for tomorrow?"

"Really? That soon?"

"Yes. Call tonight. Right now, if you can. This is urgent."

"What do you need?"

"Tell them I'm holding the guy they're looking for. From the alley, last night. They'll know who I mean. I'm prepared to hand him over, but only to the same three guys I met today. Rosser, Varley, and Breuer."

"Could be difficult, David. They're still really mad at

you. Why not deliver him to me, let me liaise? Stay out of
the firing line?"

"No. It has to be the same three guys. The same three,
or I cut this guy loose and they'll never find him."

"Oh. OK, then. I'll square it somehow. Where and
when?"

"Don't know yet. I still have to get out of the city. Tell
them to be at the Wall Street helipad at 9:00 A.M. Bring a
pilot, and enough fuel for two hours. I'll call then with
a time and location."

"Understood. Back in five."

Lesley hadn't even pretended not to listen.

"Nice misdirection, with the heliport," she said.

"Thanks," I said. "Talking of which—my hotel room,
with the ash? That was you?"

"That was me," the tall guy said.

"Really?" I said. "Good work. Subtle. I might use it
myself, sometime."

"Just glad they went for it," he said. "It was kind of
last-minute. And a bitch to do, without the smoke alarms
going off."

"How did you know where I was staying?"

"Someone told us."

"Who?"

"Can't remember now. Could have been so many
people."

"That kind of information isn't exactly commonplace."

"Depends who you know. The NYPD? They're like the

TV, the Internet, and the newspapers all rolled into one, for us. Same goes for the FBI. Nothing happens in this city we don't find out about."

"You found out pretty fast."

The tall guy shrugged.

"Wanted to make sure they swallowed you whole," he said. "Didn't know it would be the feds that found it. Didn't even know the vic was one of theirs at the time. Just didn't want any possibility of the spotlight coming our way."

"See, speed is the key," Lesley said. "Anything goes wrong, our people are motivated to tell us right away. That way, we can jump right on it. Never miss an opportunity to protect ourselves. You might want to remember that, the next couple of days."

"I hope there's not an element of distrust developing here?"

"Depends how smart you are. For instance, maybe you're thinking you could take the .22 away from my guy? Hand him to the feds without him killing Varley?"

"That never crossed my mind."

"Good. Because I haven't given you one hundred percent of the facts about that."

"Convenient time to mention it."

"See, the guy I'm giving you—he isn't really the one from the alley. That was one of my other guys. Not the cream of the crop. Now this guy—he's one of my best. French. Ex-Sûreté. Perfect for the job. Could do it in his sleep. But he's got a real loose tongue. Hand him to the feds, and it'll all come pouring out. Everything will point straight back at you."

"What if he gets caught?"

"He won't. He'll get out, or go down fighting. That's the way he is."

"You can't be sure. The feds are no mugs."

"It would be too late, then, anyway. Rosser and Breuer would have seen him pull the trigger. It would be your word against a cop killer. And he'd never see the inside of a courtroom, anyway. Trust me. None of my people ever have."

"Why take the chance? Why not just give me the real guy?"

"Look at it as an incentive. To make sure you hold up your end. Plus the real guy won't be working for a while. He needs some retraining."

"Where is he?"

"Downstairs. Want to meet him?"

"He's the one who called 911? Gave them my description?"

"He's the one. His idea, though, to give you up. We're not normally big on framing passers-by. It's an unnecessary risk. Usually just leave the body where the NYPD will trip over it. As long as it's unwashed, they don't lose much sleep."

"Then, yeah, I want to meet the guy. Alone, preferably."

"Can't do alone," she said, getting up and heading for the desk. "But don't worry. You're going to love what I've got for him."

I watched Lesley open one of the lower drawers, then the cell phone she'd given me started to vibrate in my pocket. It was Tanya.

"Deal's done," she said. "We'll be at the helipad at 9:00 A.M. tomorrow, waiting for your call. The three guys you specified and me."

"Excellent," I said. "Thanks. Any problems getting it set up?"

"Don't ask. You owe me, big-time."

"Dinner's on me, then, when this is over."

"Three dinners, minimum. Don't forget that stunt with Lavine. And you still owe me one from Madrid."

Lesley had started back before I hung up.

"We're in business," I said.

"I heard," she said.

She was carrying a lumpy, vaguely cylindrical parcel, nine inches long by four inches diameter. It was made of gray suede, held together by a fine silver chain. I heard the tall guy shifting in his chair, and I saw his eyes were glued to the object as Lesley gently laid it down on the table in front of her.

"Something you should think about," she said. "We own people. They tell us things. Your name. Where you were staying."

"You mentioned that already," I said.

"It goes further. Let me give you an example. Louis Breuer received a secret e-mail from London this afternoon. One of our guys got to it first. We'd read it before Breuer or Rosser or Varley. We know all about you. What you do. All your little trips around the world. Not a bad life, for a sailor boy."

"And your point is?"

"You need to believe, anything goes wrong tomorrow—accidentally or otherwise—we're going to know before you leave the building."

"I'm sure you're right."

"I am. Like this afternoon. You outsmarted the FBI. Got away from them, easily enough. But not me. Because my ear's to the ground. Always. I heard what you did. And I had two cars outside before you even found the door."

I allowed myself a little smile. She still didn't realize the favor she'd done me back there.

"OK," I said. "If anything goes wrong tomorrow, it won't be down to me."

"Good," she said. "'Cause there are penalties for people who let me down."

"Like what? You don't let them shoot tramps anymore?"

"Yeah. Kind of like that. I was going to tell you about it, but then I thought, why not show you?"

Lesley nodded at the tall guy. His face was blank, bordering on sullen. He paused for a moment then hauled himself up and stalked out of the room, his big feet clattering along the landing and down the stairs.

"Watch what happens next," she said. "Then see if you still have a taste for wisecracks."

THIRTEEN

I passed my test at seventeen. And learned to drive at twenty-two.

It's one of the first things the navy does when they recruit you. For intelligence work, anyway. They take your license away and make you earn it back. Which sounds fine in principle, because you know you'll not be dealing with Nissan Micras and three-point turns anymore. You'll be in modified vehicles, on private racetracks, getting to grips with the A to Z of defensive maneuvers.

There's only one snag.

They insist you understand the cars before you drive them.

I remember on the first day they showed us two groups of twenty different models lined up on opposite sides of an old aircraft hangar. One half were regular civilian cars. The others were from the motor pool. We knew the navy cars had been adapted. They would have special engines. Brakes. Tires. Suspensions. Electronics. You name it. But it was all so discreetly done that no one could tell which was which.

It was a pain, learning enough mechanics to be let loose behind the wheel. And at the time I thought I was just finding out about cars. But over the years I've seen it's the same story with people. Compare pros and amateurs in any field, and there's only ever one conclusion.

They might look similar on the surface.

But underneath, they're completely different animals.

Lesley sat and watched me, completely still except for her left hand. It seemed to be moving on its own, creeping steadily across the tabletop toward the gray parcel. Her fingertips reached it, paused, and climbed on top. Then they started to caress the soft suede, rippling across the smooth surface like a spiteful sea creature tormenting its prey.

Her fingers only stopped circling when the door opened and a man took a couple of hesitant steps into the room. He would be in his mid-twenties, reasonably tall—a shade over six feet—with jeans cut to show off his narrow waist and a pair of broad, powerful shoulders showing through a plain black T-shirt. His short blond hair was a little shaggy, like he was growing out a crew cut, and he hadn't shaved for a couple of days. The only off note was his face—it was slightly pointy, and he had beady brown eyes that were a touch too close together. They made him look like some kind of rodent.

The tall guy came in next. He didn't come over to the table this time but stayed by the door, like a sentry. George—the guy who'd brought my food and caught Julianne in the dining room—was last. He came across and stood next to the wall, near me. He was looking down, fiddling with a small video camera. The strap was looped safely around his right wrist.

"David, this is Cyril," Lesley said, nodding toward the new guy. "Actually his name isn't Cyril, but we call him that 'cause we think he looks like a squirrel. It kind of suits him. Cyril the squirrel. You Brits like rhyming words, don't you?"

"Not particularly," I said.

"Recognize him?"

"No."

"He recognizes you. Don't you, Cyril? Had to take a real close look, before he made that 911 call. Surprised you didn't see him."

"He was hiding by the time I got there," I said. "In a kiddies' playground, apparently. Not the kind of place I spend much time in."

"That true, Cyril?" she said.

He didn't reply.

"Cyril, David and I have been talking about your performance last night," she said. "We're not real impressed."

"Lesley, I—" Cyril said.

"Quiet. Don't make it any worse," Lesley said, and then turned to me. "Cyril made a mistake last night. He hasn't worked for me long, but a mistake's a mistake. Can't have my people making mistakes. And he made a big one. So now he's going to do something useful."

"Make a cup of tea?" I said.

"Maybe later. If we have any. But first, he's going to show you what happens to people who let me down."

Lesley turned the gray parcel over and I saw that the clasp on the silver chain was shaped like a tragicomic mask.

"This is me," she said, pointing to the smiling face. "And this other guy is—can you guess, Cyril?"

His face had turned pale, and the patchy stubble made his skin look as if it were covered in mold. Lesley opened the clasp, unwound the chain, and set it to one side. Then she unrolled the gray suede. It made a rectangle about eighteen inches long with a flap of the same material folded over, hiding its contents.

Lesley got to her feet and started to walk toward Cyril, casually sliding the half-opened parcel along the tabletop with the tips of her fingers. Cyril started to fidget. Lesley reached the corner of the table, stopping barely five feet away from him. She stood there for a moment, looking him up and down, and then the corners of her mouth began to creep up into the ghost of a smile.

The smile was too much for Cyril. He turned and made a dash for the door, but the tall guy was ready for him. He caught him, spun him round, and marched him right up to the end of the table with his arms pinned to his sides.

"You want to beg, now would be the time," Lesley said.

Cyril was breathing so hard he was almost wheezing, but he didn't say anything.

"Shame," Lesley said. "I like it better when they beg."

"Does it make any difference?" I said.

"Does to me," she said, grasping the corner of the suede flap and slowly peeling it back.

The parcel held a pair of rubber surgeon's gloves, which were small, even allowing for them to stretch; a coil of white elastic, an inch across, with metal hooks at each end; four long copper needles, like the kind acupuncturists use; a small hammer; two scalpels; a pair of long-nosed surgical forceps; a pair of slender, pointed scissors; a clear plastic box, rectangular in shape, containing a sewing needle and some bright blue thread; and a device that looked a little like a pair of miniature bolt cutters. It had the same kind of mechanism to multiply the force but the jaws were more rounded and it had a swollen, bulbous end.

Each item was held in place with a little loop of black elastic, obviously designed specially for the purpose. There were no gaps, and nothing extra had been squeezed in. It looked like something you might use to carry your favorite housebreaking tools.

Lesley left the parcel open in front of Cyril and went to the built-in closet at the far end of the room. She opened the right-hand door, reached inside, and hauled out a trolley like the kind they use to carry stacks of linen in hotels and hospitals. It was made of shiny wire mesh, six feet tall and two feet square. There was nothing inside it. The wheels at each corner were disproportionately large, like the ones on modern furniture. They probably weren't the original wheels, but they were very effective. The trolley was taller than her, but Lesley moved it effortlessly. It glided across the floor after her without a sound.

As she drew level I saw that the frame of the trolley had been reinforced with inch-square metal tubing, and that one of the sides was missing. Four thick, brown leather straps had been attached near the corners of the opening, six inches from the bottom and three inches from the top. With the mesh and the straps, it looked like a portable cage.

Lesley wheeled the trolley all the way to Cyril's end of the table. She left it with the open side facing the room. Cyril didn't notice. He was still staring at the strange collection of tools, completely transfixed. The tall guy eased him back a couple of steps and Lesley moved up close to him. Her left hand grabbed his groin. She squeezed. Cyril squealed. His eyes looked like they were ready to pop out of his skull.

The tall guy let go of Cyril's arms and brought the trolley in right behind him. Lesley kept hold of Cyril's groin, looked behind her at the table, and hitched him up an inch or so onto his tiptoes. The tall guy moved quickly and secured Cyril's ankles to the frame of the trolley before he could sink back down. He did the same to Cyril's wrists, pulling hard enough on the straps to break the skin. Then he nodded to Lesley who let go, leaving Cyril spread-eagled. He was quaking, causing part of the wire mesh to rattle.

Lesley reached toward Cyril's groin again, but this time he saw her coming. He wriggled his hips from side to side and tried to arc away from her, his backside retreating right inside the trolley. Lesley put her hand on Cyril's thigh and slowly ran her fingers up his leg, over the front of his jeans, and as far as the hem of his T-shirt. Then she rolled it up, revealing the kind of sculpted stomach muscles you see on the cover of fitness magazines.

"No hair," she said. "Pity."

Cyril's jeans were held up by a wide leather belt. The buckle was shaped like a motorcycle. A Harley, or maybe an Indian. It wasn't a very good replica. Lesley unfastened it, pulled the strap free of the belt loops and dropped it on the floor. The crash made Cyril jump. Then Lesley unfastened his waistband. The jeans had a button fly. Lesley undid all four, pausing each time one popped open to gaze into Cyril's face.

Lesley eased Cyril's jeans right down to the point where his ankles were strapped to the trolley. He had Calvin Klein underwear—a pair of tight black trunks with a gray stripe at the top. Lesley gently rubbed the front with the palm of her hand and the slight bulge began to grow more pronounced.

"That feeling you're getting right now?" she said, hooking her fingers into his waistband and pulling down. "Enjoy it while you can."

George released a catch and folded the LCD screen out from the side of the camera. Then he rotated a little dial with his thumb. A button in the center lit up green.

Lesley reached over to the row of tools and took out the coil of elastic. She turned to Cyril and passed it around his body, nearly level with the top of his buttocks. She joined the metal hooks together and positioned them at his side.

Then she let the loop ping back, pinning his exposed penis to his abdomen. The elastic held it upright, pointing away from his scrotum.

"Time to go, George," she said.

George hit the green button with his thumb and the camera started recording. He started off with a wide shot to show Cyril trussed up on the trolley, and then homed in on his groin. Cyril could see what George was focusing on, and the extra attention made the elastic hardly necessary.

Lesley had picked up one of the scalpels and the bolt cutter, and was holding them up in front of her. George panned across to include her in the frame.

"Since this is all for David's benefit, let's give him the choice," she said. "Which method, David? Old or new?"

"Neither," I said.

"Neither? You want me to rip his balls off with my bare hands? I suppose I could . . ."

I said nothing. Cyril yelped, and his penis twitched beneath the elastic strap. George somehow held the camera steady, his face completely blank. The tall guy was leaning on the wall near the door, arms folded, staring at the floor.

"OK then," Lesley said, putting the scalpel down. "If you're squeamish, we should go with the burdizzo. Designed for animals. Not much blood. Crushes the epididymis, and the balls just fall right off. After a few days, anyway, while they shrivel away and die."

She held the device up to Cyril's face and made a show of opening and closing its jaws. She snapped them open

easily enough, but made a real play of squeezing the handles together again. Strain lined her face and sharp tendons
bulged in her wrist. Then she winked at him. His eyes
started to roll back in their sockets.

"Look, he's getting the idea," she said, smiling and
turning to point the thing at me. "Ever seen one of these
before?"

"Frequently," I said. "All the ambassadors have them.
Standard government issue."

"This one's for rams. Perfect for humans, too. Used to
have one for lambs, but it didn't work too well. Sometimes
one ball would survive. Had to come back later and finish
it off. Couldn't get the pressure. Handles were too short.
Not a problem with this one. But you know the best thing
about it?"

I said nothing.

"The noise it makes. When it crushes the little tubes.
Like biting into a stick of fresh celery."

"Means nothing to me. I eat nothing green."

"Then I guess my special toy would be wasted on you,"
she said, and turned to tuck the device back into its space.
"This your first time?"

I didn't answer.

"Then cutting would be better anyway. Get to see right
inside. It'll change your life, believe me."

Lesley pushed the end two chairs out of the way and
reached over to the hinged flap in the tabletop. She scrabbled to get a grip on it for a moment, then pulled it right
over on itself until it was lying horizontally along the

wooden surface. There was a strip of black, brushlike material about half an inch wide fixed to the long edge, opposite the hinges. It would be to let cables run through when the flap was closed, but in that position the ends of the bristles finished exactly level with the edge of the table.

Unlike the rest of the wood, the underside of the flap was not polished. It wasn't finished at all. Instead, it was covered in brown stains, the color of old blood. There were dozens of patches. Many were overlapping. I doubt there'd been huge volumes, but it had soaked well into the grain. There would be no chance of removing it now. It had formed an indelible pattern, a little like those inkblot pictures that psychiatrists show you.

Lesley stepped aside, and the tall guy levered himself away from the wall. He came over and pushed the trolley forward so that Cyril's groin was pressing into the edge of the tabletop. He peered around the front and checked that the underneath of Cyril's scrotum was hanging down far enough to rest on the surface of the flap. The tall guy didn't touch it—he just looked. Satisfied, he locked the brakes on the trolley's rear wheels and went back to his place by the door.

Lesley slipped her jacket off and hung it on the back of the nearest chair. She took the surgeon's gloves from the roll of tools and snapped them on. A small cloud of talc puffed out from around each wrist. It smelled vaguely of lavender. Then she picked up two of the long copper needles. She gripped them carefully between her left thumb and index finger to avoid snagging the gloves and held them out for Cyril to see.

He started to wail.

Lesley picked up the hammer and stepped across, next to Cyril. His wailing grew louder and he began to thrash about, desperately straining against the leather straps. Lesley held one of the needles between her lips and reached down toward the table with the other. Before the tip had even touched him Cyril's wailing had grown into a shrill, piercing howl. A trace of blood appeared as Lesley passed the needle through the left-hand side of his scrotum and gently tapped it into the underside of the wooden flap. The blood bubbled up around the stem of the needle for a moment, then streamed away across Cyril's skin. Some got caught up in the blond hairs, but most made it down onto the rough, pitted surface. It pooled for several seconds before gradually being absorbed, adding a new, darker stain of its own.

Lesley tapped the second needle through the other side of Cyril's scrotum, took a good pinch of skin, and tugged. The needles held firm. Then she swapped the hammer for a scalpel. Her left hand kept the skin taut while she made two cuts from just below the base of his penis in a kind of upside-down V-shape, away from his body and out toward his thighs. Blood oozed over the steel blade and the tips of her gloves as she calmly worked her way down. When she finished cutting she took the remaining copper needles and tacked the flap of skin down tight, forming a neat triangular hole.

I couldn't help but stare through it at the gray, fibrous membrane inside. Lesley took the scalpel and sliced straight down the middle, leaving a single incision an inch and a quarter long. She took the forceps and guided the tip through the hole she'd made. She angled them to Cyril's left and delicately probed the inside of his scrotum. Her hand moved in tiny, unhurried circles. After ten seconds she suddenly stopped and squeezed the handles together until the latches clicked into place. She cautiously drew the forceps back out. A loop of tubing, an eighth of an inch in diameter, was squashed flat in their jaws.

"Here comes the first little guy," she said.

Cyril was silent now, and completely still. He was gawping down at himself, fascinated, not believing what he was seeing. Lesley pulled her hand back a fraction further, took out the scissors, and lined them up on the tube just above where the forceps were gripping it. Then she stopped and put the scissors down on the table.

"What am I doing?" she said. "Planned to go with the burdizzo. Forgot to get their new home ready."

Lesley went over to the cupboard where the trolley had been stored and returned with a glass jar in one hand and a stainless-steel flask in the other. The jar was five inches tall and three inches across, and had a matching lid with a spherical grip. The glass was slightly cloudy as if it had been repeatedly scoured by a machine, making it look aged, like a remnant from some ancient school laboratory.

"The little guys will be safe in here," she said to Cyril.

"Don't you worry. I'll take care of them, and you can come visit any time you like."

Lesley eased the lid off the jar and filled it with clear liquid from the flask. She didn't replace the lid, and after a moment an unmistakable stench caught in the back of my throat. Formaldehyde. Like in an old mortuary.

"Shall I write a label?" she said. "Or will you recognize them on your own? Got quite a collection going back there . . ."

Cyril didn't answer. I don't think he'd even seen the jar. He was still staring down at his groin, completely mesmerized. Lesley shrugged and screwed the cap back onto the steel flask. She picked the scissors up again, but before she used them she turned to look at me.

"You Brits appreciate irony," she said. "So how do you like this? A squirrel with no nuts."

FOURTEEN

Twelve people dropped out before the end of my training program.

Seven quit during the physical endurance phase. Two during weapons assessment. And three during unarmed combat. There was no shame attached to any of them. They all walked away with their heads held high. Because in the navy, it's better to give 100 percent and come up short than never to try anything new. As long as you give it your best shot, you earn respect.

If you get kicked out, that's another story altogether. Fortunately, in my class it only happened to one recruit. And not because of his performance. It's up to the instructors to fix that. The problem was his attitude. Specifically, one question he couldn't help but ask.

I was surprised at first. Because generally, the navy encourages questions. Have you got the right resources for the job? Could you achieve your objective more quickly? More safely? More effectively? But eventually I understood what he'd done wrong. It was actually pretty simple. I realized that once you've accepted an assignment, there's really only one thing you can't question.

Whether to do it at all.

The tall guy took me to the family room and asked me to wait while he rounded up the items I was going to need for tomorrow. Then he left me on my own with the sofa to sit on, a stack of magazines to read, and plenty of time to think about what I'd let myself in for.

Lesley's plan had a reasonable chance of success, I thought. It was simple and straightforward. Realistic objectives had been set. The necessary equipment and personnel had been promised. Commitments had been made, and assurances given.

As for me, I was perfectly clear what my role was going to be. Less sure how much to expect from the other people who were involved. And certain I was going to need more coffee. Typical of a first day in a new job.

I was hoping to lay eyes on my new partner at some point, but the only person to come near me in the next twenty minutes was George.

"It's all here," he said, dropping a battered leather Gladstone bag onto the sofa next to me. "Check it if you want."

I opened the bag and looked inside. It was neatly packed. At one side a black polo shirt had been rolled around some socks and a pair of boxer shorts. Next to the clothes were five clear Ziploc bags. The first held a watch, to replace the one the FBI had held on to. The second, a toothbrush—

still in its wrapper—toothpaste, and deodorant. The third, a dozen cable ties and a clasp knife. The fourth, money. One thousand dollars in mixed bills. And the fifth, a gun. A Springfield P9. I took a closer look.

"This is Cyril's?" I said.

"Right," George said.

"How can you tell?" I said, pointing to a blurred patch on the right-hand side of the frame. The serial number had been burned off with acid.

"Lesley said so. You want to call her on it, be my guest."

"Hotel reservations?"

"Taken care of. Online. Patrick's got confirmation."

"Who's Patrick?"

"The guy you'll be working with."

"Where is he?"

"Right here," said a voice from the hallway.

"Typical Patrick," George said, shaking his head. "Always has to make an entrance."

Patrick stayed out of sight for another moment then glided rather than stepped into the room. He hardly made a sound. He was only about five inches shorter than the tall guy, but I doubt he made five percent of the noise when he moved. He did have an advantage with his shoes, though—a pair of soft black Lacoste trainers, rather than shiny city slip-ons. They went well with the black track-suit he was wearing, but looked a little strange next to his charcoal overcoat and the tan leather suit carrier that was slung over his left shoulder.

"Been working out?" I said.

"No way," he said. "Hate that stuff. Was on my way to soccer practice. Then Lesley called. Just had time to grab some stuff for tomorrow and come down to meet you. You are David, right?"

"That's right. I am. Glad to be working with you. You all set?"

"Yeah, I'm good."

"Then how about we pick up our passenger and hit the road? I'm getting hungry."

"Sounds good to me," he said, raising his eyebrows at George.

George fetched a pair of orange-handled scissors from a drawer in the kitchen and then led the way downstairs. Julianne was back in her cage, lying on the floor in the same position as when I'd first seen her. There was no sign of anyone else, but the floor in front of the cages had recently been mopped. It was still slightly damp, with large swirling marks spiraling out from the spot where the driver had landed.

Julianne didn't react when George released the padlock but she sat up, looking surprised, when she realized it was her door that had swung open.

"What's happening?" she said. "David? Are you all right?"

"Of course," I said. "And so are you. It's over. We're leaving."

"What are you talking about?"

"We're leaving. Right now. Getting in the car. Going to the city."

"What are they doing here?" she said, pointing at George and Patrick.

"Helping us," I said. "Don't worry. We're all friends now."

"How did that happen?"

"I fixed it with their boss. Just like I said I would."

"Something's not right," she said, stepping back into the corner of the cage. "It's a trap. They're going to kill us."

"If they wanted to kill us, they'd have done it already," I said.

"Don't believe you. I'm not coming."

"Fine. Stay, then. Lock it, will you, George? I'm not wasting my time. There's a steak waiting for me at the hotel. And a hot shower. And a king-sized bed. Be seeing you, Julianne. Take care."

I turned to go. Patrick followed.

"Wait," Julianne said. "You sure this is on the level?"

She'd come out of the corner and was standing with her head tipped to one side, eyes narrow with suspicion. George had hold of the door, ready to slam it closed.

"Of course," I said. "Anyway, what have you got to lose?"

She didn't answer.

"You should listen to him, you know," George said quietly.

Julianne chewed her bottom lip for a moment then shrugged, rolled her eyes, and moved to the cage doorway.

"OK, then. But I'm not going anywhere with this on," she said, holding out her hands.

George cut the plastic tie, shoved it in his pocket along with the scissors, and led the way around toward the garage. Julianne followed. Patrick walked next to her, but I lagged behind. When they turned the corner I dodged back to the wooden shelves by the far wall. I started just beyond the spot where the passenger had lunged at me earlier, slipped my hand underneath, and slid it back toward the cages. After eighteen inches my fingers touched something round and metallic. It was the barrel of the passenger's .45. He hadn't gone back for it. Or he hadn't seen where it went.

I pulled the gun out. It was scratched and dusty, with clumps of gray fluff caught all around the trigger guard. I blew them away, stuck the barrel into the waistband at the back of my jeans, and started moving toward the garage. I caught up with the others before they were even through the door.

George popped the black sedan's trunk with the remote and turned to Julianne, looking a little sheepish.

"That better be for the luggage," she said.

George looked down at the floor. I shook my head.

"Oh, man," she said. "Why do we have to ride in there? I hate it."

"Sorry, Julianne," I said. "We don't. You do."

"What? Why me?"

"Think about it. They couldn't let you go if you'd seen where this place is. You could lead people back here."

"What about you? How come you can see it?"

"Bring the police here, and I'm in as much trouble as these guys. It's part of the deal."

"What deal? You've done a deal with these people? David, what were you thinking?"

"Staying alive has a price, Julianne. Like it or not. I just found a way to pay it. For both of us. All you have to do is get in. That way, you're forty-five minutes from freedom. Otherwise, you're back in the cage."

"But does it have to be the trunk? I really, really hate it in there. Don't you have a car with black windows or something?"

We both looked at George.

"Sorry," he said. "Black windows stop you looking in. Your problem's looking out."

Julianne sighed, went to the back of the car, and put her hand on the rear fender.

"I'm not climbing in on my own," she said.

George was closest. He did the honors.

Patrick drove. George had offered me the keys, but I declined. I wanted to get a good look around the neighborhood. I had the feeling I might need to return.

A gold Lexus SUV was waiting for us at the mouth of the driveway. I could see two people inside. Presumably a couple of Lesley's guys, sent to keep an eye on us. Then two more came up behind us in a black Grand Cherokee and we sat in line for a moment, penned in, until the Lexus pulled away.

The road near the house was narrow and uneven with a steeply domed center. There were no lights or markings, and tall trees were densely packed in on both sides. It was

like driving through woods, except for the untidy fes-
toons of power lines and telephone wires hanging down
from rough poles that sprouted at unequal intervals from
the shoulders. They gave the whole place a temporary feel,
like it hadn't been properly finished.

"So which part of France are you from?" I said, to break
the silence.

"I'm not from France," Patrick said. "I'm from Alge-
ria."

"Lesley said you were French."

"No. I speak French. And I moved to Paris when I was
a kid. My brother was a footballer. A pretty good one.
Scouts from PSG spotted him. The club paid for my whole
family to move there."

"Excellent. Did he make it?"

"My brother? No. Broke his leg. In a training match.
Had operations, physical therapists, everything. But he
wasn't the same. Never played for the first team. Never
even made it to the bench."

Patrick slowed as we approached a crossroads. The
Lexus made a right turn. We followed. This road was
smoother, and after half a mile it became much straighter
and broader. The trees thinned out on both sides and then
gave way to a row of neat, white-painted buildings. There
were shops, restaurants, a couple of real-estate offices, and
in the center, a fire station. The doors were open and inside
a guy in uniform was standing around drinking coffee while
two others polished the brass on a pair of old-fashioned fire
trucks.

"Worried about tomorrow?" Patrick said.

"Not really," I said. "Well, maybe a little."

"What bothers you? The death of Varley?"

"No. Not him. It's us I'm thinking about. Whether the FBI believes my story. How you're going to get out of the building."

"OK. Listen, David. I've been thinking about these things, as well," he said, reaching into his coat pocket and handing me a piece of paper. "Here's an address. It'll pan out if they check. Tell them that's where the kidnappers took you. You heard the guards talking, one was boasting about last night . . . you fill in the rest."

"Thanks," I said. "Might just do that."

"And the FBI building. You've been there. What can I expect?"

"Finding an exit's the main problem. The first-floor windows don't open, the ground floor's boarded up tight, and the only way out is through the garage. Today they had four guys on it, and a backup van outside. Tomorrow there could be more, given what happened."

"That's not so bad. Have faith, David. I've lived through worse. This thing is going to work out."

The last building we passed in the little town was a police station, also painted white. It was a small place. Only a single story. A light was on in one of the rooms and a patrol car was sitting on the gravel forecourt outside. Patrick saw it and instinctively checked his speed.

A quarter of a mile farther on we came to a broad stretch

of road with streetlights and white lines. An angular concrete bridge crossed over, carrying some kind of highway. A pair of heavy trucks lumbered across as we approached. We emerged at the far side and followed the Lexus up the southbound on-ramp, easing carefully around the tight curve at the top.

Patrick slotted back in line and our little convoy drifted up to a steady sixty. The leather upholstery was soft and supple, and I sank into it like I was sitting in an old armchair. The car wasn't much to look at, but I had to admit it was comfortable. Certainly a step up after Lesley's dog cage or the jail cell. The interior was warm, too, and the gentle swaying motion was relaxing. The radio was off so the only sound was the wheels drumming rhythmically against the joints in the pavement, reeling in the miles between us and the city.

I did work hard on staying awake after that, but maybe not quite hard enough. I felt my eyes slowly creep shut, and they stayed that way for twenty minutes before Patrick nudged me in the ribs and pointed at something through the windshield.

"Look," he said. "Your trick worked. Lesley didn't think it would."

The road ahead of us broadened out so that you could choose which tollbooth to line up at before using the bridge across to Manhattan. But Patrick was pointing to the other side of the highway. Over there, drivers leaving the city crossed the river before parting with their cash. That meant we couldn't see the lines of vehicles, but we got a good look in through the backs of the booths.

"See?" Patrick said. "Two people."

He was right. There were two people in each booth. One sitting down, operating the equipment. And another standing up, silhouetted against the oncoming headlights. The shape of their headgear was unmistakable. They were police officers. I checked the booths on our side. It was harder to see in, but each one definitely had only a single occupant.

"Nice job," Patrick said. "Telling them you were still in the city. Smart. They're looking for you getting out, not back in. Keep it up, and you can work with me again."

"I'm flattered," I said. "But before you kiss me, what's she doing?"

There was one officer on our side of the road, weaving her way through the traffic in the general direction of the central divider. Her progress was slow and erratic, and I saw she was handing out leaflets from a satchel she was carrying over her shoulder.

"What do you think they are?" Patrick said. "Takeout menus?"

"Hope so," I said. "I'm starving. Let's get one."

"You can eat at the hotel, if we ever get there," he said, pulling into the next lane and slipping into the shadow of the Lexus. "Let's hope these guys figure out what we're doing. They're not the sharpest tools in Lesley's shed, if you know what I mean."

We crept steadily forward, hidden from the officer's view, until we were only two cars away from the barrier. Then the Lexus stopped moving. The car at the front of their line was having a problem. Patrick held back as long as he could, but the traffic was building up behind us. Someone honked their horn. Attention was all we needed, so Patrick lifted his foot off the brake and let the car nose ahead, into the open.

I looked over to the left, expecting the officer to be several lanes away. But she wasn't. She'd turned around and was heading back in our direction. We rolled another half car's length forward, and she reached the lane next to the Lexus. She handed a leaflet to a gray-haired guy in a pickup and kept moving, straight toward us. She was heading directly for Patrick. And we were boxed in. A sign near the booth said drivers would be fined for reversing in the line. Fat chance. There was nowhere for us to go.

The officer was barely three yards away. The next leaflet was half out of her satchel. I could see my own eyes staring back at me from a black-and-white photo in the center of the page when Patrick suddenly reached down in front of me and opened the glove box. He started to rummage around inside it, urgently searching for something.

Patrick's lost it, I thought. *He's got a gun in there.*

My fingers were curled around the door handle, starting to pull, when the officer abruptly veered away to her right. She was moving purposefully now, heading for the back of our car. I thought of Julianne. She was still locked in the trunk. Had she found a way to call for help without Patrick or me realizing?

I looked around, and saw the driver of the Lexus had lowered his window. He was leaning out, beckoning to the officer. She walked over and handed him a leaflet. He examined it for a moment, then passed it to his passenger. They started arguing over it, each one pointing to things on the page. They continued to squabble until the car in front of us had cleared the barrier and we started to move again. I saw the driver finally shake his head, crumple up the leaflet, and let it drop behind his seat. He held the officer's for a moment, shrugged, and then flashed her an apologetic smile.

Patrick hauled himself upright before we picked up too much speed. His right hand was hanging on to a white plastic object he'd retrieved from the glove box. It was about three inches square and one side was covered in shiny silver indentations. As we approached the booth he held it up to the windshield, just below the mirror, and the barrier immediately whipped up out of our way.

"What is that thing?" I said. "Is it legal?"

Patrick nodded toward a board marked THIS LANE—NO CASH—E-ZPASS ONLY. Then he moved his thumb and I saw a matching logo on the white side of the square.

"Why keep it hidden, then?" I said.

"It's not hidden," he said. "It fell off. No one stuck it back on yet."

FIFTEEN

I knew the hotel was good—I'd stayed there before—but I wasn't going back for their service. I knew it was handy for our meeting the next day, but I wasn't worried about how far we'd have to drive. I'd have chosen the place anyway, whatever it was like and wherever it was located. Because, for that one night, I needed something else more than I needed comfort or convenience. I needed a garage. A particular kind. It had to be underground, away from prying eyes. And, unusually for what I'd seen of New York, one where we could park our own car.

The machine controlling the entrance barrier had developed a fault, causing it to display its instructions in German. Patrick pointed to its small LCD screen and rolled his eyes in disgust.

"Sure you're not French?" I said.

He took a ticket anyway and then coasted down the ramp, running wide at the bottom to avoid adding to the scrapes of paint on the white concrete wall.

The space we'd entered was smaller than the FBI's garage—about half the size—but it was cleaner and brighter. The fluorescent lights were closer together, casting no shadows on the shiny gray floor, and the regimented layout of pillars and parking bays was a million miles from the color and chaos of the city streets we'd just crawled through.

Most of the other vehicles were crammed in together at the far end, close to the elevator that led up to the hotel itself. A few cars and SUVs had spilled over into the center section, but farther out the garage was almost empty. The corner opposite the ramp—where people would have the farthest to walk—was completely deserted.

It looked perfect.

Patrick headed for the space at the end of the last row. He swung the car into some empty bays on the other side of the aisle then snaked backward, stopping with the rear fender about four feet from the wall. That left the hood hanging out over the white line, but Patrick didn't seem worried. He just rolled up his window, switched off the engine, and leaned down to unlock the trunk. I checked my watch. It was seven minutes past nine. Just shy of twelve hours since the detectives had disturbed me in my cell.

Julianne was lying on her left-hand side, curled up in a ball, with her back to the rear of the car. Her arms and legs were pulled in tight and she showed no reaction when I lifted the trunk lid. There was no sign of her even breathing, and her skin looked like perished rubber in the harsh artificial light.

She didn't look any better when the Jeep arrived, three

minutes later. It pulled in next to us, close to Patrick's side of the car, and kept easing backward until its rear fender was nudging up against the concrete, boxing us in tight.

"Come on, Julianne," I said, reaching down into the trunk and gently shaking her shoulder. "We're here. Time to get out."

"Wait," Patrick said. "Leave her. Let her wake up on her own."

I couldn't see why. I'd known stowaways to recover slowly before, but only when they'd been drugged or wounded, or we'd had some kind of incident en route. Nothing like that had happened to Julianne. She'd been in the trunk twenty minutes longer than I had, earlier in the day, but that was because of the traffic. It was nothing traumatic. There was no reason for her to just lie there, increasing the chances of us being compromised.

I shook her again and after a few seconds her arms loosened and her head began to appear, like a tortoise emerging from its shell. She craned her neck around and gradually started to take in her surroundings—the trunk lid, the garage walls, the Jeep. And me.

"David," she said huskily. "This is your fault."

Julianne refused any help climbing out of the trunk, but she did take my arm as we set off toward the cluster of cars surrounding the elevator. She was still looking a little green and crumpled, and her stride was shorter and stiffer than it had been at the house. The farther we walked the harder she leaned on me, but however much weight I took, it didn't make her speed up or move any more easily. The opposite, if anything. Patrick and the guys from the Jeep were pulling way out in front of us, despite changing course slightly to pass the Lexus, which had finally appeared in a space away to our left.

"What happens now?" she said quietly.

"Not much," I said. "We check in. Get a meal. Then some rest."

"What about tomorrow?"

"Take it easy. Have a lie-in."

"What's a lie-in? What are we lying about? Who to?"

"No. Lie in bed. Stay asleep. I'll see you around lunch-time."

"You want me to sleep in? Why? What will you be doing?"

"Helping Patrick with something."

"What you agreed with those people? To make them let us go?"

"Right."

"Are you OK with it, what they want you to do?"

"I'm fine."

"Is it something bad?"

"Not entirely. Neutral, overall, I'd say."

"But something big? It must be big, to trade for our lives."

"Just something they can't do on their own."

"David, this feels wrong. I don't know what they want, but they're bad people. You had a gun to your head, back then. Now it's different. No one would blame you if you didn't go through with it."

"Don't worry. I know what I'm doing. It'll come out fine."

"Are you sure? We could make a run for it. You and me. Ditch these guys and hide out somewhere, till we figure out how to make it right with the police."

"Sorry, Julianne. It wouldn't work, with the police. It has to be done this way. But trust me. By lunchtime tomorrow, it'll all be over."

The automatic announcements in the elevator had also reverted to German, which did nothing to improve Patrick's mood. He stood in the corner and muttered to himself for the few seconds it took us to reach the ground floor. The doors hadn't even fully opened before he pushed past me and veered away to the right, heading for the reception desk. Julianne and the other guys moved more slowly, taking a moment to adjust to their new surroundings. Stepping into such a bright, uncluttered space was quite a change after the cramped elevator car.

A row of abstract tapestries hung below the high windows to our left. They provided the only color or texture in the place, standing out vividly against the smooth white marble walls and floors. They were also the only things in there that weren't strictly necessary. It was a large area, but everything else in it had a practical purpose—the counter where Patrick was standing, a second bank of elevators ahead of us serving the bedrooms, glass double doors on either side leading to the bar and restaurant, and an exit to the street farther down on the right. No space had been wasted on seating areas or display cabinets or porters' stations. The result obviously wasn't to Julianne's taste—I felt her shiver as she took it all in—but I liked it. It made the place seem focused and purposeful.

It also meant that covert surveillance was out of the question.

For Lesley's people, or the FBI.

Two clerks were on duty that night. Neither had been there when I last visited, a couple of years ago, so there was no danger of them recognizing me. The one on the left was sitting down, hunched over a keyboard. It looked as if he were processing a pile of papers stacked up on the desk beside him. His hands were moving—robotically pressing the keys and sorting through the forms—but the rest of his body was absolutely still. He was completely absorbed by his work. Patrick was close enough to touch him but he had no idea that anyone was even near. You could have brushed the thin flakes of dandruff off the shoulders of his navy blue blazer and I doubt he'd have missed a beat.

The second clerk was younger and a little more animated. She was shuffling around behind the counter, gathering some documents and chatting to Patrick as they waited for us to catch up. A badge clipped to her blazer said she was Maxine, the shift manager. Her eyes did occasionally stray in our direction, but she didn't seem unduly suspicious. She clearly wasn't checking anyone against a wanted photograph or trying to match us to a description. More that she was just idly curious, and as we got closer she did nothing more sinister than fan out the wad of forms she'd collected, hand them to Patrick, and reach down for a pot of pens.

The registration forms were preprinted with the details George had given over the Net so all that was left for us to do was sign them. There were three spaces, clearly outlined in black. Even so, it turned out to be a major exercise for the guys from the Jeep. Maybe they had particularly difficult names, but they were still scratching away with the cheap hotel ballpoints long after Julianne and I had finished with ours.

George had booked me in as David Van Der Wahl from Ossining, New York. He had some idea that a Dutch-sounding name might misdirect the clerk if she heard my accent and was questioned later about English guests. I wasn't so sure. I preferred my usual approach—not speaking to anyone—but I supposed his little subterfuge wouldn't do any harm. At least he'd come up with a more imaginative name than the ones the navy usually gave me.

Maxine handed out our keys one at a time, and even though the elevators and restaurant were in plain sight, she obstinately ran through how to reach the bedrooms and where to go for breakfast with each of us in turn. She issued my key last, and by the time I'd listened to her instructions for the seventh time Patrick and the others had already started to drift away from the counter.

Our rooms were on the tenth floor. Mine was the last on the left, at the far end of the corridor. Patrick's was next door. Julianne's was directly opposite.

"See you bright and early," Patrick said, working the lock on his door and disappearing inside.

"Early, anyway," I said.

"What about lunch, tomorrow?" Julianne said when he'd gone. She was standing in the middle of the corridor, looking a little lost. "I'm worried. Will you really come back?"

"Of course," I said, sliding my key card into its slot. "Sleep well."

The door closed solidly behind me and for a moment I felt a slight pang of regret about leaving Julianne outside, on her own. She looked so forlorn, with her head tipped anxiously to one side and her big brown eyes stretched wide and fearful. Maybe I felt a little bad about lying to her, as well. After what I was planning for tomorrow there was no way they were going to let me out for lunch. I was never going to see her again, and part of me was wondering what other possibilities I was turning my back on. It was a long time since I'd been in a hotel with a woman, voluntarily, and not felt some official eye looking over my shoulder. Tomorrow's plan wasn't complex. How much sleep could I need?

But deep down, I knew I was right. If I was going down that road with anyone, it had to be Tanya. Especially now we were back in touch. And tomorrow was about more than the basic ability to stumble through a plan. It was about more than the professional pride of doing a job right. Or even the satisfaction of wiping the smile off Rosser's smug face.

Tomorrow was about redemption.

Another man's life would be taken. Mine would be reclaimed.

It deserved my full attention.

SIXTEEN

Mitchell Varley and his colleagues had seemed innocuous enough when I first met them in their abandoned office building. Devious, certainly, but not physically dangerous. Not like the Nazi from the police cell. You didn't get the feeling they were going to leap across the table and tear your head off. But with guys like these, superficial impressions don't count for much. You could say the same for lots of unpleasant species. Spiders, for example. The deadliest ones are always the most harmless looking.

Which is why I changed the plan.

I didn't call Tanya at nine the next morning, as I'd promised.

I called her at eight.

Tanya answered on the first ring.

"David?" she said. "What's wrong? You're an hour early. Is there a problem?"

"No," I said. "I've just brought the schedule forward a little. Are the FBI guys with you yet?"

"But are you OK?"

"Absolutely fine. Are they there?"

There was a pause before she answered.

"Yes," she said. "All three are here."

"Good," I said. "Because here's some good news for them. They won't be needing their copter after all. They can save some gas money. We're going to meet in the city."

"Oh. OK. Where exactly?"

"The same building they took me to yesterday. Room 3H3. It's on the first floor, for some reason, not the third like you'd think. End of the corridor. Last room but one, left-hand side."

"Got that. What time?"

"Eight-twenty. But listen. Tell them I'm set up in the neighborhood with a clear view of the room. If I don't see Rosser, Varley, and Breuer enter before that time—I walk away. If I see anyone else come in with them, or positioned in the building, I walk away."

"Got that. What about their guy?"

"He's stashed somewhere safe. When I'm happy, I'll lead them to him."

"Got that. Stand by . . ."

The phone was silent for forty seconds.

"Confirmed," Tanya said, coming back to me. "All three are en route. ETA ten minutes. Conditions understood. And David—good luck. I want you back in one piece at the end of this."

"As always," I said, hanging up the phone and shifting my position to get a better view of the garage entrance.

It took eight minutes for the first vehicles to arrive. There were five of them. Two black Fords, the Cadillac I'd seen yesterday, then two more black Fords. They swept around the corner, moving fast, only a couple of feet between each one. Then the lead car swung the other way and the others followed it into the garage, disappearing like a snake slithering into a hole.

Two minutes later a white van appeared from the opposite direction, traveling much more sedately. It trundled three-quarters of the length of the street, then drifted to the side and stopped in the same space the backup van had used yesterday. From my position, almost directly above, I couldn't see any markings on its sides but there was a picture of an engine component—a carburetor?—painted on the hood.

After another two minutes I heard activity in the hallway outside. Footsteps were approaching. It sounded like five sets, but I couldn't be sure. There was a pause, then the door was flung open. I caught a glimpse of a hand and a gray sleeve, but nothing else.

The door started to close. It was almost back in its frame when someone rammed it with their shoulder and stepped into the room. It was Varley. He was holding a Glock out in front of him, two-handed. He checked both corners to his left and then moved forward. The gun was swinging across to his right when he saw me, standing to the side of the window. He stopped instantly and snapped the weapon back, lining up perfectly on the bridge of my nose.

"Stand still," he said unnecessarily, as I showed no sign of moving. "Hands on your head."

I kept my hands down by my sides. There was no chance of him shooting me. Not yet, anyway.

Louis Breuer was next into the room. He was much shorter than I'd realized from seeing him sitting down, and he walked stiffly with a stick in his left hand. He moved to Varley's right, stopping a couple of feet from the closet where I'd found the shelves, yesterday. It was a perfect spot to triangulate on me, but he didn't draw his gun. I didn't know whether to be reassured or offended.

Bruce Rosser came in last. He saw me—I caught his eye for a moment—but pretended not to notice I was there. Then he moved between the others to the center of the room and slowly turned a full circle, like a prospective buyer assessing a new home.

"Coffee stain," he said, poking a mark on the carpet with his toe.

"Carpet's damaged," he said, examining the depressions left in the pile where the desk would have been.

"Place needs cleaning," he said, running his finger through the layer of dust on the windowsill.

"And you know what else?" he said, turning to look at me. "Something doesn't smell good. You. Three hours after you escape, wounding another of my men, you're on the phone wanting a deal. Now you're ambushing me. What kind of game are you playing?"

"What can I tell you?" I said. "If your people had done their jobs . . ."

"I want to see this guy, who you say is the real shooter."

"No problem."

"Something else you should know. We're going to take a good look at him. A real good look. You better be on the level. So had he."

"I am. I can give you the guy, where I found him, full background."

"Good. Then let's go."

"Not with a gun on me."

"Mitchell," Rosser said, shaking his head.

Varley lowered the Glock, but didn't holster it.

"Now let's hurry it up," Rosser said. "We can use my car."

"Quicker to walk," I said, moving across to the closet and opening the double doors.

Patrick stepped out. He was wearing the same coat as last night but had swapped his soccer clothes for a gray herringbone suit, white shirt, and black shoes. His arms were in front of him, fastened with a cable tie. He glanced at the three FBI men and then dropped his gaze to the floor. He looked genuinely ashamed of himself. Lesley hadn't told me he was a bit of an actor.

"This is the guy?" Rosser said. "Who is he?"

"Ask him," I said.

"Well?" Rosser said, looking at Patrick. "Talk to me."

Patrick stood in silence for a moment, then shuffled around to face the wall. His head tipped farther forward and his arms started to quiver, as if he were straining to free his wrists. I checked the others. They didn't seem too concerned. FBI agents had used cable ties themselves, all the time, before flexicuffs were invented. They work the same way. Once they're on, the only way to remove them is to cut them off. Pull against them and the little plastic teeth just lock together and the sharp edges bite into your skin.

Only, the tie around Patrick's wrists didn't have any plastic teeth. Not anymore. I'd sat in my hotel room and carefully removed them with the knife Lesley had given me. So when Patrick turned back around, his wrists were no longer secured. His left hand was gripping the flap that covered the buttonholes on his coat, rolling it back to expose the stitching. His right hand was hidden from view. It was reaching inside an opening concealed in the seam, and when he pulled it back out, a small gun was nestling in his palm. A Smith & Wesson 2213.

Twenty-two caliber, as promised.

Patrick stepped to his left and grabbed Louis Breuer by the hair, jerking his head back and locking his spine. Then he jammed the pistol under Louis's jaw and flicked the safety down with his thumb.

"Your weapons, please, gentlemen," he said. "Two fingers only. On the floor in front of you. Do it now."

Varley let go of his Glock and it fell to the carpet with a muffled thud. Rosser drew his from a holster on his belt and carefully placed it on the ground, its barrel pointing straight at Patrick.

"And you," Patrick said to Louis.

Louis fumbled and the gun slipped through his fingers, landing between Patrick's feet.

"You, too, English," Patrick said, turning to me. "I know you took one from the house."

I took Cyril's Springfield out of my jacket, held it at arm's length and let it drop.

"Easy come, easy go," I said.

"Now, kick them away," he said.

Varley's didn't travel very far, but Patrick didn't complain.

"Now, back up against the wall," he said.

Rosser and Varley shuffled slowly backward, exchanging worried glances. I went across and stood between them.

"Good," Patrick said. "Now, Mitchell Varley—two steps forward."

Varley didn't move.

"Do you want to get your friend killed?" Patrick said, savagely tugging Louis's hair.

The cane slipped from Louis's fingers and its metal handle fell down and rattled against the barrel of Rosser's discarded gun.

Varley took two small, reluctant steps.

"Now, on your knees," Patrick said.

Varley flopped down onto all fours, throwing his left hand out so it landed eighteen inches from his Glock.

"Hands off the floor," Patrick said. "Don't lean forward."

Varley straightened himself up.

"Now, hands behind your head," Patrick said. "Fingers laced together."

Varley did as he was told, and Patrick suddenly dropped his left hand to Louis's shoulder and started to propel him across the room. Louis half walked, half stumbled in front of Patrick until they were six feet away from us. Then Patrick launched Louis at the wall and stepped sideways, bringing the little .22 down and ramming the barrel into Varley's temple.

"Your other guy, in the alley?" he said, looking at Rosser. "That was a mistake. We didn't mean it. I apologize. But this, I'm going to enjoy."

The sound of the shot was uncomfortably loud in such a small, enclosed space. I normally use a silencer for close-range indoor work, but needs must. Rosser and Breuer flinched. Varley flopped down to his left. And Patrick was knocked backward, off his feet. He landed awkwardly, half on his side, with his right arm trapped underneath him. Blood was draining steadily from the hole in the center of his chest. It was seeping out faster than the carpet could absorb it. I had to be careful not to step in it as I moved in closer. Then I lowered the .45 I'd inherited from Lesley's guy and put two more rounds in Patrick's head.

They probably weren't necessary, but it pays to be thorough.

SEVENTEEN

MEETINGS. A PRACTICAL ALTERNATIVE TO WORK.

I've seen that slogan in offices from Mumbai to Montreal and Moscow to Melbourne. It's a simple observation. And it's absolutely true. People all over the world build whole careers out of sitting around, talking, secretly looking for ways to steal credit or avoid blame.

And of course, the worst offenders are always the bosses. . . .

Rosser, Varley, and Breuer had set themselves up in the boardroom, leaving me on the twenty-third floor with only Weston for company. They were busy raking over the fall-out from the Patrick incident. Searching for connections. Assessing the consequences. Reviewing their procedures. Debating corrective actions. It must have been a complex operation because they'd had to summon more guys from their main New York office to lend a hand. Then they'd spread the net to include the NYPD. Even Tanya Wilson had been dragged in. That meant London would be involved. It would be after lunch in the U.K., but that wouldn't be a problem. The desk jockeys would still be all fired up, eagerly chipping in over the spider phone and adding their slice of nonsense for the bureaucratic parasites to feast on.

I have to admit, I was starting to get annoyed. The bureau guys were obsessing over pointless details. Their desperation to nail down Lesley's exact role in their railroad case was paralyzing them. They wanted everything neatly defined, but whatever part she played it made no difference that I could see. Lesley needed to be taken off the street. She was a murderer, a kidnapper, a sadist, and a thief—minimum. They should snatch her now, and worry about which pigeonhole to file her in later. Maybe that would leave me with some explaining to do—about Cyril being the actual trigger man or the apparent deal I'd made to execute Varley—but I wasn't worried. None of that would stick. Varley was alive and it didn't matter who'd killed Raab, as long as it wasn't me. The point was, we needed to act. Speed was essential. Rosser should have already scrambled a fast-response team and sent it to secure Lesley's place before she got word from her sources and vanished. Instead, he was upstairs with his buddies, playing chairman of the board, and every second they wasted tipped the scales a little further in Lesley's favor.

"How long do these talking-shops normally last?" I said to Weston, and pointed to the ceiling.

"No idea," he said, turning back to his computer. "People don't normally bring in suspects who try and execute our senior staff."

"Really? That's a shame. Keeps them on their toes."

"Don't joke about it. Staging a mock execution—that was sick."

"There was nothing mock about it. Believe me."

"Then why do it that way? Varley could have been killed."

"No great loss, from what I've seen of him."

"You should be locked up. You're an attention-grabbing maniac."

"Attention-grabbing? Hardly. The NYPD wouldn't listen to me, remember. Nor would you. Nor would your bosses. You all had your chance. So stop complaining about how I put right what you failed to fix."

"Look, finding the guy was good work. I'll give you that. But why not call it in and let us grab him up? Or just hand him to the local PD?"

" 'Cause he'd have denied it, Einstein. And I was working alone. I don't have crime labs and technicians backing me up. I needed your bosses to hear the confession."

"You had his gun."

"Yeah. Circumstantial evidence. That's always good. Till he goes with the 'holding it for a friend' defense."

"Got an answer for everything, don't you?"

"Pretty much."

"Arrogant asshole."

"There's a difference between being arrogant, and being right. You should think about that."

"Or what? Going to break my jaw, as well?"

"That's a tempting offer. I always enjoy a bit of jaw-breaking. But ultimately, what's the point? It's not your mouth I'm listening to."

"Oh, yeah? Well, if anyone's talking out of his ass, it's you. We've got one agent in hospital 'cause of you. Another nearly killed this morning. And now . . ."

"Weston, you want to rant?" I said, getting up from Lavine's chair. "Go ahead. But do it on your own. I've got a call to make."

I could still see Weston's mouth moving, but at least with the door shut the glass booth insulated me from the sound of his whining voice. The three chairs were still inside, so I chose the one I'd used yesterday and sat down to dial the number for the hotel switchboard. A receptionist answered on the third ring. She didn't give her name, but it sounded like the woman who'd checked us in last night. Maxine. She must have been on a late-early. A bit like me.

"Julianne Morgan's room, please," I said.

"One moment," Maxine said. "Connecting you now."

The phone rang again for another twenty seconds, then Julianne answered. She sounded sleepy.

"Hello?" she said.

"Julianne, it's David."

"David? What time is it? Is it lunchtime?"

"No, not yet. But about that. I'm not going to make it, I'm afraid."

"You're not? Why? Is everything all right? Are you in trouble?"

"Everything's fine. No trouble at all."

"Then why can't you make it?"

"Something came up, and now the FBI wants my help with it."

"The FBI? Why? What went wrong?"

"Nothing went wrong. At least, not for me. Can't say the same for the bad guys, though. That's why I'm calling. I want you to get out of the hotel, right away."

"I don't understand."

"I didn't do what the bad guys wanted this morning. I went a different way. Completely stitched them up."

"You did? Fantastic. David, good for you."

"Point is, they're going to hear about it. Soon."

"So they hear. So what?"

"So they'll be seriously pissed off. Pissed off enough to maybe send someone after you."

"Me? Why?"

"Lots of reasons. In case you were in on it. To get back at me, through you. 'Cause you're a journalist. It doesn't matter why. What matters is, you're not safe where you are."

"Oh. Well, have I got time for a shower before I make my escape?"

I caught sight of a figure approaching from the far end of the room. It was Tanya Wilson.

"Better not," I said. "Safer just to leave. Have you got a place to go?"

Tanya motioned through the glass that she wanted to talk to me, smiled, then went over to chat with Weston.

"Yeah," Julianne said. "I live in the Village. It's walkable."

"Better head for home, then," I said. "Sorry again about lunch."

I saw Weston give Tanya the cold shoulder. She stood and scowled at him for a moment, and then walked over to the side wall and started looking at the train maps.

"Don't worry about it," Julianne said. "But I tell you what—if we can't do lunch, what about dinner?"

"Can't," I said, watching Tanya. "I've got plans for tonight."

"Already? You move fast. Who is she? An FBI agent?"

"Who said anything about a 'she'?"

"Come on. You can't fool me."

"It's just a work thing. Something I promised to do a while ago."

"Oh, yeah? Just business?"

"Absolutely."

Tanya's body suddenly tensed as she studied the railway diagrams and I saw her head tilt slightly to the left, as if something critical had caught her attention.

"That's what you're telling me now," Julianne said. "Wait till you've had a few glasses of red. What will it be then?"

"The same," I said. "It's not a date. Just someone from the consulate. She helped me out with a few things, and I promised to buy her dinner before I head back to the U.K. Nothing romantic."

Tanya had turned to Weston and was pointing to the lower map—the one of the entire United States of America.

"You owe someone dinner in return for a few favors?" Julianne said. "Come on, David. I'm not buying that."

"Journalists," I said. "Too suspicious for their own good."

"OK. You got me. I'll back off. But listen, you did me more than a favor. You saved my life. I must owe you a whole bunch of dinners. What do you think—can't we do at least one before you leave the country?"

"I'd love to, Julianne. But I don't know if it'll be possible. I could be on a plane back home, tomorrow."

"What if you're not? What if you're here longer?"

"OK, tell you what. If I'm here another night, I'll call you."

"Great. Only trouble is, I lost my cell. Those guys took it when they threw me in their trunk. Why not give me your number. I'll call tomorrow, after lunch, and see if you're still around."

I took a moment to think about her idea. I didn't own a personal cell phone, and there's no way I'd give my work number to a casual acquaintance. But the phone Lesley had given me was unofficial. It was untraceable, and in a few hours it would be landfill. Letting her try it tomorrow wouldn't hurt. And it was a good way to shut her up now.

"Good plan," I said, and read out the digits.

I slipped the phone back into my pocket and signaled for Tanya to come and join me in the booth.

"Briefing's over," she said, touching my shoulder then taking the chair next to me.

"Wow," I said. "Must be some kind of record."

"They want to raid this Lesley's headquarters."

"Do they?"

"They want you to go with them. Show them where it is."

"No point."

"Why not? You've been there. You know the way."

"Too late. She'll be long gone."

"Maybe. But their forensics teams might recover something."

"No chance. The place will be empty. She'll take what she can, and destroy what's left. It'll be a complete waste of time."

"You're probably right. But hey. London has agreed, and you have fences to mend. Better put a smile on your face and get on with it."

"One condition."

"What?"

"Book us somewhere nice for dinner."

"Really? I didn't know if you were serious about that, after everything that happened. And three years is a long time to wait."

"I was dead serious. But you better make it late, though, in case this raid nonsense drags on. We'll have to trail over there, fake surprise at all the empty rooms, and then haul ourselves back here again. And they're bound to want a full finger-pointing session afterward."

"No doubt about that. The blame game's started already."

"Really? Who's in the frame?"

"No one knows who's been leaking information. It's too early for that. But for the big picture, fingers are pointing at Mitchell Varley."

"Varley? Poor bastard. Both sides are after him now. Maybe I should have just let that guy shoot him, after all."

"There were a few in that room who wouldn't have complained."

"How come? He may be an arse, but how is all this his fault?"

"I'm not sure, exactly. But listening between the lines, it sounds like he has some skeletons and they're not too well buried."

"What kind?"

"Something professional. It started with a counterfeiting crew, here in New York. Years ago. The bureau tried to take it down. Varley was part of the team. Their inside man. He latched on to this Lesley and used her to get to the others. That's how their paths first crossed. She was just a lieutenant, back then, though. Sounds like she's the boss now."

"So what happened? He took down her crew? She swore revenge?"

"No. Not at all. Apparently the feds had Lesley's mob on the hook. They were ready to move. Then she pulled a really vile stunt. Some kind of trademark of hers, they say. Ritual mutilation. Of the genitals. Some poor foot soldier who'd screwed something up."

"Still does that. She's one sick puppy."

"Sick, yes. And smart."

"Not that smart. You don't need a Ph.D. to terrorize people."

"I don't think that's why she did it. Not just to terrorize. She sounds more calculating than that. I think it was a test."

"Of what?"

"Her people. To flush out any traitors. Or infiltrators."

"Sounds a bit far-fetched."

"No. Because she always does it when new recruits are around, apparently. She knows no one with a conscience would be callous enough to just sit and watch something like that."

"More likely she's just a psycho."

"Maybe. But either way, Varley bit."

"You're joking. He blew his cover?"

"Believe so."

"Cardinal sin. The idiot. What happened?"

"Lesley was wounded, but escaped. So did the other bad guys. Apart from the foot soldier. He died. And none of the other agents made it, either. I don't know how many there were, but they left behind some friends. And friends with long memories."

"Oh, dear. Varley's in deeper shit than I'd thought."

"He probably is," she said, opening the door. "But now you better get moving. They want to form up in the garage at nine-thirty. That's less than ten minutes, and Rosser's getting uptight."

"Don't worry," I said, following her out. "They can't leave without me. What was up with the map, by the way? Just now?"

"Oh, that. It was weird. I thought I recognized some-one. There are photos around the edge."

"Really?" I said, moving over to the map. "Which one? Show me."

Tanya pointed to the photo in the top right-hand corner. It showed a man's face, in his mid to late thirties. An arrow connected his picture to a point on a railroad just south of the Canadian border.

"Who is it?" I said.

"He doesn't look familiar?" she said.

"No. Why? Should he?"

"I think it's a guy called Simon Redford."

"Who's that?"

"A Royal Marine. We met him in Spain, when we were there together. You don't remember him? My brother knew him, too. Same regiment."

"No. Definitely not."

"Strange. Maybe I met him before you arrived?"

"Maybe. But why would he be here? All these guys were murdered by some serial killer, apparently. Some-thing to do with trains."

"I don't know. But they've gone outside, now, Simon and my brother. Could be anywhere."

"As civilians?"

"No. He went to work for some private security firm. They both did. In Iraq."

"So what do you think? Is it him?"

"I don't know. But it really, really looks like him."

"Ask this guy," I said, nodding toward Weston. "He's working the case. Should know the victims' names."

"I did," Tanya said. "He wouldn't speak to me."

"Oh, really?" I said. "Maybe I should ask."

Weston was working on his laptop, pretending not to listen, and he kept up the act as I moved in behind him.

"Agent Weston," I said, as I leaned over his shoulder and slammed the screen down hard on his fingers. "Perhaps you would like to show my colleague some professional courtesy?"

He tried to wriggle free, but I just leaned down harder.

"Of course," he said eventually, through gritted teeth. "What does she want?"

"Speak to her," I said. "She's right here."

"I want a name," Tanya said. "The man in the photo I pointed to."

"I'll need to look it up," he said.

I flipped the screen back up and gave Weston a minute to locate the file.

"Dmitry Blokhin," he said. "Illegal immigrant from the Ukraine. Deserter, on the run from their army."

"There now," I said. "That wasn't so hard."

"And it's just *Ukraine*," Tanya said. "Not *the Ukraine*. They hate that, you ignorant pig."

I needed a bathroom break on my way downstairs, so I stopped on the first floor and found some restrooms near the elevators. I didn't exactly rush, so it was past 9:41 A.M. by the time I reached the garage. Rosser and Varley were already there, standing next to one of the black Fords that had escorted the Cadillac when they arrived. Rosser looked impatient. Varley just looked angry.

"First you were an hour early," he said. "Now you're late."

"No pleasing some people," I said.

"We have a job for you," Rosser said. "If you want brownie points, do it without anyone else getting killed."

"Depends what it is," I said. "Might not be possible."

"I have two teams ready to roll, outside," Rosser said. "I want you to escort them to the premises where you apprehended the suspect in Raab's shooting."

"Why don't I give them directions?"

"I want you to take them there, personally. Wait outside till you get the green light. Then go in. Look around. You're the only one who's been inside. I want to know everything that's missing or out of place."

"I hope you've got a lot of paper. It'll be a long list. She'll have had a two-hour head start, minimum, by the time we get there."

"Then so be it. Just get it done."

"Since you ask so nicely. And am I traveling alone, or will I have a babysitter?"

Varley stepped aside, and I saw Weston sitting behind the wheel.

"Oh, well," I said. "At least it'll be a quiet journey."

*

The first FBI team entered Lesley's house via the garage. The second—with Weston trailing behind, still wearing his suit—went in through the front door. I stayed in the car and figured the odds of Lesley not having booby-trapped the place.

Twenty minutes passed without any explosions then Weston reappeared, heading back down the path. He was flanked by two agents in full urban assault kit, which made him look like an alien abductee.

"Better come inside," he said. "There's something you should see."

It turned out I was wrong about the house being completely empty. Something had been left behind, in Lesley's office. It was the metal trolley that Cyril had been strapped to. Inside it was a glass bottle. The same cloudy, industrial kind she had used yesterday. Its lid was off, so you could smell the formaldehyde, and a label was attached to the side.

Two words were written on it, by hand, in green ink.

DAVID TREVELLYAN.

EIGHTEEN

My friend Jeremy was a born victim.

I first met him two weeks after I started at high school. He'd missed the beginning of term because he was still recovering from a recent kicking. He appeared in the corner of the classroom one morning and I remember thinking he might as well have BULLY ME tattooed on his forehead, the way he behaved. The local thugs just gravitated toward him. I had to step in and save him on several occasions over the years, when people were taking too much from him or it looked like he was going to get seriously hurt again. I could have stopped the trouble altogether without too much effort, but I didn't think that would be right. I wasn't going to be around for the rest of his life and he needed to learn how to stand up for himself. The problem was, he had no instinct for it. No idea how to spot danger coming or stop it in its tracks.

Most of the skirmishes he got into were fairly low level until one day I overheard a couple of kids threatening to beat him up after school if he didn't give them money. So, straightaway, he emptied his pockets. It was as if he were hearing their words but not understanding what they meant. It was such an obvious mistake. I could hardly believe what I was seeing. And after he'd sent out a message like that I knew there was nothing for it. I was going to have to take the long way home.

I left the school gates at the same time as Jeremy then hung back, drifting between the various groups who walked the same way as him. The journey started uneventfully. Nothing happened until we came to an alley, half a mile from his house. Then my heart sank. He walked straight into it without even looking. I turned the corner and saw the two kids who must have been waiting there. They'd already caught him, about twenty feet away. One was holding him, the other was standing with his fist pulled back, ready to strike. He was too far away to grab so I picked up a rock—a big chunk of flint with sharp, shiny edges—and hurled it at the kid's head. He looked around at the last second and it connected with the middle of his forehead. He tumbled backward, blood already oozing from the wound, and the other kid turned to run. But the passage wasn't long enough. I reached him with ten yards to spare.

Jeremy was so happy to get his lunch money back I don't think he really understood the point I was trying to make. I told him threats are like smoke. They're like the first wisps that appear before a fire really catches hold. And there's only one way to deal with them. Stamp them out before they grow into something bigger.

That method worked for me when I was a kid, and I've stuck with it ever since.

So you can imagine how I felt that afternoon, locked in an FBI debriefing while Lesley was left to slink away unopposed . . .

The rickety typist's chair I'd sat on yesterday had been relegated to the far corner of the boardroom and was now half hidden under a tangle of navy blue overcoats. But that wasn't a problem. Eight more chairs had been brought up and shared out along each side of the big granite table. I headed to the right, where two empty seats separated Tanya from a plump forty-something in a gray suit. The backrest of the one nearer her was stained, so I went to swap it with its neighbor.

"Hey," the plump guy said. "Someone's using that."

"Yeah," I said. "Me."

The double doors opened again and a guy hurried in with four large coffees wedged into a cardboard tray. He left one in the place to my right and took another round to Varley, who was sitting on his own at the center of the long side of the table. Then the new guy came back and flopped into the seat next to me, leaving two cups unclaimed.

"Which one of those was for Rosser?" I said.

"Why would one be for him?" he said.

"Come on, which one?"

"That one. Why?"

"I'm guessing black, no sugar?"

"Right. But what's that to you?"

"That's just how I like it," I said, taking the cup and passing the other one to Tanya.

"Hey," the new guy said. "That's . . ."

"Yes?" I said, turning to look at him.

"Hot. Maybe. Still."

"Gentlemen," Varley said. "And lady. Time to get under way. I guess you don't all know our English friends, so let's start with a quick round of introductions. We'll go clockwise. Ivan?"

"Ivan Sproule," the plump guy said. "FBI Special Operations, working for Mitchell out of New York."

"Brian Schmidt," the guy with the coffee said. "Also FBI Special Ops."

"David Trevellyan," I said. "Yesterday, in league with the devil. Today, innocent bystander slash tour guide."

"Tanya Wilson," Tanya said. "British Consulate."

"Lieutenant Byron McBride," the guy opposite Tanya said. "NYPD intelligence task force. I'm pulling together a citywide response to the spate of homicides involving elderly and vagrant victims."

"Detective Rosenior," the next guy said. "NYPD intell, working for Lieutenant McBride."

"That just leaves me," Weston said from his seat opposite the plump guy. "And our English friends certainly know who I am."

Varley stayed with Weston for his first set of questions, which involved asking for a full account of the raid on Lesley's house and then picking it to shreds. How had they entered? Where had they searched? How long had they taken? What had they found? How had they documented the scene? Could they have missed anything? How could

he be sure? Had they taken photos? Had forensics un-
earthed anything later? Varley was relentless, firing his
queries and driving Weston over and over the same
ground for a full twenty minutes.

The police officers were next to come under the micro-
scope, but Varley came at them from a different angle. This
time he wasn't interested in one specific case, but pushed
them for detailed breakdowns of the previous year's crime
figures. How many vagrants had been murdered, precinct
by precinct? What were their age groups? Gender? Reli-
gion? Previous occupations? Cause of death? How many
had made it into the press? State or country of birth? How
many had been cleared? The barrage was exhausting, and
Varley tired of it first. McBride was still going strong, wading
through his endless reservoir of statistics when Varley cut
him off and turned to me.

"Mr. Trevellyan, you recently infiltrated the criminal
organization of the woman known to us, but not exactly
loved, as Lesley?" he said. "Is that correct?"

"Yes," I said. "She tried to recruit me."

"And she raised the subject of Agent Raab's death with
you?"

"She did."

"What did she say about it?"

"That one of her operatives had killed him."

"The individual you brought here this morning?"

"You heard him say that for himself."

"Did she say why they targeted an FBI agent?"

"She said they didn't. They had intended to kill an

ordinary vagrant, but her operative failed to establish Raab's true identity before pulling the trigger. Which I guess you could take as a testimony to Raab's skill in working undercover."

"Why did they want to kill a vagrant? How was her operation linked to Raab's case?"

"I don't believe it was. I think she was involved with identity theft. It had nothing to do with the railroad killings."

"Why do you think that?"

"Because Agent Raab had a stolen Social Security card in his wallet when he was found, and I saw a similar card in someone's possession at Lesley's house. That can't be a coincidence."

"Maybe not. It's an interesting angle. We should follow up on it. Make absolutely sure there's no connection."

"I'll get right on it," Schmidt said.

"Good," Varley said. "Now, let's recap. Based on Lesley's conversation with Commander Trevellyan and the confession from her operative that I heard myself, we can be confident we know who killed Mike Raab. Anyone unhappy with that?"

No one responded.

"Agent Weston searched Lesley's premises and found no evidence that Raab was deliberately targeted, or that the gang had been acting on information received from within the bureau. Anyone disagree?"

Silence.

"Lieutenant McBride has thoroughly analyzed all the

available data, and has identified no pattern or trend consistent with the targeting of federal agents in New York. Anyone disagree?"

Silence.

"OK. That being the case, I conclude that Agent Raab simply fell victim to an unrelated criminal act perpetrated by Lesley's organization, which we know to be both extensive and vicious. As, in a sense, did Commander Trevellyan. Anyone disagree, now's the time."

Again, no one spoke. Everyone was still except for Weston, who looked down at the floor.

"All right then. This is what we're going to do. Kyle, now we know that Lesley's involvement was only coincidental, I want you to get moving with the train thing again. Pick up where Raab left off. I don't want any more bodies."

"Sir," Weston said.

"Ivan, work with Commander Trevellyan. Get an up-to-date description of Lesley and all her known associates. I want it with every field office and every PD nationwide before the end of the day. I don't care that Mike was only caught in her crossfire. She's still going to pay."

"Sir," the plump guy said.

"Brian, you're on this new ID theft theory. I can't see how it could be connected to Mike's case, but it could still be significant. It should be followed up in its own right. Cooperate fully with D.C. And get help from Commander Trevellyan if you need more detail."

"Yes, sir," the coffee guy said.

"David, are you happy with that?"

"Not entirely," I said. "I know it didn't cause Agent Raab to be targeted, but you do still have a leak. So does the NYPD. People have been passing all kinds of information about me to Lesley, for example. Who knows what else they're giving her?"

"You're right. But don't worry. We're on it. Standard procedure is to bring in a team from another office to do a deep-dive investigation. They're on their way. It'll be a pain in the ass, but they'll probably want to talk to you, if that's OK?"

"Of course," I said.

"Excellent. So, Ms. Wilson, Lieutenant, Detective, thank you for your time this afternoon. I appreciate your input and—"

Lieutenant McBride's cell phone began to ring. He excused himself and answered the call.

"Sorry, guys," he said, closing his phone after ninety seconds. "I asked my office to let me know if anything came up that might be related."

"And was it?" Varley said.

"Don't think so. Just another vagrant found dead this morning."

"Not missing any more agents, I hope?" I said.

"Better not be," Varley said.

"Well, if you are, remember I've been with you all day."

"Don't say that. You're making me nervous. McBride, what do we know about this guy?"

"Don't worry, you're pretty safe," McBride said. "The vic was seventy-six. Born in Brooklyn. Name of Charles

Bromley. Died of blunt force trauma. Found by a jogger in Central Park. Oh, and he only had one arm."

"Thank goodness," Varley said. "All my guys have a full set."

"What was his middle name?" I said. "The victim. Was it Paul?"

"Does it matter?" McBride said.

"It might."

"Hold on then. I'll check."

"His middle name was, in fact, Paul," McBride said after a moment on the phone. "How did you know?"

"And his Social Security number?" I said. "Was it 812–67–7478?"

McBride shrugged and made another call.

"You've got some explaining to do," he said when he hung up.

"That's the name and number I saw on the card at Lesley's house, yesterday," I said. "One of her thugs had it."

"Not possible," McBride said. "The ME was clear. Time of death was after midnight."

"They must have already snatched the guy," Weston said. "Took his card, and kept him holed up somewhere, like a room you never went in. Then brought him back to the city and killed him during the night."

"That just about works," Varley said.

"No," the plump guy said. "It doesn't. That's not it at all."

"Explain it, then," Weston said.

"Something's been bothering me ever since I heard a

card was found on Raab's body," he said. "It didn't make sense, killing him and leaving the card behind. But now I understand. They're doing the opposite of what Mr. Trevellyan thought. They're not stealing identities. They're creating them."

"You know, he might be right," I said. "I've heard of something like this before. In Africa, or somewhere. It's clever."

"What is?" Varley said.

"It's a Social Security scam," the plump guy said. "Lesley must have a guy inside the department. What he does is create hundreds, maybe even thousands of dummy accounts. Then they skim off the payments for a bunch of people who don't exist."

"Thousands?" the coffee guy said. "Could be big money. How much do retired people get?"

"Don't know," the plump guy said, unclipping a PDA from a holster on his belt. "But I can find out. I'll Google it, now. OK. Here we go. It's taking me to the Social Security Administration Web site. It says the maximum payment for a retired worker is $2,185 per month, and the average is $1,079."

"They'd stick somewhere around the average," the coffee guy said. "To avoid attention. But how many fake accounts do they have? That's the key."

"Sorry," the plump guy said. "Dead end. There's no way to tell."

"Can't you estimate?" Tanya said. "How many people receive Social Security over here?"

"Give me a second," the plump guy said. "Here we go. In New York, 1,996,230. And that was in 2005, so there'll be even more now."

"OK," Tanya said. "And how accurate is that data?"

"Federal standard is 99.96 percent," the plump guy said. "Which isn't bad."

"Not bad," Tanya said. "But even so, point-zero-four percent of almost two million is a fair few dummy accounts."

"Around eight hundred," I said.

"And if each one receives, say, thirteen thousand dollars a year?" Tanya said.

"Wow," the coffee guy said. "That's well over ten million dollars, annually."

"If all your assumptions are right," Weston said. "And if all the false accounts are fraudulent, not just mistakes. And if all the fraudulent ones are tied to Lesley."

"They will be," Varley said. "Trust me. She doesn't tolerate competitors."

"But even if it's half that amount, it's still huge," the plump guy said. "And dead easy. Once it's set up, the money will keep rolling in all on its own."

"I just don't see it," Weston said. "Surely they have auditors."

"Of course they do," I said. "That's why people are getting killed."

"If it's like previous scams, the department will randomly check X-number of accounts every month," the plump guy said. "The inside man will match the list against the dummy ones he set up. And any time he sees they're investigating one of his, he'll warn Lesley."

"So?" Weston said.

"So Lesley will have a suitable homeless guy killed," the plump guy said. "Plant a fake Social Security card on the body. The police find it, the victim's new identity works its way back through the system, and the investigators take that as proof their records were legit all along."

"That's why they moved Agent Raab's body," Tanya said. "Remember how it had been dragged to the front of the alley? David practically tripped over it. Lesley wanted it found in a hurry."

"Sounds almost foolproof," Varley said. "Lieutenant, can you tell how many victims' records were being audited at the time they died?"

"Not right now," McBride said. "But give me a week. I'll get the new parameters added to the database."

Give the guy a week. He'll add the new parameters. Which is fine, from an admin point of view. But if you were Lesley, would you be scared?

NINETEEN

Some skills, the navy can teach you.

Others, they can only develop. There has to be something already there, inside you, for them to work with. I first figured that out when we were learning about close-target reconnaissance. Surveillance, as most people think of it. The approach was that before we could try out any techniques for ourselves, we had to go on loan to the army for a week. We were told they needed untainted "volunteers" to be tracked by a group of trainee spooks who were taking their final assessments. It seemed like an easy enough assignment. All you had to do was walk around a different city center each day and carry out a number of mundane tasks like posting letters or buying groceries. Our brief was to keep our eyes and ears open, and every evening give a written report on how many tails we'd spotted and where. We were warned the spooks could be anywhere. In cars, on foot, riding bicycles, walking dogs, sitting in cafés. If they could observe us without being detected, they would pass their course. But as usual with the navy, there was something they weren't telling us.

Being stalked by the army guys wasn't just the end of their evaluation. It was the start of our own. If you couldn't pick up, instinctively, when you were being followed, you never made it to the next stage. Because there are a lot of things you had to know to make you effective in the field. But only one thing you had to have. A kind of sixth sense.

Useful, if you wanted to pass your assessment.

Vital, if you wanted to stay alive afterward.

The table Tanya had booked for us turned out to be at Fong's. That was the same restaurant I'd eaten at two nights ago, just before walking into the whole debacle over Raab's body. And as good as the place was, choosing to go back so soon did seem a little strange. The feeling that I wasn't getting the full picture was still gnawing at me when I arrived, exactly at nine-thirty, and I knew it wouldn't go away until I'd asked Tanya what she'd been thinking of when she made the reservation. But as it happened, I couldn't ask her anything. Because she didn't turn up.

I had the same waiter as last time. He gave me the same table. And when Tanya's apologetic text arrived he gave me the same half amused, half pitiful look you always get when you eat out alone.

I ordered the same meal. The same wine. And I was staying in the same hotel, so I decided to complete the whole déjà vu experience by walking back the same way. Except that by the time I reached Raab's alleyway, I had a strong feeling I was no longer on my own.

Five people had left Fong's around the same time as me. Two couples and one single male. I wasn't too concerned about the couples. They'd been in the restaurant before I arrived, sitting together, and I watched them hang around at the edge of the sidewalk chatting for a few moments before they drifted off in the opposite direction. The guy was much more interesting, though. I hadn't seen him inside, eating or working. He'd just appeared from the side of the building, near the staff entrance, and then loitered in the shadows until he saw which way I was headed. He set off in front of me and walked fast until he was twenty feet ahead. Then he slowed his pace to match mine, carefully keeping the gap between us roughly constant.

At the first corner he turned right, the way I was planning to go. I followed him into the next street and found he'd stopped ten feet from the intersection and was standing sideways, looking toward me and laboriously trying to light a cigarette with a spluttering old Zippo. As soon as he saw me he snapped the lighter closed and moved off again in the same direction, quickly stretching the gap back out to twenty feet. The same thing happened at the next corner, except that this time he'd paused to fiddle with the heel of his right shoe. So, when I reached the mouth of the alley, I decided it was time for a test. Without breaking step I dodged sideways into the gloom and flattened myself against the wall.

Nothing happened for half a minute. Then I heard footsteps coming back toward me. One set, fast and light. I looked down and scanned the layer of garbage on the alley floor until I spotted something suitable—a section of wooden banister rail, about four feet long. I crouched down, took a firm hold, and when the guy from Fong's hurried into view I scythed it around in a low arc toward the street. It connected with his shins, halfway between his knees and ankles. He shrieked and cartwheeled forward, not quite bringing his arms up in time to save his face from plowing into the sidewalk.

I stepped out of the alley and checked both ways, up and down the street. There were no pedestrians. No vehicles were moving. No windows overlooked us. No one had seen what happened. I leaned down to check the guy's pulse and breathing. Both were fine. He was just stunned, so I moved on to his pockets. He had a wallet, cash, a cell phone, and two sets of keys. Nothing of any use. The only thing worth taking was a Browning Hi-Power 9 mm, which he'd tucked into the waistband of his jeans.

The smart move at this point was clearly to dial 911 and walk away. I'd stood at this very spot two nights ago, and could hardly believe the trouble I'd brought on myself by getting involved in someone else's problems. I took out my phone. It was the one Lesley had given me. Lesley, who'd left that glass jar with my name on at her house that morning. How had she been intending to fill it? I looked down at the guy on the sidewalk. I had no idea who he was. Where he had come from. Or why he was following me. Maybe Lesley had sent him? Because if she had, that changed everything. There was no way I could let that pass.

I needed to be sure. And if I handed the guy to the police, the chances were I'd never find out.

I reached down, grabbed the guy's collar and dragged him into the alley. He was still pretty groggy so I took a moment to call up the main menu on my phone. I picked the option to create a new contact, typed Lesley (*personal cell*) and entered *917* followed by seven random digits. Then I put the phone away, sat the guy upright, propped him against the wall, and retrieved my piece of wooden banister.

"Evening," I said, when he looked as if he could focus again. "How are you feeling?"

He grunted and wriggled forward, reaching for his gun and trying to stand up at the same time. I pushed him back down with my foot.

"Move again, and I'll hit you in the head with this," I said, showing him the banister. "Understand?"

He grunted again, but stayed still.

"Good," I said. "Now. What's your name?"

He didn't answer.

"OK," I said. "No problem. To be honest, I don't really care what your name is. What I really want to know is, why did Lesley send you after me?"

He didn't speak, but a flicker of recognition showed in his eyes.

"Actually, don't worry about that, either," I said. "I already know why she sent you. I double-crossed her, killed one of her guys, and now she wants to pay me back."

"Right," the guy said, at last.

"She wants to give me her special treatment. Just like Cyril."

"Right again."

"I thought as much. So, here's my real question. What were you supposed to do once you caught me?"

"Like I'm going to tell you. Go ahead. Hit me with that thing. No way am I talking."

"Oh, I don't know. An adult human has 206 bones. I doubt I'd have to break more than five percent of yours before you were singing like a canary. But hey. It's late, and I'm tired. Let's cut out the middleman. Why don't we just call Lesley and ask her?"

I took out my phone.

"You're shitting me, now," he said. "No one knows her number."

I showed him the contact entry I'd just created.

"I used to be her partner, remember?" I said. "Of course I know her number. Now before I call, here's one last question. Her special treatment? Remind me. Does she save it for people who betray her? Or do people who fail her get it, too?"

He didn't answer.

"OK," I said. "I'm calling her now. And I'll be sure to mention that you're right here, helping me."

"Please," he said. "Don't."

"So, what were you supposed to do when you caught me?"

"I wasn't supposed to catch you. Only tail you. In case you didn't go back to your hotel."

"People are waiting there?"

"Yes. Two in the lobby. Two in your room."

"How did they know where I was staying?"

"Lesley's contacts. In the feds. And the police. Someone told her."

"What about Fong's? No feds or police knew I was eating there."

"You don't get it. She owns people, everywhere. Cab drivers. Limos. Bars. Hotels. Restaurants. And she's generous. Someone'll be buying a new car off calling you in to her, minimum."

"And the guys at my hotel. What are they supposed to do with me?"

"Take you someplace."

"Where?"

"An old building. In the basement, there. A couple of blocks away. Lesley owns it."

"You know the address?"

"Yes."

"Then what?"

"Beep her. So she can come down and do the you-know-what. Turn you from David to Davina."

"Tonight?"

"As soon as we could lay hands on you."

"Good," I said. "Now shut up."

I dialed Varley's number.

There was no answer.

I tried Lavine's.

It was switched off.

Weston's.

No answer.

I tried Tanya's, to get the details for Rosser and Breuer. Her line was busy.

I knew I couldn't trust anyone else in the bureau or the NYPD, so that left me with three choices. Hang around the alley hoping someone would answer their phone before a cop car came by. Handle Lesley myself. Or walk away.

"Who knows Lesley's beeper number?" I said to the guy on the ground. "Just the guys at the hotel?"

"No," he said. "I've got it, too."

"Good," I said, handing him the phone. "Now. Call your buddies. Tell them tonight is a trap. Lesley is going to dish out some special treatment, all right, but not just for me. To all four of them, as well. Tell them to run for their lives. And then take me to this old house."

Lesley's guy took me to a side street tucked away off Canal Street, three blocks to the east. It had no visible name. He paused for a moment then led me right to the far end, moving slowly as both the remaining streetlights had been broken. We stopped in front of an old tenement building—the last structure standing on the right-hand side. It was a complete ruin. The steps up to the entrance were chipped and pitted. The doors were boarded up. All the windows were smashed. Every inch of the walls was daubed with graffiti and a tide of empty cardboard cartons and plastic bags had drifted several feet deep along the frontage.

The guy tugged my sleeve and set off down a narrow

flight of steps to the left of the main set. They led to a recessed door. It was made of steel. I guessed it was new because it hadn't been vandalized yet. I waited while the guy fished for one of his sets of keys and used them to work the lock. He pushed the door and it swung back, silently. I followed him inside. He hit the lights and I saw we were in a long, rectangular room. It was easily forty feet by twenty-five. The floor and walls were covered in shiny white tiles, and the ceiling was divided into a series of sloping red-brick vaults.

I moved farther into the room, toward a rusty industrial-sized boiler that sat in the far corner. It clearly wasn't working—the place was freezing—but a maze of pipes still led out from the top and meandered their way through a series of holes in the walls and ceiling. Four piles of clothes were neatly folded on the floor in front of it. They were all men's. Next to those lay the remains of a bed mattress—just the springs and frame, no material or stuffing. The only other thing I could see was attached to the wall on the other side of the boiler. It was a metal ring, four inches in diameter, eight feet from the ground. Two lengths of chain were hanging from it. And there was a shackle at the end of each one.

"Hospitable kind of place," I said.

The guy didn't answer.

"Let's not waste any more time," I said. "Lesley's pager number. What is it?"

He told me, and I made the call.

"OK," I said. "I've whistled. Let's see if she comes running. How long should she be?"

"Don't know," the guy said. "I don't know where she's coming from."

"Better get ready then, in case she's around the corner. You get in the boiler, where the coal would go, and keep your head down. I'll stay out here."

"You're not going to . . . ?"

"I'm not going to do anything. To you, anyway. Unless you come out before Lesley gets here. Then I'll shoot you in the head. If you come out after Lesley gets here, or make any kind of noise, you know what she'll do. But if you wait quietly till we've gone, you're free to walk away. You've played your part. I've got no axe to grind with you."

Lesley must have been holed up somewhere nearby because it only took her twenty minutes to arrive in the cellar. She made no sound creeping down the outside steps. She just appeared in the doorway, paused for a moment with one hand leaning the frame, then launched herself into the room like a model strutting down a catwalk. Her eyes were fixed on me. I was in the corner next to the boiler, arms behind my back, leaning slightly forward to keep a realistic tension on the heavy chains. She stopped in the center of the room, leering at me, then suddenly the smile disappeared from her face.

"Where are my people?" she said. "They should be here."

"The reception committee from my hotel?" I said. "They decided not to hang around."

"Why? I told them to wait."

"I guess they heard about Cyril. Thought you might be planning another demonstration."

"The fools. There'll be no more demonstrations. Tonight it's your turn. I was going to let them watch."

"Really? Maybe we should postpone, then. Wait till you've got a big enough audience?"

"No. It's happening tonight. But don't worry. People will still see it. George is going to tape the whole thing. Maybe I'll have him put it on the Internet. Then everyone can enjoy it, all over the world."

I heard a shuffling sound from outside and then George stumbled into the room. He was moving backward, helping the tall guy from Lesley's house to carry a bright yellow hand truck. They set it down inside the doorway and the tall guy wheeled it toward the remains of the mattress. There were two things on it. A vehicle battery—heavy duty, probably from a truck or an SUV—and a polished mahogany box. It was ten inches wide, eight deep, and eight tall. On the front there was a rotating switch and a round, brass-edged dial. Two long thick cables snaked out from the side and lay in a coil on top of the box. One was attached to a large crocodile clip. The other was fixed to a wooden handle, twelve inches long, with a pointed bronze tip.

The two men wouldn't catch my eye but Lesley moved over until she was almost close enough to touch me. She reached into her coat pocket, pulled out the bolt-cutter device she'd brandished in front of Cyril, and started into her routine of opening and closing its jaws.

"Remember my burdizzo?" she said. "What it does?"

"I remember," I said. "But it's only fair to warn you. There's no way on earth I'm going to let you use that thing on me."

"David, don't worry. I have no intention of using it on you. There's no need. Because you're going to use it on yourself."

"On myself? I don't think so. On the scale of unlikely things that's pretty much off the chart."

"I understand, David. Most people in your position think that way, to start with. But their views always change. Yours will, too."

"You think?"

"I know. See my wooden box? Can you guess what it's for?"

"Making coffee? That would be useful, about now."

"It's for changing people's minds."

"It won't change mine."

"You know what I might do, that would be funny? Get you to go on tape right now, swearing you'll never use the burdizzo on yourself. Then, in a few minutes, when you're begging me to hand it you, that'll make an amusing contrast, don't you think? Before and after?"

"Doesn't strike me as funny. But why not bring your box over here and we'll find out?"

"Oh, no. It doesn't come to you. You go to it. First I'm going to cut off all your clothes. Slowly, one by one. Then John and George are going to strap you to the mattress.

Naked, obviously. That's when I fire up the box. The clip goes—well, you can imagine where. The probe goes wherever I choose. And you go to hell on earth."

"Are you sure? Because I hate it when people over-promise and underdeliver."

"See the switch? That controls the power. It's set to minimum, right now. Sixteen thousand volts. That's where we'll start."

"And?"

"It goes right up to thirty-two thousand."

"Is that a lot? I never paid much attention in science class."

"It's more than a lot. I can't wait to show you. But you know the best thing? The current. One-thousandth of an amp."

"Means nothing to me. Physics was never my strong suit."

"It means there's no danger of accidentally killing you. We can keep going for hours. All night. As long as I want."

"I see. That must be the benefit of understanding all these little details. The control it gives you. Is it important, would you say? Knowing all the relevant facts?"

Lesley slipped the burdizzo back into her coat pocket and swapped it for a pair of dressmaker's scissors.

"Because I think there's one fact you don't know," I said. "One that's more important than everything else you've told me."

"So come on," she said, stepping in close and pulling my shirt tight, ready to cut. "Share."

"I could," I said. "But I have a better idea. Remember at your other place, with Cyril? How you thought show-ing was better than telling? That idea stayed with me."

I dropped the chains and grabbed her right hand tight, crushing her fingers into the scissors so she couldn't stab me or release them. Then without letting go I spun her around, whipping my elbow over her head and forcing her arm up until she was pushing the scissor blades into her own throat. At the same time I grabbed the Browning from my waistband and looked across at George and the tall guy. Neither had moved.

"On the floor," I said. "Both of you. Right now."

George was the first to respond. He went for his inside pocket, trying to draw his old Army Colt. I fired twice. Both bullets hit him in the chest, throwing him backward and leaving a bright crimson smear on the tiles where he slid. The tall guy reacted a moment later, springing to-ward me, arms outstretched. I fired again, hitting him in the head and shoulder. I felt Lesley's body tense and press back harder against mine as he went down. I spun her around and shoved her away from me. She staggered but stead-ied herself after four steps. Her chin was up, shoulders back, eyes blazing. The scissors were still in her hand. I willed her to use them, but she stayed stock-still. She wasn't going to give me an easy excuse.

I lifted the gun and lined it up between her eyes. Her lackeys were on the floor, but she was the one who deserved the bullets. There was no doubt where the blame lay. My finger began to squeeze the trigger. A fraction of an ounce more pressure and she would be dispatched, too. I imagined her lying on her back, dead. As Raab had been when I found him. But then I thought back to the scene in the alley, earlier. There was nothing left to mark the spot where he'd fallen. Not even a vague impression in the trash. It was like a fresh tide of garbage had swept in and scoured away every last trace of his death, and wiped the slate clean for Lesley's successors. If she disappeared, too, there would be nothing to stop them from dumping more helpless victims in similar places, all over the city, wherever they chose. Ten million dollars a year is plenty of incentive to keep the machine running. Unless Lesley was around to help the FBI dismantle it.

I looked at her face across the end of the barrel for another few moments, then lowered the gun. And hoped that this time, Varley would pick up the phone quickly.

There's only so much temptation a man can take.

TWENTY

In my world you are surrounded by deceit.

You spend most of your working life lying to people. About who you are. Where you're from. Why you're with them. What you do. Who you work for. What you believe in. It makes for some interesting conversations. Because you know that for every lie you tell, you're told a dozen in return. It changes the way you relate to people. You don't just hear their words. You scan everything they say for contradictions. Check their facts for discrepancies. File minute details away in your head for future confirmation.

You end up convinced that everyone is hiding something from you. Friend, as well as foe.

Which experience shows is not too far from the truth.

Tanya had promised to send a car to drop me at the airport the next morning. That was fine by me—better than having to put my hands on $60 cash for a cab, and the consulate drivers are trained not to annoy their passengers with mindless chatter. The only question was what kind of car it would be. Tradition dictates that you sit in the back, which makes their cramped little X-types a pretty unappealing prospect.

I crossed my fingers, came out of the hotel, and saw that I needn't have worried. A long-wheelbase XJ limousine with diplomatic plates was sitting at the side of the road, engine running, waiting for me. It was a little ostentatious with its dark green livery and black privacy glass, but at least it would be comfortable. And I got another surprise when I opened the door. A nice one. Tanya was inside.

"I'm sorry about last night," she said.

"Don't worry about it," I said. "Everything worked out in the end. You missed Varley's reunion with Lesley, though. It was a treat. Very emotional."

"That's not what I meant. I'm talking about the restaurant. Having to break our date."

"I know. That was a shame. But if you had to work, you had to work. Don't be too hard on yourself. It catches up with all of us, eventually."

"To be honest, I wasn't really working. I just exaggerated a little, when I sent you the text."

"So what were you doing? It must have been good, to outgun me and a kung pau chicken."

"Talking to my brother. And a few other people."

"About what?"

"My friend. Simon. The guy in the photo. Who they found dead, by the railway."

"The guy you thought was Simon."

"No. I know it was Simon. I'm sure of it now."

"How?"

"Because of what Agent Sproule said. The fat guy, at the debrief. About Lesley planting fake IDs on those corpses."

"She was planting U.S. IDs so she could rip off their Social Security money. The railway guy had Ukrainian papers. How would that work?"

"Not the scam part. The way she used fake IDs to change people's identities. To throw the authorities off the scent."

"How do you know the Ukrainian papers were fake?"

"I don't. Maybe they weren't. That doesn't matter. The point is, that was really Simon's body they found, but the FBI doesn't believe it."

"Tanya . . ."

"Just listen. I spoke to my brother. He's back in Iraq. Simon went with him. And another Brit, called James Mansell. They were working together. Then Simon and James were moved to another team, guarding a hospital."

"Why?"

"Emergency replacements. The hospital team was originally all Americans, but a couple of them got killed."

"The hospital was hit?"

"No. It happened on a day off. They strayed out of bounds, got caught up by a mob—quite gruesome apparently. But that's not the point. Simon and James took their places. They worked at the hospital for maybe two days, then the whole team was pulled out. Called back to the U.S."

"For what reason?"

"Training, they were told at first. But when they got back to New York, where the firm's based, they were all fired. The whole team."

"Why?"

"Didn't say. Their boss just gave them three months' money and told them to vacate the building."

"Seems a bit odd."

"Doesn't it just."

"So what did Simon and James do about it?"

"Simon said they were going up to Canada. With the other squaddies. They were pissed off, but had plenty of money so they didn't need to find more work yet."

"Canada?"

"Yeah. A lot of vets end up there, apparently. At least for a while. Canadians seem much more sympathetic. They have support groups, retraining programs, legal help for deserters, that sort of thing."

"Maybe they're still up there, getting counseling."

"No. I spoke to my brother and everyone else I could get hold of. Simon and James were in regular contact with quite a few people. But guess when that stopped?"

"When?"

"The day before the FBI found the alleged Ukrainian. Not a single word from either of them since then."

"That's suspicious, Tanya, but not conclusive."

"And something else. Do you know which U.N. country was controlling the sector Simon was working in?"

"Let me guess. Ukraine?"

"Got it."

"That's an interesting coincidence, but it still doesn't prove anything."

"Right. So, will you help me?"

"To do what?"

"Prove it's Simon. Get justice for my friend."

"How?"

"I don't know. Go up there. Get hard evidence that it's him."

I paused for a moment. A trip upstate with Tanya could have possibilities. There was plenty of unfinished business between us, after all. Part of me wanted to say yes. But realistically I knew her idea would never fly. Her friend was history, and anyway, I was needed elsewhere. There would be real work waiting for me. More than enough of it. There always was.

"I can't, Tanya. I'm on my way home. London is expecting me."

"I'll take care of that. Your head wound will buy a few more days."

"No, Tanya. I've got to get back. I can't go traipsing around the country, chasing a ghost."

"Why not? You went nuts over someone you thought was a tramp. I helped you, then. So why won't you help my friend, now?"

"How can I help him? He's dead. We can't bring him back to life."

"No. But if we can identify him, I can bring him home. Like Dog, remember? When he was killed in Morocco?"

"Dog was killed in the line of duty. The navy brought him home."

"How naïve are you, David? The navy didn't bring him home. I did. They wanted to leave him in Africa, to save money. You were in the hospital. You didn't hear about it. You couldn't have done anything, anyway. So I came down and made them do it."

"I thought you came to visit me."

"That, too. But I knew Dog was your friend. I knew you wouldn't want him left behind. I knew it was the right thing to do. So I stood up, David, whether you knew it or not. And now I'm asking you to stand up. I really need you to do that. Please don't tell me you're walking away."

I was tempted. Very. And this news about Dog tipped the scales even further. But still, I knew I'd be doing it for the wrong reason. If I stayed it would really be to steal another couple of days with her. She didn't need me on a job like this. If she was serious about resolving it she should be getting the specialists involved. Not someone who'd only be along for the ride.

"I'm not walking away, Tanya. But I'm the wrong person for this kind of work. I'm no use with crime scenes and forensics. The FBI are experts at that stuff. They're the ones you should be talking to."

"They won't listen. I've tried."

"So make them listen. Don't just nag at them. Find something positive to engage them with."

"Such as?"

"Use your brain. Think it through. You reckon the Ukraine IDs were planted?"

"Right."

"So go back to Simon's body. Get someone to check his dental work. Vaccination scars. Surgical scars, if he has any. All that stuff is done differently in the U.K. It's a dead give-away."

"I don't know. It sounds a bit tenuous."

"OK then, how about this—how did Simon and this other guy get back to the States?"

"They flew."

"On a commercial flight, or does this firm have their own planes?"

"They do have planes, but Simon said they took a regular flight because of the short notice."

"Good. Which airport did they use?"

"JFK, I think."

"Excellent. The INS fingerprints every foreign national who arrives there. The FBI can get access. Ask them to compare the prints from the railway victim with the passengers on Simon's plane."

"Much better. That would put it beyond doubt. Excellent, David. Thanks."

"No problem. Just let me know how it works out. I'm in your corner. And let me know if the feds give you any grief. I'll make some calls. See if Weston needs any more help closing his computer."

TWENTY-ONE

I can still remember what my new commanding officer said to me when I first stepped into his office in Canberra, thirteen years ago.

"I like to rattle cages, me."

I remember wondering what on earth he was talking about. Was it a threat? A confession? Had he confused me with someone else? But I soon found that this was his motivation technique. Or what passed for it. He thought he could get the best out of people by frightening them. Only no one was exactly quaking in their shoes. A few people felt sorry for him, certainly. But the net result was that he ran the most inefficient and unpopular unit anywhere in the Royal Navy. Even the torpedo refurbishment plant in the Falkland Islands had a better reputation. No one wanted to stay a moment longer than necessary, so I did what most of the others did. Kept my head down, bided my time, and transferred out at the first opportunity.

The whole experience wasn't a total waste, though. It did teach me two things.

You can bully people all you like, but they'll only go the extra mile if they want to.

And you don't have to be the boss to take advantage of that.

Regular travelers all have strategies for dealing with long-haul flights. Some are pretty complex. Others are simpler, but just as effective. My personal routine, for example, has been honed to perfection by years of experience. I eat in the airport. And I sleep on the plane.

The breakfast they serve in the old Concorde room at JFK is pretty good. Not quite the whole nine yards, but big enough to last until we land in London. I like to take it slow, savoring every mouthful, and then move over to the armchairs for the last part of the ritual. A second refill of coffee, and a good hour catching up with the U.K. papers.

I was coming to the end of the final broadsheet with ten minutes to spare when a stocky man in a gray suit eased his way through the gaggle of passengers loitering near the reception desk. He paused, scanned the room, then came across toward me. He stepped in close so no one else could see and took out a Homeland Security ID for me to inspect.

"Someone would like to speak with you," he said.

"Really?" I said. "Who?"

"A woman from your consulate. She says it's urgent."

"Does she have a name?"

"Wilson. Ms. T. That's all her ID said."

"Oh, that's all right. I know her. Tell her to come in."

"No can do. She's not traveling today. Not permitted this side of security. You'll have to come with me."

I checked my watch.

"Well, OK," I said. "But she better make it quick."

Tanya was waiting for me by the self-service machines in the check-in hall. Two other people were with her. The first was Agent Weston. And as I moved closer I realized the second, allowing for his swollen, discolored face, had to be Agent Lavine.

"No one told me Herman Munster would be here," I said. "Who let him out?"

"Now David, I want you to take a deep breath," Tanya said. "Count to ten before you say anything."

"Why?"

"Because I know you probably won't believe me. This isn't what I meant to happen. It was London's idea."

"What was?"

"You're not going back today. You have to stay a little longer."

"How much longer? What for?"

"Turns out we've got a bigger problem than we thought. I talked to London. Brought them up to speed. And you were their solution."

"Solution for what? Is this about your friend?"

"Partly. There's more to it, now. But look, we can't talk here. Come back to the car. I'll fill you in properly."

"Let me do that," Lavine said. "I'll fill him in permanently."

I'd expected Tanya to still have the Jaguar, but they'd obviously switched to Weston's car at some point during the morning. It was the one we'd used yesterday to raid Lesley's house. Lavine was in the passenger seat this time, so I climbed into the back with Tanya.

"I'm listening," I said.

"It started with your idea, funnily enough," Tanya said. "We got the INS records for the plane Simon and the rest of his team were on. We did the comparison. And we got a match straightaway."

"Simon."

"Yes. I'm afraid so."

"Well, I'm sorry you lost your friend, Tanya, I really am. But what's that got to do with me? These two geniuses notwithstanding, the FBI are world experts on serial killers. They'll get the guy who did it."

"We don't think it was a serial killer," Weston said. "Not in the accepted sense."

"There's an unaccepted sense?" I said.

"Stop it," Tanya said. "We didn't just test Simon's prints. We also checked on the other four railway victims. And got four hits. From a military database. I ran the names past my brother. He confirmed it. They were the four U.S. guys from Simon's team in Iraq."

"Someone took out that whole team," Weston said.

"Except for James Mansell," Tanya said. "The other Brit. He's still out there somewhere."

"Unless his body hasn't turned up yet," I said. "Maybe it got eaten by a bear."

"Alive or dead, we need to find him," Tanya said.

"Someone needs to find him," I said. "It doesn't have to be me."

"London wants you on the team," Tanya said. "The FBI has agreed."

"Reluctantly," Lavine said.

"I'm not a team player," I said.

"No shit," Lavine said.

"Stop squabbling, both of you," Tanya said. "One marine is dead. Another marine is missing. The navy wants something done about that. And they want you to do it, David. So what's your problem?"

"They're not marines anymore, Tanya," I said. "They're ex-marines. No offense to your brother, but these are guys who put their wallets before their regiments. You go outside to make money, this is the sort of thing that happens. End of story."

"Never thought I'd agree with him, but David has a point," Lavine said.

"Sorry, Tanya," I said, opening the door. "This is no good. I'm going back to London. I need to sort this out with the brass, face-to-face."

"Wait," Tanya said, sliding out of the car behind me. "Please. Don't go."

"Why not? Simon's been identified. That's what you said you wanted."

"It was. But now we know about James Mansell."

"What about him? If he's alive, he can take care of himself. If not, the FBI will find his remains and you can bring him home. Either way, you don't need me."

"Think about it, David. All his companions were killed. If he's alive, he must be in danger."

"That's his problem."

"Mine, too. Because I know about it. That means I can't just ignore it. I'm obligated. I've got to do something. And I need your help."

"Why you? What makes it your responsibility?"

Tanya closed the car door, took my arm and led me to the other side of a concrete pillar, fifteen feet away.

"Will you just trust me on this?" she said.

"Why?" I said. "It makes no sense."

"I'm only asking you to hang around for a few more days. A week at the most. Until we know Mansell's safe."

"What if he doesn't want us butting in? Maybe he wanted to disappear."

"If he's alive I just need to find him and warn him. After that, it's up to him."

"Why? Who is he? An ex-boyfriend?"

"No. Nothing like that. I've never met him in my life."

"Then why do you care so much?"

"Because he's in danger."

"Everyone's in danger, Tanya. Give me the real reason."

She didn't answer.

"Explain it in a way I can understand," I said. "Or I'm on the next plane home."

"I can't," she said. "I'm in an impossible situation."

"Is this London nonsense? Is it classified?"

"No."

"Then what is it?"

"If I don't say, you won't help. If I do say, you'll hate me and you won't help. What can I do?"

"I'm not going to hate you, Tanya," I said, taking her hand. "Whatever it is, just tell me."

Tanya pulled her hand away, closed her eyes for a moment, and started to sway slightly, like someone in a trance.

"OK," she said, finally. "Here goes. After Morocco, did you ever hear what happened? Officially?"

"No. There was never a proper report."

"There was. Only I made sure you never saw it."

"You did? Why?"

"The ambush that killed Dog? I knew about it. Well, I didn't exactly know. I'd received a tip."

"When? Who from?"

"The day before. A local informant. Someone new. I didn't know if he was reliable, so I wanted to verify his story before passing it on."

"It checked out?"

"It rang true enough. But I was too late. It took too long. When the bomb went off under your truck I was actually on the phone, trying to reach you."

"So you made sure the threat was credible, and then you sent up the flares?"

"Yes, but—"

"And the report—did it censure you?"

"No."

"Were you disciplined?"

"No."

"Demoted?"

"No. But that's not the point. The report judged what I did. Not what I could have done. And looking back, I'm sure I could have been quicker. If I'd got to you five minutes sooner . . ."

"That's ridiculous, Tanya. You did the right thing. Dog would have said the same. Let it go."

She didn't respond.

"And even if you were wrong, what's done is done," I said. "Life goes on."

"Not for Dog," she said.

"So what do you think? By warning James Mansell you can make amends, somehow?"

She didn't answer.

"What do you think will happen?" I said. "Dog will spring back to life?"

She stayed silent.

"You can't change the past, Tanya," I said. "However hard you try. I'm sorry. You'll just have to find another way to deal with it."

A car horn sounded, to our left. I looked around and saw that Weston had rolled down his window.

"Hey," he said. "Hurry it up. We need to get moving. Varley called. He wants us back at the office."

Tanya turned to go and as she brushed past me I glimpsed the trace of a tear nestling in the corner of her right eye. It reminded me of the hospital, in Rabat, when I'd woken up and found her in my room. Maybe she'd come to Morocco out of guilt that day, but she'd still been there for me. And the way she blamed herself for what happened may not have been logical, but in a way I could understand it. Ultimately, you feel what you feel. You have to recognize it, deal with it, and move on. Sometimes, people need help with that. Especially in our business. The only question is, are they worth enough of your time?

I slid onto the backseat just as Tanya was about to slam the door.

"Changed my mind," I said, cupping her hand with mine. "Too much paperwork in London. Rosser's complaints will still be ringing in their ears. Better to let things settle. Around a week should do it."

Mitchell Varley was back on his throne, lording it over the boardroom table. Tanya and I were on the left-hand side, in the places we'd used for the debriefing. Weston and Lavine were sitting opposite us. But that was all. There was no one else to soak up Varley's questions. And worse than that, no one to fetch the coffee.

"OK then, gentlemen," Varley said. "Things are moving on. Yesterday, we discounted Lesley from our railroad investigation. Which is a shame, since she's now in custody. Today, we've uncovered new facts about the case. Disturbing new facts. It seems we're not talking about a lone serial killer anymore. Or even a gun for hire. The victims weren't random, as we'd assumed. They were part of a group. There's some kind of connection here we don't fully understand."

No one responded.

"So," he said. "How do we proceed from here? I want options. Bartman—you first. And welcome back, by the way."

"Thank you, sir," Lavine said. "I think we should go back to the crime scene evidence first. And start again. Whatever's going on here, it sounds structured. Organized. We're talking about professional hits, now, obviously. Not a whacko. Not an amateur. We need to go much deeper than we thought."

"Just with the evidence?" Varley said. "Or should we revisit the scenes, as well?"

"Just the evidence to start with," Lavine said. "We won't find anything new at the scenes. It's been too long. But I guess it might be worth a quick look, to see if the choice of locations can tell us anything. Maybe throw some light on the killer's training, background, or whatever."

"OK," Varley said. "Get someone on it. What about witnesses?"

"None came forward," Lavine said. "But it sounds like the stakes are higher now. Maybe we should think about a reward?"

"Not yet," Varley said. "That would bring out too many

cranks. We'll save it for a last resort. Just get the local PDs to go with a straight recanvass for now. So, Kyle? Over to you."

"I was thinking about these planted IDs," Weston said. "Especially the Ukrainian ones. Where did they come from? Are they real, or fake? Did they make them, or steal them? And when?"

"Good angle," Varley said. "Could definitely lead somewhere."

"And don't forget the basics—follow the dollar," Weston said. "These guys had just been paid off. Three months' money. Their line of work that could be, what, fifty grand each? Three hundred thousand dollars? That's a decent motive right there. And no one looked at it before, 'cause we thought they were bums."

"You're right," Varley said. "Get the full financials on all of them. Including the company they worked for."

"Good call," Weston said. "Must be people there who knew about the payoff."

"We're moving on that already," Lavine said.

"I'd focus on the employer, if it was up to me," Tanya said. "Not so much on the money. I'm not sure the payoff's all that relevant."

"Three hundred grand isn't relevant?" Weston said.

"You have to understand how it works, over there," Tanya said. "I've been thinking. Something about how the people were moved around between jobs sounds fishy to me."

"What's your problem with it?" Varley said.

"When my brother first went back, he was on convoy protection," Tanya said. "The others were, too. My brother's still doing it."

"What kind of convoy?" Lavine said.

"Captured ammunition," Tanya said. "On its way for destruction."

"Ouch," Lavine said. "Rather them than me."

"Exactly," Tanya said. "They get all sorts of bonuses, because of the risks. And because it's so critical to keep the ammo out of the insurgents' hands."

"And yet Redford and Mansell were pulled off these ammo convoys to guard some hospital?" Varley said.

"Right," Tanya said. "So what does that tell us about the hospital work?"

"It was more important than protecting the convoys," Varley said.

"Exactly," Tanya said. "And the whole team was pulled out of the hospital under some bogus cover story. Then they were fired. And a few days later, they started being killed."

"I see where you're going," Varley said. "It doesn't sound like a coincidence."

"No, it can't be," Tanya said. "That's why I think the company holds the key. Someone there knows something."

"Did your brother give you the name of the company?"

"He did. Tungsten Security."

"Contact details?"

"Kelvin Taylor. Chief operating officer."

"We need to run his background, pronto."

"I ran it already," Lavine said. "Nothing stands out."

"So who is he?" Varley said.

"Ex-military. Served in Iraq during the first Gulf War. And Kuwait. Mustered out shortly after. Went back to do charity work. Set up some kind of humanitarian project. It's still running. The only U.S. program to survive. He may have got married over there as well, but his wife never surfaced Stateside if he did."

"What's his involvement with Tungsten?"

"He set that up, too. It's basically your garden-variety private security contractor. Current climate, they can't make money fast enough. Balance sheet's more than healthy. They're awash with cash. List of government contracts as long as your arm. No employees with criminal records. No red flags on file. Nothing to help on any systems. It's going to take a coordinated effort to unravel."

I listened to Lavine's words in disbelief. In a literal sense I knew how we'd got to this point. Stumbling across Lesley's victim dragged me into her scheme; finding that the body belonged to an agent bounced me into the railroad case; the connection with the security firm suggested something larger was going on. But what I couldn't comprehend was how I'd been plucked from the departure lounge at JFK and dumped on the verge of a full-scale FBI frolic. Staying on to help Tanya fight her demons was one thing. I was thinking about time spent in restaurants. And bars. And other, more secluded places. Not in offices. Not sitting through endless meetings. Talk of corporations was a bad sign. Any mention of conspiracies and government contractors was worse. Interagency cooperation was only a sentence away. Task forces would be proposed. I knew how it would end up. If I let the FBI go down that road I'd never get away. I'd be stuck here for months, and at the end I'd have absolutely nothing to show for it. I needed to head them off at the pass. Something more direct was called for. It was time to shake the tree.

"So the whodunitometer isn't working," I said. "What a surprise. Tanya, how do we contact this guy?"

"I have his cell number," she said. "My brother knew it."

"Perfect. I'll give him a call. Pop around, have a chat."

"No," Varley said.

"Yes," I said. "You guys stick to your paper trails. Leave the infiltration to me. I'm the only one who's trained for it."

"We're not going to infiltrate," Varley said.

"You're not," I said. "Not with your track record."

"We can't, because everyone at Tungsten is a suspect. We may need to arrest people."

"We may need to do more than that."

"Absolutely not. Anything we find needs to hold up in court. No way are you going in on your own. If you go, all four of you go. Keep an eye on each other. This one stays above the line. No exceptions."

I sighed and pulled out the phone Lesley had given me.

"What's his number, Tanya?" I said.

"You're a bit gung ho," Weston said. "Somewhere you'd rather be?"

"Yeah," I said. "The other side of the world."

TWENTY-TWO

The navy loves to use role play in its training exercises.

That can be embarrassing at first. Pretending to be a businessman or a plumber or a traffic warden in front of twenty other people makes you feel like you're back in grade school. But after a while the awkwardness wears off and the value starts to show through. Doing something is always better than being told how, and seeing other people perform gives you plenty of food for thought.

The first time we tried it we were given a clear scenario. We worked for a company that wanted to build a new refrigerator factory in one of the ex-Soviet republics. We had to meet a group of their government officials at a hotel in London to haggle over state subsidies. We were suspicious that they had offered our competitors a better package, so we were sent with a list of questions to test the theory. And at the same time, we had to avoid revealing any details about ourselves that would strengthen their hand. To make the exercise realistic we were told to bring our suits and briefcases. Then we were taken to a location in the City and sent on our way.

Everything that happened in the hotel was videoed, and reviewed afterward. All of us did a pretty good job. Evil communist schemes were revealed, our lips remained tight. We were ready to pat ourselves on the back when the instructors passed a piece of paper around to each of us. These detailed everything we'd given away about ourselves. The lists were long. At first no one could understand, because nothing on the sheets corresponded with the recordings of the meetings. Then the real point became clear. The information they'd gathered about us hadn't been spoken. It had come from our coats, which they'd politely hung up. Our jackets. Briefcases. Anything that had been out of our sight or opened or left in plain view.

The lesson was, information can come from everything people show you.

Whether they mean to, or not.

Tungsten Security had two sets of premises. Their operational base wasn't in the most promising part of New York. It was built on a scruffy, unfashionable patch of land in Queens that had been clawed back from the marshes when Kennedy Airport was first developed in the forties, but the isolated compound was in no way run-down or neglected. And it hadn't been starved of money. In fact, the people who'd fitted the place out had burned through an even bigger pile of cash than the decorators at the company's official headquarters I'd seen on Fifth Avenue. They just hadn't been as concerned with esthetics.

The line of five drab, olive-green warehouses sat un-invitingly alone at the far end of a long, straight service road. It was easy to find. There were no other structures within five hundred yards in any direction. The reinforced mesh fence separating the buildings from the surrounding land was sixteen feet high, with four gleaming strands of razor wire sloping toward us at the top. Another fence ran parallel to it, twenty yards inside the perimeter, identical except that the wire faced the other way. Nothing taller than a blade of grass grew in between, and posts set at regular intervals on the far side carried an array of floodlights, security cameras, infrared beacons, and motion sensors.

There was no mention of the company name. And no signs to welcome visitors.

The only obvious way in was through a pair of stout metal gates. They were wide enough for heavy trucks to use, so Weston's Ford felt pretty small as he coasted up to them and stopped inside a hatched area marked on the road with yellow paint.

A small notice on the vertical bars said WAIT.

"What is this place?" Weston said.

"Did I miss something?" Lavine said. "Are we at Gitmo?"

The outer gate slid silently aside and Weston rolled forward until his window was level with an intercom mounted on a steel pillar. A second box was attached higher up, for truck drivers. Weston reached out with his left hand but before he could press any buttons the gate started to close behind us again. The gaps on both sides were blocked with the same mesh and razor wire as the main fences, leaving us completely caged in.

"See?" Lavine said. "A guy will come out, now, with orange jumpsuits for us to wear. You wait."

"State your name and business," a voice said through the intercom. It was male, and had an Australian accent.

"FBI," Weston said. "Kelvin Taylor is expecting us."

"Building one," the voice said.

The buildings each had a four-foot-tall number stenciled in white paint above their main door. We emerged through the inner gate in front of building number three. Number one was at the far end, to our left, with a pair of old, battered Toyota Landcruisers and a shiny silver Prius parked outside.

"What do you think these places are for?" Tanya said.

"Don't know," I said. "Presumably building one will be their admin block, if that's where they're meeting us. And if this is where their people prepare for deployment, they'll need a warehouse and an armory."

"There," Weston said, nodding at number two as we trundled past. "No windows."

"See the roll-up doors on three?" Lavine said. "That'll be their workshop. They'll need to prep their vehicles for different climates."

"And the others?" Tanya said.

"Didn't get a good look," I said. "Accommodations? Briefing rooms? More storage?"

"Who knows?" Weston said.

"Maybe the place is just a front," Lavine said. "Could be what this whole thing's about. Could all just be stuffed full of drugs and illegal immigrants."

"Could be," I said. "Let's ask Mr. Taylor. . . ."

The doors to building one swung open automatically, but as we followed Lavine inside I got the impression we'd be dealing with people who weren't big on hospitality. The space we entered was more like a cell than a reception area. The gray paint on the floor was wearing thin, the walls were bare, unfinished cinderblocks, and the three fluorescent lights on the ceiling had no covers to diffuse their glare.

A plain metal table had been placed in the center. Its legs were bolted to the ground. A man was sitting behind it, keeping one eye on us and the other on an oversized flat-panel monitor. He was wearing shiny black paratrooper boots, sand-colored utility pants, and a matching short-sleeved shirt with fake epaulets. It had a logo on the left pocket—a bold, capital W with some kind of dog's head superimposed on it—and a stenciled name label stuck to a Velcro patch on the right. It said SMITH. A cordless headset with a boom mike was hooked behind his left ear. When he finally stood up to greet us, you could see a Sig Sauer pistol in a holster on his right hip.

"Good morning, folks," he said. It was the same voice we'd heard on the intercom. "Still is morning, just about. And Mr. Taylor is already on his way over. Just need to see some ID while we're waiting. . . ."

He was happy with Weston's and Lavine's, but raised his eyebrows when he saw the card Tanya had returned to me in the car along with my wallet and other papers.

"Royal Navy?" he said. "You're a bit off the beaten track, aren't you, mate?"

"Telling me," I said. "Tried to go home this morning, but this lot couldn't manage without me."

He was still trying to decide whether I was joking when a door opened behind him and a slender, gray-haired man appeared. He was wearing an identical pseudouniform, but his was a little darker as if it hadn't seen much outdoor action. The name badge said TAYLOR, which saved him the trouble of an introduction.

If Lesley's hit man had been a squirrel, this guy was a mouse. It wasn't that he was particularly small—five eight, five nine at the most—but there was something about the nervous energy in his wiry limbs and tight, pinched face that made him seem jumpy and unsettled. And the impression grew stronger as he guided us through the main office, darting between rows of steel desks like an animal in a laboratory maze. We had a struggle to keep up as he scuttled around the final few banks of metal filing cabinets and disappeared through the door to a meeting room.

The tables in the meeting room were also made of metal. There were four. Each was wide enough for two people. They were arranged in a diamond shape with only their inner corners touching, leaving a square gap in the center. The space had been used to display a Plexiglas sphere. It was two feet in diameter, and was sitting on a wheeled wooden frame like the kind that hold ancient globes in libraries and museums. A chunk of rock was suspended inside. It was a rough pyramid shape, with patches of pitted gray occasionally visible through a thick, uneven crust of white and yellow crystals.

"Interesting," Tanya said. "It looks like a tiny mountain peak, covered in snow. Maybe the Eiger or somewhere like that."

"It could have been, once," Taylor said. "This piece is from Austria, not far from there."

"What is it?"

"Wolframite. Iron-manganese tungstate. It's a mineral."

"Is it valuable?" Lavine said.

"Depends what you value," Taylor said. "We use it as a symbol."

"Of what?"

"Wolframite was the original source of tungsten."

"As in your company name?"

"Exactly. Tungsten has the highest melting point of all metals. Did you know that? Nearly sixty-two hundred degrees. Seems appropriate, given what we do."

"And convenient," I said. "If your office ever burns down."

"Well, let's hope that never happens," Taylor said, taking a seat on the far side of the rock. "Now, make yourselves at home. Let's get down to business. How can I help you?"

"We're interested in a team of contractors you recently let go," Lavine said.

"Can you be any more specific?" Taylor said.

"More specific?" I said. "How many entire teams have you fired in the last couple of weeks?"

"I'm not sure," Taylor said. "It's a busy time for us. I'd need to check with HR. Perhaps if you tell me exactly what you need, I could get back to you in the next couple of days?"

"Agent Weston," Lavine said. "Have you still got that buddy in procurement, at the Department of Defense?'

"Sure," Weston said. "Matter of fact, I owe him a call. I was waiting till I had something to talk about."

"Want to start this conversation again?" Lavine said.

"One," Taylor said. "One team. Six people."

"Why fire them?" I said.

"There was a complaint from the client."

"About what?" I said.

"An allegation of inappropriate treatment of civilians."

"Expand on that," Lavine said.

"The guys were working at a hospital. In Iraq. Top team. Flagship contract. One night, three teenagers were brought in. Gunshot wounds. Took the rounds when their car—which they'd stolen—tried to run a roadblock. A U.S. Marine got hurt in the process. Story is, my guys heard about it, came on the ward, and tried to set things straight right there."

"But you don't believe that," Lavine said.

"No. My guys are professionals. And they're on good money. They wouldn't put all that on the line over some marine they'd never met."

"More likely to do it over someone they did know," I said. "You lost a couple of guys recently, didn't you? The ones Redford and Mansell were brought in to replace."

"First thing I thought of, myself. But no. We've got investigators on the ground. They took a real good look, and it didn't fly."

"So why fire them?" I said.

"The client insisted. Lose the guys, or lose the contract."

"So you chose the contract," Lavine said. "That's cold."

"Not really. What we're doing over there is more important than the short-term welfare of a handful of individual personnel."

"Why not move them to another contract?" I said.

"It doesn't work that way. We're not a typical operator."

"Meaning?" Lavine said.

"We're there for principle, not profit. Our goal is the long-term advancement of the region, not the maximum percentage. We're trying to give something back to a people who've been hit pretty hard, you know? Which means we only take on certain kinds of contracts. Ones that will benefit the local population as well as ourselves. Things like hospital security. Mine clearance. Ammo disposal. Prisoner transport."

"So?" I said.

"To win that kind of business, your reputation is everything. There's no room for anyone with the slightest question mark over them."

"Even if they haven't actually done anything wrong?" I said.

"Look, it's not like we just cut these guys loose. We gave them three months' money. And there's plenty of other work for them, over there. They'll get other jobs if they want them."

"Three months' money?" Weston said. "What's that in dollars?"

"Ballpark? Somewhere between $40K and $60K each. Can't remember the exact package all our guys are on."

"Big numbers," Weston said.

"Above average, yes. But that's what we're about. Above-average people, above-average risks, above-average rewards."

"The team you let go," Lavine said. "Who actually fired them?"

"You mean who sat in the room and gave them the bad news? Me."

"Who else knew?" Lavine said.

"A couple of people in HR. Another couple in operations. Why?"

"We'll need their names," Lavine said. "And a list of people with access to your payroll system."

"What's that—"

"Excuse me a minute, guys," I said. "I need to use your bathroom. No need to call anyone. I saw it on our way in."

No one was speaking when I came back. Lavine had moved to the far side of the wolframite globe. Tanya glowered at me, as if she were annoyed I'd left the room. Taylor was standing with his back to the others, staring blankly out of the window. He looked pale. In his place at the table was a line of four-by-six photographs. If he was telling the truth, the last time he'd seen the people in those pictures, they'd just finished being his employees. And they'd still been alive.

"He was lying," Lavine said, back in the car. "He knew something. You can forget all that friend-of-the-people bullshit. I mean, please."

"It's about the money," Weston said. "Always the same."

"It's not about the money," I said. "I agree with Tanya. It's about the hospital. Something happened over there. Someone did something. Or saw something. We just have to figure out who. Or what."

"How?" Tanya said. "Asking Taylor didn't do much good."

"We can start with this," I said, taking a CD out of my jacket pocket.

"What is it?" Lavine said.

"Debut album from a new Icelandic band," I said. "Björk's brother-in-law. Played the Bowery Ballroom the other night. Heard of them?"

"No."

"Go ahead. Put it on the stereo. It'll help us concentrate."

"Don't think so."

"Well, you're probably right. It might not sound too good. Because it's not really music. It's actually Tungsten's phone bill. Brand-new, fresh out of the envelope."

"On a CD?"

"Of course. Itemized corporate phone bills always come on CD. Unless they want twenty boxes of paper every month."

"Where did it come from?"

"The phone company, would be my guess."

"I mean, how come you've got it?"

"Use your imagination."

"So you didn't really need the bathroom, back there," Tanya said.

"You stole it?" Lavine said.

"That makes it compromised," Weston said. "We can't use it."

"You can't," I said. "But we can. Tanya, could you get some people to take a look?"

"Sure," she said. "Drop me at the consulate. I'll get them straight on it."

"What's it going to give us?" Lavine said.

"Who knows?" I said. "Maybe everything. Maybe nothing. We'll let you know in a couple of hours."

"Worth a try, I suppose," Weston said. "Call us when you're done. Meantime, we'll head back. Check on the other hares we've got running."

"You can drop me at a hotel on the way," I said. "I'll need a room, now that I'm staying a while."

"No problem," Weston said. "Which one? Same as last night?"

"No," I said. "I fancy a change. My favorite room's not available in that place."

"Want us to have a word?" Lavine said. "When we ask, rooms get made available."

"Wouldn't work this time," I said. "They're not done repairing it after the bureau's last visit."

TWENTY-THREE

A few years ago I remember there was a craze for "magic pictures."

They were really just psychedelic blotches that people would stare at for hours, willing their eyes to somehow make coherent images out of the brightly colored speckles. Intelligence analysts wouldn't admit it, but the bulk of their everyday work is very similar. It all hinges on the same skill. Identifying hidden patterns. Only they're not trying to conjure people's faces and mountain ranges out of paint splatter. They're looking for bomb plots and assassination attempts in financial transactions. Currency transfers. Phone calls. E-mail traffic. Internet searches. Passenger manifests. Freight receipts. University registrations. Job applications. Tax returns. Red-flagged purchases. Even old-fashioned letters and faxes.

It's a similar story for us, in the field. Only we have less material to work with.

Less support.

And less time to join the dots.

*

The first guy was waiting near the crosswalk, half hidden behind a street vendor's refreshment stand. He wasn't buying anything. Or eating anything. Or reading anything. He was just waiting, watching the traffic. And occasionally glancing across at the disused store, fifteen yards away. That's where the second guy was, prowling up and down, keeping track of the cars' reflections in the blank glass.

The lights changed, but neither guy made a move toward my side of the road. The lights changed again, and a BMW 5 Series approached. A woman was driving, on her own. The first guy stiffened. The car drew nearer. The guy's weight shifted forward, and he took half a step toward the street. Then he suddenly relaxed and melted back away from the curb. The car cruised past and I saw there was a baby in a child's seat in the back. It was fast asleep.

The lights went through three more cycles and the first guy remained like a statue until another car caught his attention. It was an Audi A6. Another woman was driving. Again, she was on her own. She picked up a little speed, trying to get through the intersection without having to stop when he sprang out into her path. She hit the brakes. The tires screamed. The car's nose pitched down as if it were trying to burrow into the asphalt. The front fender hit the guy below the knees, flipping him into the air. He came down headfirst onto the hood, stuck to the shiny metal for a moment, then slithered forward and tumbled limply into the gutter.

The driver jumped out and raced to the front of the car. The vendor ran to join her. The people who'd been waiting to cross the street quickly gathered round, anxious for a glimpse of blood. And beyond all of them, the second guy peeled away from the store window and casually drifted across the sidewalk.

I crossed the street, heading for the back of the car. The second guy didn't see me. He was too focused on the crowd. He reached the open driver's door without anyone noticing him. He reached inside. The woman's briefcase and purse were lying on the floorboard, on the passenger's side, where they'd fallen. The guy stretched across, hooked his fingers through the handles, and smoothly backed out of the car. It had taken him less than two seconds, and no one else had seen what he was doing.

I let him get clear of the trunk before hitting him. I didn't want him to land on the car, or make any noise when he fell. My fist made a good clean contact and he went down like a stone, the side of his face banging against the base of a mailbox. I quickly checked him over. He was breathing, but out cold.

The woman's purse had rolled a few feet away across the sidewalk so I retrieved it, scooped up her briefcase, and tossed both bags back into the car. I took the keys from the ignition and found the button to lock the doors. Then I dropped my shoulder and waded into the gawking crowd.

"Let me through," I said. "I'm a medic. Out of the way."

"Don't touch him, man," one of the onlookers said. "He'll sue you."

"He won't," I said.

"Is he dead?" the driver said. "Have I killed him? I

didn't see him. He came out of nowhere. Just stepped out . . ."

"Don't worry," I said. "He's not hurt at all. Not yet, anyway."

I took hold of the guy's fake Armani lapels and hauled him up until he was slumped on his back across the Audi's hood.

"Stop," the same onlooker said. "You can't move him. He might have a neck injury."

"He might now," I said, leaning down and pressing the point of my elbow into the guy's throat, just above his collarbone.

"The hell are you doing? How's this going to help him?"

"It's a new resuscitation technique, from England. Twenty seconds. Thirty max, and he'll be awake. Trust me."

It actually took fifteen. The guy started to twitch. Then wriggle. Then thrash about, clawing at my arm and trying to wrench it free. I let him squirm for another moment then took hold of his right hand, locked his wrist, and flipped him over onto his front.

"See?" I said, handing the keys back to the driver. "It was a scam. This guy, to make you stop. His buddy back there to grab your stuff."

"Well, I'll be . . ." the onlooker said.

"I don't believe it," the driver said. "I was so worried. The assholes."

"Want to stick one on him?" I said. "I'll hold him."

A phone started to ring. I realized it was mine.

"Excuse me a moment," I said, pulling the phone out left-handed.

It was Weston.

"Got a breakthrough," he said. "Where are you?"

"Shopping," I said. "I need clean clothes."

"Time for that later. We need to move. Where can we collect you?"

"Back where you dropped me. In five."

"Be there," Weston said, hanging up.

I put the phone away.

"Feeling better?" I said to the driver. "OK then. Time to call 911. These guys have done this before. They need to be stopped. Now that's up to you."

Weston's Ford was already waiting at the side of the street when I got back. Tanya was in the backseat. She looked a little confused.

"I don't see it," she said. "That doesn't prove anything, either way."

"What doesn't?" I said, getting in.

"Tungsten made another set of payoffs," Weston said. "A year ago. To another team of six guys."

"How do you know?" I said.

"Our forensic accountants found it. They started digging this morning. Got an early break. But listen to this. The other team—it was also assigned to the hospital right before getting fired."

"So the hospital is the link."

"No. It can't be."

"Why not?"

"Because none of the six we just found out about are dead."

"So?"

"If the hospital was the link, they'd have been killed, too."

"No. That's backward. If the payoff money was the link, they'd have been killed."

"See?" Tanya said. "It's totally inconclusive. The hospital and the money are both common factors. And at this moment, there's just no evidence to place one above the other."

"Has any money been taken from the current six?" I said.

"Not from two of them," Lavine said. "We're still checking the others."

"Not very convincing," I said. "Whereas both teams were definitely working at the hospital. That's the clincher. Something about the place got them fired. Has to be."

"Right," Weston said. "They were fired because of the hospital. But not killed because of it. It has to be two separate things."

"Taylor called them tough clients," Lavine said. "Maybe he was right about that."

"Otherwise, why bring the team home?" Weston said. "Why pay them off? Why not just kill them in Iraq?"

"That would be cheaper," Lavine said. "Easier. Less risky."

"Could make it look like another mob got them," Weston said. "Or an ambush. Or friendly fire. No one would think twice. And there's no one like us over there to sniff around."

"Will you three stop speculating?" Tanya said. "You're wasting time. Let's just talk to this guy. We should get it from the horse's mouth."

"Which guy?" I said.

"From the original team," Tanya said. "Five have gone overseas again, but one of them's here in New York."

"Didn't we tell you?" Weston said. "I spoke to his wife before I called you. That's how we knew about him working at the hospital."

"So where is he?" I said. "Your office?"

"No," Weston said. "At his job. He works construction, now."

A framed, five-foot-square artist's impression was attached to every panel of rough blue hoarding that separated the pedestrians on East Twenty-third Street from the spindly steel skeleton rising out of the narrow lot on the other side. There were eight pictures altogether. Each one gave a different vision of the finished building, from a grand marble-lined lobby to a serene Japanese roof garden, complete with tiny bronze sculptures.

Weston pulled up next to a designer couple power-snacking at a granite breakfast bar, and we had to walk past the view from one of the balconies to reach the foreman's compound.

"How tall is this place going to be?" Tanya said, staring at the pictures.

"Not tall enough," Weston said, hammering on the wooden gate. "Except for maybe the penthouse. Won't see the Chrysler, lower down. The Met Life's in the way."

"And the Empire State's not that high," Lavine said.

"Shame," Tanya said. "Three buildings, each the tallest in the world at one time, all from your living room window. What a view that would be."

Eventually the foreman ambled across to talk to us.

"Yeah?" he said. "What? I'm busy here."

"FBI," Weston said. "Looking for Julio Arca."

"Not here."

"His wife said he was working today."

"He is. Not back yet."

"When do you expect him?"

"Don't know."

"Where did he go?"

"The park. 'Cross there. With the other guys."

"His coworkers?"

"No. Guys in suits. Like you."

"Like us? How many?"

"Two."

"When did they go?"

"Don't know. Ten minutes ago. Fifteen maybe?"

"What does he look like, this Julio?"

"Like a regular guy."

"Age?"

"Thirties, I guess."

"Height?"

"Five ten, maybe."

"Hair?"

"Buzz cut. But he had a hard hat on."

"Mustache? Beard?"

"No. Shaved."

"Clothes?"

"Boots. Coveralls, like me. And a fluorescent vest."

The little park was swarming with people. They were sitting on benches, sprawling next to statues, lying on the grass, walking their dogs, lining up to buy coffee from an outdoor café. Some were on their own. Others were in groups. Some were wearing suits. Several were in work clothes. But none matched the description we had for Arca.

The path from the gate at the southeast corner was one of six that radiated out from an ornamental fountain on the far side of the café. Another oval path crossed in front of us, a few yards in. Lavine paused when he reached it.

"Better split up," he said. "I'll go straight on. Kyle, you go left. Dave and Tanya, you go right. You on the air?"

Tanya patted her bag.

"Good," he said. "RV at the fountain if you don't find anything."

Weston was the first to come through on the radio.

"On me," he said. "Statue, southwest corner. Code blue."

Lavine reached him just before us.

"What have you got?" he said.

"Found him. But there's a problem. I think we're too late."

Weston led the way round the outer path until we reached another monument. From a distance it looked like a giant candlestick, but as we drew closer I saw it was actually a stout, white flagpole with a five-pointed star at the top. Seven people were gathered around its square stone base. A woman, eating sandwiches. Another listening to an MP3 player. Another on the phone. Three teenagers, sitting together at the far corner, talking. And one man. He was leaning back against a carved plaque. His hard hat was lying on the plinth next to him, upside down. Clumps of fresh mud had fallen from the cleats on his work boots and the leather on the toes was torn and scuffed. His yellow vest was rucked up under his arms as if he'd slumped down from a standing position. His neck was twisted sharply to the right. His eyes were shut. And his tongue was lolling out from his mouth like a giant pink slug.

"See what I mean?" Weston said.

"How did this happen?" Lavine said.

"Must have been the two guys he left his job with," Weston said. "I already checked for them. No sign."

"What about these people?" Tanya said. "Someone must have seen something."

"Wouldn't count on it," I said.

"Kyle, call it in," Lavine said. "I want the place sealed off. Nobody leaves. Everyone gets questioned. Twice. See if there's any CCTV from the streets or the park. Or the construction site. Get forensics here. And the ME. Tell them to put a rush on it. We'll make a start with these guys."

"Hang on a second," I said. "Who checked his vitals? Or are we just making assumptions, here?"

"Kyle?" Lavine said.

"No," he said. "I pulled back and called you guys."

"You don't think . . . ?" Tanya said.

I stepped forward and reached toward his neck with two fingers. But before I made contact the guy's right arm whipped up and his fingers clamped tight around my wrist.

"Afternoon, Julio," I said. "Or should we call you Lazarus?"

Lavine and Weston wanted to arrest the guy on the spot, but I persuaded them that a sandwich and a coffee at the park café would be a more productive option.

"OK, then," Lavine said, after taking a swig of cappuccino and munching through a couple of biscotti. "I'm ready to talk. What was that about, back there, Julio? Are you a Boris Karloff fan or something?"

"Relax, man," Arca said. "I was just checking you out."

"Checking us out? Who do you think you are?"

"A guy with a cell phone."

"Meaning?"

"You think people don't talk, because we're not in the service now? You think I don't know six more Tungsten guys got canned, the same as me? And five are dead?"

"Let me see the phone," Weston said.

Arca took a small silver Motorola from his coverall pocket and put it on the table. Weston picked it up and prodded a couple of buttons.

"It's not the phone that called Raab," he said. "But your wife called you. Right after we spoke to her."

Arca didn't reply.

"She told you we were coming. That's why you tried to run. Doesn't make you look good, Julio."

"Five guys are dead," Arca said. "My wife gets a call out of nowhere. You tell her you're the feds. How does she know?"

"So you set this up with your boss? You're getting paranoid."

"He established a viable cover," I said. "Headed for a populated area. Created a diversion. Observed our reactions. Pretty smart, I'd say."

"We'll come back to that," Lavine said. "But right now, tell me why you got fired from Tungsten."

"Don't know," Arca said.

"You got fired from a job paying you a couple of hundred grand a year, and you didn't ask why?"

"Oh, yeah, we asked. Fed us some 'client complaint' bullshit."

"Why did the client complain? What did you do?"

"Nothing."

"What about your buddies?"

"Nothing."

"So they fired you for no reason. How'd that make you feel?"

"Great."

"Yeah?"

"Yeah. They gave me fifty-five grand. The chance to retrain. Now I got money in the bank. I don't have to go overseas to earn a living. And people don't try to kill me every day."

"What did you do at the hospital?" I said.

"In Iraq? Premises team."

"There was more than one team?" Lavine said.

"Right. There were three teams. Premises—that was us. Supplies—they guarded the medicine trucks coming in. And close protection—they went with the doctors when they were off-site."

"What about the team that just got fired?" I said.

"Premises team, the way I heard."

"These overseas guys, they have weird traditions," I said. "They can be very sensitive. Easy to offend. Are you sure . . ."

"I know about their traditions. We get training before we go over there. I'd been three times, already. And we did nothing wrong. None of us."

"Then did you see anything strange? Out of place? Maybe something that didn't hit you till later?"

"No. Nothing like that. It was a hospital. Sick people, funny smell. It was boring. Why are you asking me these things? When are you going to ask me about James Mansell?"

"Why ask about him?"

"Because he killed those other guys."

"He did? Why? How do you know?"

"Look. Six people get payouts. They go freeriding together. Nothing unusual about that. Lots of guys do after their final tour. But then five of them don't come back. You do the math. And do it quick. I'm the only ex-Tungsten guy left around here. Don't want him coming back for my slice of pie."

Lavine kept himself under control until Arca had disappeared through the trees. Then he slammed his palm down on the table so hard it sent a wave of leftover coffee slopping into his saucer. People glanced at us from other tables. Tanya fidgeted, uncomfortable with the attention, and began to chew her lower lip. Weston stayed still, but I saw his knuckles whitening around the arms of his chair.

"What now?" he said.

Tanya shrugged.

"Anyone got a quarter?" Lavine said.

"Feel a big tip coming on?" I said.

"I'm thinking about James Mansell," he said. "Heads, he's in mortal danger. Tails, he's a mass murderer."

"But which?" Tanya said. "Or maybe both?"

"Doesn't matter right now," Weston said. "Either way, we've got to find him."

"Agreed," Tanya said. "But how? Arca was useless as a lead. Tungsten was a dead end. And now we're looking for one guy who could be anywhere in the whole of the United States."

"Or Mexico," Weston said.

"Don't forget Canada," Lavine said.

"Anywhere in the world, then," Tanya said. "And that's some haystack for the four of us to comb through."

TWENTY-FOUR

When I heard that expression as a kid I always thought it was stupid. How could a needle possibly end up in a haystack? And why would anyone care?

When I got a little older I thought, *So a needle's in there, and we need it back. No problem. Get some matches. Hay burns. Needles don't.*

Later still I thought, *Why waste time on a fire? Use a magnet. Make the needle come to you.*

Eventually, when I thought about it a little more, I put it all together. It's not about whether you need matches or a magnet, at all. It's about knowing where to get the right tools for the job.

Tanya's phone rang as we were trudging back through the aimless clusters of people still frittering their time away in the fading afternoon sunshine. It was Lucinda, her assistant at the consulate. They'd finished crunching Tungsten's phone records ahead of schedule and wanted to talk her through the results. Tanya listened intently. A satisfied smile spread across her face. And finally she said if they could knock out five copies in the time it would take us to collect Weston's car and get over to Third Avenue, she'd stop by and collect them herself.

The detour via the consulate didn't add much journey time. The traffic was light for a Wednesday, and Weston left the engine running while Tanya ducked inside to pick up the stack of fat manila envelopes. She got back in the car without a word, and no one broke the silence until we were away from the curb and moving again.

"I better call the boss," Lavine said, taking out his cell phone. "Tell him we're coming in."

The call lasted the rest of the way back to the FBI garage.

"Varley's not here," he said, after Weston had finished tucking the car neatly into its bay. "He's gone to sort out some other crisis. So there's no point going all the way upstairs. May as well just head for the twenty-third."

Tanya wouldn't part with the reports until Lavine had collected the chair from his desk and wheeled it into the glass booth with the others.

"You can skip section one," Tanya said, when everyone had finally opened their plastic binders. "That covers landlines. People have seen too many cop shows to use a regular phone for anything suspicious. They always use their cell phones for that. Psychologically it seems like no wires, no records. The fools."

"Section two's just a list of numbers," Weston said.

"Correct. We pulled out the numbers of all Tungsten's

own handsets. Then we looked at the itemized records and identified all the calls from company cell phones to other company cell phones, and from company cell phones to company landlines. Everything not on that list was a cell phone call to someone outside the company. That's all in section three."

"Long list," Lavine said.

"Correct again. So we narrowed it down. First with a reverse directory. Then with Google. That took care of 95 percent of the numbers. My people called the rest. Said they were from the phone company, checking records, if anyone answered. They kept trying, or took the details off their voice mail greetings if no one picked up. Tedious work, but worth it. Take a look at what we found. That's section four."

"Six numbers," Weston said. "With dates against five of them."

"That shows when the last calls were made from Tungsten to those numbers. The dates don't stand out?"

"They do to me," I said.

"They should to all of you. They're also the dates that Simon and the four Americans were killed."

"They all received a call from the same cell phone the day they died," Weston said.

"Correct."

"From someone going after the money," Weston said.

"Not necessarily."

"It had to be," Lavine said. "But who?"

"Don't know. We only have the originating number, not a name. We called it, but no one answered."

"Voice mail?" Lavine said. "Did you leave a message?"

"No. It didn't go through to a mailbox."

"What about the sixth number?" Weston said.

"There's something about it . . ." Lavine said.

"It's the only one we couldn't account for. It received its last call from Tungsten the day after Simon's, but before two of the Americans."

"It's James Mansell's phone," I said.

"I think so, too. It has to be. Which means . . ."

"Mansell's dead as well," I said.

"Oh, no," Lavine said, standing up and striding toward the door. "It doesn't. Stay there. Don't move. There's something I've got to show you."

Lavine rummaged through the clutter on his desk for over a minute, then came back into the booth brandishing a blue Post-it note.

"Take a look at this," he said.

It was the same number.

"Where did you get that?" Tanya said.

"In Raab's paperwork," Lavine said. "It's the number of the guy he was planning to meet, Sunday night. When he was killed."

"It was Mansell that Mike was due to meet?" Weston said. "No. How could that be?"

"Mansell must have survived the attacks on his buddies," Tanya said. "Then tried to get help when he realized the trouble he was in."

"Needing help, I understand," I said. "But how on earth did he end up in touch with Raab?"

"It makes sense, if you think about it," Lavine said. "It's standard procedure. Mike's team floods everywhere they work with flyers. They ask people to call a hotline. The calls are screened. Anyone genuine would have been passed up the chain."

"All the way to Mike?" I said.

"Absolutely," Lavine said. "Mike was a hands-on guy. He liked to judge for himself whether people were on the level."

"It does fit," Weston said. "We know Mike was meeting someone with a British accent, remember. That's why the NYPD suspected you. One reason, anyway."

"Then why meet in an alley?" I said. "Why not an office, or police station?"

"To keep the killer in play," Lavine said. "In case he was watching. Mike didn't want to scare him off."

"So what went wrong?" Tanya said.

"Mansell must have arrived after Mike was already dead," Lavine said.

"He would have seen what happened, and figured the Tungsten guy got there first," Weston said. "The same guy who killed his buddies."

"Then he would have run, figuring there was a leak from the bureau," Lavine said. "He'd have thought, how else would the Tungsten guy know about his meeting with Raab?"

"That's pretty much the same assumption we made," Weston said.

"And it's not impossible," Lavine said. "Tungsten is hooked up with the DOD. Why not with the bureau, as well?"

"I'll tell you something else it explains," Weston said. "Why Mike didn't put up a fight."

"Right," Lavine said. "That part never sat right with me. But now we know. When this guy from Lesley's scam walked into the alley, Mike thought it was Mansell."

"It explains a lot," Weston said. "And it proves Mansell is alive. Or was, at least up to Sunday night."

"Poor fellow," Tanya said. "His friends are dead, he's been scared off the bureau, and he thinks the guy from Tungsten is still after him."

"The guy from Tungsten probably is still after him," I said.

"Then we've got to find him," Tanya said. "And stop him. Fast."

"We need a warrant," Weston said. "Then we can go back to Tungsten's compound. Tear the place apart."

"How long will that take?" I said.

"A day?" Lavine said. "A couple of days? We need to convince a judge. Which will be hard, since we can't use any of this evidence. You poisoned the fruit, my friend."

"We could be a little more direct," I said.

"And what, break in?" Weston said.

"No," I said. "We have Mansell's number. We could use that."

"I already tried," Lavine said. "I called it as soon as we found it in Mike's papers. There was no answer."

"Same for us," Tanya said. "That's why we couldn't identify it, remember?"

"Where did you call from?" I said.

"Here," Lavine said.

"The consulate," Tanya said.

"If you were Mansell, would you have answered those calls?"

"I guess not," Lavine said. "I didn't know what he was likely thinking, when we tried it."

"So where should we call from?" Tanya said. "How do we make him answer?"

"We can't," Weston said. "Forget the phone."

"We don't call him," I said. "We text him. From Tanya's cell phone. Then he gets the message without having to answer."

"My cell?" Tanya said. "Why? What do we say?"

"We tell him the truth," I said. "He's friends with your brother. You heard he's in trouble. You want to help."

"The truth," Weston said. "That'll work."

Tanya sent the message. A minute passed. Two minutes. There was no response. Weston and Lavine exchanged glances. Tanya gazed at the floor.

"We should get started on the warrant," Weston said.

"You're right," Lavine said, getting to his feet. "Sorry, guys. Worth a try. Come on, Kyle."

Tanya stayed in the booth, with me.

"What now?" she said.

"We try again," I said. "Put yourself in Mansell's shoes.

What's he thinking? When he sees the message, what's he afraid of?"

"A trap. The Tungsten guy, trying to finish what he started on the railways."

"Could be. Or?"

"A crooked fed. Because he's going to think his meeting with Raab was betrayed. He's got no way of knowing about the wires being crossed with Lesley's guy."

"Right. So this time put in some details that only you would know, because of your brother. And tell him the thing with Raab wasn't what it seemed. That there's no problem between him and the bureau."

Tanya poked awkwardly at the tiny keys until she was happy with the message.

"Sent," she said. "I hate texting. I hope he answers this time."

We waited five minutes. There was no reply.

"What now?" Tanya said.

"Try again," I said. "Tell him you work at the consulate, and you can get him out of the country in one piece if he needs you to."

"Done," she said after a moment, dropping the phone on the chair Weston had been using. "I don't know why teenagers like this so much."

Thirty seconds later there was a sound like a cartoon arrow hitting a target.

"It's him," Tanya said, snatching the phone back up. "Look."

this is james. do need help

"OK," I said. "Go ahead. Reply."

where r u, she sent.

nyc. in danger

am also in nyc. go to nearest police station. will meet u there

no police

ok. come to consulate. 845 3rd ave. round corner from grand central. ask 4 me

no2 dangerous

"Not exactly bending over backward, is he?" she said.

"Frightened people need to feel some control," I said. "Give him the choice. Ask him where he'd feel safe."

where then? can't help if can't meet, she sent.

bulldog pub. w4th st. know it?

i'll find it. when?

tonight?

ok. time?

21:00

ok. c u later.

sit at bar. i'll find u. COME ALONE

ok. will be ALONE

"Excellent," I said. "He's on the hook. We just need to reel him in. Then we can take some time for ourselves."

"Don't get ahead of yourself," Tanya said. "Plenty can still go wrong."

"I didn't know you were such a 'glass half empty' person."

"I'm not. I'm more of a 'what glass are you talking about?' person. As in, down to earth. You're already dreaming about tomorrow. I'm still wondering whether to tell Tweedledum and Tweedledee about tonight."

"Do you want to tell them?"

"Not particularly."

"Do you know what Mansell looks like?"

"Yes. Lucinda pulled his record. He looks a bit like you, actually."

"Could we borrow Lucinda for the evening? Get her to sit with me while I keep an eye on you?"

"Mansell said come alone. He seemed clear on that."

"You will be alone. I'll be with Lucinda. Couples are less conspicuous. And if you tell the feds they'll bring dozens of guys. Probably helicopters and everything."

"Seems a bit OTT just to meet a friend of my brother's."

"Shocking waste of tax dollars."

"And it would be nice to see their faces in the morning, when we bring Mansell in all safe and sound."

"Especially if he dishes the dirt on that hospital first . . ."

TWENTY-FIVE

When I began my training, there was one exercise that nobody was looking forward to. Withstanding interrogation. There were too many rumors about exactly how realistic the experience was going to be. But when the course schedule was finally handed out I could see no mention of it. I remember sitting with the paper in my hand, studying each of the titles, wondering where in the jargon it was hidden. And obviously no one was stupid enough to ask.

The exercise after the fake fridge company was also based in the field. Each of us was dropped in a different town in Devon and given four hours to get hold of the full names, addresses, passport numbers, and bank account details from a pair of civilians. It didn't matter who they were, as long as the information was genuine. It sounded pretty straightforward. We all set off happy, confident of another tick in the box. Plus an afternoon in a nice seaside pub if we worked fast enough.

Ten minutes after jumping down from the bus we'd all been snatched back off the street. We were each thrown in the back of a van. Sacking was tied roughly over our heads and we were driven to an abandoned abattoir. What happened next wasn't nice. But it did teach us two things. How to keep our mouths shut, at least for a while. And that circumstances are rarely as they first may seem.

I never forgot the first part.

I should have paid more attention to the second.

The consulate Jaguar had dropped Lucinda and me outside the Broadway branch of Rhythm & Booze at dead-on 7:30 P.M. We mingled with the little group of early-evening drinkers that was gathering outside until the car was well out of sight. Then we made our way toward the rendezvous point, circling the area and looking for anyone who could be watching the place from a vehicle, a building, or on foot. Lucinda thought I was paranoid, the length of time we took, but I made her stick with it. She wasn't the one who'd be facing Lavine the next morning.

The Bulldog itself turned out to be a typical theme pub—a square, characterless multipurpose unit clumsily dressed up to look like something it wasn't. There were fake Yorkshire flagstones on the floor, a rectangular mahogany and brass bar tacked on to the back wall, a pool table and one-armed bandits to the left, and four dingy booths in a row on the right. We checked that no one was lurking there or in the restrooms, and by 8:00 P.M. were settled on hard wooden chairs at the side of the drafty doorway. I had a bottle of Newcastle Brown on the round table in front of us. Lucinda had a gin and tonic.

Twenty-three people entered the pub over the next hour. Seventeen were men. Nine were on their own. Five were in the right age range. And none of them looked anything like the photo of Mansell that Lucinda had brought in her purse.

Tanya arrived at a minute to nine. She stood on her own near the door for a few moments, gazing around the room as if she were taken by the oversized photos of wartime London that were plastered all over the walls. Then she stepped up to the bar, took the middle one of the three remaining stools, and ordered a drink.

"Looks different, doesn't she?" Lucinda said.

"A little, maybe," I said.

The truth was she looked very different. It wasn't just the jeans and casual blouse, or the way she'd left her hair untied. It was her whole manner. She seemed tense and twitchy, like someone on speed. That wasn't like her at all. It brought home to me how much the need to exorcize the ghosts of Morocco must be eating away at her. I just hoped Mansell would show his face. And if he did, that her spikiness wouldn't scare him away again.

"Who is this guy we're supposed to meet?" Lucinda said.

"No one special," I said.

"Then why are we bothering?"

Good question, I thought. *Ask Tanya, and her overactive sense of guilt.*

"He's a U.K. citizen," I said. "He's in danger. Needs our help."

"We help lots of citizens," Lucinda said. "But they usually come to us. What's different about this guy?"

"Hold on," I said. "Watch this. We have a possible contact."

A man was sidling along next to the bar, looking mainly at the floor but occasionally glancing up at Tanya. He was short and fat, in his forties with thinning hair, saggy jeans, and a Chelsea soccer shirt at least two seasons out of date.

Lucinda sighed.

"You have no idea what it's like for a woman in a pub on her own, have you?" she said. "It's just a creep hitting on her. Happens all the time."

The guy put his hand on Tanya's shoulder and leaned in close to whisper something in her ear. I couldn't hear her reply, but it must have hit the spot. He didn't hang around. And none of his pals tried their luck, either, after that. Which was just as well.

At nine thirty Tanya took out her cell phone and labored through the process of sending a text. She tapped out another at ten. And at ten thirty, and eleven. Then thirty minutes later she stood up, put the phone away, and headed for the exit. The door hinged inward, and as she pulled it open Tanya curled her first two fingers around the leading edge.

"Phase two," I said to Lucinda. "Time to go."

Lucinda and I stood close together at the edge of the sidewalk and stared in opposite directions, arms poised as if waiting to flag down a cab. Tanya was on our left, strolling casually back toward Broadway. Nothing developed for thirty seconds. Then another guy came out of the pub. He paused next to Lucinda and also looked down the street. But he was only interested in one direction. Tanya's. He watched her intently for ten seconds then started after her, sticking to the shadows. He was moving just fast enough to draw level before the end of the block.

"Creepy guy," Lucinda said. "But too short for Mansell."

"So who is he?" I said.

"What do you think? Pervert?"

"Don't know. Could be. Let's find out."

We moved off together, keeping pace with the guy from the pub. I felt for my phone and held down the 3 key with my thumb. It was set to speed-dial Mansell's number. Five seconds passed. Six. Then the guy reacted. His left arm twitched, reaching for his pocket, and I heard a brief snatch of muffled ring tone.

Tanya was closer and she heard the phone, too. She stopped and turned. Both the guy's hands disappeared into his coat pockets. He silenced the ringing with his left, and pulled something out with his right. It was small. Brown. Wooden, with brass ends, like a flattened tube. There was a button halfway down its long edge. The guy pressed it and a four-inch blade scythed out from the side and locked into place. He lifted the knife up. The steel was gleaming orange under the streetlights. The point was level with Tanya's throat.

I was too far away to reach him. If he moved now Tanya would be dead before I could make up half the distance.

"Stop," I said. "Armed police. Drop your weapon or I will fire."

The guy froze, but the knife stayed in his hand.

I kept going. I was nearly there.

"Armed police," I said. "Drop your weapon. You've been warned."

He slowly turned to face me, raising the knife and angling it toward my chin.

"Now, it seems you have two problems," he said, in a flawless BBC accent. "You don't look like a policeman. And you don't look like you're armed. So tell me again, why I should drop anything?"

"We're looking for a missing person," I said. "Another Englishman. We're worried about him. All we need to know is who you are, and where you got that phone. Tell us, and there's no need for anyone to get hurt."

"Firstly, I'm not English, you presumptuous ass. I don't care what happens to your countrymen. And secondly, who is going to hurt me? You? Or these women?"

"No one wants to hurt you. We just want your help."

The guy snorted disdainfully.

"OK," I said. "If that's not a good enough reason, how about money? Put the knife down and we'll talk. Dollars, pounds, euros—whichever you prefer."

The guy pursed his lips, nodded thoughtfully, and began to lower the knife. He traced an imaginary line down the center of my body from my throat, past my chest and stomach and as far as my waist. Then he lunged at me, thrusting forward and trying to drive the blade back up under my rib cage. I jumped back and shot out both arms, crossed at the wrists, trapping his hand and stopping him an inch short of skewering me. The guy tried to pull away so I grabbed his wrist with my left hand, forced it over, and jabbed one knuckle from my right fist into the fleshy part of his forearm. He yelled. The knife clattered onto the sidewalk. I kicked it aside and flicked my right fist up square against his cheekbone, disorienting him. Then I punched him hard in the solar plexus, doubling him over, and slammed my fist upward into his face to stand him upright again. He was sagging now, bleeding heavily from the mouth and nose, barely able to breathe. The job was nearly done.

I drew my arm back, ready to unload the final blow, but before I could launch it his whole body was suddenly bathed in light. It was coming from the street. I realized a car engine was running, close by. It was stationary. Then a door opened, followed by another a second later. I heard footsteps. Two sets. One moving straight toward me, the other peeling away to the right.

"NYPD," a woman's voice said. "Stand still. Nobody move."

"The phone," I said to the guy. "Where did you get it? Tell me and we'll help you. We can make this go away."

"Shut up," the officer said. "Hands where I can see them. All of you. Do it now."

Tanya and Lucinda complied straightaway. I gave the

guy another couple of seconds to answer, then let go of his wrist and raised my own hands. He staggered sideways, slumped against the wall, and struggled to get his arms up to chest level.

"You, in the leather coat," the officer said. "Turn and face me."

"Can't do that," I said. "Can't turn my back on this guy. He's a psychopath. Wanted by the FBI. Multiple homicide."

"Shut up. Turn around. Do it now."

"Listen to me. My name is David Trevellyan. I'm working with the FBI. Special Agent Lavine is in charge. His number is in my phone. I'm going to reach inside my jacket and—"

"No. Don't move. Hands where I can see them."

"David, quick," Tanya said. "Stop him."

The guy from the pub was smiling. But not an ordinary smile. A fervent, ecstatic smile. And his right hand was moving again. It was snaking back toward his inside pocket. This time the officers didn't bother with a warning. They just fired. Two rounds each. Tight pattern, to the center of his chest. After that—epiphany or not—there's really no way back.

"Too slow," Tanya said. "Damn it. We needed him alive."

"Maybe not," I said. "Look at his hand."

The officers had shredded a number of the guy's vital organs, but they'd missed the thing he'd been reaching for.

Mansell's phone.

TWENTY-SIX

My first cellular phone was enormous.

It was so big it had to be fixed permanently in my car. I remember watching it being installed. The engineers had to dismantle half the interior, like customs officers searching for drugs. They put in amplifiers, speakers, microphones, antennas, miles of wiring, separate fuses, a big cradle for the handset. And even then it didn't work very well. Today's phones are much better. They're smaller. More powerful. More reliable. Easier to use.

And able to do more than just make calls.

Lavine thought the events outside the Bulldog were significant enough to bring back his boss, so Varley was called in for the next morning's meeting. That meant heading up to the boardroom. The three FBI guys were already there when Tanya and I arrived, just shy of eight thirty. Varley was waiting in his seat. Someone had left a tray of coffees on the table next to him. Weston was helping himself to one. And Lavine was busy setting out piles of papers in the places we'd each used last time we'd met.

I gathered up the thicker pile he'd left near my seat and started to flick through it. The top sheet was a list of calls. Next were transcripts of text messages, including the ones Tanya had sent yesterday about meeting Mansell. The rest were photographs. There were seventeen. They'd been blown up to eight by ten inches, leaving the color washed out and the images grainy and fragmented. Typical of a low-resolution camera-phone.

"Morning," Varley said. "Come on, join us. Grab a coffee. Take a seat. Don't want to waste any time, today. Bartman, lead off, please."

"Thank you, sir," Lavine said, holding up the thinner stack of papers. "This is the list of calls made from one of the phones recovered in last night's incident. It corresponds exactly with the records David acquired at Tungsten's offices, and it shows a call to each of our previous victims shortly prior to their deaths."

He paused and looked in turn at each person in the room, as if inviting questions. No one spoke.

"So, it's safe to conclude we know who murdered the five ex-Tungsten employees," he said. "The owner of that phone. The same guy now lying in the morgue, courtesy of the NYPD. Anyone disagree?"

No one spoke.

"Which is great news," Varley said. "Case closed. A little unorthodox. Not quite the result I'd expected, but good work anyway, guys. Let's chalk this one up to Mike. We should have more than coffee in here. And of course special thanks go to you, Ms. Wilson."

"To me?" Tanya said. "Why?"

"Your input was crucial," Varley said. "Recognizing the crime-scene photos was a huge break for us. We may never have found the link to Tungsten without it. You put us on the right track."

"Don't mention it," Tanya said. "I'm glad to help catch the man who killed my brother's friend."

"Oh, my," Varley said. "Aren't I the sensitive one. I forgot how you knew the guy. I hope this leads you to some sort of closure."

"Thank you," Tanya said. "I'm sure it will. I'm just sorry that no one will stand trial for it. Doesn't feel like proper justice, this way."

"The guy's dead," I said. "That works for me."

"No, I'm with Ms. Wilson," Varley said. "The outcome was regrettable. Obviously we can't go back and change it now. But what we can do is make sure the case holds together. So Kyle, first thing, I want you to sit on forensics."

"Sir," Weston said.

"Make sure they stay the course on this one," Varley said. "It would be nice to tie the guy in a little tighter than just the phone calls."

"He also had Mansell's cell," Weston said.

"He did," Varley said. "That's got to be significant. But what else do we know about him?"

"Not much, to be honest," Lavine said. "His name's Salif Hamad. Iraqi citizen. Entered the U.S. legally, eight weeks ago, via JFK. Employed by Tungsten Security, which is no surprise. But there's a lot else we don't know. I wouldn't be hanging the flags out yet, if it was me."

"What's on your mind?" Varley said.

"A few things," Lavine said. "Like we think he killed the other five guys, but why did he do it? We can't put this to bed without knowing why."

"The money," Weston said. "Hamad worked at Tungsten. He could have had access to all kinds of records. We need a full workup on the guy. See what shape he was in, financially. Also, we need to follow up on the warrant. Find out exactly what his job gave him sight of."

"I'm still not convinced about the money," Tanya said.

"We can't rule it out just yet," Varley said. "Stay with it, Kyle. Anything else, Bartman?"

"Yes," Lavine said. "Mansell. If he's alive, we should find him. Something doesn't add up. If Hamad had Mansell's cell, I want to know how he got it. And when."

"I see where you're going," Weston said. "Mansell contacted Mike. To set up the meeting. If he'd lost his cell, how did he make the call?"

"That's exactly what I'm thinking," Lavine said.

"I can answer that," Tanya said. "These other papers—they're from Mansell's phone?"

"They are," Lavine said.

"OK," Tanya said. "If we compare the two lists of calls, what do we see? Let's start with my brother's friend, Simon Redford, whose body you found. A call comes in to his phone from Hamad, the morning of the day he died. Four minutes later, Redford called Mansell. They talked for eight minutes. There was no further activity on either phone until later that afternoon. Then Mansell tried to call Redford ten, twelve, fourteen times. All were unsuccessful. And straight after the last try, he called this toll-free number. See that?"

"It's the hotline number Mike set up," Weston said.

"I guessed that," Tanya said. "So this is what I think happened. Redford told Mansell about the call from Hamad, and how they were going to meet. Then maybe Mansell heard about another freerider being killed, or maybe he just got nervous when Redford didn't answer his phone. Either way, he was spooked enough to call for help."

"But why call us?" Varley said. "How would Mansell know the hotline number?"

"He got it from the flyers Agent Lavine told us about yesterday," Tanya said. "You were away somewhere when we discussed it. Anyway, Redford was the third to be killed, remember. Then the next day, look, Mansell himself took a call from Hamad. After that there's nothing till you guys found the number in Mike's paperwork and started trying it yourselves."

"So you think Mansell met with Hamad?" Varley said. "He was that stupid, after what happened to his buddy?"

"After what he thought happened," Tanya said. "My guess is he went looking for answers. He got some, of a sort. And it only cost him his phone, not his life, unlike the others."

"And if he didn't have his cell, he couldn't warn the other two," Lavine said. "That explains how Hamad could still pick them off, one at a time."

"Wow, back up," Varley said. "How do we know it didn't cost Mansell his life? I still don't see a compelling reason."

"Thinking about it, we don't know," I said.

"No, we don't," Weston said. "Yesterday, we assumed he'd survived because he called Mike. But based on that sequence from Tanya, he could have been killed any time after he set up the meeting. Especially if he ran into Hamad."

"We have no proof Mansell ever made it to the alley," Lavine said.

"And everything else would have unfolded the same whether Mansell made it or not," Weston said. "Mike was in place ahead of time. Lesley's guy stumbled across him by chance. David showed up. We just don't know about Mansell, either way."

"I'm sorry, Tanya," I said.

"None of that's conclusive," Tanya said. "He could easily still be alive. We must keep on looking for him."

"We'll look," Varley said. "But I want the focus on Hamad. What was behind his killing spree? Stealing payoffs? Or is there more to it?"

"We know Hamad took Mansell's phone," I said. "We should focus on that. Forget everything else."

"Why?" Weston said.

"Because he didn't take anyone else's," I said. "So

there's something special about Mansell's phone. And if he was after Mansell's money, why not take his ID, or something with his bank details?"

"He probably did," Weston said. "We won't know till we search his place and his work. He'll have them stashed, somewhere. That's why we need the warrant."

"No," I said. "We need to pull in Taylor. The boss we saw at Tungsten. He blanched when he saw the photos of his dead employees. We should show him the pictures from Mansell's phone. We know he was hiding something. That might loosen him up."

"Chat to him about holiday photos?" Weston said. "Sure. The dam will really bust open."

"We don't have cause to pull him in," Varley said. "Not yet. So here's the plan. Kyle—fast-track that paperwork. I want a team all over Tungsten, first thing in the morning. Bartman—get onto the NYPD. I want Mansell top of their missing persons list as of five minutes ago. David and Tanya—contact the cell phone providers. See if they've got any GPS data on either of those phones. Any questions?"

No one spoke.

"OK then. That's it. Reconvene at noon. And Mr. Trevellyan—last night you took a gamble. It paid off, in a sense. You were lucky. But I don't want you going off on your own again. Are we clear?"

I shrugged.

"Are we clear?"

"Depends on them," I said, nodding toward Weston and Lavine. "I tried to get them involved yesterday, but they had forms to fill in."

Weston and Lavine trotted away to start on their tasks, trailing out of the room behind Varley like a pair of obedient schoolboys. I stayed behind and started on the leftover coffees. Tanya watched me for a moment then excused herself and left the room. She was looking a little flustered about something.

"You OK?" I said, when she returned a couple of minutes later.

"I'm feeling a little paranoid, to be honest," she said. "I thought I saw a couple of guys watching my place last night. And again this morning."

"Really? What did they look like?"

"Well, they were male. Early twenties. Nothing really distinctive about them."

"What about their clothes? How were they dressed?"

"I don't really remember."

"Their height? Build?"

"I'm not sure. I got more of an impression than anything."

"OK, well, I'll stop by later, if you like. See what's what."

"No. Don't worry. I'm probably just tired. I didn't get much sleep."

"Because of Mansell?"

"Partly. And I was a little freaked out, with Hamad

getting shot. That kept me awake for a while. How about you?"

"I slept like a log. Nearly missed breakfast."

"How could you eat breakfast, after what happened? A guy died, right in front of our eyes. We watched his lifeblood literally drain out onto the pavement. I was so close it nearly went on my shoes."

"Tanya, he wanted to die. You saw him smile. He knew they'd shoot him if he went for his pocket. Suicide by police, they call it. Not the way I'd do things, but it was his choice. You've got to respect that."

"Respect it? You're warped. Anyway, let's stop talking about it. I don't want that picture in my head all day. And we should be getting on with this phone company GPS thing."

"Why?"

"Because Varley told us to."

"And?"

"David, why do you always go looking for trouble?"

"It's hardly trouble. Being told off by Varley's like being savaged by a piece of lettuce."

"You're so awkward. Why can't we just do the job we've been given? Do you want to be the only one with nothing to say?"

"I'd rather have something useful to say. The whole GPS thing is nonsense. Varley just wants us out of the picture while he tries to wrap things up his own way."

"Even if that's true, is it a problem?"

"Yes."

"Why? Because he doesn't do things the same way as you?"

"No. Because he's got a different agenda. He's soft-soaping you, Tanya. He's only bothered about his railroad case. Making sure nothing comes back to bite him. Finding Mansell is on the back burner. And he'll leave it there, if we let him."

"Maybe. But how do we change that?"

"Go after Taylor."

"Why?"

"Because there's only one link between everything that stinks in this whole affair—the teams that were fired, the people who were killed, the hospital where they worked, and Hamad who pulled the trigger. It all points straight back at Tungsten. Nothing else ties it together."

"I agree. But to arrest him, we need evidence. That's why they're also working on the warrant."

"Which won't be here until tomorrow. That's too late. Taylor will have buried everything by then. Tanya, you need to ask yourself something. About Mansell. Are you really serious about this whole thing?"

"Of course. Absolutely. I know you think it's silly but—"

"Then we need to lift Taylor today. This morning. Right now. And you know what? That's exactly what we're going to do."

"How? We can't force him."

"We don't need to," I said, taking out my phone.

"What are you going to do?"

"Call and ask him to meet us."

"Seriously?"

"Seriously."

Taylor answered on the first ring.

"Yes?" he said. "What?"

"Good morning, Mr. Taylor," I said. "This is David Trevellyan. We met at your office yesterday."

"Yeah, I remember. What can I do for you?"

"Thing is, I've got a bit of a problem. Turns out we both do. I was hoping we could get together, and see if we could find a way around it?"

"What do you mean?"

"Remember I'm working with the FBI at the moment? Well, they're a pretty suspicious bunch. And they've got the idea you weren't quite straight with us when we met."

"That's baloney. I told you everything I know."

"I believe you, Mr. Taylor. Really, I do. Trouble is, the feds are also pretty stubborn. I'm struggling to convince them. It's me against them. And right now they're drawing up warrants for your phone records, computers, premises, vehicles, the whole nine yards."

"Are we on tape? Why are you telling me this?"

"Because if they go down that road, it'll take weeks to wrap it up. Months, maybe. I've seen your place. And the fed's comb is pretty fine."

"Tell them to go ahead. Knock themselves out. They won't find anything."

"Maybe. Maybe not. But here's my problem. I don't

want to hang around for months making sure. My day job's back in London. The longer I'm out of the loop, the harder it'll be to get back in."

"Like you said. Your problem."

"Yours, too."

"How so?"

"Hard to imagine a business surviving, these days, without computers. Or phones. Not having any vehicles could be problem. And what about your clients? They could get jumpy, with all those crime lab people wandering around, in and out of meeting rooms. . . ."

"Are you threatening me?"

"No. Just giving you a heads-up about what's on the cards, unless we figure out a way to stop it."

"So how do we do that?"

"We meet. You and me. Off the books. I'll talk you through what's eating the feds. Then, if you can give me something to work with, I'll feed in the right answers. Save you a lot of hassle. Save me a lot of time."

"And if the investigation closes quicker, you'll take the glory."

"If things work out that way, who am I to demur?"

"Now I see what you're doing. OK then. I'll meet you. When?"

"As soon as possible. They've started the paperwork. It needs to be before lunch."

"Today?"

"The task force is penciled in for tomorrow morning."

"Are they crazy?"

"Be ready in an hour. I'll come to your office."

"Today's an out day. I'm at my apartment."

"See you there, then. Twenty minutes."

Tanya had turned away and moved over to the far window while I was talking, but as soon as the call ended she spun around and almost ran back toward me.

"David, what are you thinking? You've deliberately compromised the whole investigation. How can this possibly help?"

"What did I compromise?"

"The whole case. You told Taylor about the warrants, the raid, everything."

"They were already expecting those things."

"You don't know that."

"I do. At Tungsten's offices, did you see a metal carrying case down on the floor next to the filing cabinets?"

"About twelve inches tall? Yes, I did."

"Do you know what was inside?"

"How could I? I don't have X-ray eyes."

"A portable degausser. I checked when I went to the bathroom."

"What's one of those?"

"A device that wipes computer hard drives. Permanently."

"That doesn't mean anything. There are new regulations here. You have to wipe hard drives now, before you dispose of them. To safeguard employee data and so on. Having one could be perfectly legit."

"Tanya, you don't believe that. Think about it. Whether this is about stealing money or the hospital or something we haven't even thought of yet, someone organized is at the heart of it. They'll be prepared for things going wrong. Whole teams of ex-marines don't end up dead by chance. They obviously have a backup plan, and now they're executing it. Step by step. If we leave them to it there'll be nothing left to find."

"Now they know we're coming, will they leave anything anyway?"

"That doesn't matter. That's not what my call was about. It's thrown a monkey wrench in the works. I've given them a decision to make. How they respond to it will tell us more than any search."

"And what about Taylor? If they're so well prepared for contingencies, what will he tell you?"

"Anything I want to know."

TWENTY-SEVEN

I was sent to a company in France once, where the entire office was obsessed with milk.

A list had been drawn up to determine who had to fetch each day's supply from the local shop. It sounded easy. But the system never worked. People would forget to pay their dues, so the club ran short of money. Others would say they couldn't find time to leave the premises. Or they might refuse to go because someone else had missed their turn the previous week. And so it went on until a kind of anarchy broke out. Factions sprang up that brought their own provisions. They refused to share. Then tried to steal from each other if they didn't have enough. The organizers took steps to hide their supplies. One old guy went to incredible lengths to conceal his. He'd secretly decant his milk into all kinds of unlikely containers, then distribute them all around his workspace.

I wasn't interested in the milk—I drink my coffee without—but the job was so boring I needed something to amuse myself. So I came up with a game. Trying to locate each day's hiding place. I was considerate, though. I didn't root around in the old guy's stuff. All I did was watch him. I would drop a hint about being thirsty then deliberately hang around in different areas of the office and observe his reaction. I wasn't concerned with the exact spot—which bookcase, not which book—and my method worked every time. It formed the bones of a strategy I would use for years to come.

It might not tell you the precise location of the thing you're searching for.

But it will confirm the direction you should look.

Taylor opened the door to his apartment the moment I knocked and then stepped aside, gesturing for me to come in. He didn't say a word—just stood back and waited. I guess that was a favorite act of his, because as hallways go his was pretty unusual. Apart from the external door the space was completely circular. The floor was covered in five-bar chequer plate like you find in factories and warehouses, only his was polished to a flawless shine. The paintwork was plain white, and if you looked carefully you could just see the outline of concealed, curved doors set into the walls on the right and the left. A corridor led through an archway in front of us, presumably to the bedrooms and bathrooms. The center of the space was filled by a spiral staircase. The frame was gleaming metal. All the bolts and structural parts were exposed, and the treads were textured to match the rest of the floor.

"There's nothing to see down here," Taylor said, when

he'd finished enjoying my reaction. "Let's go up. After you."

The higher floor of Taylor's duplex had been knocked through to form a single, continuous rectangle. The floor, walls, and ceiling were made from some kind of granite-like material. It was crisp white with tiny silver flecks, and it must have been somehow molded in place like an inner skin because there were no joins or seams visible anywhere.

All the power cables were carried externally in round zinc-coated conduits. These were connected to heavy, industrial-style switches and ran up to three parallel lighting bars hanging on chains from the ceiling. The one on our right was above a dining table. It was made of green-ish glass with flowing irregular edges, three-quarters of an inch thick, supported by adjustable metal trestles. Eight chairs surrounded it. They were covered in suede. There was one in each color of the rainbow, plus one in plain black.

"Is that a dumbwaiter?" I said, nodding toward a square steel hatch set into the right-hand wall.

"Sure," he said. "The kitchen's downstairs."

The other two lighting bars were on our left, hanging over a large white leather sofa. It was L-shaped. The two segments were the same length, and it was set up so you'd be equally comfortable watching TV or looking out of the floor-to-ceiling windows opposite us.

The TV was huge. At least fifty-two inches, set into rather than hung on the far wall. There was no sign of any cable boxes or DVD players to drive it. But whatever AV equipment Taylor had hidden away, it would be hard-pressed to compete with the view. First your eyes were drawn to the lavish green of the park, twenty-one floors below. Then the jagged gray and brown buildings of the Upper West Side. And finally the cold blue of the Hudson. Individually each swath of color was fascinating. Together they were hypnotic. No wonder Taylor didn't feel the need for pictures on his walls.

"Do you live here alone?" I said.

"At the moment," he said. "Why?"

"I'm just looking at what you've done with the place. It's hard to be so focused if you've got to compromise with someone."

"That's true. Can I get you a coffee?"

"Please. No milk, no sugar."

"I've got a pot brewing downstairs. It'll be ready in a minute. Meantime, take a seat. Let's talk. Tell me what's got the feds all riled up."

"Down to business already. OK then. Well, remember your dead ex-employees? We talked about them yesterday. It turns out they were killed by someone from Tungsten."

"No way. Who?"

"A guy called Salif Hamad."

"Hamad? I got a call about him, this morning. He's dead."

"I know."

"Hamad killed those guys? Are you sure?"

"Oh, yeah. No doubt."

"Salif Hamad. Would you believe it? Such a quiet guy. But if it was Hamad, it kind of begs the question, why are you here? The feds aren't going to get their warrant, now."

"Want to bet?"

"What's to search for? You've got the guy. End of, surely?"

"Sorry, Kelvin. This isn't going away. Not yet. The feds are suspicious people. They hate mysteries. Who did it is only half the story. They'll keep on coming till they find out why."

"Why has nothing to do with us."

"I believe you. But the feds think otherwise."

"How come?"

"Hamad worked for you. The other dead guys worked for you. They don't think that's a coincidence."

"Of course it is. And you need more than a coincidence to get a warrant."

"They do have more."

"Like what?"

"I have it here. I can show you. But before I do, I want to get something straight."

Taylor's phone began to ring before he could reply. He excused himself, answered it, and listened for a few moments.

"Sorry," he said. "My housecleaner's on the way up. I need to go let her in."

His feet clattered down the metal steps. The door opened. Footsteps came into the hall. Two sets. Both heavy.

Then the door closed again and Taylor started back upstairs without a word being spoken.

"I'm back," he said, emerging from the stairwell. "Sorry
about that. What were you saying?"

"Does your housecleaner come up here?" I said.

"Yeah, she will. But not for an hour or so. She does downstairs first. And don't worry. She doesn't speak English. So,
you wanted something?"

"Yes. Assurances. I'm taking a big risk. No one
knows I'm here. If anyone finds out what I'm showing
you . . ."

"Understood. And don't worry. Discretion is my biggest
virtue. Now, let's see what you've got and maybe we can
help each other."

I took out the set of photos Lavine had given me from
Mansell's phone and handed them to Taylor.

"It looks like Iraq," he said, studying the first one.

"It is," I said.

"Where did you get them?"

"One of your ex-employees took them. On his phone."

"Which one?"

"James Mansell."

"I remember him. He wasn't one of the five victims,
though?"

"We're not sure. We know Hamad tried to kill him. If
he succeeded, we haven't found the body. But he certainly
took Mansell's phone. He had it with him, last night, when
he died. He was trying to protect it."

"Strange."

"Very. And the question the feds are asking is, why did he want the phone so much?"

"No idea. Call records? People's numbers?"

"No. The FBI have analyzed everything. There must be something else."

"I can't imagine what."

"They're thinking, maybe the photos?"

"Surely not. How could someone's vacation snaps be worth five lives?"

"I don't know yet. Have a look. Tell me what you see. If I can convince the feds the photos aren't significant . . ."

"Got you," he said, starting to thumb his way through the pile. "I'll try. Let's see what we have. Guys in their barracks. Guys in the desert. More guys in the desert. Some girls—not ours. Guys in vehicles. One of our convoys. One of our trucks."

"What's that Arabic writing on the back?"

" 'Danger. Keep Back. Authorized to use lethal force.' "

"Is that normal?"

"Completely. All private contract vehicles have signs saying it. In English, and in Arabic."

"Oh. OK. Keep going."

"This next one is, this one is, well, it looks like it could be the inside of one of our trucks."

"What are all the containers?"

"Organ carriers, for transplants. Big on the black market."

"Valuable?"

"Very. That's why we have to guard them. Those and the drugs, obviously."

"Why would Mansell photograph them?"

"No idea."

"They don't look like regular ones. Usually they're like picnic boxes."

"Right. These are special. The country's in a mess right now, so most of the organs have to be flown in. They need built-in monitors, fluid pumps, all manner of gizmos. Because of the time from harvesting."

"OK. So what about the rest. Anything?"

"I don't think so," he said, glancing at the remaining pictures. "They just look like souvenirs."

"I see."

"So that's cleared things up? We're good?"

"No. Sorry, Kelvin, but that's nowhere near good enough. I can't go back to the FBI with 'they look like souvenirs.' I need more."

"There is no more. I looked at the pictures. I told you what I saw."

"The SWAT teams are suiting up, right now. They might not wait till tomorrow morning. . . ."

"So, stop them."

"Then give me something to work with."

"Like what? There's nothing in those pictures. They're irrelevant."

"Then I'll see you in the morning," I said. "And I'd wear old clothes, if I were you."

"No, wait," he said. "Forget the photos. Let's try another approach. We work with the government all the time. It's a complex machine. Sometimes the wheels get a little jammed up. I'm thinking, maybe that's the kind of situation we have here?"

"I don't know. What do you do, in that kind of situation?"

"We unjam the wheels. Lubricate them. Get them moving again."

"How?"

"Money usually works."

"How much?"

"Depends how many wheels are jammed."

"Say, three? Aside from me."

"A hundred thousand. You keep whatever's left."

"How about a million?"

"Don't push your luck."

"I wonder if they'll raid this place, too?"

"Five hundred thousand."

"Imagine them checking these walls, digging around for concealed hiding places. . . ."

"Seven fifty. Fifty now, the rest when the case is closed."

"I keep whatever's left, after the wheels are moving again?"

"Right."

"How about the coffee?"

"Forget the coffee. I've got the fifty downstairs. I'll go get it."

"Thanks. And tell your guys they can stop hiding."

"What guys?"

"The guys you just let in. Unless it really was your housecleaner. And she's got four legs."

"Oh. The metal floor. Not the best for subtlety."

"No."

"OK, this is embarrassing. We still good?"

"We are. What if I'd not taken the bribe? You couldn't meet me here alone. Only a fool would have done that. And I don't do business with fools."

TWENTY-EIGHT

Halfway through my first month in the navy there was a fire.

It was at our training barracks. We had to move out for two weeks while they repaired the place. The nearest available alternative was a university residence hall. It was in the middle of the holidays, so most of the campus was deserted. There was just us, plus the last dregs of students on the floor above. They'd stayed on for some kind of summer school.

The students didn't seem very dedicated. They were more interested in partying than studying. Always playing loud music. Drinking. Running around, making noise, annoying everyone. Well, annoying me, anyway. I remember one night water started to drip through my ceiling. I went to investigate. Turned out someone had taken a garbage can from the kitchen, filled it under the tap, and leaned it against my upstairs neighbor's door. They knocked, he opened, and finished with twelve gallons of soaking garbage around his ankles.

I remember thinking it was pretty stupid, at the time.

Funny how your perspective can change, though, later in life.

Taylor had no need for his bodyguards once we'd reached our agreement, so they walked out of the apartment at the same time as me. It was strangely disconcerting because the two guys looked almost identical. One appeared from the bedroom corridor, then another, as if I were seeing double. I guessed the pair would be in their late twenties. Both were around six two, with broad shoulders and the kind of muscles in their arms you get from working outdoors, not visiting the gym. Their skin was deeply tanned. Blond stubble bristled on the top of their heads. They had the same kind of clothes as the guy we'd seen at Tungsten yesterday, minus the name patches. Both had Australian accents. One carried a canvas utility bag slung over his right shoulder, and neither showed any awkwardness about standing and talking with someone they'd been ready to kill ten minutes before.

"Need a ride?" the guy with the bag said as Taylor's door closed behind us.

"Please," I said. "Just a couple of blocks. Saves me finding a cab. Only thing is, I don't get on too well with elevators. Any chance we could take the stairs?"

"Twenty-one floors?"

"Come on. It is down, all the way. And I'll even carry your bag."

The guy sighed and looked back at his twin.

"OK," he said, finally. "We'll walk. But don't touch my stuff."

The door to the stairs was to our right, next to the third elevator. I was nearest so I moved across and gave it a push. It opened more easily than I'd expected. The self-closer was broken. That was a piece of luck. It meant I could bring the timetable forward a little. I didn't want Taylor leaving before I could get back and see him again.

"After you," I said, moving aside to let the guy with the bag go first. I stepped through immediately after him and took hold of the handle on the other side. I paused. Then I heaved the door back toward its frame, twisting my body and shifting my weight like a hammer thrower.

My timing was just right. The steel skin of the heavy fire door crushed the second guy's nose like it was made of paper and only slowed down when it connected with his jaw. The impact sent him staggering backward and he went down in a sprawling heap like he'd fallen twenty feet off a building and landed on his face.

The guy with the bag heard the thud. He stopped, four feet in front of me, right at the top of the stairs. He started to turn. I waited until he was facing me. Then I launched myself forward, swinging my back leg up and driving the ball of my foot into the base of his rib cage like a battering ram. He fell back, gasping for air, hopelessly off balance. His arms were flailing, desperate for anything to grab onto. His right hand glanced off the smooth wall. His left grazed the metal banister rail, scrabbling for grip, but he just couldn't hang on. Both arms ended up stretched out behind him. That was just as well. They took some of the sting out of his fall. But even so, the back of his head caught the sharp edges of four, five, six bare concrete steps before he came to rest.

I followed him down, retrieved his bag, and checked inside. There were three things. A clear, heavy-gauge plastic sheet, folded into a square. A black body bag, standard U.S. Army issue, rolled up. And a metal case containing a syringe. It was filled with some kind of clear liquid. I put the syringe case in my pocket, replaced everything else, and slung the bag over my shoulder. Then I took hold of the guy's hands, swung him over the same shoulder, and carried him up to the landing.

Next I went to check on the second guy. He'd rolled onto his front and was trying to drag himself across the carpet toward Taylor's apartment, groaning softly each time he moved. He wasn't aware I'd come back, so I let him get within touching distance of the wall before rolling him onto his side and slamming the heel of my hand into his temple. That put an end to his crawling, so I eased him into a sitting position and shuffled him over until his head and shoulders were against Taylor's door and his backside was twelve inches out from its lower edge. Then I fetched the bag guy. I lugged his unconscious body through the lobby and lowered it down onto the second guy's lap. They ended up back against chest, like one was sitting on the other's knee. The bag guy's head lolled sideways, so I had to roll it around onto the second guy's shoulder. His oozing blood left a blotchy stain on the white surface of the door, but I wasn't too worried. I was going to give Taylor more to think about than smudged paint.

I took the syringe out of its case, stepped to the side, and reached across to the doorbell. It was set into the center of the door, above Taylor's printed name card and below the lens of a security peephole. I kept my finger on the button for a full two seconds. The sound was harsh and mechanical, like the old-fashioned windup kind. Not what I'd expected at all. There was silence for ten seconds. Then a light pair of feet started down the spiral stairs. They came nearer, scurrying across the metal floor like a couple of mice. And stopped.

"Who's there?" Taylor said.

"Your cleaners," I said. "They forgot to do upstairs. Thought they better come back."

Taylor opened the door. That was a mistake. The bodies fell backward, deflecting off his legs as gravity pulled them to the floor. I heard a sharp intake of breath, and two near simultaneous thumps as their skulls hit the checkered tile. I gave Taylor a couple of moments to register what had happened. Then I stepped into view.

"I don't know what your boy had in here," I said, holding up the syringe. "But if you don't want it pumped straight in your heart, get down on the ground. Hands behind your head. Lace your fingers. Do not look at me. Do not move."

Taylor hit the floor as if his legs had been swept from under him. I put the syringe back in its case, slipped it into my pocket, and stepped in through the doorway. The bodies were in the way so I hauled them to the side and shut the door. I made sure it had latched, then felt in my pocket for the sheaf of cable ties I'd taken from Lesley's. I isolated four. My fingers worked them free. I used two to bind the identical guys' wrists. The other two secured them to the frame of the spiral staircase. Then I turned back to face their whimpering boss.

"Good, so far," I said. "Now, on your feet."

"Where are we going?" he said.

"Upstairs."

"Why?"

"There's nothing to see down here. And we need somewhere private. We have something to talk about."

Taylor went up the staircase ahead of me, hesitantly, one hand on the rail. I kept my distance, just in case, but he didn't try anything. He just labored his way to the top, took a couple more steps, and then waited for instructions. I directed him to the dining end of the room and put him on the violet chair. That was in the middle of the long side, with its back to the sofas. I sat opposite, on the yellow chair, giving him only me and the blank white wall to look at.

"Take a minute to think," I said. "You've made some mistakes, this morning. Serious mistakes. So now you have to choose. Either you put them right, or you pay the price. And it's only fair to warn you. The price is going to be high."

"How do I put them right?" he said.

"Tell me the truth."

"I did."

I took out the wad of photos, pulled out the one showing the organ containers in the truck, and put it down on the table.

"So why did you choke when you saw this, the first time?" I said.

"I didn't choke. I just took a second to recognize it," he said.

"I'm going to ask you one more question. Before Tungsten, were you in the army?"

"Yes."

"Special Forces?"

"No."

"Airborne?"

"No."

"Infantry?"

"No. Why?"

"Because I'm getting the feeling you weren't much of a fighting soldier. Not much combat experience. Is that fair?"

"Modern armies stand or fall on their staffwork. Don't belittle it."

"I'm not. I'm just thinking, you saw those guys downstairs? The one guy's face? The back of the other guy's skull? Now look at these."

I held up my palms, then the back of my hands.

"If I can do that to those guys, on my own, without getting a single scratch, what's going to happen to you if you don't give me what I want?"

Taylor stared down at the tabletop. But the only thing on it was his reflection, and that didn't offer much comfort.

"So, here's your choice. Talk to me about this," I said, tapping the photograph. "Or end up in this."

I undid the canvas satchel and took out the body bag. I held it up so he got a good look, then gripped one end and flicked the roll toward him so it unraveled across the width of the table. The final eighteen inches cascaded off the far side and dangled down onto his lap.

"Your buddies brought it for me," I said. "But it looks more like your size."

Taylor sat in silence, mesmerized by the strip of black rubber as if it were a giant tentacle about to grab hold of him. Then he snapped his eyes away, shoveled the end back onto the table, and reached across for the photo.

"They were organs, going for transplant," he said. "But we weren't bringing them in."

"Who was?" I said.

"Nobody. We were bringing them out."

"Out? Where to? The U.S.?"

"Obviously."

"So back in your office. You talked about being a principled operator. Giving back to the people. But behind it all, you're just a bunch of organ smugglers."

"Don't lay your tabloid-headline morals on me. Yes, we make money. Yes, what we do is technically illegal. But, hey, what we do saves lives, and that's good enough from where I'm sitting."

"Save lives? Wake up, Taylor. You steal people's organs."

"We don't steal them."

"You buy them then. Who from? How much? What happens if they say no?"

"We don't buy them."

"So what do you do? Make them?"

"You've got no idea what state that country's in. Bizarre as it sounds, there are spare organs literally lying at the side of the street. Back here, people are dying because there aren't enough. So we put the two together. No one loses. Innocent Americans win."

"What do they win? Someone else's body parts? Who had no choice about donating?"

"They get to stay alive. And I'm not apologizing for that to anyone."

"These spare organs. They're not still encased inside people's bodies, by any chance?"

"You're an asshole. This is how it works. We don't just protect that hospital. We provide surgeons and doctors. Pro bono. Patrols scoop up the victims. Our guys save as many as they can."

"And the rest you tear apart? Carve up for spare parts?"

"You've got to be realistic. You can't save them all."

"So, the unlucky ones. You just help yourselves to their innards. Like vultures."

"What would you do? Leave the organs to rot? Do you know what life on dialysis is like? And that doesn't always work, anyway. Ten thousand Americans die every year from kidney failure as it is."

"How do you get them back here? The organs."

"By plane."

"What about customs?"

"We're licensed government contractors. They're our planes. No one looks twice."

"Once they're here, how do you sell them? On eBay?"

"We don't just sell them. It's like I said. We do this to save lives. We only work with our own patients. We do the diagnosis, the treatment, the convalescence. Our approach is completely holistic."

"Don't the hospitals blow the whistle? Or do you bribe them to look the other way when you wheel in your crates of meat?"

"We don't use hospitals. We have our own facilities."

"What kind of facilities?"

"Private clinics."

"Private. Pandering to line-jumpers."

"No. Mothers. Fathers. Normal people who just want to stay alive and see their kids grow up. The regular channels let them down, because the fact is—and this is truly sad—the system can't deliver. It's inadequate. So they turn to us. And for every one we help, a space is freed up on the list for somebody else. Everybody wins. There is literally no downside."

"How many clinics are we talking about?"

"Five."

"In New York?"

"One is. Around the corner, on Sixty-sixth Street. It was our first."

"And the others?"

"Boston."

"All of them?"

"No. One in Chicago. And Washington. And Miami."

"All dedicated to saving lives."

"Yes. If you ask me, it's the only good thing to come out of the whole war."

"So why do the FBI have five ex-Tungsten guys in their morgue?"

"You should talk to James Mansell about that. The ass-hole. He was new to the hospital detail. Strayed somewhere he shouldn't have. We didn't know how much he'd seen. Obviously we couldn't take the chance."

"So you canned the whole team. Clinically excised them. Brought them home, paid them off, sent them on their way."

"Right."

"Then how did five of them end up on the slab?"

"That's Mansell's fault again. He sent us a copy of this picture. Wanted more money. A lot more."

"One guy tried it on, and you wiped out the whole team. That's a pretty holistic approach, I guess."

"It wasn't my call. I wouldn't have done it that way."

"No. You'd have just killed Mansell. Or had him killed."

"If it was necessary. As a last resort."

"You're like a saint, in comparison. So, who made the call?"

Taylor didn't answer.

"Don't go shy on me now," I said. "I'm in no mood to compromise."

"OK," he said, "but this is hard for me. Because the Tungsten you see today, it's not the way I set it up. Things have changed."

"In what way?"

"I have new partners, is the easiest way to say it."

"Since when?"

"Three months ago."

"Who?"

"I don't know their real names. Iraqis."

"You employ large men with automatic weapons. Why let anyone muscle in?"

"It's not that simple. They found out what we were doing. We thought they'd try and shut us down. It's happened a couple of times before. And you're right. We're well placed to deal with that. But these guys were different. They didn't want us to stop shipping organs. They wanted us to ship more. And they were ready to help."

"And you let them."

Taylor shrugged.

"They're well connected, locally. Tripled the supply of suitable donors. Even sent their own surgeons over here, to pick up the slack. We're averaging one transplant per day, per clinic, since they came on board. Mainly kidneys. Some livers. Now we're talking about diversifying. Into corneas, that sort of thing. All in all, it's ninety percent good."

"And the other ten?"

"Day to day isn't an issue. It's how they deal with problems that sucks. They overreact. Have different ideas about what you can and can't do."

"I know all about that. So who are they?"

"I told you. I don't know their names."

"Where can I find them? The bosses. Back in Iraq?"

"No. They're here. They work out of the clinic on Sixty-sixth Street."

"Hamad's one of theirs?"

"Yes. Their fixer. He came over a month after they did. Most of the wild stuff is up to him."

"And you stood back and let him get on with it."

"What could I do? I've had my concerns from day one. But the other directors . . ."

"Head down, mouth shut, take the money."

"Exactly. Why kill the golden goose? And be honest— would you have done it differently?"

"Oh, yes," I said. "Pretty much all of it."

TWENTY-NINE

We didn't return to our barracks straight after the fire incident.

Instead, we were sent to an army base in Wiltshire for a hostage rescue exercise. None of us could see why. If anyone was being held captive in an embassy it wouldn't be our job to get them out. Blowing holes in walls and smashing through windows isn't up to us. But that kind of speculation is pointless. In the navy, you go where you're told. And besides, it sounded fun.

The briefing for the first exercise was pretty basic. They told us eight terrorists were holding two hostages in an abandoned vicarage. As far as they knew, the terrorists were dispersed throughout the premises and the hostages were in a windowless room on the second floor. I was allocated to the first rescue team. There was me, another navy guy, and four special ops soldiers who weren't too keen on working with us.

The navy guy and I created a diversion, pretending to attack through the basement. The soldiers went through four separate ground-floor windows, entering simultaneously and tearing through the building like wildfire. We came in after them and helped with the sweep. Between us we found the terrorists—only six, it turned out—and neutralized them easily enough with orange paintballs. The hostages were harder to track down. They'd been moved to a tiny cupboard in the attic. One was injured. She was barely conscious, and bleeding badly. Her companion was in a blind panic, convinced she was going to die. The soldiers slapped on a battlefield dressing and started to haul them out. Only by the time we reached the front door, all of us were covered in sweet-smelling red jelly. Because the hostages were already dead. The women were the seventh and eighth terrorists. And no one had found the remote detonator in the casualty's shoe.

We didn't have to take part in any more hostage exercises after that. In fact, there weren't any. The whole thing had been staged. The soldiers had been in on it from the start. And the point wasn't to teach us how to storm a building. It was to hammer home something entirely different. To take nothing and no one at face value.

Or, as I've found over the years, it's usually the person you're least expecting who causes the most trouble.

It was a ten-minute cab ride back to the FBI building so I made sure to use the time carefully. First I called for someone to come over and scoop up Taylor and his boys. Then I settled back to think. If I could make sure every angle was covered, there was a chance I could get Varley to sign me off the job after the 12:00 P.M. conference. That way I could

take the rest of the afternoon for myself, have dinner with
Tanya, and be back in London by suppertime tomorrow.
Or suppertime the next day, if things went really well. Only
I'd been as far as JFK already, yesterday morning. I didn't
want anyone pulling the rug out again today.

I was expecting some heavy flak after visiting Taylor
on my own, and I could see I was right about Varley's reaction before the meeting even started. He crashed through
the boardroom doors, stomped over to his place, and sat
there glowering at me until Tanya arrived. He let me talk
first, but I guess that news of the arrests had reached him
through the grapevine because he interrupted, sniped, and
criticized at every turn as I brought the others up to date.
Weston and Lavine weren't much more constructive. But
as the briefing wore on they began to see the possibilities.
Bringing down organ smugglers is hard to beat for headline potential. Especially when the operation spans five cities. Coordinating something like that is a dream for career
development. A task force would be needed. Leading roles
would be up for grabs. Practical details started to dominate
the discussion. And no actions were coming my way. There
was no mention of James Mansell, so no need for a British
presence in general. They had Taylor in custody, so no
need for me in particular. Things were looking good.

Until I realized I was looking in the wrong direction. If
anyone was going to trip me up, it wouldn't be the FBI. It
would be Tanya.

"I don't agree," she said, out of the blue. "What you're
proposing, it'll take too long. It's turning into a circus. We

should hit the New York clinic now. This afternoon. There's no time to delay."

"We can't do that," Varley said. "We need confirmation that no other agencies are already into this. They could have people in there, undercover. Then we need surveillance. As of now, we have no idea what we'd be walking into. Or whether the big fish are even there. And we need foolproof cooperation from the other cities. It's no good taking one crew down and letting four more walk away."

"And something else," Weston said. "The other end. Iraq. We need someone to sweep that mess up."

"What a jurisdictional nightmare that'll be," Lavine said.

"I'm not a fool," Tanya said. "I understand the big picture. But while you're worrying about 'what if this' and 'what if that' the people we really want will be long gone. David proved that. Look how Taylor reacted."

"We don't know who's involved," Varley said. "We don't know how many there are. We don't have names or faces. And you've picked out targets?"

"Yes," Tanya said. "The people who ordered the five murders. They're the ones that count. Lives are worth more than money, however much we're talking about."

"Agreed," Varley said. "And we're going to take them. Because I know what you're thinking. They're to blame for your friend's death. Well, the way I see it, they're to blame for Mike Raab's death, as well. Lesley's guy pulled the trigger, but Mike's path only crossed because Tungsten was dropping bodies everywhere. These guys, they're top of the list. We'll get them. Have faith."

"Those are just words," Tanya said. "I want action. We're not going to get anyone, sitting here. I want us to do something, now."

She was starting to sound alarmingly like me.

"OK," Varley said. "What?"

"We know they're at the clinic," Tanya said. "A few streets away. Taylor told David. So we find another reason. Tax evasion. Operating without a medical license. Immigration issues. Anything. Then throw a net over the others later, when you're ready."

"No," Varley said. "And don't obsess over *later*. We're not talking days. As soon as we're done here, we'll get onto INS. Kyle will get the tech crews rolling. I'll liaise with the other cities, personally. I'll talk to the overseas guys, as well. Then, when we know the who and the where, we'll move. It'll be tomorrow morning, at the latest."

"What if Taylor warns them before tomorrow?" Tanya said.

"We'll up the watch on the airports," Lavine said. "All flights in and out of that region."

"And Taylor can't warn anyone," Varley said. "He's in jail. They're holding him in solitary."

"What if he already did?" Tanya said. "David left him alone in the apartment. He could have phoned before you picked him up."

"The phone was broken," I said.

"How do you know?" Tanya said. "Did you check?"

"No. I broke it," I said.

"What about their cell phones?" Tanya said.

"They lost their cell phones," I said.

"All three of them?" Tanya said. "Doesn't seem likely."

I reached into my pocket and laid the three phones on the table.

"What if his disappearance spooks them?" Tanya said.

"Tanya, I know you're frustrated," I said. "And no one cuts more corners than me. But this is not the time. The organ smuggling, the hit on Simon, finding Mansell, they're part of the same thing. We've led the horse to water. Now leave it. It's up to these guys to make it drink."

Varley took Weston and Lavine downstairs to hit the phones, leaving me to keep an eye on Tanya. He didn't trust her to stay away from the clinic until we reconvened at 5:00 P.M. The conversation left me wrong-footed. One minute he was shooting me daggers, the next swearing me in like I was his deputy. All I needed was a tin badge. It was a strange role to give me. And not one I was interested in playing.

I went across to the window and watched the city drift by for a couple of minutes. Looking down through the glass made the streets seem remote, like a museum exhibit. Which reminded me of something. I turned and headed for the door. Tanya came with me. She stayed close all the way down in the elevator and through the garage, but she didn't open her mouth until we'd climbed the ramp and stepped out onto the sidewalk.

"What next?" she said.

"Don't know," I said. "Should we walk? Or take a cab?"

"To the clinic?"

"No. To the Museum of Modern Art."

"Why there?"

"I heard they've got a helicopter in one of the displays."

"What do you want with a helicopter?"

"Nothing. But in an art gallery? It sounds interesting. And we've got to do something till five o'clock."

"We're not going to the clinic?"

"No."

"Why not?"

"There's no point. The only reason would be to find out what's happening and work out if it's a problem. But we know what's going on already. We're in a different phase now. It's time to pass the baton."

"Not good enough, David. We need to at least go and look."

"No. Why?"

"They'll be getting ready to run. If we lose them now, we'll never find Mansell."

"No. It's more likely we'd just spook them."

"We don't have to go in. We could just drive by. Find something to convince Varley."

"No. We're not going anywhere near that place. Neither of us. Have you got that?"

Tanya didn't reply.

"Is that clear?" I said. "The risk is not justified."

"Risk?" she said. "Listen to you. Since when have you worried about risk? When we went to Tungsten's place? Rooted round their office? Stole their mail?"

"That wasn't a risk. That was a tactic."

"When you made me meet Hamad, then? Got into a knife fight with him? Or when you went to see Taylor and his thugs? No. But now Varley wants to take the reins and you think there's a chance to sneak back home . . ."

"Tanya, your judgment's impaired. Your head's still stuck in Morocco. The answer is no. We stay away from the clinic."

"This has nothing to do with Morocco."

"Your obsession with finding James Mansell, then."

"It's not an obsession. . . . David, wait. See those two men? They're the ones who were watching me this morning."

"Which ones?"

"Black car, four bays down on my right. Reading newspapers."

I saw it. A black Cadillac Deville with no license plate at the front.

"Sure?"

"One hundred percent."

"OK. Let's see if they're happy with just watching. This is what I want you to do. Lean over and kiss me on the cheek. Softly, like we're friends saying good-bye. Then I'll head into the garage. You take a couple of steps—no more than two—and take out your phone. But don't hold it to your ear. Keep it low, like you're texting. Ready?"

"I guess . . ."

Nothing happened for twenty seconds after I moved out of sight. Then a car door slammed. I heard an engine start. A man came into view, walking fast. He was a fraction over six feet tall, slim, in his early twenties with short dark hair, black leather bomber jacket, and mid-blue jeans. He was heading for Tanya. He sneaked right up behind her, hesitated for a moment, then grabbed her. He locked his arms around her waist. She started to struggle. The Cadillac appeared. It pulled in next to them, snaking across to our side of the street. Its trunk lid was already swinging open. The guy on the sidewalk started to wrestle Tanya toward it, lifting her half off her feet.

The driver rolled down his window and gestured impatiently. He looked jumpy and inexperienced. I didn't want him escaping while I was still disentangling Tanya so I stepped up to the car and punched him hard, just to the side of his ear. He went over sideways, sprawling across the front seats and revealing a small black Colt .38 that had been wedged under his left thigh. I paused to check he wasn't moving. Then I heard a voice behind me.

"Hold it." A man's voice. He sounded nervous. "Don't turn around."

I turned around. The other guy had moved back, out of reach, almost pressing into the little booth at the top of the ramp. He still had one arm around Tanya's waist. A black .38 was grasped in his free hand. Another Colt. It matched the driver's. Only this one was pressed against Tanya's right temple.

"On the ground," he said. "Or she's dead meat."

I reached down behind me, through the car window, using my body to hide the movement. My hand found the waistband of the driver's jeans. I traced my way down his leg until my fingers brushed against metal. I felt for the textured surface of the handgrip, took hold, and smoothly withdrew my arm. The safety was on the top left of the frame, at the rear. I held my hand out so the guy could watch me flick it down. Then I pointed the gun straight at his face.

"This is what's going to happen," I said. "I'm going to shoot you in the mouth. Twice. The first round will sever your spinal cord, just where it joins your brain. That way, no nerve signals can reach your trigger finger. The second is just for insurance. Then I'm getting lunch."

"I don't think so," the guy said. "I'm going to blow her brains out."

"What do you fancy, Tanya?" I said. "I feel like a big sandwich. Pastrami and Swiss, maybe. I had a great one the other day. Are there any good delis around here?"

"It won't work, the mouth thing," the guy said. "Shoot me, and she dies."

"Shut up," I said. "I don't know who you are, but I do this for a living. And in three seconds' time, you're going to lose the back of your skull. Unless you put your gun down. One . . ."

The guy didn't move.

"Two . . ."

His hand started to shake.

"Normally I don't bother with three," I said. "I just pull the trigger on two. But I've got a feeling about you. I don't think you came to kill anyone. So put the gun down. There's still time to straighten this out."

He didn't react for fully five seconds. Tanya closed her eyes. She didn't breathe. Then the guy started to sag. He lowered his right hand. The gun slipped from his grip. It hit his foot and clattered six inches across the sidewalk. He dropped down onto his knees. For a moment I thought he was trying to retrieve his weapon, but he'd just lost his balance. He fell forward again, landing on all fours. And then he puked. Three long gut-wrenching torrents, flooding the ground in front of him and spattering up his sleeves.

Tanya turned to me, holding her hands out like a shield against the stinking puddle. She looked half shocked, half disgusted. Finally she opened her mouth, but before she could speak her phone began to ring.

"It's Lavine," she said, holding the handset away from her mouth. "He's got a lead on Mansell. The NYPD have picked him up. Or someone that might be him. They want us to go and see. They're still bogged down prepping for the clinics."

"Excellent," I said. "Maybe this has a happy ending, after all. But tell him to send someone to sit on these guys till we get back."

"David, let's not waste time. You're not going to make a

big deal out of this, are you? I mean, no harm's been done. They're only kids. Couldn't we just let it slide? Or leave it to the police?"

"Why? Do you recognize them?"

"No."

"Have you had a row with anyone lately? Someone in your building?"

"No. I only moved in a couple of days ago."

"At the consulate?"

"Of course not."

"What about work? Anything that could come back and haunt you?"

"No. Nothing. I haven't been here long enough. I've had no problems at all. Until you turned up."

"Then, no. We can't let it slide. They were stalking you. They tried to snatch you off the street. And they know where you live. Where you work. That's not something you turn a blind eye to. Ever."

"OK. I guess you're right. I'll tell Lavine to send some people."

"Good. And Tanya—tell him they'll need a sponge. I'm not spending time with this guy till he's been cleaned."

THIRTY

I don't remember a great deal about my grandfather.

He died when I was too young. I've seen photos of him, and heard stories from relatives. But I never got a sense of what he was really like until a couple of years ago when his few remaining possessions found their way through to me, sealed up for years in his old army trunk.

It turned out the old man had been fascinated by the *Titanic*. He'd built up a whole hoard of books and articles and clippings about it. Accounts of how it was built, in Belfast, near where he was born. The night it sank. The conspiracy theories. The expeditions to find the wreck. Biographies of the survivors. Histories of its sister ships. I read every word. But it wasn't the technical details that struck a chord with me. It was how that final night must have felt for the passengers. One minute, their ship was indestructible. An unsinkable engineering marvel. The next it was a metal coffin on the way to the ocean floor. Their world was turned on its head. In an instant. With no warning.

I've had that feeling, myself. On more than one occasion.

And, as with icebergs, you never know when it's going to strike.

The trip to pick up James Mansell was a complete waste of time. The NYPD's "ninety percent match" turned out to be a sad, confused drunk with an English accent. He'd been spotted dancing naked in the turtle pond in Central Park. The police had fished him out, dried him off, covered him up, and taken him to their station house. That part was easy enough. Getting an ID was another story. They were going nowhere until Lavine's bulletin came through. Then they saw the chance to palm him off on the bureau. Which seemed like a good idea, until we got there. When Tanya realized what they were trying to pull I was lucky to get her out without any blood being spilled.

The dead end at the police station set the tone for the rest of the afternoon. Tanya was too disappointed to speak much on the way back to the FBI building. She preferred to sit and stare silently at the traffic. Every street we tried was completely choked with it. There was no obvious reason why. There was no construction work. No accidents. It was as though the other vehicles had come out specifically to get in our way. There were so many we only just made it back by five o'clock. And just as we were jumping out of the car, Lavine phoned. They weren't ready. Coordinating with the other cities was taking longer than expected. He wanted to postpone the meeting till 8:00 A.M. tomorrow. Which I didn't mind, in itself. It would give us a chance to interrogate Tanya's stalkers. Only Tanya chose that moment to remember some critical task she had to complete at the consulate. Something so important there was no way she could leave it till the morning. The only upside was a clear shot at dinner. A good chance to cheer us both up.

Tanya had suggested Fong's. She was probably thinking we could pick up where we'd left things on Tuesday, but I wasn't so sure. The same restaurant three times in five nights would be a stretch, even if the previous visits had ended happily. So instead we settled on a French place I know not far from Union Square. The food's good, the service is discreet, the tables are large and well spread out, and the lights are always turned down low.

Ideal if you have to wait a while, for any reason.

We'd agreed on eight o'clock. I arrived on time. Tanya didn't, but I wasn't worried. I figured that after her previous no-show she wouldn't be more than five minutes late. Ten at the outside. There was plenty to keep me occupied. Thinking about spending time with her again, outside work. The assortment of other diners, subtly shepherded together near the window to make the restaurant look extra popular. The waiters, silently gliding around with their order pads and plates of food. The solitary barman, halfheartedly flicking a bar rag over a stack of wine glasses, and a pair of youths, eyeing the twenty-inch chrome wheels on a BMW coupe parked across the street.

My phone rang at eight fifteen. I went outside to

answer. I'd expected Tanya, calling with an apology, but it turned out to be Lavine.

"News," he said. "The Iraqi doctors from the clinic? We traced them. There were four. But they already left the country. Flew out of Newark on Monday."

"Only four?" I said. "Are you sure?"

"That's just New York. It's the same story in Boston and D.C. Four medics in each place, all flew out three days ago. We're still checking Chicago and Miami, but I'm assuming we'll find the same thing."

"Did anyone come in to replace them?"

"None that we can see, but we did link four other Iraqi nationals to Tungsten. They also bailed out Monday. Via JFK. Probably the ringleaders Taylor talked about. So it doesn't look like they're just changing shifts. More like they're folding their tents altogether."

"Does Tanya know?"

"I just called her cell. No answer. I'll try her landline in a minute."

"Any other agencies involved?"

"No. Not a one. Wasn't on anyone's radar."

"But we didn't start sniffing till yesterday. So why cut and run on Monday?"

"My guess is they weren't running. They were leaving because they were ready. Which means we're looking at a whole new scenario."

I checked the street. No one was in earshot.

"The organ thing," I said. "Maybe it's not just a gold mine."

"No," Lavine said. "More like a direct pipeline into five major cities. It gave these guys access to people. Locations. Technology. Expertise. And who knows what else."

"I've seen this before. A team moving in on the back of something else. Time to worry is when the key players pull out."

"Right. Means whatever they're planning, it's about to happen."

"They just leave the bare bones behind. Expendable nobodies. Drones, to press the button."

"It's a standard terrorist MO. They keep the key assets safe. Ready to go again, somewhere else."

"But if they pulled out on Monday, we're almost out of time. They won't wait much longer. Too much risk. Another day, maybe. Two, max."

"That's cutting it fine. We don't even know what their target is."

"Taylor might. I'll talk to him again. If he knows, he'll tell me."

"He won't. He's in the wind. His lawyer got him out. Took two minutes, after the job you did on him."

"What job? I didn't touch him."

"That's not what he says. But it's beside the point. He's gone."

"Did he get his possessions back?"

"I think so. Why?"

"I could call him. Set something up."

"I already tried. He didn't answer."

"He might do, if he sees my number. Or Mansell's. I hung on to the SIM after we dumped his calls."

"Maybe. But listen. Could you hold off on that, at least till tomorrow? When we couldn't reach Taylor, I spoke to Varley. He's trying to bring the schedule forward on the raids. It could spook them, if Taylor thinks you're still one step behind."

"OK. If we move fast on the raids. Because this is going to be huge."

"We don't know that. There's no need to scaremonger."

"We do know. Think about it. How much does a black-market kidney cost? Including the surgery?"

"I don't know. One hundred fifty thousand dollars, maybe? Why?"

"Taylor said they were doing one procedure a day. They have five clinics. That's $250 million a year, even if they stop for Christmas. You'd want a pretty big bang to turn your back on that amount of bucks."

The two youths had moved farther down the street. They were lurking near another row of parked cars. I strolled to the end of the block to take a closer look. I saw one of them hook a piece of gum out of his mouth and stick it to the top of the aerial on an old, square Chevrolet. Then they moved on to the next car in line. It was an XKR in slate-gray metallic, gleaming as though it had just rolled out of the showroom.

The guy who'd been chewing the gum leaned on the Jaguar's front wing with both hands, fingers spread wide like fat starfishes. He pressed down for ten seconds before straightening up and looking to see how much grease and filth had been transferred to the paint. His pal nodded and started to idly pick at the tip of the windshield wiper. Then they noticed me watching them. Instinctively I began to melt away, but I stopped. Because something struck me. I wasn't working. I was on my own time. There was no need to be invisible, that night. It didn't matter who saw me, or if anyone remembered my face afterward. I could stare at those guys as blatantly as I liked. I could even go over and encourage them to show a little more respect for other people's vehicles.

The idea was growing on me. But before I could act on it my phone began to ring again. And this time, it was Tanya.

"David, I'm so sorry," she said.

"You're not coming," I said.

"No."

"Why not? What is it this time?"

"Don't be cross, David. I'm in trouble."

"Why? What happened?"

"Inside my apartment. Two guys grabbed me. Now they're holding me."

"Are you hurt?"

"No. I'm OK. So far."

"Good. Now, where are you?"

"At the clinic."

"They're holding you at the clinic? On Sixty-sixth Street?"

"Yes."

"Have they said what they want?"

"Yes. You. They want you to come here, to the clinic, on your own."

"Me?"

"Yes. They say if you come alone, inside one hour, they'll let me go."

"They asked for me by name?"

"Yes. But David, don't do it. Find Mansell. I'll be—Ow. Someone just hit me."

"Don't be silly, Tanya. I'm coming to get you. Don't worry. This will all work out fine. Now, tell me. How many people are holding you? One. Two. Three. Four."

"Yes."

"Which part of the building are you in? The basement. Ground floor. First floor."

"Yes. Ow. They hit me again. They say our time's up."

"OK. Stay strong then, Tanya. I'm on my way. There's nothing to worry about. And whoever these guys are, they're going to pay."

"One more thing. They're going to text a photo of me to your phone. To remember me by. Because they say if you don't make it here inside an hour, or don't come alone, you won't recognize what you find."

"Tell them not to bother," I said. "I won't be needing it."

THIRTY-ONE

Dead-letter boxes went out with the ark, but the navy still trains you to use them.

It's not that unreasonable, if you think about it. Often the simplest solution is the best, and it's unwise to always rely on technology. And whether we thought we'd ever need the skill or not, we were sent into a south London housing estate, in pairs, to practice. One person to leave a coded message, the other to retrieve it.

My role had been to retrieve. I waited until the agreed time, then approached the drop. I walked past twice, to be sure no one was watching. But when I was happy the coast was clear, I found there was no package to pick up. I was annoyed, rather than worried. I assumed the other guy had screwed up, so I pulled back to our rendezvous point to share my thoughts on his performance. I was fifty feet away when someone sprang out at me from a gap in a broken-down fence. It was a guy from the next group up on our course. He said my partner had been mugged by a bunch of local youths and dragged into a lockup garage around the next corner. There were eight of them, and they'd been laying into him with baseball bats. He was hurt pretty bad.

We moved silently forward and peeked around the end of the fence. I could see the garage. It was on its own, surrounded by crumbling, gravel-strewn tarmac. A trail of blood led to a single vehicle-sized door at the front, which was now closed. The guy from the course wanted to rush it. With two of us he thought we'd be OK. I wasn't so sure. There was no way of approaching silently or under cover. We had no weapons. No knowledge of the youths' objectives or disposition. Nothing to force open the door. No information on the area or surroundings. And strong odds we'd end up giving them three hostages instead of one.

I pulled out my phone. It was the right decision to make. The whole scenario had been staged. The emergency procedures were drummed into us every day. We all knew the backup facilities that were available to us. The question was, did you have the presence of mind to use them when it really counted? Or would you become John Wayne and make the situation worse?

Varley, Weston, and Lavine were already in their mobile command center when I got there, twenty minutes after I sent the balloon up. It was tucked in at the end of a row of maintenance vehicles behind Temple Emanu-El on Sixty-fifth and Fifth. All three were in the control room. Weston was nearest the front, sitting at a console. The others were standing behind him. They were all staring at an array of flat-panel monitors. There were nine, arranged in a square that covered the whole end wall. None of them were working.

The central panel flickered into life just as I walked in. It showed a dainty four-story building, only two windows wide with ornate stone carvings around the frames and a sloping roof covered with embossed copper sheeting. The hulking, utilitarian offices that bore down on each side made it seem tiny and out of place, like a slice of old-world Europe sandwiched between two concrete cubes.

"The external camera's online," Weston said.

"That's the place?" I said.

"It is," Lavine said. "Looks respectable, doesn't it, for a human chop shop."

"It does," I said. "But we can soon change that."

"That won't be easy," Varley said. "We have no ground-level access at the back. No approach for a vehicle. First- and second-floor windows are heavily barred. There are no skylights."

"What about a cellar?" I said.

"There's no access to one. And we can't blast through from the neighboring buildings. Old place like that, there's too much risk of collapse."

"That just leaves the front," I said.

"Right. The front door, and the two dormer windows on the roof."

"What about inside?" I said. "Any idea where they're holding her? She told me the first floor on the phone, but she could have been moved."

"Nothing yet. But we've got surveillance teams in both office buildings. Kyle, any word on the fiber cameras?"

"Any minute now," Weston said. "They've finished drilling through. The cables are all in place. Wait—the first camera's coming up now."

As we watched, a shadowy, indistinct picture spread across the bottom left-hand monitor. I had to look closely, but could just about make out three rows of shelves piled up with bedding and towels. They were leading away from us, toward a distant flight of stone steps.

"It's the basement," Weston said. "There's not much light. The others'll be better."

One by one, brighter pictures filled the other screens until finally eight were in use. I held on, waiting for the ninth, but it remained stubbornly dark.

"OK," Lavine said, after a moment. "This is what I see. Basement: storage. Access by stairs only. Ground floor: reception desk, waiting area, two offices."

"No," Weston said. "One office, one consulting room. Look at the walls. The diagrams and posters."

"You're right," Lavine said. "One's a consulting room. Also we have stairs and an elevator. A large one."

"Big enough for a gurney," Weston said.

"It would have to be, I guess," Lavine said. "OK. First floor: I don't know. It looks like a room within a room. I can't see inside."

"It'll be their OR," Weston said. "It's an old building, drafty, they probably had to make it self-contained. Only way to guarantee it's sterile."

"Makes sense," Lavine said. "And again, stairs and an elevator. Leading to the second floor: two beds, hospital style. Vases. Flowery decor. Must be their recovery ward."

"Right," Weston said. "Looks like a nurses' station in the corner."

"And finally the attic," Lavine said. "Two small bedrooms. A bathroom. Functional, not fancy. Must be for the on-call staff."

"Right," Weston said. "But staff? Where are they?"

"Where's Tanya?" I said. "I didn't see anyone in the whole place."

"Must be in that OR," Varley said. "It's the only room we can't see into."

"That's where I'd go," Lavine said. "It's self-contained. No external walls or windows. It'll even have its own oxygen supply."

"How would you see out?" Weston said. "You wouldn't know what was going on."

"CCTV," Lavine said. "See the cameras? Both sides of the front door. More at the back. They'd just need to reroute some cables and hook up some monitors."

"How are we for sound?" I said. "Have we got any ears in there?"

Weston picked up a headset from his console, pressed a button, and repeated my question.

"Nine," he said, after a moment. "Two parabolics and seven probe mikes. Not a whisper on any of them."

"But they wouldn't reach the OR anyway," Varley said.

"So we still have to assume that's where everyone is. Agreed?"

No one replied.

"Good," Varley said. "Now, time check?"

"Tanya told David one hour," Lavine said. "That means we have twenty-four minutes remaining."

"I don't want to take this to the wire," Varley said. "They may not be that precise. Or they could panic, we could hit a snag, anything. So, Kyle. The office buildings. What's their status, please?"

Weston made another call on his headset.

"Red and blue teams are in position on the roofs," he said. "They're roped up and ready to go, in case you need both of them. All civilians are contained within the buildings. No one is being permitted to leave. All exit points are secured by our own people."

"Good," Varley said. "Now, the NYPD?"

Weston checked with someone else.

"They're ready," he said, covering his microphone with his hand. "Covert units are in place on Fifth and Madison, both sides of the junction. But they're getting jumpy. Worried about the number of people. They want to start intercepting the pedestrians right away."

"Tell them no," Varley said. "It's too risky. The clinic guys could have eyes on the street. They don't deploy till I say so."

Weston passed on Varley's orders.

"Done," he said, turning back to us. "They're standing by. Waiting for your green light."

"And the chopper?" Varley said.

"In place," Weston said. "Two minutes and we'll have their live pictures."

"All right," Varley said. "So. That just leaves you, David. Are you good to go?"

"Always," I said.

Varley decided to go with both roof teams. Eight agents. That was a big number for such a small building, especially with the lack of confirmed targets showing up on the monitors. The whole setup was a nightmare. It screamed of a trap or an ambush. But we were concerned about time. We still couldn't see into the OR. We couldn't hear anything. There was no telling what the kidnappers would do if we were forced to go in.

And they had Tanya.

I walked across East Sixty-sixth Street, directly opposite the clinic, until I reached the edge of the sidewalk. I forced myself to move slowly and smoothly, but it was nearly impossible. With each step I took another tortured vision of Tanya squirmed its way into my head. I imagined her tied up. Hooded. Thrown on the ground. A gun pressed to her head. A finger on the trigger . . .

I pushed the thoughts away and opened my jacket. I held it wide, to show anyone watching that I wasn't armed. I let ten seconds crawl by. I lifted up my shirt, to show that my waistband was clear. Five more seconds ticked away. I turned around to show I had nothing tucked in the back of my jeans. Another ten seconds. Then I stepped up to the door, paused, and knocked twice.

I was at the clinic, alone. Unarmed. It was less than an hour since Tanya's call. If the kidnappers were true to their word, it was time to let her go.

Ten seconds passed. Fifteen. There was absolute silence from inside the building. No one moved. No one came to open the door.

I raised my arms, held them out by my sides for a moment, then slowly knocked two more times. As my knuckles rapped against the wood for the last time I heard something, high above me. A pair of muffled explosions, one right on top of the other. It was the agents blowing the two dormers out of the pretty copper roof. My diversion had been a success. The kidnappers hadn't complied. Now they'd lost the chance to negotiate. I just hoped Tanya hadn't lost an awful lot more.

Another four agents streamed out of the office building to my left. One handed me a Glock. The next fixed a shaped charge to the clinic door, checked everyone was clear, and hit the button on his detonator. The door dissolved into a cloud of sawdust and the first agent was through the gap before the final few splinters had landed on the sidewalk.

Two agents dived through the door to the basement. The others stormed through reception and crashed into the consulting room. I could hear a commotion above me, but no gunfire. It would be the two roof teams swarming through the upper floors, working their way down to join us. The plan was to coincide in the hallway, but I wasn't concerned about that. Tanya had said she was on the first floor. That meant there was only one place I was interested in going. Up the stairs.

My way was blocked by an agent, on his way down. The moment I saw him I knew something was wrong. It was more than annoyance over me ignoring our instructions. I could tell by the tilt of his head. The stoop of his shoulders. The distance he kept away from me. The tired way he removed his goggles before speaking.

"Commander Trevellyan?" he said. "Sorry to tell you this, sir, but we've found your friend. At least, I think we have."

THIRTY-TWO

Every couple of years the navy brings in a new initiative. The last one was a health screening program. A series of examinations was to be held at the same time as the regular psych evaluations, presumably to keep the costs down. It was billed as a benefit, but that didn't fool anyone. Its real purpose was obvious. To minimize sick leave. It was as if we were the machines, and the bosses wanted as little downtime on the production line as possible.

The scheme was optional. I'd estimate about half a percent of people took up the offer. Even that figure might be too high. Worrying about whether you may or may not get sick at some point in the future is not a typical mind-set in my line of work.

I didn't go, myself. The way I saw it was that if something bad was waiting around the corner, I'd rather not know. And that didn't just apply to health matters.

My view had made sense, back then.

I wasn't so sure, anymore.

*

I passed four more agents on the stairs, on my way up to the first floor. All of them were carrying equipment—guns; an aluminum stepladder; a folding metal arm with a kind of claw on the end, like a larger version of the things park keepers use to pick up rubbish; a video camera on an extending pole. But none of them would look me in the eye. And I noticed something else. They were all breathing through their mouths.

The closer I got to the top of the stairs, the more I understood why. The hallway had stunk of disinfectant, like most hospitals do. The odor had lingered as I began to climb. But once I'd reached the midpoint it gave way to something else. A harsh metallic tang that coated the roof of my mouth and clung to the inside of my nostrils. It was unmistakable. The heavy, cloying stench of blood. An unhealthy smell. The kind that humans are programmed to avoid.

The final three agents were gathered outside the entrance to the OR. I walked toward them, and the stink grew worse with every step I took. They watched grimly as I drew closer and finally all three backed away, leaving me with a clear view through the door.

The body had been left neatly on the operating table. Its head was missing, but taking that into account, I figured the person would have been around five feet eight. Tanya's height. The hands were also missing, but I could see one severed wrist peeping out from under the blood-soaked theater greens. It was slender and delicate and hairless, like a young woman's. So were the feet. They were still present. And both big toes were bent slightly inward, as if she'd been used to wearing pointed shoes or boots.

Something had been left on her chest. A stainless-steel kidney dish. A small object was propped up inside. It looked like a computer memory stick, but I couldn't get close enough to check. Not without wading through an unbelievable amount of blood. I'd never seen so much in one place before. I didn't know a person contained so much. The stout pedestal holding up the operating table had literally become an island at the center of a sticky, red lake. It was almost perfectly circular, and had already flowed around two trolleys of electrical equipment and a yellow surgical-waste bin. No way was any part of me going to be next.

A sudden agitated rustling sound behind me broke my concentration. I looked around and saw four people in white paper suits emerging from the staircase. They had clear plastic bonnets on their heads, like hotel shower caps, and similar covers stretched over their shoes. Their faces were hidden behind thick breathing masks, and each one was carrying an aluminum tool case like an artist or a fisherman.

"My name's Maher," the first of them said. "Dr. Melvyn Maher. Now. You, in the leather coat. Step back. This is my crime scene. Go and wait at the MCC with the others."

"Sorry," I said. "I don't feel like cricket."

"What? Are you part of this investigation?"

"No. I just came to laugh at the clowns."

"Who are you?"

"Nice outfit, by the way. It could do with some color, though. Red might suit you."

"Are you threatening me? I'll have you removed."

"You can try. But the remains of my friend are lying in that room. And until I know who's responsible, I won't be leaving."

Varley's patience with the forensics crew lasted just less than an hour. Then he summoned Dr. Maher to the command center. I followed him to the control room. Weston and Lavine were already there.

"I know you've just got on this, Doc," Varley said. "But something's way out of whack, here. That's obvious. So I need an early heads-up. What can you give me?"

"Nothing," Maher said. "It's too soon. We're still processing. I wouldn't want to draw any conclusions at this stage. You'll have to wait."

"Nobody's going to wait, Doc. Talk to me now."

"Don't pressure me. You're being unreasonable."

"Kidnappers and murderers can have that effect. Now give me what you've got. Qualify it later if you need to."

"And if you run off down any blind alleys as a result?"

"Forget ass covering, Doc. That's not what this is about. The buck stops with me."

Maher looked down at the table and silently chewed his upper lip.

"I think this is unwise," he said, after a moment. "I

want you to know that. But if you insist, there are a few things we can be reasonably certain of. Three so far, I believe."

"Sometime today, Doc?" Varley said.

"OK, then. Don't rush me. First thing. Let's start with the victim. I understood you were aiming to rescue a woman hostage?"

"Correct."

"Well, the body in the OR isn't hers. It's male."

Weston, Varley, and Lavine exchanged puzzled glances.

"Are you sure?" I said.

"Of course," Maher said. "It's hardly the kind of thing I get wrong. He was skinny and slightly effeminate, yes, but certainly not female."

"So it's not Tanya," Weston said. "She could still be alive."

"Are you anywhere with an ID?" Varley said.

"There was nothing helpful on the body," Maher said. "And the head and hands had been removed, presumably to hinder identification. But fortunately we're a little more resourceful than that. One of my technicians hacked into the building security system. Only one person swiped in, but not back out again. His name was Kelvin Taylor. It gave his position as a director of the parent health care company."

"Kelvin Taylor?" Weston said. "We know him. Naughty."

"He should have stayed in jail," I said.

"This is unconfirmed, remember," Maher said. "Nothing's guaranteed till we hear back from the lab. We need a DNA match to be sure who he was. Assuming we have a reference sample, of course."

"Understood," Varley said. "But put a rush on it, will you, Doc? It could be important."

"What about Tanya Wilson?" I said. "The hostage. Any trace?"

"Not at this stage," Maher said.

"They must have taken her somewhere," I said. "Any indication?"

"Nothing, I'm afraid," Maher said. "But we'll keep looking."

"Keep us posted," Varley said. "Meantime, what else?"

"Second thing. Cause of death."

"Let me guess. His head was cut off."

"No. Seems that nothing in this case is as it appears on the surface. The decapitation occurred postmortem. So did the removal of the victim's hands."

"How do you know?"

"The blood tells us. Think about the vessels in the neck and wrists. If the heart had still been beating when any of those were severed, blood would have been forced out under considerable pressure. It would have sprayed in a series of diminishing arcs, leaving a completely different pattern. Very recognizable. Whereas in this case, you can see from the extensive pooling that the blood literally drained out of the victim."

"So why the chop job?"

"I don't know. We may not be able to make sense of it till we find the missing body parts."

"Then what did kill him?"

"Preliminary findings suggest exsanguination due to the introduction of a catastrophic blood thinning agent."

"Bleeding to death?"

"Yes. But no ordinary bleeding. The blood was thinned to such a colossal extent it would have escaped from the vessels even without them being cut."

"What can do that?"

"I'm not sure. A drug of some kind, I'd imagine. But nothing I've encountered before. Nothing that acts so fast, anyway. We found a syringe in the sharps bin with traces of an unidentified clear liquid, and several unopened vials in the controlled-drugs cupboard. No labels, obviously. We'll know more at the lab, but it looks to me like an extreme derivative of heparin or possibly warfarin. Both are commonly available. They're used legitimately as anticoagulants."

"I thought warfarin was rat poison."

"That's one use. Bait is doused with the drug, and if rats ingest it in high enough concentrations they die from massive internal bleeding. It's a hideous way to go, even for vermin. The same thing happened to this victim. But in his case, the drug was administered intravenously. And it had been altered to increase the potency. Probably by a factor of many thousands."

"Would Taylor have known what was happening to him?"

"Most likely. He probably would have seen the first

traces oozing out through his pores before he lost consciousness."

"Human ingenuity never ceases to amaze me, Doc. So, down to your last point?"

"Yes. Well. This is where it gets difficult. We just don't have sufficient data. All I can definitely tell you is this. There was more going on in the clinic than illegal organ transplantation. But exactly what? I need time in the lab to be certain."

"Best guess?"

"No guesswork. But I can tell you that we found components from miniature detonators. The kind that are activated by radio signals. We're still looking for traces of explosives."

"Any sign of a transmitter?"

"None. But it doesn't look like the usual cell phone–based type. We're thinking in terms of Wi-Fi."

"So we're looking at an Internet bomb factory?"

"That seems likely. We need to confirm the volatile material involved, but it would appear that someone has used the place to construct a series of compact devices. And given the presence of the victim and the lack of anyone else, there's a strong likelihood the devices have already been planted. Or are in transit."

"And you're only telling me this now?"

"We need time to analyze. Rushing helps no one. A false conclusion can be more dangerous than—"

"Any indication as to targets?"

"Nothing. But we're still looking."

"David, what about Taylor? Think back. Everything he said. Was there anything that could give us a clue?"

"No," I said. "But he may not have known. He said the people from Iraq took over the organ smuggling a few weeks back. They brought their own doctors. This murder, the drug, the explosives—it could all be their doing."

"Damn," Varley said. "And we can't ask him now. Look, are there any bombs out there, or not? We need to know. And if so, where? And how many? And how big? Doctor, this is your top priority. Put everyone on it. I don't care about anything else."

"What about Tanya?" I said.

"I'm sorry, David," Varley said. "We need a handle on this first."

"Then why not start with the memory stick?" I said.

"What memory stick?" Varley said.

"The one from the OR," I said. "Left where we couldn't miss it. Now we know bombs are involved, I bet it's some kind of warning. If you want the target, that's where I'd look."

"Doctor?" Varley said.

"I agree," Maher said.

"And you were going to tell me, when?" Varley said. "Christmas? When the bombs have gone off? When I'm up to my ass in casualties?"

"I'd be at the lab right now, analyzing it," Maher said. "If I wasn't here, answering premature questions."

"Where is it?" Varley said. "The stick."

"Right here," Maher said. "In my case."

"Hand it over."

"No."

"Right now, Doctor, please."

"I can't. There's a dozen reasons why not. It would compromise the chain of evidence, for a start. And there may be prints, which would be lost if you started pawing at it. The chip could contain viruses, or other malicious code. Untold damage could be done. You can't just blunder in."

"What brand is it?" I said.

"I didn't note that," Maher said. "Why?"

"It could be significant. Is it all bagged up?"

"Of course."

"Can I just have a peek? For a second? Through the plastic?"

Maher sighed. Then he flipped open his metal case, took out a two-by-three-inch evidence bag, and gingerly handed it to me.

"Sandisk," I said. "One gigabyte. Probably came from Radio Shack."

"Is that important?" Maher said. "What does it mean?"

"That you should get out more," I said, tossing the package across the table to Varley.

THIRTY-THREE

Time was, you wanted to threaten someone, you'd leave them a note.

You could use a pen and paper, and write with your "wrong" hand. Or you could type. Or cut the letters out of newspapers. If it was for a whole community, you could phone a radio station with a handkerchief over the mouthpiece.

But now we have computers.

The application of technology really is universal.

Varley told Weston to dig out a stand-alone laptop, and as soon as it had booted up he slotted the memory stick into a USB port at the side of the machine. The end of the stick flickered blue, and after a moment a dialogue box opened on the computer screen. The title bar read REMOVABLE DISK (E:). A note said the disk contained video files, and a series of options was listed underneath.

"Click on the bottom one," Maher said. "*Take no action.* Then give the thing back to me and let me take it to the lab."

Weston chose OPEN FOLDER TO VIEW FILES. Another window opened. It contained a single icon. The image looked like a quarter of a DVD superimposed over a strip of movie film. Beneath that was a file name. Or rather a number: 320. There was no extension. The description was *InterVideo Media File*, and the given size was 10,082 KB.

"That's a chunky file," Weston said. "Shall I play it?"

"No," Varley said. "Let's absorb the information via ESP."

Weston double-clicked on the icon and an image appeared like the front of a 1950s television, filling the screen. It was blank. At first it was silent, but after a moment you could hear a soft heartbeat. It sounded human. It started quietly, almost subliminally, and grew louder by the second.

"Like *Dark Side of the Moon*," Lavine said. "Cool."

The figure three appeared. Then a two. Then a zero. The digits were white. They swelled up until they filled the screen and shrank back to the center in time with the steady pulse. Out and in, out and in, hypnotically, for fifteen seconds. Then the numbers were replaced by images. A one-legged child leaning on an improvised wooden crutch. Burned-out cars strewn by the side of desert roads. An old lady cowering in the shattered remains of her home. A filthy hospital corridor crammed with listless amputees on stretchers. Each new scene emerged from the center of the last as if pushed out by the relentless throbbing heartbeat until at last the screen faded to red. The number 320 returned. And then text started to appear, scrolling from left to right, one letter at time like an old vidiprinter display.

> *Each day that passes, you crush a little tighter*
> *the heart of our nation.*
> *Now, we strike back in symbolic vengeance.*
> *Leave our soil, or more shall drown in their own blood.*

"David was right," Varley said. "It is a warning. But it's the weirdest one I've ever seen."

"Talk about cryptic," Lavine said.

"Strike at the heart of our nation?" Weston said. "Symbolic vengeance? That can only mean one thing. An attack on D.C."

"That gives them hundreds of targets," Lavine said. "Which one? Or ones?"

"No need to panic," Varley said. "We have contingencies for this. They're well rehearsed. All we need is an idea of the time frame."

"What about this number?" Weston said. "Three twenty? Why does it keep flashing up all the time?"

"I don't know," Lavine said. "Three twenty. That's the area code for Minnesota. Could that be what they take as the heart of the nation? It's kind of in the middle. East to west, anyway."

"Or an Airbus 320?" Weston said. "Another hijack?"

"No," Maher said. "It's not a number. It's a date. Like 9/11."

"March 20?" Lavine said. "Why pick that?"

"Where were those photos taken, do you think?" Maher said.

"Iraq, obviously," Lavine said.

"What happened to Iraq on March 20?" Maher said.

No one answered.

"Two thousand three?" Maher said.

Silence.

"Shock and awe got your tongues?" Maher said. "That's when we invaded the place."

"Are you sure that was the date?" Varley said.

"Certain," Maher said.

"Then it can't be a coincidence," Varley said. "But March 20? That's tomorrow. We've got less than twenty-four hours."

"Much less," I said. "If they're really being symbolic."

"Of course," Varley said. "The time, as well. They'll go for 3:20A.M."

Lavine checked his watch.

"That's less than four and a half hours," he said. "We've got no chance."

"Yes we have," Varley said, getting to his feet. "Make the call. Right now. You know the codes. Kyle, get the car. La Guardia, on the double. Doc, you get to the lab. David, are you coming with us?"

"No," I said. "I can't help feeling we're missing something."

"Yeah," Varley said. "The chance to save lives, if we don't haul ass."

"Think about it," I said. "Something here doesn't add

up. Why did Tungsten use Tanya to deliver the warning, for a start?"

"I don't know," Weston said. "But it does seem strange."

"We know she was curious," Lavine said. "Maybe she went snooping around and they caught her?"

"I can't see it," Weston said. "That video must have taken time to produce. They must have had a plan for delivering it. Relying on catching a snooper wouldn't work. And was Tanya really stupid enough to go down there, alone?"

"No, she wasn't," I said. "And anyway, she told me they were waiting at her apartment."

"Which begs the question, why would Tungsten be staking her out?" Weston said.

"Good questions," Varley said. "I don't know the answers. We can unpick it later. But right now, stopping the bombs is our priority."

"You should hold fire until we're clear about what's going on here," I said. "You have hordes of guys in Washington. Can't you put them on it?"

"No," Varley said. "This is too high-profile. We need to get our boots on the sidewalk."

"Here's another thought," I said. "Why ask for me in particular?"

"Tanya knew you," Lavine said. "She trusted you."

"But Tungsten didn't," I said. "Why would they want me at the clinic? They didn't know I existed when they made that video. Delivering it was critical. Why make that hinge on me?"

"Time's up," Varley said. "We've got to move. Come with us, David. We'll piece it together on the plane."

"No," I said. "You go. I'm staying here. I'll figure it out, myself."

"If you must," Varley said. "But be honest. This is about guilt for losing Tanya. Talking isn't going to help you find her."

"I won't find her in D.C.," I said.

"You won't find her here, either," Varley said. "Face it, David. It's been too long."

"I told her I was coming for her," I said. "And that's a promise I'm not about to break."

"You're one guy, on your own," Varley said. "What will you do? Sit around and wait for them to call? Forget it, David. Come with us. Help us do some good."

Waiting for them to call wasn't part of my plan. And if it had been, I wouldn't have got very far. I'd switched my phone to silent before setting off for the clinic. Old habits die hard. Varley's comment reminded me. I pulled it out of my pocket. I was going to switch it back to normal when I saw an envelope symbol was bouncing around the screen. A new text had arrived.

having fun playing with my boys? hope so. i'm having fun playing with your girl

I showed Lavine.

"Doesn't sound good," he said. "Who's it from? Do you recognize the number?"

"No," I said. "I've never seen it before."

"Call it back," Weston said. "See if anyone answers."

I dialed, then hit the key to activate the phone's tiny built-in speaker.

A recorded voice answered after one ring. It was Lesley's.

"Please choose from the following three options," it said. "If you're David Trevellyan calling in a panic about your soon-to-be-late friend Tanya, press one. If you're the FBI wanting to know the difference between your head and your ass, press two. Everyone else, please call back later. I'm having too much fun to come to the phone right now."

I looked around the table and saw three shocked faces. Dr. Maher just looked confused.

"I don't understand," Lavine said. "I thought the Tungsten people had Tanya. If Lesley has her, why did she send David to the clinic to find Tungsten's message?"

"The woman is obviously working with Tungsten," Maher said. "Surely this clarifies things?"

"No, it doesn't," Weston said. "It does the opposite. Lesley and Tungsten are totally separate. Completely unrelated. We proved that."

"The evidence suggests otherwise," Maher said.

"Wait, back up," Lavine said. "How can Lesley have her? She's in jail. After her run-in with David on Tuesday night."

"Enough," Varley said, slamming his palm on the table. "Come on. We've got bombs to find. I don't get this, either, but we'll make some calls from the car. Now move it, all of you."

Twelve chair legs scraped across the floor as Weston, Lavine, and Maher got to their feet. I stayed where I was, looking at the phone, trying to force all the pieces back into place in my head. I was still holding it three seconds later when another text arrived. It was from the same number.

sorry i missed u. 2 busy 2 talk. u can have tanya back when i'm done with her. meantime have attached picture. promised before but 4got. am i bad?

I pressed the button and a blurry image slowly filled the screen. Dark thoughts started to form in my mind. I looked at the photograph for another moment, then handed the phone to Weston.

"Ignore her face," I said. "Look at her right wrist."

"A leather strap," he said. "And a metal frame. Like that wheelie-cage thing. At Lesley's house."

"Or could it be that cellar place?" Lavine said. "That had white walls, too."

"No," Weston said. "I can see a window."

"Give me some car keys," I said.

"You're going there?" Lavine said.

I didn't answer.

"You can't go on your own," Weston said. "It's the same deal as here. She's a hostage. We need to send a team."

"Forget it," Varley said. "There's no time. And we know who we're dealing with, remember. If Lesley has her, we don't need hostage rescue. We need a mop and a bucket."

"I'll still be needing those keys," I said.

"Where is it?" Lavine said, sliding his Bart Simpson ring across the table. "Westchester, somewhere? I'll call the local PD. Have them meet you there."

"I'd rather you didn't," I said.

THIRTY-FOUR

No one ever lost anything during our navy training.

That wasn't because we were particularly careful with our stuff. Or due to any fines or punishments we might have suffered. It was because of the quartermaster. He was the most practical person in the barracks by a country mile. Whenever part of anyone's kit was missing he didn't waste time getting angry. He wasn't interested in where it had last been seen or if you'd sold it or who might have stolen it.

To him, there was only one reason you couldn't find something.

You were looking in the wrong place.

The first time I was taken to Lesley's house it took fifty minutes, in the trunk of her car. Driving myself that night in Lavine's, it took thirty.

The Westchester County police were already there, waiting, when I arrived. I could see red and blue lights beckoning to me through the foliage as I took the final corner. They were coming from a squad car. It was parked sideways, blocking the entrance to her yard. I slid to a halt next to it and saw three more cars lined up nearer the house. I looked for the officers. I counted eight. They all had shotguns and flak jackets, but their body language seemed pretty relaxed. Almost bored. One was on his own, down by the garage entrance, leaning on the doorframe. Another was squatting on the ground outside the open front door. Five of them were hanging around in the space between the fence and their vehicles. And the final guy was ambling across the gravel, toward me. I jumped out of the car and moved around to intercept him.

"I'm Officer Rossi," he said. "I'm in charge here. You the English Navy guy? Commander Trevor-Lyon?"

"Trevellyan," I said, showing him my ID.

"Well, sir, looks like you've wasted your time. Nobody here but us."

The knot in my stomach wound itself another notch tighter.

"You've checked inside?" I said.

"Every room, top to bottom," he said. "Looks like no one's been here since CSU cleared the place."

"When was that?"

"Tuesday. Late p.m."

"And after that? Have you kept the house secure?"

"No, sir. No one asked us to. We drove back out, just now, when the Bureau called."

I set off toward the path.

"Are you going to take a look, anyway?" Rossi said.

"That's why I came," I said.

"Do you want me to show you around?"

"No, thanks. I know where I'm going."

"OK. If you're sure. One thing, though. I've got to ask you to take care if you go in the home office. First floor. End of the corridor. We've still got a situation going on in there."

The officer at the front door looked over to Rossi, then shuffled aside to let me pass. I made my way straight through the hall, down the stairs, and into the basement. I figured that if Tanya had been brought to the house, they probably would have kept her in one of the dog cages, at least for a short while. She was intelligent, resourceful, and well trained. The way she'd chosen her words on the phone showed she was thinking on her feet. If there was a way to leave a note or sign, she would have found it. I was confident of that. But there was nothing down there for me. The basement had been completely stripped. Even the cages were gone.

I headed back up the stairs and kept going until I reached the landing. I could see Lesley's office door was shut this time. It was stuck to its frame with yellow and black tape. I held down the handle, burst it open, and continued into the room. A cluster of numbered, yellow evidence markers had appeared on the floor, like a crop of angular plastic fungi. They were in a wide, flat U-shape where the end of the table would have been. The crime scene guys must have been busy with their ultraviolet lights.

The laboratory bottle had also been replaced with an evi-

dence marker, but the trolley was still there. It was in the
same place it had been when I was here with Weston.
And the leather straps were just as empty. Tanya wasn't
attached to it. And if she ever had been, there was no sign
of her now.

I took out my phone, pulled up the picture of Tanya,
and held the screen next to the trolley. The frame looked
similar, but I couldn't be sure it was the same. The image
was too small and too dark and too blurred. There was
nothing to say Lesley didn't have two trolleys. Or more.
And nothing to pinpoint the location. The photo could
have been taken anywhere. I felt as if I'd been tricked. No,
that wasn't right. Cheated. Out of the only thing that really
mattered just then. The only thing that Tanya and I really
couldn't afford to lose. Time.

Officer Rossi was waiting for me in the hallway.

"Find what you need?" he said.

"No," I said.

"Sorry to hear that. Anything I can help you with?"

"The woman who owns this house. Does she have any
other places around here? Homes, offices, shops, garages,
storage facilities? Anywhere with some privacy?"

"No, I don't think so."

"Then there's nothing you can do. I'll head back to the
city. Thanks, anyway."

"I could do a search online? There's a terminal in the
car."

"There's no point. Records of anything she owns will

be well hidden. I need firsthand information. From someone who knows her. And I've got the perfect people in mind."

"Will they play ball? The way I hear it, the woman's pretty brutal."

"Oh, yes. They will. They're dying to. They just don't know it yet."

I waited until I was around the corner, out of sight, then called Lavine.

"Did you find her?" he said.

"No," I said. "The house was untouched. Lesley must have another place her people can use."

"Any idea where?"

"Not yet. So I need a minute with those two guys. The ones I caught at your office. They obviously work for her."

"David, it's better if I don't know things like that."

"I've got no choice. I need your help. You put them in the system. You can find out where they're being held."

"Be reasonable. Talk about compromising my position."

"How about we talk about Tanya's position. How compromised that might be."

"Fair point. I'll call you back."

Lavine was back on the line before I reached the freeway.

"I've got bad news," he said. "And I've got really bad news. Which do you want first?"

"I can always rely on you to cheer me up, Lavine," I said. "Give me the really bad news."

"The two guys you were asking about? Both are dead. They're gone, David. I'm sorry."

"When?" I said.

"Ninety minutes after they were popped."

"They lasted that long? How did it happen?"

"Their throats were cut. I don't have the ins and outs. But it has Lesley written all over it. She can't have trusted them to keep quiet, I guess."

"Damn. I'll have to lean on Lesley herself, now. And she'll be a much tougher nut to crack. Anywhere with witnesses, anyway. Where is she now?"

"Yes. Lesley. That brings me to the bad news."

"What is it? She's dead, too?"

"Not dead. But just as hard to talk to. We're nowhere near finding her. The NYPD has turned up nothing. Same story for our guys. We're chasing shadows."

"Tell me you're joking. Tell me now, and I'll spare your wife and children."

"I'm as pissed as you, David. And you should have heard what Varley said."

"Do we even know what happened?"

"She pulled a switcheroo. Feigned illness, swapped IDs with another sick prisoner, and broke out of the secure hospital. The oldest trick in the book."

"When?"

"Yesterday morning. It took them thirty-six hours to

get to the bottom of it. We've only just got the full picture, ourselves."

"So what's been done about it?"

"Our field office is all over it. The NYPD has pushed descriptions out to all their patrols. They're staking out that tenement building you found of hers, and searching for any more property she could own. And they're going to recanvass Tanya's building. They're still trying to get a solid lead on the guys who snatched her. I'll keep the heat turned up. As soon as I know anything, you'll know."

"OK. Understood. Just make sure it's soon."

"What will you do now?"

"Don't know. Head over to her apartment myself, I guess. Try and put my hands on someone there. I'm only forty minutes out."

"Sounds like you're clutching at straws."

"Got any better ideas?"

"Just don't do anything you'll regret."

"Me? Never. But how about you? Found anything that goes bump in the night?"

"Nada."

"Did big-head Maher come up with anything, now he's back at his lab?"

"No. Well, yes. But nothing useful."

"Such as?"

"Something about that weird blood drug."

"Have they put a name to it?"

"No. They're nowhere with that yet. But it's obviously

some deliberately made thing. And the surgeons were from Iraq, so Maher's wondering if it's part of some different procedure they have over there. He's trying to find someone to check with."

"What did he find, then?"

"Nothing. He's just curious about the quantity involved. They found another whole bunch of vials in the basement. All used."

"Empty medicine bottles? Sounds pretty normal for a clinic."

"But you saw how strong the stuff is. Taylor took a whole vial. That means they'd only need a tiny bit for any patients they didn't want to kill. So either they had millions of patients, which we don't know about, or they threw most of it away."

"It's probably just a scam to charge more. Private clinic. Desperate patients. It's a license to print money. Do you know what the busiest piece of equipment in that place was?"

"No. What?"

"The credit card machine. Check it, if you don't believe me."

THIRTY-FIVE

The navy spends its training budget on all kinds of strange things.

I was once sent on a course to learn about how I learn. Seriously. It seems there are different ways, and knowing which one suits you is allegedly beneficial. For example, some people favor an auditory style, which means they like things explained to them in words. Others are kinesthetic. That's a fancy way of saying they learn from experience. And the final group are visual. Breaking ideas and concepts down into pictures and diagrams is the key thing for them.

It turned out I was a visual person.

Only it's not just textbook illustrations I respond to.

I took the curving on-ramp far faster than strictly necessary and kept my foot on the gas until the tires started to squeal. I'd hoped it was late enough for the highway to be clear, but I saw another vehicle trundling through the junction, making me drop a little speed. It was an old van. Its dull silver bodywork looked rough, as though it had been badly resprayed, and a crude picture of a woman had been painted on the side. She was half sitting, half lying back with one knee raised. Her clothes were all leather and fishnets and her wild purple hair flowed all the way back to the rear doors. I couldn't help wondering who it was based on.

I pulled onto the main highway and moved straight into the left-hand lane. I saw a picture had been painted on the far side of the van, too. It was another figure, in the same pose as the purple-haired woman. But this one's clothes were all torn open and inside them lay a grinning skeleton. It still had its head and hands, but somehow it reminded me of the body I'd seen in the OR. The two paintings could be before and after shots, like some government health warning against the mystery blood drug.

The silver van rapidly dwindled to nothing in my mirrors, and after it disappeared I didn't come across another vehicle for twelve or thirteen miles. There was no other traffic on either side to distract me. Nothing to divert my imagination from what Lesley might have in store for Tanya. Or what she might already be doing to her. My foot leaned harder on the gas and the heavy sedan swayed through the next set of bends. I was moving fast, but I had no idea if I was heading in the right direction. My only leads had gone up in smoke. No one had a clue where Tanya was. I certainly didn't know where to look. And all the time the car's wheels were thumping tirelessly on the road like the ticking of a giant clock, counting down what few minutes I had left to find her.

The toll plaza had been busy on Saturday when Weston brought me back from Lesley's, but now, with no one around, it looked like a field the day after a festival. There was debris everywhere. Coffee cups, soda cans, food wrappers, newspapers. All kinds of rubbish that people must have jettisoned while they were inching along in the queues, earlier in the day.

A slight breeze was blowing across to my right, stirring up the lighter items. It caught an A5-sized piece of paper and set it dancing, holding it level with my window for a second. It was an advertisement for a mobile dog-grooming service. I looked around and saw dozens more lying discarded on the ground. They were from a whole range of different places. But none were takeout menus. And none had my picture on them, this time, either.

I wondered what had happened to all the flyers the NYPD were handing out on Monday. Some would have been discarded straightaway, I guessed. Others would have been held on to, at least for a while. Some might still be in people's cars. I wondered how far they'd been taken. I imagined them radiating out from that point on the highway, trampled on floors and stuffed into door pockets. I pictured a map with tiny colored dots to show their final destinations, like the one of the railroad victims in the FBI's office. In my mind, these dots were also red. Only I could see hundreds, scattered randomly all over the country.

I thought about the image. What it could mean. And then, once again, I picked up my phone and called Lavine.

"Anything?" I said.

"No," he said. "We've got two and a half hours left. Varley's going nuts. It's chaos. So much for well-rehearsed protocols. More like setting a bunch of monkeys loose in a banana plantation."

"Then listen. I've got another question. The medicine vials Maher's people found. At the clinic. Were there all different types? Or just the mystery ones."

"Just the mystery ones," he said. "Why?"

"How many were there?"

"It doesn't mean anything. We already thought about it. We figure they disposed of the other kinds in the normal way, and hung on to the mystery ones because they aren't licensed here."

"I understand that. But how many were there?"

"Let me check. Seventy-two."

"Were they all used?"

"No. Sixty-five were used. Seven were unopened."

"The sixty-five, does that include the one they used on Taylor?"

"I think so. Let's see. Yes, it does."

"OK. So that makes sixty-four used on patients. Have you heard from the other clinics? Did they find any vials?"

"David, I don't have time for inventory queries. Can't this wait?"

"No. It can't. Think about it. There are five clinics. What's five times sixty-four?"

"Three hundred twenty. OK, that's weird. I'm putting you on hold for a minute."

He was back after two minutes.

"Boston and D.C. did find vials," he said. "There were sixty-four hidden away in both places. All were used. We've got to assume it's the same for the others."

"I think we do."

"Three hundred twenty vials. That number again. But you were expecting it?"

"Yes."

"How come?"

"Because I know what they're doing."

"You do? Then talk to me. Stop wasting time. The bombs. Where are they?"

"Nowhere. There aren't any. You're on a wild-goose chase."

"We aren't. Maher found detonators. Bomb-making equipment."

"He did. But no explosive. And he said *miniature*. Focus on that."

"Prepacked explosive, so no trace. And powerful, so small size."

"No. Something else altogether."

"Maher's people are on this, you know. They're the best. And they're thinking there must be a large number of devices. Each one too small to do much harm on its own. But coordinated, so that together they could take down a power grid, say. Or a telecom network. Or the water supply. It's a recipe for maximum chaos."

"No. Look at what they had at the clinics. The drug. Remote triggers. And one other thing. Something unique to them."

"What?"

"Access to the inside of people's bodies. It wasn't just ripped-off organs they were putting back in there."

"They planted bombs inside people? You're crazy."

"Not bombs. Devices for releasing the drug. They put them in during the operation, alongside the new organ. They lie dormant till a signal triggers them. Then a whole vial's worth of the drug gets dumped directly into the bloodstream. And you know what happens next. Ten pints of the red stuff pours straight out through the poor bastard's skin, like water through tissue paper."

"Is that even possible?"

"I've heard of similar things, for cancer and diabetes."

"Using mechanical devices? With remote control? Nationwide?"

"Not so far. They've used polymers, up to now. For gradual diffusion."

"Any proof they've made the leap?"

"It's the only thing that makes sense."

"I don't know. It doesn't tally with the video."

"It does. They said people would drown in their own blood. And you saw Taylor."

"Taylor didn't drown."

"Not literally. But you get the picture."

"I still don't buy it. Think of the resources you'd need."

"You've seen the drug they developed. That shows a high degree of competence in itself. And the guys they brought over were transplant surgeons. Implanting things in people is their day job."

"It still seems like—"

"Lavine, stop talking. You believe me, or you don't. You save these people, or you don't. Either way, I don't care. I don't know them. I'm not interested in them. Stay in D.C. Look for your nonexistent bombs. Knock yourself out. Just call me when you have news about Tanya."

THIRTY-SIX

There was a moment when I thought my career in the navy was over before it even began. It was at the end of the first exercise I'd been sent on, away from barracks. I was sitting in the course supervisor's office with two other people. My training officer, who'd been summoned especially for the meeting, and the psychologist who'd been observing me for the previous two days. I remember looking at their faces and thinking that absolutely nothing good was about to happen.

The course had been all about teamwork. There were thirty-two other people in the group. They were all up for jobs in the civil service. The Home Office, Inland Revenue, Employment Service, that kind of thing. All their written exams were out of the way. Now they just had to show how well they could work together. It was the final hurdle for them. It felt like the final straw for me.

We had to sit through two full days of role plays and discussions and debates. *Your plane has crashed in the jungle. What should you do? Your ship is sinking. Which two people should you save? You have to market a new soft toy. What kind should it be?* And if that wasn't painful enough, they forced a group feedback session on us between each exercise. *How fully did you involve the quieter members of the group? How do you feel about the inclusiveness of your performance? How could you encourage everyone to contribute more actively?*

At least there was no hugging.

The psychologist's verdict wasn't complimentary. He left no room for misunderstanding about that. Every word he uttered for half an hour was carefully chosen to show exactly how badly he thought of me. By the time he left the room I was half expecting to be arrested as a menace to society. But when the door closed behind him my training officer's stern face broke into a huge smile. He roared with laughter. And then he took me for a drink.

The navy works in strange ways. I know that now. But at the time I had no idea what the assessors had been told. They thought they had to rubber-stamp me for a staff role. Not out of mischief. But because people are naturally inclined to give you the answer they think you want. They have to be really certain of themselves to dig in and contradict you. Especially when you're paying their wages. So with a lot of external tests, the navy runs things backward. You have to fail to pass. And that one I failed with flying colors.

So in the end, whether he meant to or not, the psychologist did me a favor. A huge one. He opened the door for me to work on my own. That freed me from depending on other people to make progress. And from feeling responsible for what happened to anyone else.

Until Tanya went missing, anyway.

Then I was back to doing both.

The night doorman at Tanya's building rolled over the minute he saw my consulate ID. He gave up her spare keys immediately. He didn't even ask me to move my fingers away from the expiration date at the bottom of the pass. Which was lucky, since it had run out at midnight on Sunday.

I saw no one in the corridors or elevators on my way up to Tanya's floor. And no sign of the police doing any canvassing. Maybe they'd already finished, and found nothing. Or maybe they hadn't started yet. Either way, I wasn't encouraged.

There was a fresh scratch in the gray paint around the lock on Tanya's door. It was half an inch long and roughly curved, as if someone had been careless with their key. I couldn't say it was significant. But equally, I couldn't rule it out. Tanya could have done it herself. Or the previous resident. Or the kidnappers. Or even the police. Without equipment and people and time to run tests, there was just no way of knowing.

I've lost count of the number of offices and houses and flats I've rifled through in my career. I'd lost count before the end of my first year. It's the kind of thing that feels alien the first few times but quickly becomes tediously routine. The fear of being disturbed or leaving some telltale sign of your presence soon passes, and instinct and training take over. You learn to anticipate the likely places where people try to conceal things, thinking they're clever. Mundane, scattered items form patterns before your eyes, revealing your suspect's true character and habits. Normally I wouldn't turn a hair, walking in uninvited through someone's front door while they were out. But stepping into Tanya's apartment felt very different. Partly because what I was searching for was so intangible—signs of who had ambushed her and where they might have gone after the clinic—but mostly because this time the job wasn't professional.

It was personal.

Tanya had only been at that address for five days and she'd hardly had time to scratch the surface of making it her home. The kitchen drawers and cupboards were empty except for one box of imported tea bags. A carton of milk stood on its own in the cavernous fridge. Two takeaway Thai food containers lay in the trash, accompanied by plastic cutlery and a couple of diet Coke cans. Five heavy cardboard boxes were lined up against a pair of bookshelves in the main room. They were still sealed up with wide strips of packing tape. There was no sofa. No chairs. No TV or stereo. No pictures on the walls or blinds at the windows. But more unhelpfully, no signs of a struggle. No cryptic messages. And nothing left for me to interpret or decode.

I'd imagined walking into Tanya's bedroom a thousand times, but never under these circumstances. Pulling back her duvet felt intrusive, not intimate. I moved on to her wardrobe, then her bathroom. I felt like a pervert, rooting through her personal things, but I carried on anyway. And turned up absolutely nothing. I kept on looking until I was certain there was nothing there to work with. Nothing I could uncover on my own, anyway. Maybe a forensics team could take things further, but with the facilities at my disposal I'd hit a dead end. Again. And now, I was out of ideas.

I could only hope Tanya wasn't out of time.

I moved back into the main room, perched on the windowsill, and called Lavine.

"I've scoured her place," I said. "No luck at all. How about the NYPD. Anything?"

"Kyle's talking to them now," he said. "I should know in a minute. Hold on."

I swiveled around and looked out of the window, just for something to do. There wasn't much of a view. The apartment was in the wrong part of the building for that. All I could see was other people's light spilling out and throwing shadows down to the courtyard, seven floors below.

"Have you thought about my idea?" I said. "About the drug implants?"

"We've been kicking it around," he said.

"And?"

"Varley's not convinced. He thinks it's not spectacular enough."

"But that's the whole point. Spectacular's out of fashion. No one can top 9/11, so attacks are becoming more personal, now."

"I don't know. Varley thinks it lacks impact."

"He didn't see Taylor's body, though, did he? Neither did you."

"No."

"Well, picture this. You go to bed with your wife, everything perfectly normal. You wake up in the morning and she's dead. But that's not all. The bed is soaked with her blood. Saturated with it. So are you. Like you've bathed in it. The room stinks. It's all over the floor. It's flooded out of the door and down the stairs and filled half the hallway. It's dripping through the ceiling of the room below—"

"Stop it, now. You're exaggerating."

"Or it could be your parents. Your kids. Neighbors. Friends . . ."

"OK. I'm getting the picture."

"It's about taking terror out of the public space and bringing it into people's homes. Taking their sanctuary away. No one would feel safe. Anywhere. At any time. Tell me that doesn't have impact."

"Maybe you're right. Let me talk to him again."

"You don't need to talk about it. You need to find a way to stop it happening. What about patient lists? Client records from the clinics?"

"That's a nonstarter. Maher told me there was no paperwork recovered at all. From any of the sites. And all their computers were wiped, as well."

"Computers? Wait a minute. Didn't Maher say the devices were rigged for Wi-Fi, not cell phones?"

"Yes. That's his theory."

"Then that's the answer. Talk to the phone companies.

And whoever pipes in the cable TV. Shut down the broad-band at source. That way, you'd stop the signal getting through. Whether they're bombs or drug implants or any-thing else we haven't thought of."

"Shut down the Internet? We could do that, I suppose. We've done it before. But here's the problem. What if the devices work the other way around, like burglar alarms? It might be stopping the signal that sets them off. What-ever they are."

"So. We're no further forward."

"No. Oh, hang on. Kyle's off the phone. Let me talk to him. Give me a second."

I could see that quite a few rooms were still lit up, all around the courtyard. Maybe seven out of every ten. Quite a few people must still have been awake. They must have been awake earlier, when Tanya was taken. I thought about going around and knocking on their doors. The police might have drawn a blank before, if they'd even tried, but jogging memories is a gift of mine.

"OK, I'm back," Lavine said. "This is how we stand. The NYPD is throwing everything they have into finding Lesley. They've brought in all their specialist squads. Organized Crime. Vice. Narcotics. Major Case. Computer Crime. Everyone. A bunch of our own guys are backing them up. Varley's even reached out to the DEA, to see if they know anything."

"When will we hear?"

"I don't know. Lesley's a slippery customer."

"So basically no one has made any progress."

"No."

The light went out in one of the apartments, opposite. Then another, almost immediately. I would have to get moving if I wanted to talk to people, tonight.

"Look, thanks anyway," I said. "But I've had an idea at this end. A long shot, but I'm going to give it a try. Call me if anything breaks."

"Will do," he said.

Two more lights went out, away to my left. The useless, lazy bastards. People who'd just been sitting around in their snug little apartments, paying no attention to anyone else's problems, when all Tanya needed was for one person to have opened their eyes. Now they were heading off for a cozy night's sleep without a care in the world. Maybe there was a case for jogging memories a little more vigorously than usual. I pushed back from the windowsill and started toward the kitchen. I'd only taken four steps when my phone rang again. Lavine's number flashed up on the screen. But when I answered, it was Varley's voice I heard.

"Listen to this," he said. "Hot off the press. The body you found at the clinic? It wasn't Taylor. Maher's come up with a new ID."

"Who was it?" I said.

"No one we've heard of before. A guy called Darius Metcalf."

"What's his connection with Tungsten?"

"There isn't one. He does have a sheet, though. Small-time stuff. He's just some junkie asshole. They probably picked him because he was scrawny enough to pass for Taylor. The weedy little runt."

"So Taylor is still alive?"

"As far as we can tell."

"Where is he?"

"We don't know."

"Why the elaborate cover? Why not just slip away with the others on Monday, before anyone was even looking for him?"

"We're thinking he wasn't looking to run. He was looking to stay, under the radar."

"What for?"

"We're thinking he's the trigger man. Or he knows who is. Which means he's the way we're going to stop these explosions."

Forget that, I thought. *He's the way I'm going to find Tanya.*

We already knew someone at Tungsten had made Tanya call me. To lure us to the clinic. To find their video. And now, it appeared, to set up Taylor's cover at the same time. That was a neat move. We hadn't seen it coming. But the key is what happened next. They didn't just kill Tanya, or even let her go. They gave her to Lesley. And that didn't happen on its own. Taylor and Lesley must have been in contact, to arrange the handover. They must have spoken today. This evening. In the last few hours. Taylor could get in touch with Lesley when it suited his own ends. So he could get in touch with her for me.

If I could put my hands on him.

"Let me help you find him," I said. "You've tried his apartment? His office?"

"They're the first places we looked," Varley said. "We're still sitting on them."

"No fruit?"

"Nothing from his work, but a neighbor saw him leave his building. Yesterday afternoon. Less than an hour after he was released. Two big guys were with him, in some kind of desert uniform. He was carrying a satchel. Like a laptop bag. But no other luggage."

"Any idea where he was going?"

"No. That's why I'm calling you. You spent the most time with him. Any thoughts about where he might run?"

"Nothing comes to mind."

"You were at his apartment. Anything there that could help? Pictures of holiday cabins? Ski equipment? Scuba stuff? Anything at all?"

"No. The place was sterile. Immaculate."

"You spoke to him. Any idea how we could contact him?"

I checked my pocket before giving him an answer. I did have one idea. But I wasn't sure if it was the kind of thing I could share. The FBI is too conventional. Taylor was the last strand in Tanya's lifeline. It was frayed enough, already.

Smoking him out was going to need a different approach.

THIRTY-SEVEN

In training, the emphasis is all on preparation.

The instructors are constantly asking, *What's your situation? What's your objective? What's your exposure? What's your time frame?* It's a relentless process. You're always being pushed to plan, check, adapt, implement, and review. Then go again, if necessary.

In the field, the emphasis is all on speed. The ability to think on your feet. To react. Improvise. Make it up as you go along. For some jobs, you're on the road or in the air before the background reports have even been opened, to make sure you're in the right place when you're needed.

That's the kind of reality that drives the instructors crazy.

But for the agents, it's what gives you your edge.

I perched back on Tanya's windowsill and switched the SIM card in my phone with the one I'd taken from Mansell's. Then I started to type a message.

hi I sent to Taylor.

No reply.

guess who's back?

No reply.

got a game 4 u. want 2 play?

No reply.

3 questions. guess how i got my phone back? guess where i am? guess how much $ i want

This time Taylor did respond. He sent a single character.

?

am working with fbi. fun! but not 4 u if u don't answer my qs

ok. where r u?

66ᵗʰ st. inside clinic. taken more photos. haven't shown fbi. yet

$?

50k. tonight

2 hrs

I checked my watch. I couldn't wait two hours. It would be too agonizing. And more to the point, neither could Tanya.

no I sent. *30 mins*

need 2 hrs 2 get $

cant stall for 2 hrs. calling fbi now

wait. 1 hr?

I thought about it. One hour would be hell, but I couldn't afford to overplay my hand. Taylor was Tanya's last chance. If I scared him off, that would be the end of the game. And I did have some arrangements to make.

ok 1 hr I sent.

where will u be? will send cash

who with? mechanic, like last time? no thx. i'll collect. where?

swan hotel. e 12th. rm 1012. come alone

no. will send 2 guys. 1 stays with u, 1 brings back the $. then he brings u the photos & u let both go

ok. but want phone as well, not just photos

deal.

Varley said he knew the Swan Hotel. He remembered it from a surveillance assignment, early in his career. And he agreed with me when I said we should send more than two agents. Taylor had caved in far too easily. I'd barely made a single threat. He was clearly in no mind to roll over and pay Mansell off. More likely he had something up his sleeve. Something nasty. Which made this one occasion when it would pay to go in mob-handed.

My approach to his sole remaining witness hadn't boosted my popularity any, in Varley's eyes. He had cut me some slack, given the outcome, but there were still severe limits to his spirit of cooperation.

"One last point, Commander," he said, once the logistics were squared away. "Where are you planning to be when my guys take Taylor down, tonight?"

"I hadn't really thought that far ahead, to be honest," I said. "Where would you like me to be?"

"I don't care. Be wherever you like. Just make sure it's not within half a mile of the Swan."

"You don't want my help? In a purely supportive, backup-type capacity?"

"How can I put this so there's no room for ambiguity? No. Every step of the way you've been reckless, irresponsible, insubordinate, and rash. We cannot afford to fail at this point. There are no more second chances. Hundreds of lives are at stake."

"I understand."

"So. Where are you planning to be?"

"I'll stay here. At Tanya's apartment. I'll wait by the phone."

"Good. I'll call you back when we have him."

Old habits die hard. As soon as Varley had cleared the line I called information and asked for a number at the Swan.

A sleepy receptionist answered on the fourteenth ring.

"Swan," he said. "Help you?"

"Hope so," I said. "I need a room. For tonight."

"How many people?"

"One."

"How many nights?"

"One."

"Two hundred and forty-eight dollars. Need a card number."

"No problem. But while we're talking, could you see if room 1012 is free? I'm sure I had that one last time."

"I'll have a look. No. It's taken."

"That's a shame. Never mind. Oh, hang on a minute.

Let me think. Ten twelve. Does it look out the back of the hotel?"

"No. Over the street."

"Really? Oh, wait. You know what I've done? Confused it with the one my brother had. I was in the one opposite. Any chance that's free?"

"Ten eleven? Sure. No one in there. You want it?"

"Yeah, why not. It's as good as any. I'll be over in ten."

The reception area at the Swan was made up of two intersecting ovals. They were on different levels, and a pair of elliptical steps was formed where the shapes joined. The door from the street brought you in at the higher level, to the side of a long curved counter. It was made of heavily grained wood, and had been finished with a pale blue wash to match the carpet and walls. The lower area was a mess of orange. It was overstuffed with furniture. There were five ocher chesterfield sofas. Mounds of contrasting scatter cushions. Clusters of stained wooden coffee tables. A forest of stylized artificial potted plants, the color of virulent carrots. And one man.

I'd never seen him before, which simplified things. He was in his late thirties, with beige Timberland boots, loose jeans, and a tan leather jacket. His face was rough and weathered, and his fine blond hair was cropped close to his skull, betraying a smattering of gray. He was sitting on the center sofa, leaning back comfortably as if he were expecting to be there a while. An open newspaper was spread out on his lap. But he wasn't reading it. His eyes were fixed on me. They'd locked on the moment I walked in, so I took a moment to check that Tanya's Yankees cap was properly pulled down over the back of my head before approaching the check-in area, wheeling her travel-scarred Rimowa suitcase behind me for cover.

There was no sign of anyone behind the desk. I waited a moment, then rang the bell. It was made of heavy brass, eight inches in diameter, with a well-worn disk at the top to press down on. It made a deep, reverberating sound like the striking of an old-fashioned clock. I waited for the note to die down and then gently pushed against its base with the tips of my fingers. It moved slightly. Which meant it wasn't fixed down.

It took a full minute for the receptionist to drag himself away from his back room and shuffle out to help me. His hair was brushed forward over his left eye, his tightly stretched skin was almost transparent, and his crumpled blue shirt was a couple of sizes too large for his scrawny arms and neck. He crept forward cautiously until he got to the counter. Then he stood and rubbed his tiny, beady eyes for a moment as if he were having trouble focusing.

"You the guy on the phone?" he said.

I nodded, and he reached down to pull a registration card from a drawer. I leaned forward, placed my forearms flat on the countertop, and watched as he struggled to fill it in. He took a print of my credit card and checked a computer screen. Then finally he took a fresh card key, ran it through the validator, and handed it to me.

"Here you go," he said. "Enjoy."

I turned away, and swept the bell off the countertop with my right hand as I went. It clanged down onto the floor and began to roll toward the steps. The guy on the sofa heard it. He didn't react until I was approaching the elevators. Then his hand went for his jacket pocket. But he wasn't reaching for a gun. I was watching. He was going for his phone.

I figured that if Taylor had a lookout in the lobby, there was a fair chance he'd have someone watching his corridor as well. Taylor himself and three of his guys could recognize me. So I didn't go straight to the tenth floor. I went up to the twelfth. I counted the rooms. There were twenty. I found 1211 and 1212. They were just over halfway along the corridor, marginally closer to the stairs at the far end than the elevator I'd just used. I carried on past them and started to make my way slowly downward.

The fire door on the tenth floor was stiff, but I eased it open far enough to peek through. I could see all the way along to the elevators. The corridor was deserted. The layout was the same as the twelfth, but there was something different about 1012. The floor outside it was covered in something shiny. Heavy-duty plastic sheeting. And it extended beyond the neighboring two rooms.

It looked as though Taylor were preparing something for his guests.

I pulled out my phone and dialed 911. An operator picked up after six seconds. I ignored her request for my details and told her they had two officers down in the doorway of a building. I gave an address. It was the office opposite the Swan. Then I hung up, switched my phone to silent, and took a tight hold on my room key.

I heard the first siren after less than two minutes. Then another joined in. And another two. They grew louder and louder until there could be no mistake. They'd arrived, right outside the hotel. Directly under Taylor's window. I slid through into the corridor and started toward my room, only slowing down when I reached the plastic sheet. I didn't want to end up flat on my back.

Seven more paces and I was close enough to slide the key into the lock. It clicked. The light changed from red to green. The door swung open. I darted inside. The door eased smoothly back into its frame. I held my breath and listened. I heard nothing. I looked out through the spyhole. The door to 1012 was still closed. It stayed that way for the next two minutes.

I checked my watch. It was just 1:48 A.M. Another twenty-seven minutes until the agents were due to arrive.

Twenty-seven minutes that Tanya may not have.

THIRTY-EIGHT

The navy's psychologists always seem fascinated by dreams.

They home right in on them, every twenty-four months, when you go for your evaluations. But it's not just the shrinks who are interested. Over the years I've heard all kinds of people spend hours discussing what happened in theirs. And then speculating endlessly about what they're supposed to mean.

One of the most common dreams, according to what I've been told, involves people who witness a chain of events. They can see that a bad thing is about to happen. They want to stop it. But for some reason they can't. Something external prevents them. They could have been tied up. Or made to watch through a window. Or maybe they're a passenger in a moving car. But whatever's holding them back, they all reach the same conclusion. That it reveals a sense of underlying helplessness in their lives.

I'd never had that feeling myself.

But after looking out through that spyhole, I had a good idea of what it's like.

*

The first of Varley's agents stepped into the corridor at exactly 2:15. But he hadn't sent twelve of them, as agreed. He'd sent ten. I watched them approach, all swollen and distorted by the tiny fish-eye lens. The first four filed quietly past me and backed up against the wall on the stairs' side of Taylor's door. They drew their weapons. Another four mirrored their positions on the elevator side. That left one pair. They were directly in front of me. The right-hand guy stepped forward. He knocked, firmly.

"Mr. Taylor?" he said. "We're here. James Mansell sent us. You should have something for us. Can we come in?"

There was no reply. Nothing happened. I counted to fifteen. Then the agent stepped forward and knocked again.

I couldn't hear any instructions being given, but the two agents simultaneously raised their hands. They both took a step back. They opened their jackets, took out their Glocks and laid them on the plastic sheet. Their Glocks. The FBI's signature weapon. I couldn't believe they hadn't thought to carry something else. It was a dead giveaway. Absolute naïveté. Which made me worry. If they were so lax over gun choice, how would they have handled the sentry, downstairs?

Taylor's door eased open a crack. The agents were focused on it. So were their eight buddies. That's where they expected the threat to come from. But they were wrong. Instead, the doors to 1010 and 1014 flew open. A man burst out through each one. They were wearing Tungsten uniforms. And they had silenced .38s in both hands.

The Tungsten guys didn't waste any time. They started

shooting straightaway. With their silencers in place it sounded like someone swatting flies with a loosely rolled magazine. I couldn't count the shots—they came too fast, one on top of the other—but the eight flanking agents went down like pins at a bowling alley. Only the central pair was still standing. They were left like statues, frozen rigid with shock. The one who'd spoken snapped out of it first. He ducked down, trying to recover his weapon. The other one followed a split second later. But they were too slow. Their fingers were still scrabbling forlornly on the shiny plastic when two more guys appeared from Taylor's room. They kicked the guns away, grabbed the agents by their wrists, and dragged them inside.

The uniformed guys were still in the corridor, checking that none of their victims was breathing. I saw them gather up the spent shell cases as they went. They pocketed the two discarded Glocks. Then they lined the bodies up on separate plastic sheets and carefully hauled them, one at a time, into their own rooms. They took four each. After the final bodies had been removed the guys returned with something shiny in their hands. Aerosols of some kind. They started spraying randomly, swinging their arms in big lazy circles, and I realized they were using air fresheners. To cover the smell of the gunfire, I guessed, in case any other guests came past. They squirted away for thirty seconds, then one of them tipped his head back and pretended to sniff the breeze like a giant rabbit. He grimaced, and mimed that he wanted to stick his fingers down his throat. I knew how he felt. The other guy just smiled. Then they swapped a silent high five, glanced up and down the corridor one last time, and disappeared into Taylor's room.

If the two captured agents were going to stand any kind of chance, the FBI would have to send its backup team in there, right away. Someone would have to get them moving. And let them know what they were up against. Varley would be best placed. I grabbed my phone. It would mean revealing I'd broken our agreement, but that couldn't be helped now. His number rang, but he didn't answer. I tried Lavine. Same result. Then Weston. His was still ringing when the door to 1012 swung open.

Taylor and one of the Tungsten guys came out. I hung up and watched them go into 1010. They stayed inside for less than a minute, then hurried over to 1014. The uniformed guy stayed outside the door. Taylor was out of sight for thirty seconds. He reemerged, phone in hand, scowling. He shook his head, and led the way back to his own room.

I redialed Weston's number. He was engaged. I tried Varley again. I let it ring for longer this time, hoping the noise would be annoying enough to make him answer. But it didn't work. And I didn't get the chance to try Lavine because of more activity across the corridor. I saw Taylor's door twitch. Twice. Then, slowly, it opened. One of the agents appeared. He moved forward, taking tiny hesitant steps. His arms were tied behind his back. One of the Tungsten guys was holding him by the collar. And a pistol was jammed against his temple.

Taylor followed, backed by two more Tungsten guys.

All five of them were staring at my door. Taylor hit a button on his phone. He lifted it to his ear. I wondered who he was calling. Seven seconds later I found out. It was me.

"I know you can see me," he said. "Come out of the room. Now."

I hung up.

He called back.

"I know you're in there," he said. "I just spoke to my guy in the lobby. He saw you check in. I'm a little surprised you didn't come knocking before, with your buddies. I didn't have you down as a coward."

I didn't reply.

"So come out of the room, or this guy dies," he said.

I didn't reply.

"What?" he said. "You don't believe me?"

"No," I said. "I believe you. I just don't care."

"You don't care. You're just going to stand there and watch me shoot him?"

"That's a tempting offer. I do like a good shooting. But I've seen eight today, already. So maybe I'll just lie down, watch a little TV."

"I will pull the trigger."

"No you won't. You'll get one of your lackeys to do it. But either way, go ahead. Fill your boots."

Taylor was silent for a moment.

"Got anything else for me?" I said. "Or shall I put the kettle on?"

"If you won't come out, we'll come in," he said, nodding at my door.

The guys either side of him raised their pistols.

"Five seconds," he said.

"Then what?" I said. "Those are only .38s. Low muzzle velocity. The silencers will soak up another 10 percent. And this is a fire door. I'll take my chances, thanks."

"OK. I didn't want this, but I'm out of patience. Here are your options. Room 1005. Mother, father, and eighteen-month-old daughter. Room 1015. Mother, and two teenage sons. Come out, or pick one. Then explain to their families why they're vacationing at the morgue."

I disconnected him and redialed Varley's number. It started to ring. Taylor looked at his watch. Varley wasn't answering. Taylor started to fidget. Then he moved away, to his left. Toward 1005. The pair of Tungsten guys followed him. Their bodies stretched and curved into distorted crescents as they reached the outer fringes of the spyhole's range, but they didn't quite disappear. I could still see what they were doing. The phone was still ringing. And still Varley didn't respond.

So, in the end, I had no choice. This was no dream. There was nothing to hold me back. It was no time to stand around, watching, while three innocent people were murdered in their sleep. Not to mention the 320 slightly less blameless ones who wouldn't survive the night if I let Taylor walk away. And Tanya. I had to hold on to Taylor to stand any chance of finding her. Even if it meant losing the upper hand.

I let the phone ring two more times.

Then I hung up and opened the door.

THIRTY-NINE

Right from the start we knew Navy Intelligence was training us for one thing. Infiltration. The ability to worm your way into a close-knit group, extract secret information, get word back to your own side, and get out again in one piece. So it came as no surprise to find that they'd set up one of the other recruits to spy on us. Especially after all the other tricks they'd pulled. Although, to be honest, she gave herself away pretty cheaply. The type of questions she asked. The places she was spotted. The way she tried to buddy up to you for a few days, before moving on to someone else.

After three weeks an emergency announcement was made. A security breach had been uncovered, it said. We were all summoned to the briefing room, that same morning. I remember everyone sidling past the chief instructor, not making eye contact but feeling smug, confident they were in the clear. And how that feeling changed when everybody was handed a file. It was thick. It gave details of everything that had been leaked. Only it hadn't come from the person we'd all suspected. The real culprit turned out to be the quietest guy on the course. The one we'd all talked to, trying to bolster his confidence and save him from getting thrown out.

At first I thought the moral would be the usual "trust no one." But the real point soon became clear. That people will only talk voluntarily if they don't perceive a threat. Tongues will only wag when people believe they're in a position of strength.

Even if, in reality, they're not.

You could see the surprise creep across both agents' faces when we reached the elevators and Taylor hit the UP button. They fought it back, and gave nothing more away for thirty seconds. Then surprise turned to confusion when the doors opened and Taylor stepped inside.

"Don't play poker, do you?" he said, as the Tungsten guys herded the agents in behind him. "What did you expect? Down?"

He hit the button for the fourteenth floor.

"But don't worry," he said. "Your backup buddies won't be hanging around long. Any minute now they're going to hear about my car getting spotted on the FDR. They'll go after it. Chase shadows the rest of the night. Last place they'll look for you is right here, in the same building."

The elevator doors opened and Taylor led the way down the corridor. He stopped halfway along. Two of his guys took the agents into 1410. Taylor slipped his satchel off his shoulder and let himself into 1412. That left me alone with the two guys who had done the shooting. The silencers were gone and their .38s were safely holstered. It was a tempting moment. But Taylor's confidence was sky-high, and I wanted to keep it that way. I checked my watch. It was 2:34. No time to cover any ground twice.

The guy who'd done the rabbit impression was the first to move. He produced a key and opened the door to 1414. A light flickered on from inside the room. The other guy took my elbow and guided me through, in front of him. He steered me past the thin wooden closet and kept shoving until we reached the foot of the double bed. The rabbit guy was standing on the other side, looking around at the furniture. Then he took hold of a dressing-table chair, picked it up, and thoroughly checked it over.

"An elephant couldn't break it," he said. "Bring him."

I sat down on the chair. Between them the two guys bound my wrists and ankles to its metal frame. They used four of the cable ties they'd taken from me, downstairs. Each one checked the other's work, pulling all the ties a couple of clicks tighter. They dumped the rest of my possessions—the gun I'd inherited from Lesley's guy, one last cable tie, my wallet, ID, room key, and key to Tanya's apartment—on the dressing table. Then they perched on the bed behind me.

I couldn't help wondering if Tanya was tied up somewhere, as well. Attached to a chair, like me. Or still strapped to one of Lesley's trolleys . . .

"Is there a kettle in here?" I said. "I could really use a coffee."

No one answered.

A picture of Lesley's shiny wooden box crept into my

mind. I could almost hear her voice. All her talk of volts
and amps . . .

"Room service?" I said. "Maybe a snack, while we're
waiting?"

Neither of the guys replied. They seemed happy to just
sit in silence. I couldn't see my watch, but ten or eleven
minutes must have crawled past without any activity. I
stared at the wall and tried to fend off all the images that
kept forming in my head. Then I heard a light knocking
sound. It was coming from a door in the side wall, between
the closet and dressing table. The rabbit guy jumped to his
feet and opened it. A man stepped through. His hair was
combed back and he was wearing a black suit with wide
chalk pinstripes, like a Chicago gangster. It took me a
moment to recognize who it was.

"Taylor?" I said. "What the hell have you got on?"

He came over and stood next to me.

"You struck me as a smart guy when we talked before,"
he said. "So I'll level with you. I'm looking for a little
bonus. Some information."

"Information only I have?"

"No. Several people have it. But you could save me the
trouble."

"I could save you some trouble. My lifelong ambition.
And if I give you this information, I go free?"

"No. You die. In this room. In around thirty minutes'
time."

"Well, then, it may just be me, but I'm not really seeing
much of an incentive."

Taylor went back into his room and reappeared ten seconds later carrying an old-fashioned doctor's case. The brown leather was worn into holes where it folded and the metal clasp at the top clearly didn't work anymore. Taylor laid it down on the dressing table and levered it open. He took out a glass vial full of a clear, colorless liquid and placed it next to the bag. Then he pulled out a brass syringe. It was huge. He curled two fingers around the curved flanges on the side of its wide body, slipped his thumb into the loop at the end of the plunger, and held it out at arm's length.

"Trying to compensate for something?" I said.

"Bigger than average, I know," he said. "It's European. An antique. It came from some old veterinarian, over there. Holds eighty milliliters. More than you really need for humans. But when I go to work with this baby, you don't need to worry about air bubbles. Because you know what I'll be injecting."

He tapped the needle against the top of the vial.

"Is that the stuff you implanted in your patients?"

Taylor nodded.

"Then you can't use it on me," I said.

"Oh?" he said. "Why not?"

"You'd end up with 321 victims. One too many. Ruin the symbolism. Everyone would laugh at you."

Taylor smiled.

"Don't worry," he said. "My guys will sit you in the bath, first. Your blood will just trickle away down the drain like watered-down cranberry juice. No one will know. Except you, obviously. If you force us down that road."

I didn't reply.

"We don't have to go that way," he said. "You could be sensible."

I took a moment to glance up at Taylor. I could feel the time slipping away from me. I wanted to move on him. Find out what he knew. But I could see it was too soon. He wasn't ready for the close. I only had one chance. I couldn't afford to blow it. And I still needed a way to free myself from the chair.

"I never really did well with sensible," I said.

"Maybe I can change your mind."

"You can try. But I have to warn you. It wouldn't be the first time. And it's never worked before."

Taylor put the syringe down on the dressing table. Then he stretched across, picked up my gun, checked it was loaded, and placed it carefully on the other side of the vial.

"There," he said. "Have a look at your choices."

He reached down to my left wrist and unfastened my watch.

"He can't escape?" he said.

"No," the rabbit guy said.

"The ties. They're tight enough?"

"They are."

"The chair. He can't break it?"

"No."

Taylor added the watch to the collection of items in front of me, laying it down so that one of the straps was touching the syringe and the other was nestling against the barrel of the gun.

"We're going next door, now," he said, picking up his bag. "There's something we need to do. It'll take us ten minutes. That'll give you time, on your own. To think. Then you can tell me how you'd like your life to end."

FORTY

One thing really annoyed me about our training regime, at first.

It was to do with the instructors. They never gave us accurate information. If they told us to run twenty miles, they'd change it to twenty-five. And then thirty. If they sent us to steal five people's credit card numbers, they'd really want ten. Or probably fifteen. For a while I thought they were just disorganized. That, or plain sadistic. But then it dawned on me. There was a message hidden in the chaos.

Don't count on anything being over. Ever.

No matter how good or bad it's looking.

The rabbit guy was right about two things. The cable ties were tight enough. And the chair was too strong to break. But when it came to me not escaping, there was another factor he'd completely overlooked.

The length of my legs.

As soon as the connecting door slammed shut behind Taylor I tipped the chair back and held it balanced on the toes of my right foot. I shifted my left leg to the side until my thigh was clear of the cushion, pushed down hard, and wriggled the cable tie over the tip of the shiny metal leg. The same thing worked for my right ankle. Then I levered myself to my feet, suspending the chair behind me like some kind of cumbersome backpack.

I folded my arms up until my wrists were level with my shoulder blades and leaned forward to transfer some of the chair's weight onto my back. I held tight with my right hand and slid my left about nine inches down the leg. Then I shifted my grip to my left hand and brought my right down until it was roughly level. I heaved the chair back up as high as I could and took hold with my right hand again. This time I straightened my left arm out all the way. I felt the cable tie slide smoothly down the metal. It reached the very end of the leg. Then it snagged on something. A kind of rubber foot, presumably designed to stop the chair from slipping on the floor. I snapped my wrist around in a sharp circle once, twice, three times until finally the tie worked itself clear. The chair spun around to the side, suddenly supported in only a single place, but I grabbed hold again before it hit the floor. Then I wrestled my right hand free and silently lowered it down.

I checked my watch. Two minutes twenty had ticked away. I picked up the gun, removed the magazine and emptied it onto the bed. I ejected the final round from the chamber, slotted the parts back together, and returned it to the exact same spot on the dressing table. Then I scooped up the bullets, dropped them inside one of the pillowcases at the head of the bed, smoothed out the duvet, and came back for the syringe.

The needle was broad. It was a tight fit, but I managed to force it into the catch on the cable tie around my left wrist. I kept pushing until the little plastic tongue was bent back, safely out of the way. I did the same for the ties on my right wrist and both ankles. Then I replaced the syringe and got ready for the hard part. Reversing the process I'd just gone through. I had to reattach myself to the chair before anyone caught me.

Taylor came back a minute early and found me sitting with my chin on my chest, snoring gently.

"Wake up," he said. "It's decision time."

"Oh, yes," I said. "Well, I was thinking we should do it in the Caribbean. On a beach. With a cold beer in my hand. Something like that."

"Not ready to be sensible?"

"No."

"I thought you might say that. So. I've got something new to put on the table. The chance to see your friend, one last time."

"Tanya?"

"You have other friends who've been kidnapped recently?"

"Is she here?"

"No. But if you cooperate, I'll take you to her."

"I want to see her first. Then we'll talk."

"No. Something here needs my attention. You tell me what I want to know. I'll finish my work. Then we'll go."

"How do I know she's still alive?"

"You know who's holding her?"

"Lesley."

"Correct. And what are the odds, would you say, of Lesley missing the chance to kill you while your friend watches? As long as you're breathing, nothing will happen to her. Nothing terminal, anyway."

"I want to talk to her."

"That's not possible."

"Why didn't you tell me this before?"

"I only just thought of it."

"But you knew Lesley had her."

"True. But I wasn't expecting you to fall into my lap. And when you did, for you to need extra persuasion. You're an unusually stubborn man, Mr. Trevellyan. The syringe has more of an effect on most people."

"But how do you and Lesley even know each other?"

"We're old friends."

"Rubbish. The FBI's been buzzing around Lesley for years. They keep tabs on all her friends."

"And yet they hadn't heard of me."

"No one had heard of you till your guy left those bodies by the train tracks."

"I've been out of the country."

"And then you only hit the limelight when Lesley's guy accidentally killed the agent who was working the case."

"The fickle hand of fate. How can you plan for something like that?"

"Level with me. We were certain there was no connection between you. Were we wrong?"

"No. You were bang on the money. Truth is, I'd never heard of Lesley, either, until yesterday. Then she reached out to me. Completely out of the blue."

"Why you?"

"Lesley was locked up because of you. She escaped—she's a resourceful woman—and wanted revenge. For the jail thing, obviously, and the millions of dollars your meddling has cost her. Only her operation was down the pan. The NYPD was all over it. And the feds. Parts she couldn't control. So she needed a new partner. Fast."

"The first part I can understand. I like a good bit of revenge, myself. But how did she wind up at your door?"

"She talked to her sources—the ones that were left—and reviewed her options. I may be a late entry, but I'm top of the FBI charts right now. So she heard about me and thought we could help each other. Mutual benefit, she called it."

"Why did she go after Tanya? Not me, direct?"

"No one knew where you were. You'd moved hotels, apparently, and not told the FBI where you'd gone. So she needed bait. And a substitute, in case she failed to reel you in. She likes her fun dirty, or so she led me to believe."

"OK. So, Lesley wants revenge. That part's clear. But what's in it for you?"

"Taking you out of the game. The FBI are predictable. I got the measure of them a long time ago. Any agent I can't fool, I bribe. You, on the other hand, are a loose cannon. I wanted you out of the picture."

"By dragging me to the clinic?"

"For starters. Then you were supposed to be running all around the city, looking for Tanya. So when you turned up here and refused to talk, I improvised. Added a little icing to the cake."

"Lesley's not the only resourceful one, then. I'm impressed. So, is it far, to where she's holding Tanya?"

"Answer my questions and you'll find out. Continue to annoy me, and you won't."

"What do you want to know?"

"At last. Now you're being sensible. So. Back to the FBI. They didn't respond to my warning in the way I expected. I need to understand why. Start with the visit to the clinic. They found the memory stick?"

"Your ultimatum? Yes."

"What action did they take?"

"They flew to Washington."

"Why?"

"The wording was ambiguous. They thought you'd planted bombs there."

"That's interesting. Something to tighten up on, next time. If there has to be a next time."

"I take it we're not talking about bombs? Conventional ones?"

"No."

"You've been implanting capsules of that drug? Remotely controlled? In your patients? Three hundred and twenty of them?"

"Yes. Hammurabi pods, I've named them. Ancient justice, modern technology."

"That's fine. But when you talk about them, remember who your audience is. Less history. Less symbolism. More facts. More specifics. Then perhaps fewer people will get hurt."

"Perhaps you're right. But tell me, what did the FBI do when they got to Washington?"

"Launched into their standard bomb-threat protocols, they said. I can't tell you what those are because I didn't go with them."

"No, you didn't. That's interesting, in itself. Why did you stay behind?"

"To look for Tanya, just as you planned. Then my thoughts strayed back to your video. I put two and two together."

"And you sprang into action, single-handed?"

"No. I called them. The FBI bosses. I tried to fetch them back."

"But they didn't come? And they only mustered up ten people? Raided one building?"

"I don't think they really believed me."

"Well, at least you can go to your grave knowing you were right."

"That's a comfort. But on that, let me ask you something. The FBI. I told them to shut off your patients' broadband. If they had done it, would that have helped?"

"Of course. Without a signal, nothing would happen."

"The devices weren't set to go off at a certain time? Or if they lost contact?"

"No."

"Why not? That would be a lot easier."

"If you just wanted to kill a lot of people in a messy way, yes."

"Which differs from what you're doing, how?"

Taylor glared at me.

"You fool," he said. "How can you ask me that? You saw the video. You saw what I want."

"Yes, I saw it," I said. "You want vengeance. People drowning in blood. That seemed clear."

"How stupid can you be? Vengeance is not the goal. It's a language. A means to an end."

"What end? More money, somehow? Haven't you sucked enough out of the place?"

"My mission in all this is to bring an end to the killing. That should be obvious, even to a government puppet like you."

"You're killing people because you're against killing people? You don't see a tiny discrepancy there?"

"Do I have to spell it out? The people who are going to die, they're dying anyway. What I'm doing is taking their pointless, inevitable deaths and giving them a purpose. Individually their passing means nothing. By molding them together, symbolically, I can save thousands of other lives."

"Really. And who made that your job?"

"Everyone has a purpose in life, Mr. Trevellyan. A unique part to play. You have yours. This is mine."

"How do you know? Maybe your purpose is running your clinics? Saving all those innocent Americans you were so worried about."

"I thought so, too, at first. I was saving lives. A handful. And that was enough. Until I woke up to the full potential of what I'd created."

"What woke you? Your new partners waving dollar bills under your nose?"

"I've told you, it's not about the money. The golden goose is dead now, anyway. My clinics are finished because of this. And there are no new partners. I misled you about that. I brought those guys in myself, because the old help was too slow."

"So what raised the stakes?"

"It's hard to give it a name. Call it fate, if you like. I had a very special opportunity. Only I was too blind to see it. I was happy messing around in the foothills instead of heading for the summit. So I was given a wake-up call. That's the way I see it."

"Who called? Your bank? Your broker?"

"My wife. In a way."

"Oh, OK. Blame your other half. That's original."

"Your FBI friends didn't tell you about her?"

"Nothing specific. Just a rumor you'd got married."

"We did. Seven years ago. And then, because I had my head in the sand for so long, she was taken from me."

"She was kidnapped? You're being coerced into this?"

"No, for goodness' sake. She was killed. By the U.S. Army. And you know when?"

"Obviously not."

"March 20, 2008. What do you think about that?"

"Well, it's a terrible shame and everything. But really, so what? Dozens of people were probably killed that day."

"Are you brain-dead? The date? The fifth anniversary of the invasion? My wife, an Iraqi? Me, an American? And me, the only person on the planet with the resources to end the war without wasting a single extra life? Apart from the worthless fools who've interfered, of course."

"You think there's a connection?"

"Of course there's a connection. The tragedy is my wife had to die to make me see it. And now she's gone, I'm going to use every means at my disposal to make her death count for something."

"Including your clinics? Using them to acquire your targets?"

"Acquire, monitor, and control. Otherwise how could I be sure I have the correct number of serviceable devices? In the right places? At the right time?"

"Yeah. That would be tough. And the trigger signals. What sends them? A Web server, somewhere?"

"Correct."

"Is it already set?"

"No. Server activity is kept to a minimum. Everything's done at the last moment."

"Isn't that a bit risky? If it was me I'd want it primed well in advance."

"Then you'd get caught. The FBI monitors every byte of traffic anyone transmits. You've got to keep it invisible, until it's too late to stop."

"How do you set it?"

"I log in, over the Net."

"Remote access? I know about that. It's a nightmare. What about hackers?"

"Impossible. Only two machines are authorized. Mine, and a backup. Security's embedded into their software. The server won't respond to anything else."

"What if somebody steals one?"

"It wouldn't help them. The software expires every twenty-four hours. Plus you need an eight-digit access number from my security token, which changes every minute, and a twelve-digit PIN number from two separate Tungsten employees."

"That's what you were doing just now? Loading today's software? Logging on?"

"Right," he said, checking his watch. "Now. Five minutes to go. Time to arm the system. Do you want to see?"

"No," I said.

"Well that's too bad. Stay there. You're going to watch."

Taylor slipped the gun into his pocket and fetched his laptop from next door. It was large and heavy with a rubberized outer shell, such as the kind field engineers use. He brought it back, dragging a chair in his other hand, and as he put it down on the dressing table his phone began to ring. He wedged it under his chin so he could open his computer and talk at the same time.

"That was Lesley," he said, when the call had ended. "There's a change of plan. We're not going to her. She's coming to us. Here."

"When?" I said.

"Now. All her usual places are too hot, apparently. The NYPD is staking out everything she owns. Someone must have really put the wind up them. She's fuming. And absolutely paranoid. She's seeing cops behind every tree and lamppost."

"Where is she now?"

"Around the corner. Three or four minutes away. I should just about be done when she gets here."

"Is Tanya with her?"

"Yes. Don't worry. You'll be making your fond farewells very soon."

This changed everything. There would be at least five FBI sedans scattered around outside the hotel, left there by the dead and captured agents. No one would have moved them, yet. Regular people might not realize the significance, but Lesley would spot them in a millisecond. Especially if she was already extra suspicious. Which meant it was no good getting Taylor to call back and warn her about them. She hadn't known him long enough. She'd just take it as proof of a trap.

I had three or four minutes. That wasn't enough time. The 320 people in Taylor's crosshairs would have to take their chances. Those cars were a dead giveaway, and they were there because of me. I had to be in the street outside before Lesley saw them. Otherwise my plan wouldn't be Tanya's salvation. It would be her death sentence.

I started to loosen the ties around my wrists.

Taylor ran his finger over the trackpad. The screensaver melted away and a Web page sprang into view. There were two tabs at the top. The one on the left was active. It was labeled MONITOR. The screen was taken up with five dials, like the instruments on a car dashboard. There were four small ones in the corners, and a larger one filling the center. The background to all of them was green, and each one had a needle that pointed to a scale around the edge.

"There," Taylor said, jabbing his finger toward the central dial. "Three hundred twenty. All devices are in Wi-Fi range. We're ready."

Three hundred and twenty devices. He meant 320 people. Soon to be 320 corpses. Three hundred and twenty lives I'd have to sacrifice to rescue Tanya. Those were terms I'd take in a heartbeat, but how would she feel? She had been tortured by one death on her conscience after Morocco. For three years. If three hundred died so I could save her, could she live with herself afterward?

Taylor clicked on the second tab—CONTROL—and a picture of an old-fashioned light switch appeared in place of the dials.

It was in the off position.

I made the decision. I was going now. I'd get down to the street as quickly as I could. But I'd stop Taylor on my way. For Tanya's sake.

"All we have to do is drag this . . ." Taylor was saying when I pulled my arms free of the ties and elbowed him in the side of the head, knocking him flying off his chair.

The rabbit guy was the first to react. He ran toward me, trying to wrap his arms around my body. I watched him coming in the mirror. I waited until he was one step away then twisted sideways and drove my right fist deep into his stomach. He doubled over, the momentum carried him forward, and the bridge of his nose slammed straight into the sharp edge of the dressing table.

He went down without another sound.

The other guy had a hand on one of his .38s. He was too far away to reach, so I scooped up my chair and hurled it at him, across the room. It felt good. I hadn't done that to anyone since I was at school. And I hadn't lost my touch. The backrest caught him square in the face and sent him staggering backward long enough for me to move in and smash my left fist into his jaw. The impact spun him around, bouncing him off the bed and onto the floor.

I caught movement out of the corner of my eye. It was Taylor. He was back up, on his knees, going for his computer. That left no time for finesse so I just drove my heel down into the other guy's throat as I passed him, crushing his larynx and leaving him to choke in silence.

Taylor was kneeling next to the dressing table. He was

drawing his left hand away from the computer. I checked the screen. The switch had been dragged down, into the ON position. A row of digits had appeared underneath it, like the display on an old LED watch. They read *00:02:01*. Two minutes, one second. And counting.

"Thought you'd like to see it," Taylor said, pulling my gun out of his pocket. "Now. Turn around. Hands on the wall."

Lesley would still be at least a block away. I hoped.

"How do you stop it?" I said.

"Right click on the display. Select 'cancel.' But that's not really on your agenda, is it?"

I took a step toward the computer. Taylor raised the gun and aimed at my chest. I took another step. He pulled the trigger. The gun clicked harmlessly. He looked puzzled, and tried again. Twice. There were two more clicks. Then I put my hand flat on the side of his head and shoved, sending him tumbling sideways onto the floor.

I reached the computer and followed Taylor's instructions to cancel the countdown, but all that happened was another window appeared. It read, WARNING: *This action will stop the program from activating the remote field devices at the time you previously specified. Are you sure you wish to cancel?*

I clicked *Yes.*

Another box appeared. *Enter Password.*

I turned to Taylor. He was back on his feet, fiddling with his phone. I took it from him, threw it on the floor, and ground it into pieces with the heel of my boot.

"You probably could make me tell you," he said, nodding at the screen. "Given time. But not in a minute twenty. So go ahead. Guess."

I typed *Tungsten*.

Incorrect password.

I typed *3/20*.

Incorrect password.

I typed *Retribution*.

You have entered 3 incorrect passwords. The system is now locked. Your request has not been accepted.

"You weren't far wrong with that last one," Taylor said. "But it's over now. Your chance has gone. All you can do is wait and watch."

A cartoon image of a rocket appeared on the screen. It was red with an oval, cigar-shaped body and curved fins at the side, like a shark's. It was sitting next to a fuel pump, and as I watched a curly pipe floated across and slid its nozzle into the rocket's tank. Then a little door opened halfway up the rocket's body, revealing another timer. It was set at thirty seconds and counting. The rocket started to fidget on the spot and with each passing second its movements grew more frenzied, as if it were desperate to break free from the screen and fly away.

Which made me think.

"Taylor," I said. "The signal. It hasn't been sent yet, has it?"

"Of course it has," Taylor said. "I sent it. You tried to cancel. And you failed."

"But you keep your Web server quiet till the last

moment. You told me. And that error message. It said 'the program.' As in, the one running on this machine."

"So?" he said, looking away. "Just computer semantics."

I reached down and pulled a .38 from one of the rabbit guy's holsters. And I heard a noise. From the door, behind me. Someone was opening it. I spun around, expecting to see Lesley. Hoping to see Tanya. But actually seeing one of the other Tungsten guys, from 1410. He was already speaking as he came into the room.

"Boss?" he said. "Got part of a text—"

I shot him twice in the chest, watched him fall, and turned back to the computer. The countdown was hovering on two seconds. It turned to one. I pulled the trigger again. Three more times. Three bullets tore into the keyboard. And I put one into the top edge of the screen, where the Wi-Fi aerial is usually housed, just in case.

Then I grabbed Taylor by the collar and ran.

I could see all five black Fords before we were even through the hotel lobby. They'd been left in a loose horseshoe around the entrance. Lined up like a firing squad, I thought. They couldn't have been any more obvious. I checked both ways, up and down the street. There was no sign of Lesley. No movement at all, of vehicles or pedestrians. Nothing to show whether she was still on her way, or had already gone.

I pulled Taylor back into the shadows and willed her car to appear.

Taylor broke the silence, after two minutes.

"You were too late," he said. "You failed. You couldn't stop me."

I looked at my watch. My eyes were drawn to the second hand. I thought it must have stopped, but realized it was just crawling around as if it were made of lead. I followed it all the way around the dial. Twice. That made it 3:27. And then my phone rang.

It was Lavine. I spoke to him for fifteen seconds. Taylor saw the expression on my face and broke into a triumphant smile.

"It's started, hasn't it?" he said. "They've found bodies."

"Body," I said. "Just one. A block from here."

It was Tanya's.

FORTY-ONE

Losing one of your own is always traumatic.

I was introduced to it early in my career. One of our people was killed while I was in Hong Kong, on my first assignment. He was on their headquarters staff. Some of the others had worked with him for years. I remember wondering how they would react, and being surprised at how calm and unemotional they were. And also feeling uncomfortable when they invited me to his funeral. I'd hardly known the guy. So I declined, and straightaway the station chief called me to his office. He wanted to explain something. It wasn't just a funeral, he said. It was an alibi. Because in our branch of the service you don't waste energy on tantrums or hysterics. You don't get mad. You just get even. Quietly. Efficiently. And permanently.

The killer's body turned up that afternoon, crushed in the mechanism of an automatic car wash.

At least the police thought it was him. They found his remains unusually hard to identify.

*

Tanya's death was officially being handled by the FBI, though inevitably it was overshadowed by their panic over Tungsten. Building a case against Taylor took priority with their bosses, along with keeping a lid on the media, recovering the money he'd squirreled away, hunting down the organ smugglers, and treating the clinics' victims. But if their eyes were looking in other directions, that suited me fine. London, too. They cut me all the slack I needed. Complications were found with my head wound. Consultations at numerous hospitals were needed. Compassionate leave was granted. You name it. Lucinda, Tanya's assistant, took care of the official explanations. I just made sure one thing was clear. I wasn't leaving the United States until Lesley had been found. And made to pay.

It was beginning to look as if I were in for a long stay. How could I infiltrate an organization that had completely dissolved? The FBI could find no trace. Nor could the NYPD. Their internal affairs departments couldn't unearth Lesley's informers. We talked to the DSS, but her people had already been pulled out. We tried the banks. Forgers. Weapons suppliers. Car dealers. Realtors. Moving companies. Her known enemies. Homeless people. Everyone and everything we could think of. And we were getting nowhere.

Ten days later I was sitting with Weston and Lavine in their office, trying to conjure up some new angles, when my phone rang. It was Julianne Morgan.

"Hey, David," she said. "Good to hear your voice. You still in town?"

I was tempted to fob her off. I was in no mood for socializing. But it's not every day you share a dog cage with someone and then save their life. And there was something else about her. She was a journalist. An investigator, of sorts. A good enough one that Lesley had snatched her off the street a fortnight ago. She must have struck a nerve to warrant a response like that. I decided it was worth a shot. She might be able to dredge something up that could help me.

"Sure," I said. "I'm just tying up some loose ends. How about you?"

"The same. I just finished a story. A big one. So I'm looking to celebrate. And you promised to let me buy dinner, last time we spoke."

"I did. You're right. That would be nice. When were you thinking?"

"How about tonight?"

"Works for me."

"Great. I'm going to the gym first. Should be done by eight?"

"Eight's fine."

"OK, so where to meet? Do you know Esperanto's? In the Village?"

"I can find it."

"That's fine then. See you there."

The main dining room at Esperanto's was on the first floor, but they wouldn't let you up there until you were ready to order. If you were still waiting for anyone you had to stay downstairs, in the bar. Which was tiny. About the size of a normal coat closet. It was too small for tables. You had to stand, sandwiched between the staircase and the counter, being constantly jostled by a noisy throng of overly cheerful customers.

Julianne was forty minutes late. And when she arrived, she wasn't exactly rushing. She just strolled in, saw me, waved, and waited for me to push my way through the crowd. At least she showed some enthusiasm when I did finally reach her. She threw her arms around me, hugged me tight, and kissed me on both cheeks. She must have just showered. I noticed her hair was still damp. And that it smelled of coconut.

A waiter was standing at the top of the stairs, between us and the tables. They were divided into three regimented blocks of twenty. The nearest ones had red and yellow table-cloths. The central group had red and blue. The farthest had red and green.

"Good evening," the waiter said. "Spanish, French, or Italian?"

"English," I said. "And American."

Julianne giggled.

"No, sir," he said, gesturing to the tables. "Your choice of cuisine?"

Add in the white of the walls, and the color scheme suddenly made sense.

"Any preference?" I said to Julianne.

"Me? No."

"Then let's go with Italian," I said, with an eye on the table in the far corner. It would give me the clearest view of the whole restaurant. I didn't know if Julianne had invited any other guests.

Julianne let the waiter take her jacket. Her blouse was slim and tightly fitted, her slacks had no pockets, and she was wearing boots. That just left her purse. It was unzipped. She was holding on to it as we sat down, then I saw her lean it against the table leg on her right-hand side. I nudged it with my foot, knocking it over. She reached down and retrieved it. But not before I'd caught the glint of metal near the top.

The waiter came back for our order, and then Julianne excused herself. I left it a moment and then followed her. The corridor leading to the restrooms was long and dingy. I had to press myself against the wall to let an older woman squeeze by, coming from the other direction.

"You haven't seen a little girl, have you?" I said. "I'm looking for my daughter. She's six years old."

"No," the woman said. "Sorry."

"She didn't just go in the bathroom?"

"No. That was a tall lady. Good-looking."

"Five eleven, white blouse, black slacks?"

"Sounds about right. Why?"

"That's my wife. She'll know where the kid is. I'll just wait outside."

I moved up to the restroom door and listened. I could hear a soft electronic beeping sound. A cell phone keypad. Julianne was texting. Then the toilet flushed. The lock slid back. The door started to open. I let it move an inch and then shoved it, hard, with my right hand. It slammed back into Julianne's face, breaking her nose. Blood spurted onto her blouse, scarlet and soggy against the crisp white cotton. I pushed her back, stepped into the tiny space, and locked the door behind me. Julianne snarled. And dropped her phone in the toilet.

Julianne's purse had fallen on the floor. I leaned down to grab it and she tried to kick me. I blocked with my forearms. She pulled back, but I kept hold of her foot. Then I lifted and twisted at the same time, throwing her sideways. Her head smashed into the wall, dazing her for a moment. I grabbed the purse. I slid my hand inside. My fingers closed around wood and metal. It was the handstock of a small revolver. A Colt Detective Special. Only this woman was no detective.

Julianne straightened up and looked me straight in the face.

"You know what I'm going to ask you," I said.

She didn't answer.

"Where is she?" I said. "Lesley."

"How would I know?" she said.

"Because you work for her."

"I don't. I'm a journalist."

"Maybe. Maybe not. But either way, you do work for Lesley."

"Who told you? They're lying."

"I don't think so. It's a good source. Your hair."

"What the hell has my hair got to do with it?"

"It smells of coconut. You just washed it."

"So?"

"It smelled the same in Lesley's cage. When we first met. You told me you'd been in there for three days. No hair smells that fresh after three days. You were a plant. I should have realized at the time."

"That's ridiculous. I got too close. I was kidnapped."

"It's all right. I know what you were doing. It all makes sense, now. Gently pumping me for information, when we talked. Getting us caught, when we escaped. Testing my nerve, at the hotel. What were you planning for tonight? To serve me up as dessert?"

She didn't react.

"Drop the pretense, Julianne. Drop it now. And tell me where she is."

She didn't answer.

"OK," I said. "Take a minute. Think carefully. There's something you have to understand. Lesley killed my friend. For no good reason. She did it just to get back at me. That means there is nothing—nothing—I will not do to find her."

"I can't tell you," she said. "You know what she'll do to me."

I thought of Tanya's face, the last time I'd seen her. Her hair, loose, fanned out against the stainless steel. The porcelain wedge under her neck, like a pillow. And the lines of crude blue stitches the pathologist had left when he'd roughly sewn her back together.

I do, I thought. *And it wouldn't be enough.*

"Is she in the city?" I said. "Tell me that much."

"Yes," she said.

"Tell me where, and she'll be dead by midnight. I guarantee."

She didn't reply.

"Otherwise I might start thinking, who could have told Lesley about Tanya and me?" I said. "Who knew I was meeting someone from the consulate for dinner that night?"

She didn't reply.

"I might start thinking, do I really need you?" I said. "You just texted someone. I could wait for them. Let them take me to her."

Still she kept silent.

"So let me make this as simple as possible," I said, raising the gun. "Tell me where Lesley is. Or I'll shoot you in the head."

She gave me an address in the Bronx.

"Thank you," I said. "Now, let me check one last thing. Just then, did I say, 'Or I'll shoot you?'"

"Yes, you did," she said. "Why?"

"I'm sorry about that. I should have said, 'And . . . '"

I pulled the trigger, twice, then checked my watch. It was eleven minutes before 9:00 P.M. Over three hours to midnight. It wasn't far to the Bronx. Plenty of time to keep the other promise I'd made.

DIE TWICE

Obliged to leave New York City in the aftermath of his previous mission, ex-Royal Navy Intelligence agent David Trevellyan is summoned to the British Consulate in Chicago. To the same office where, just a week before, his new handler was attacked and shot by an operative gone bad.

Assigned the task of finding the rogue agent and putting an end to his treacherous scheme, Trevellyan soon finds that once again his only hope of saving countless innocent lives lies not within the system, but in his instinct to do what's right—whatever the personal cost may be.

Die Twice, the next book in Andrew Grant's gripping David Trevellyan spy thriller series, is out now.

An extract follows here.

He had two guns, as I expected. His service weapon and a back-up. A factory-fresh Beretta M9/92F and an ancient, scratched Walther PPK. One under his left arm, the other strapped to his left ankle.

Both still in their holsters.

There's a strict protocol for bringing the career of a fellow professional to a premature end. It demanded that I take out the Beretta. Place it in his right hand. Curl his index-finger through the trigger guard. Release the safety. Discharge at least one round. Give him the final dignity of appearing to whoever found his body that he'd at least gone down fighting.

I'd always followed those rules before. With an Armenian. Two Iranians. A Peruvian. A Ukrainian. Even a Frenchman on one bizarre occasion. But that evening I left the guns where they were. I didn't even loosen the straps that held them in place. I just left him lying face down on the strip of coarse office carpet, picked up the green metal flask he'd been so desperate to take and walked away.

He was from Royal Navy Intelligence, just like me.

The insult I'd paid him was deliberate. Calculated. Unmistakable to anyone from our world.

And only ever paid to a traitor.

ONE

I come from a small family. My mother was an only child. My father had one sister, but they weren't close. We didn't see much of her even when I was a kid. Partly because she still lived in Ireland and my parents found it a nuisance to get over there. But mostly because the two of them didn't get on. My dad is very practical and down-to-earth. If he can't see or touch or taste something, it doesn't exist. My aunt is the absolute opposite. Her life is barely her own. She abdicates all personal responsibility and just drifts happily along, governed by an endless stream of signs and omens and portents and premonitions.

The premonitions in particular drove a wedge between the two of them. He thought she was some kind of crazy, half-pagan simpleton. She thought he was too stiff and stubborn to see the world in front of his nose. And so any time the family was together, they fought. Relentlessly. Not physically, obviously. It was more subtle than that. At some point, soon after we arrived, she would announce a prediction. We would be waiting for it. He would denounce it. Then the duel would begin. There'd be endless pointed looks. Barbed comments. Contrived, cynical observations. The level of sarcasm would ratchet higher and higher until one was proved right and the other descended into days of impenetrable sulking.

Believe me, those visits were always fun.

My own views fall somewhere between the two. I certainly don't believe that the future is already set. We're not helpless; our destiny is ultimately in our own hands. But take some time to think, mix that with a little experience, and it's not too hard to see what's waiting around the corner.

In some circumstances, at least.

Mainly the ones involving bosses and their stupid plans.

I knew no one was following me, but I still had the cab from Midway drop me half a mile from my destination. But this was no random paranoia. Old habits die hard. The first thing you always do when you're sent somewhere new is tap into the service grapevine. To find out how the land lies in your next city. It's quicker and more efficient than any corporate intranet I've ever come across. And from what I'd been hearing about the current state of play, a little extra caution would not be out of place.

The ride in from the airport felt strangely flat. I had no idea why I'd been sent to Chicago, but that wasn't unusual. You begin lots of assignments without the slightest clue about what you're going to be asked to do. And the way a mission looks on paper is generally a million miles from how it plays out in the field. For me, that's part of the excitement. Like being a handed a Polaroid photograph, fresh from the camera, and watching as the image gradually takes shape on the warm, shiny paper. But the familiar feeling of promise and anticipation was completely missing that morning. Normally I love the first glimpse of a new place, but as I watched the cityscape morphing out of the traffic haze, it left me absolutely cold. Because I knew I wasn't going to have anything meaningful to do here. I was just passing through. Quickly, I hoped. I should have been called straight back to London. This detour had the feeling of a wrong turn about it. The sense that the fallout from my last mission—or the debacle that followed it—had knocked me off the freeway and shunted my career into an obscure backstreet. I needed to get back into the thick of things, to put the record straight. And to find some real work to do. Something to keep me from dwelling too long on absent friends.

My orders were simple: report to a liaison officer called Richard Fothergill. I'd never worked with the guy, but I'd heard him talked about often enough over the years. The prospect of meeting him was the one ray of sunshine cutting through the heavy, swirling clouds that had filled the sky since dawn. And not because he was supposed to be nice. His reputation made him out to be pretty much the opposite. Which actually seemed like a good thing, that morning. I had no wish to add to my circle of friends after what had happened when my previous liaison officer, Tanya Wilson, had resurfaced in my life during the case

I'd just closed. The main reason, though, was that Fothergill sounded like a very unusual person. Because although he worked in liaison now, he'd started his service life in the field. He'd made a transition that most observers would tell you is impossible. Which, statistically, it is. I've checked. And from what I've been told, only sixteen people have ever managed it.

I figured the Hancock Center was a suitably innocuous location so I baled out and found a good spot, near the flags and the fountains. I paused there for five minutes, watching the shoppers and tourists and office workers bracing themselves against the wind. I waited until I was certain that no one was paying me any undue attention. Then I walked north for another block, crossed the street and made my way back up the opposite side of Michigan Avenue.

It took me twelve minutes to reach the Wrigley Building. The public entrance to the British Consulate is on the thirteenth floor but I took the elevator to the fourteenth, to an office marked with our usual cover name: UK Trade & Investment. The receptionist was expecting me. She checked my ID and then came out from behind her desk and led me to a row of doors on the right of the lobby area, away from the main corridor. There were four. They looked like cupboards from the outside but when she opened the nearest one I saw it led to a clear cylinder, about seven feet tall and three across. The segment facing me slid open and she gestured for me to step inside. It was unusual for people to make me bother with this kind of thing, but after what had apparently happened here in the last couple of days I supposed a bit of stable-door-bolting was inevitable. I complied, and immediately the curved glass slotted back into place behind me. I heard a gentle hiss and dry, bottled air swirled around me for a full twenty seconds. The sound died away. I waited while the machine sniffed for incriminating particles. Then an indicator light above my head turned from red to green and the panel ahead of me swung aside, releasing me into the narrow, grey corridor on the other side.

The office I wanted was at the far end, on the left. The door was standing open so I gave a cursory knock and stepped straight inside. The room was larger than I was expecting. Around twenty feet by thirty. Not a bad size for a liaison guy. In fact, the biggest I'd ever seen. There was a glass desk to my left, completely bare, with a high-tech chrome and black mesh chair behind it. A round glass coffee table to my right, covered with newspapers, and surrounded by four black leather chairs. A densely woven Oriental rug filling most of the floor space between the two areas. And another man, directly ahead of me on the far side of the room. He was on his feet, his back towards me, gazing out at the river from the central one of three large windows. He was around five feet eleven with thick, glossy, grey hair clipped neatly above the collar of his blue pin-striped jacket. When he turned to greet me, I saw that his lined face looked sombre and dignified, like a statesman or a judge. I put him in his late fifties. He was smart. Imposing. The kind of person a corporation or government department would put on TV to break the worst kind of news. The only thing that jarred was his left arm. It was in a sling. But it wasn't the injury that struck me. I'd already heard the rumour about his recent brush with a 9mm bullet. Fired by a fellow officer. In that very room. No. It was the material he'd used to support it that caught my eye. It was fine, blue, pinstriped wool. Exactly the same kind of cloth as his suit. A haute couture bandage. I couldn't see this guy cutting it easily in the field any more. He must be spending too much time behind his desk. Or in front of a mirror.

"Commander Trevellyan?" he said, offering me his hand. "David?"

"In the flesh," I said, as we shook.

"Delighted to meet you," he said, taking my arm and guiding me towards the easy chairs. "Shall we sit? My name's Fothergill, by the way. But please, call me Richard."

"Any chance of a coffee around here, Richard?"

"I'm sure we could round some up for you," Fothergill said. "Be pleased to. We've heard a lot about you—word spreads quickly. Especially from New York. The Big Apple's a very leaky place, you know. You should remember that. Though I doubt you'll be rushing back there any time soon."

I didn't reply.

"No trouble en route, I hope?" he asked.

"None," I said. "Why? Should there have been? It's hardly an arduous journey."

"Nothing untoward at LaGuardia?"

"Nothing. I used the Marine Terminal. It's small. Quiet.

There was no problem at all. I wish all airports were like that."

"Well, that's good. It's a relief, actually. I'm just glad we were able to pull the right strings. Get the NYPD to back off for long enough to get you out."

"We?"

"Well, the New York people did the actual string-pulling, obviously. But I'm happy we're here to offer you a port in a storm, as it were. No use them getting you out if you had nowhere safe to go."

"Are you confusing me with someone else? No one got me out of anything. I'd finished what I was doing over there. And the police had no reason to be sniffing around me."

"Of course," Fothergill said, pulling a newspaper from the bottom of the pile and placing it in front of me. "Whatever works for you. I completely understand."

The paper was a copy of yesterday's *New York Times*. It was folded to emphasize the story beneath a double-width photograph. The picture showed a house festooned with crime-scene tape. The headline read: Butchered in the Bronx: woman, men massacred in unexplained, savage attack. I didn't need to read the report. I knew they wouldn't have got the details right. And what happened in that house didn't strike me as unduly savage, given the circumstances. So instead I took a moment to glance around the room, checking the walls and furniture for signs of bullet damage. I wanted to know if the story about how he'd been injured was true. Being shot in your own office by a colleague did seem a little unusual. And embarrassing. But then, I'd known this guy less than two minutes and already I was beginning to understand how it could happen. Only, if it had been me pulling the trigger, he'd have been left needing more than a fancy sling.

"Interesting story," I said, thinking of the last time I'd seen Tanya. "Someone must have had a pretty good reason to do all that."

"A very good reason," he said. "I hear the first officer to respond lost his breakfast, the scene was so brutal. Which is something for a cop used to working the Bronx."

"Really?" I said. "I wouldn't know. I've never been there."

Well, I'd been there once, actually. To one house. To take care of one piece of business.

"Of course you haven't," he replied, tapping the side of his nose. "Of course, the NYPD think otherwise."

"They've been wrong before," I said.

"Not this time. I understand they're very confident."

"How so? I heard there were no survivors. No witnesses. No usable forensics."

I knew there were none. I'd gone out of my way to make sure.

"But they do have the victim's identity," he said. "And that tells them a lot."

"Which victim?" I asked. "Weren't there several?"

I remembered each one's face. Their clothes. Their smell. What they'd been doing as I tracked them through the house.

How they looked as I lowered them, lifeless, to the ground and moved on to the next one in line.

"There were eight or nine, they think," he said.

"I'd say more like seven," I said. "From what I heard."

Only four of them had been any good, though. The others should have found another line of work.

"It's the woman they're focusing on," he said.

And why not? That's exactly what I'd done. Though for an entirely different reason.

"How chivalrous," I remarked.

"No," he said. "Just practical. A lot of things stand out about her."

"I'm sure they do."

"I'm serious. The way she was singled out, for example. She was the last to go, you know."

I did know. Because I'd planned it that way. I hadn't wanted any interruptions.

"Are they sure about that?" I replied.

"Yes," he said. "They're certain."

"Then maybe she was hiding when—whatever it was—all kicked off. Maybe the others were trying to protect her."

They didn't try very hard. But it wouldn't have mattered if they did. Nothing and no one could have saved her that night.

"That's what the NYPD think," he said. "That the men were her bodyguards."

"They didn't do a very good job, then," I said. "They hardly put up a fight. By the sound of it. She should have hired more carefully."

I remembered the misplaced sense of peace in the house, when the final guard was dead. The stillness. The silence. The inevitability, once the last obstacle had been removed.

"The police don't think it was the guards' fault," he said. "They're not blaming them at all."

"Why not?" I asked.

I felt like I was back there, moving from room to room, feeling her presence, knowing the end was near.

"They were all ex-military," he said. "Well trained. Heavily armed. No trace of drink or drugs. None of them had been sleeping on the job. They were just overwhelmed."

"Implying a number of attackers, then, surely?" I commented.

I'd had her in my sights once before, and then stood aside to let the authorities take their shot. I wasn't going to make that mistake again. And she had known it.

"No," he said. "Just one. A professional. Someone who does this kind of thing for a living."

I had warned her. She knew I'd be coming.

"They don't know that," I said. "The police are just fishing."

"No," he said. "Look. These guards were killed one at time. Silently, so as not to alarm the others. Or the neighbors. Some had their necks broken. Others were stabbed, neatly, between the ribs. One was suffocated. They were picked off methodically to give—someone—access to this woman."

He was right. It had been methodical. A means to an end.

Collateral damage. Nothing more. And no worse than you can expect if you sign up for the wrong side.

"That proves nothing," I said.

"And there's the way she was killed," he said. "Someone physically dragged her out of her panic room. Then shot her in the head. Twice. From close range."

I hadn't wanted to touch her, but there had been no choice. She wasn't dignified enough to come out on her own.

"Probably a mob hit," I said.

"No," he said. "The police think not. She wasn't on her knees when she was shot, for a start. Mob guys always make their victims kneel, apparently. Whoever did this wanted to look her in the eye when they pulled the trigger."

He had it backwards, this time. I didn't want to look at her, particularly. I wanted her to look at me. To know who was pulling the trigger. And to have no doubt as to who was being avenged.

"Maybe this guy took more pride in his work," I said.

"But it wasn't brutal enough," he said. "There was no sadism. If one outfit was moving in on another, they would have wanted to send a message. Something depraved. Psychotic, even. It's the same the world over. But whoever did this was cold. Calculating. Like a surgeon cutting out something malignant."

Now he was back on the money. The woman had been malignant. Like a virulent tumour, corrupting everything she touched. There was no way, in all good conscience, that I could have let her survive.

"Well, we could speculate all day," I said. "But whoever killed her, I expect she deserved it."

"I'm sure she did," he said. "But the point is, this was personal; the woman was executed. This specific woman. Who you just happened to know. Very well, I understand."

"I did?"

I knew her only too well. And I wish with all my heart that the day I met her had never dawned.

"You were a recent house guest of hers, apparently," he said.

"Really?" I said. "Who was she? I didn't see any names in that report."

"The police withheld it. My sources could only give me a first name."

"Which was?"

"Lesley. But I think you knew that."

Lesley. An ordinary name before I met her. Now a name I'll never forget.

"Lesley?" I said. "That's pretty common-sounding. There must be lots of Lesleys in a city the size of New York."

"Come on, David," he said. "I've played along with this for long enough. We all know what you did. And you're with friends here."

"Nice try. But I'm admitting nothing."

"Of course not. That's the first rule. But you wouldn't be worthy of the uniform if you'd just stood back, after what this woman did."

I didn't reply.

"I understand, David," he said. "I do. Working here isn't that different to life in the field. The liaison community, well, we're a pretty tight bunch. I heard about what this Lesley did to Tanya. And I heard that you guys were close."

I wasn't happy that we'd become fodder for the navy gossip machine. And I had no idea what he'd heard about us. But, whatever it was, I could guarantee it fell a long way short of the truth.

"Besides, Tanya had a lot of friends," he said. "We'd all have done the same thing. Given the chance."

I bit my tongue.

"Look, David, even London approves," he said. "Unofficially, of course. That's why the NYPD were kept at arm's length for so long. But there's a limit to what they'll turn a blind eye to. They were straining at the leash. You dump the worst horror show anyone's ever seen in the middle of their patch and leave them looking like they can't catch the perpetrator. The press are slaughtering them ten ways till Christmas. They're humiliated."

"They'll get over it. Or they'll just frame someone. Some lowlife they've been trying to rid themselves of for years. It's happened before. Whoever's behind this probably did them a favour."

"They don't see it like that. Seriously, we needed you out of there. Pronto. I was genuinely worried we'd left it too late."

"I left because I was ready. No other reason. My only question is, why am I here? I should be back in London. It's time to get back to work."

"It is. And that's exactly why you're here. Your next job is here."

"It can't be. You never work the same country twice. It's a rule. You know that."

"Technically, it's a convention. But that doesn't matter. The point is, you're still off the books. Officially, you don't exist. And that's what's important right now."

"Why?"

Fothergill took a moment to reply. He licked his lips, and I saw his eyes track across to a point on the wall in the shadow of the radiator below the left-hand window. To a patch of paint that was slightly lighter than the rest. A recent repair. Around an inch and a half square. The kind of area a bullet could still make a mess of, even after passing through someone's arm.

That second, I knew what was coming my way. House-cleaning. Again. The most distasteful task there is. And I realized something else in the same moment. That there was another difference between my aunt and me.

It gives me no pleasure when my premonitions turn out to be right.

None at all.